The Gilded Web

The Gilded Web

J. R. Glover

A novel dedicated to my wife,
an inspiration for the writing of this book
Hattie
1992

iUniverse, Inc.
Bloomington

The Gilded Web

iUniverse books may be ordered through booksellers or by contacting:

iUniverse
1663 Liberty Drive
Bloomington, IN 47403
www.iuniverse.com
1-800-Authors (1-800-288-4677)

ISBN: 978-1-4620-2153-6 (sc)
ISBN: 978-1-4620-2154-3 (ebk)

Printed in the United States of America

iUniverse rev. date: 05/31/2012

Table of Contents

[illegible]

Chapter One

The Event

Life is full of truisms, such as "honesty is the best policy; the grass is always greener on the other side of the fence" and things of this sort. Life also consists of placates which make no logical sense like, "The trip back is always shorter than going," which is a vain attempt to appease one's sense of impatience. Jeremy was hoping that the latter would prove to be accurate in spite of what common sense dictates. After all, juniors in college should be rational, right?

But man . . . I was tired—dead tired. And, right now the drive home was about as appealing as a mustard sandwich. Still I hoped and drove. The brand new black 1980 convertible roadster given to him as a graduation gift by his father, sped through the ink velvet night.

Jeremy was so preoccupied with his own musings, that he forgot about Rod in the seat next to me until he snored, or more like snorted. I knew that he was knocked out after driving over 300 hundred miles. What a pal! I don't think any two friends could be any closer than Rod and me. I didn't even think about his being black, although we did nothing to pretend that we weren't different. We just kind of accepted that as a given. Aren't all people different anyway? Jeremy smiled as he remembered that this was not always the case between them.

At 21 years of age, Jeremy was a rather ordinary looking guy with a rugged handsomeness about him. His heavy dark brown eyebrows were framed by a wrinkled brow and thick locks of sandy colored hair, bleached even lighter after two weeks of Florida sunshine. His thin and wiry six-foot frame was slightly slumped at the shoulders as he battled a little driving fatigue.

He had been at the wheel for over five hours and knew that pretty soon he would have to rest for a while. Jeremy is a rather easy-going person prone to quick laughter and mild-mannered ways. He knew that these laid-back characteristics, so natural to him, would soon be challenged in the dog-eat-dog world of investments on Wall Street following graduation. This warning had come from his dad, himself a well-respected and successful broker in upstate New York. The lines in his brow deepened ever so slightly with resentment at the thought of this. As much as he disliked the thought, he knew his father was probably right.

Different occupations often call for certain kinds of demeanor and personalities. He hated the thought of a professional "Game Face." Ministers should be cordial and smiling; school teachers, like surrogate parents; lawyers, trusting enough to even be lied to if necessary. All so phony. So artificial. He didn't relish his childhood ways being changed by a society which often lacks authenticity. Why can't people just be real? Be themselves? His dad was nicknamed "bulldog" on the Market, but at home he was as placid a person as you could find. A Jekyl and Hyde of sorts.

"Hey dude," a voice shattered through my thoughts.

"This ain't finals week, you know," Rod was saying.

"What's the serious look about?" Rod was awake.

"Aw, nothing really," Jeremy replied, "Just thinking about the rest of my life after school." Rod sat up straight for an instant, changed positions and relaxed again.

"Yeah, but don't let it depress you. You'll be okay," he said. "It's gonna be tough, though, meeting all of those middle-class expectations laid on you. Me? I'm the first person in my family who'd have a college degree. Man, I'm a celebrity in my neighborhood!" Jeremy smiled. Rod was good at helping me to keep things in perspective. Here I was troubled by the thought of an adult role, while my friend would face an uphill battle for the rest of his life overcoming the disadvantage of being black in a white culture. My concerns pale by comparison.

The boys lapsed again into the easy silence that comes when two people are truly comfortable with each other. In his own way, Rodney thought, Jeremy was as trapped as he was. While their situations were different, both would have something to prove after graduation.

Rodney was not always this open-minded. When he first enrolled at Waynesville State University three years ago as an engineering major, he brought with him some disillusionments and bitterness that a life of poverty instills. He had thought that all whites were blessed and all blacks were cursed. Even his high school counselor, Mrs. Vernor, encouraged him to attend a trade school or a vocational school because he had to take the ACT twice before passing. Man, I'll never forget her icy look and casual matter-of-fact advice. Now, he was a Junior in college!

At five feet nine and 185 pounds, Rod was built like the athlete he was. Barrel-chested and bronze, he was a striking figure. His short haircut was neatly cropped. After his freshman year in college, Rod had to give up football in favor of academics because he refused to opt for a less challenging degree. Since he wasn't on an athletic scholarship anyway, the decision was not that difficult. Since neither of his parents were college graduates, he was determined to give Mom and Dad something to rejoice about as well as to prove to himself that he could do it, in spite of Mrs. Vernor!

Strangely enough, the boys' friendship grew out of a fight they had in their second month of school. Having been made roommates in the dorm at Halverson Hall, the result of an intentional cross-racial dorm policy at the school, they were polar opposites.

Jeremy was raised in a bed chamber suburb with its insulated and elite community school system, while Rod came from an inner city school system replete with truancy and discipline problems. There were no blacks in Jeremy's hometown, so he had no experience relating to African Americans. All he knew of blacks was what he had heard, tales that were related by friends or by what he saw on television or read in the papers.

Unfortunately, what he saw and read in suburbia was largely biased and sensational types of news. Always something negative. You couldn't trust blacks as far as you could throw a Volkswagen! The unfortunate thing about this was that Jeremy had no other frame of reference by which to judge the trueness of falseness of these perceptions.

Rodney, on the other hand, lived in a poor black neighborhood in the inner city. Although he went to school with some white students, they were mostly poor inner-city whites who were bussed in as part of the longstanding desegregation plan for the city. These whites, however, were very different from Jeremy. In many ways, poor whites who go to school with blacks, are discriminated against themselves. So, in some cases there were similarities.

But like Rod once told one of his white classmates, "The difference is that you can go on to college, get an education, put on a suit, move on the other side of the tracks and Bang! You're in. Me? My color follows me wherever I go."

Away from school, however, black and rival white gangs fought continuously. One thing that Rod learned was that somebody had to always be on the bottom. When a poor white calls a black a "nigger," Rod was told that was their way of saying, "Yes, even though I'm poor, I'm still white." Rodney knew all about racism first hand. Jeremy was told that blacks were poor because they were not very intelligent and lacked motivation. Put these ingredients in the pot, turn on the fire, and the pot begins to boil a strange soup indeed! Still, Rodney thought then, he liked the whites in high school better than Jeremy's kind.

Several incidents happened that would change their lives and thinking forever. One such situation occurred in their room on a weekend after playing volleyball and basketball all day. Rod took off his watch and there was a light circle around his wrist where the watch had been. Jeremy poked fun.

"Man look at that," he laughed pointing to Rodney's wrist, "I didn't know you all could tan. I thought the sun just bounced off blacks' skin." Instantly, Rodney jumped on Jeremy. Caught by surprise, Jeremy was not quick enough to duck a hard right thrown by Rodney. His lip was busted and bleeding. Rodney was now ready to fight for his life, because Jeremy was taller than he was and s-t-r-o-n-g. He expected a furious onslaught and braced himself for the coming attack. It never came. Rod will never, ever, forget the puzzled look on Jeremy's face as he sat there and wiped at his mouth.

"What the hell did you hit me for? You've got about one minute to explain and it better be good," Jeremy shot at Rod, anger building by the second. "I don't know if I can take you," retorted Rod, "but nobody, including you, is gonna insult me or my people with racist slurs and remarks. Where do you get off, anyway?"

There was genuine confusion written all over Jeremy's face. Incredible as it seemed, Rod believed his roommate was sincere. "If I had called you a name out of place, like a coon or a nigger or something like that, I'd deserve to be hit. But I didn't call you or your people anything like that. I never believed half of that crap I grew up hearing," Jeremy continued, his voice quivering in anger.

Looking down at his classmate's bleeding lip, Rod realized that he was too quick on the trigger. Society had conditioned him to predictable responses of defensiveness. He felt bad after he realized that Jeremy's remark was probably a careless reflection of his childhood and was really said in jest. He went to the bathroom, wet a wash cloth and brought it back and handed it to Jeremy.

"Man, I thought it was a dig," he said apologetically. "When somebody says something derogatory about my race, they include my mom and dad as well. Jeremy, you can't just go around saying things like that. You could get hurt real bad. What if I had said that whites try to tan because their skin was sick looking. It's the same thing. You'd be insulted too. God made my skin just like he did yours. Skin is just skin."

"I never thought of it like that before," said Jeremy, "I guess it would make a difference. But don't be so damn defensive all the time. We ought to be able to joke together. Sometimes even if it is about our races as long as it is not meant to be demeaning." Rod hesitated a moment, pondering Jeremy's words. "Yeah, I think you're right.

We ought to be able to be real. But, look! Remember our Language Arts course last semester about trigger words?"

Jeremy thought back. Rod was right. Some words carry with them implicit meanings that sometimes invoke emotional responses from the ones who hear them based upon their past experiences and background. "Patriotism" may be interpreted differently by blacks and whites, for instance. Very few blacks get goose bumps from hearing the "Star Spangled Banner" being played, but they nonetheless fight and die in combat to defend what it represents.

"It's a crazy mixed-up world, huh," said Jeremy. "Here we are in 1980, near the end of the 20th Century, with technology enough to build space stations and to explore the galaxy, yet you and I who live in the same room and go to the same classes live in the middle ages as people." Rod nodded his head in agreement.

"Yeah, it's messed up all right."

Both boys eyeballed each other as if for the first time. "Rod, I spoke out of ignorance, and I'm sorry, " Jeremy said, extending his hand. "Naw, man," replied Rod, "I had no business hitting you. You didn't lay a hand on me. I apologize," he said.

The two shook hands. Black man, white man—Americans—learning to live together in a land that was native to both. What a shame! Yet, there is always some good that can be found in any bad situation, for Jeremy and Rod began in the smallest of ways to become friends.

The hour was getting late as the car hurled itself down the dark country road. The night was like a velvet blanket sprinkled with an occasional cluster of stars like sparkling diamonds. Only at long intervals did the glare of oncoming headlights interrupt the serene silence of the night as they passed by on the other side of the highway.

The boys had earlier decided that 600 miles a day between them would be about as much as they would push themselves. They were fast approaching this limit.

"Hey Rod," Jeremy said, cutting into the silence. "We're close to our time limit. The trip indicator almost reads 600 miles. Check the map and see where we are. We'll stop at the next town." Rod retrieved the map from the glove compartment and turned on the map light. After some quick calculations, he determined that they should be approaching the Georgia and Tennessee state line. They agreed to stop at the next town, get a late meal and a hotel room. They would leave early the next day after getting the car checked out.

"You know that Ft. Lauderdale was my first trip south," Rod remarked to Jeremy. "Well, I told you you'd love it. We've gone down there for years now when my folks vacationed. Let's go back for a few days next year after graduation. Chances are we won't be seeing much of each other after that."

"I heard that," retorted Rod, "Chicago and Buffalo aren't exactly next door to each other."

The boys began to laugh and exchange tales about the past two weeks. They certainly had enjoyed themselves immensely, and had even run into some other kids from Waynesville U. All in all, it was a most memorable trip. "You know, it's too bad that more of my people don't get to do things like this. Can you imagine me going back to Chicago and talking to the brothers about Fort Lauderdale?!" Rod finished. They laughed, yet Jeremy understood all too well.

"One day it might happen, Rod. We have to believe that," he replied. "Yeah, what is life anyway without hope," said Rod. Just at that instant they passed a road sign. The next town was 12 miles ahead, and they noticed that the gas gauge was getting low. "Looks like we'll be just in time," Rod countered.

Several minutes later, they came to the county line and in the distance they could see a few lights scattered on the hillside. "Sure isn't Buffalo," Jeremy noticed, "Our campus is almost that big." Rod expressed the desire to stop at a bigger city, saying he was not crazy about being in a small southern town. But the next big city was just too far away and they were too low on gas. Anyway,one night was no big deal.

"Man,look at that, "Jeremy said, peering back momentarily, "Yeah, I saw it," Rod exclaimed, "population 595." Just then an object flashed in front of the speeding car and there was an audible thump.

"Oh, hell," cried Jeremy, "Rod! I think we hit something." Rod strained to see. "What was it? I only saw a flash." By the time Jeremy was able to stop the car, they had travelled several hundred feet from the point of impact. Nervously the boys sat in the car, stunned and afraid. what if it was a pedestrian? What if they had killed someone? Maybe it was just an animal of some kind,or just their imaginations running wild. Perhaps it was fatigue. They sat in panic-stricken silence.

"Let's check the car," suggested Rod, "if we really did hit something, we will soon find out." Unbuckling their seat belts, the boys opened the doors and climbed out. The pitch blackness enveloped them. The only sounds were those of crickets and locusts harmonizing out of tune and rhythm.

"Geez," exclaimed Jeremy, "I can't see a thing. Rod get the flashlight out of the glove compartment." Reaching through the open window, Rod opened the glove compartment, retrieved the flashlight and returned to the front of the car. "We shouldn't have pushed ourselves so hard," Jeremy was muttering, "we just shouldn't have." Rod turned on the flashlight and the beam cut through the velvet darkness like a knife. It splashed onto the front of the car. Sure enough, on the driver's front fender was a large dent. And there was blood!

"Damn," whispered Rod, "Damn." Their suspicions were now confirmed. "No question about it. We did hit something," said Jeremy, "but what?" Turning off the light, the boys climbed back into the car, distraught. "Maybe we're making a mountain out of a molehill," Jeremy suggested, "Let's just go back and take a look." Rod nodded his head in agreement, and they backed up, turned around and began making their way back up the road.

Driving slowly, Jeremy checked the road ahead drenched in the light of the head lamps, while Rod checked alongside the car with the flashlight. They saw nothing. "I know we've gone back past the spot," Jeremy was saying, "We should have found something by now." Rod had an idea. "Cut the engine, and let's see if we can hear anything," he suggested. "If something or someone is hurt, it ought to make some kind of sound."

Jeremy killed the engine. Silence. Only typical night sounds invaded the boys' ears. Nothing. "What do you think?," asked Jeremy. "Dunno," muttered Rod. "Damn," Jeremy repeated. "Man, let's get outta here," Rod countered, "I ain't seen a thing and neither have you. We've got to get home." They sat in stony silence for a few moments. "Yeah," Jeremy said, "but what about the blood? What about the blood, Rodney?!" An eternity passed it seemed.

"You would have to mention that," Rod conceded, "we can't ignore the blood."

After picking each other's brains about what to do, they finally at long last agreed on a plan. They would report the incident to the local sheriff as any law-abiding citizen would do. They would not be able to live with themselves never knowing. Rod hated the idea. "I don't like it either," said Jeremy, "do you have any other suggestions?" Rod shook his head, "Nope." Turning the key in the ignition, the boys headed toward town, disappearing into the night.

Chapter Two

Circumstance

Silence stole the moment like a shadowy creature lurking in the darkness. No one spoke. Neither dared. The town lights grew larger, closer, as their car pushed forward through the stillness. It was approaching midnight as the boys rolled into town. The streets were deserted except for a few stray cats and an occasional dog crossing the road. It was a sleepy little place with dirt roads and old wooden buildings. A general store with a large padlock on the front door. Only sparsely scattered lampposts gave off whatever light was visible. A small dingy hardware store on the left. To the right sat an old wood frame building which simply had a sign painted over the entrance Post Office. The boys saw lights in a building straight ahead with a few cars parked outside.

This road, they reasoned, was probably the main strip. They were in the heart of town! The building with the lights on turned out to be a small fire station.

"Let's go in and ask where the Sheriff's office is, " said Jeremy quietly. "Uh-uh," replied Rod, "let's find it on our own. A stranger looking for the sheriff at midnight ain't too cool. Besides, it can't be too hard to find. Let's just keep looking."

Rod definitely, was going to be as low-key as possible in this situation and Jeremy even confessed to a little nervousness. As they turned a corner slowly onto another narrow avenue, they consoled each other. After all, they had done absolutely nothing wrong.

Bright lights now loomed ahead. "This is obviously the Business District," offered Jeremy, "we ought to find some thing real quick." They did.

"This is their night spot," observed Rod, "no matter where you go, folks will party." Cars lined the street. "I bet when they close up, everything stops in this town. I wouldn't be surprised if they pulled in the fire hydrants and rolled up the sidewalks," Jeremy joked. For the first time in a while, the boys dared to laugh. They felt a little better. Laughter works miracles in lifting the spirit.

"There it is," said Rod pointing down the street, "three police cars under the light pole on the left."

Jeremy nodded and slowed the car to a crawl.

"Last thing we need now is a ticket," he chuckled, "The sheriff is probably the judge too."

Again laughter, but this time twinged with apprehension. Pulling to a stop, the boys get out of the car, look pensively at each other for a moment and walk up the steps to the front door. "Well," said Rod, "let's do it." Jeremy opened the door and the two stepped inside.

"Ain't seen y'all two before," a voice from out of nowhere greeted them.

They turned to the left and looked at a tall, skinny officer seated at a small desk behind a revolving fan. "You boys lost or something?" He was looking at Rod especially hard, Jeremy noticed. Too hard. He had dark brown hair that was too stringy and very thin on top. A front tooth was chipped and his hairy mustache was badly in need of trimming. He had a big Adam's Apple that moved up and down when he talked. His voice was a rich baritone and his southern drawl was thick. He pointed in Jeremy's direction.

"You, come over here and sit down. The cat got your tongue or something? How can I help you if you don't say nothin'?"

Rod stayed by the door as Jeremy walked over to the desk and sat down. He didn't like this man already. His arrogance, attitude and the way he kept looking in Rod's direction made Jeremy a little wary.

"What about my friend?" Jeremy said nodding towards Rod. "Don't you have another chair somewhere? We're both here to see the Sheriff."

Pointing to a chair against a wall on the other side of the room, the deputy tells Rod to sit there. "Now don't fall asleep, son," he said to Rod. "This won't take long."

He chuckled to himself. A real smart ass, Jeremy thought. He could tell Rod was upset, but to his credit he didn't say anything.

"My name's Willie Joe. I'm the Sheriff's Chief Deputy. Call me Mr. Bivens." He lit his pipe and inhaled deeply. "How can I help you son?" he said peering at Jeremy with brown piercing eyes buried in deep sockets.

"My friend and I are on our way back to school from a vacation in Ft. Lauderdale," Jeremy began.

"Ft. Lauderdale, Florida?" interrupted the Deputy wide-eyed, "you're puttin' me on. Since when did colored folks start takin' vacations in Florida?" he questioned looking in Rod's direction in a mocking sort of way.

The man's an out-and-out racist thought Jeremy. Just what we didn't need.

"Look, Deputy Bivens," Jeremy said impatiently, "Can we please talk to the Sheriff?!"

Deputy Bivens told Jeremy that the Sheriff was busy in the back trying to get home because he was working much later than normal and that he handled all routine matters. Jeremy insisted that the matter was not routine and repeated his desire to talk to the Sheriff. He knew that he and Rod, who continued to sit quietly, would be making a mistake to confide in this jerk, who Jeremy believed probably didn't have a high school diploma.

"All Right then, if you insist," said the Deputy getting up out of his seat. "But keep an eye on your friend over there. We don't want him runnin' off nowhere. You know how they get when the law's around. Nervous and jittery. Be right back," he chuckled as he turned toward the back room.

Rod made an obscene gesture with his finger. I winked reassuringly at him and we both smiled.

After a brief moment, Deputy Bivens came back with the Sheriff. He was much shorter than Willie Joe and much heavier. A portly kind of man with an immaculate uniform and confident gait. His hair was snow white and he appeared to be in his late fifties or early sixties. His face was round and friendly with crinkles at the corners of his eyes. He smoked a bulldog pipe and his complexion was ruddy.

"Howdy, boys," he smiled. "What seems to be the problem?" He motioned for Rod to come over and join us.

I felt an immediate sense of relief. We all sat down at the desk as Rod pulled up his chair.

"Willie, I want you to stay by the radio in the back while I talk to the boys," he said, "and please, Willie, don't eat all of my chocolate chip cookies."

"Yes sir, Sheriff Relliford," he said, "I'll take care of everything. Don't worry." He left hurriedly. The Sheriff called back over his shoulder, "and Willie, close the door." Willie did as he was told.

"My name is Toby Relliford what's your's?" he asked looking at both of us.

"I'm Jeremy McCutchin and this is my friend Rodney Blake."

We all shook hands. "Nothing much going on in the back room," the Sheriff told us, "but when I came in and saw Rodney sittin' way over there, I knew that ol' Willie was up to his usual antics. He never did care much for the coloreds around here. We'll have to work on his manners, huh?" he said smiling at Rod.

"Thanks, Sheriff," Rod replied, "but that's okay. Nobody's perfect."

The Sheriff nodded. "Well put, son. Now what's the problem that brought you to see me?"

The boys related the whole incident to Sheriff Relliford without sparing even the slightest detail. The Sheriff listened intently and scribbled some notes on a pad. When the boys had finished, he pushed the intercom button and told his Deputy to bring in three cups of coffee. Rod and I had cream and sugar. The Sheriff took his black.

We talked further for a time, and then Sheriff Relliford stood up and began pacing slowly.

"Boys," he began, "I don't see much of anything to worry about right now. You absolutely did the right thing. You could have kept on going if you wanted to. I want to commend you both for your honesty and concern. We don't get a lot of that around here much anymore. People just aren't what they used to be."

We agreed and assured him that it was the same up north as well. He too shared our concern about the blood on the car, and because of it, he thought it would be best for us to stay around a couple of days and see if any accidents were reported.

"News travels fast in small towns like this," he was saying. "If somebody doesn't come home in a day or so, I'll get a call for sure from their family. I suggest you just sit tight for a day or two just to be on the safe side. Okay?"

Rod and I both agreed.

"It was probably just a deer or something you hit," the Sheriff volunteered, "We have 'em running all over the place. They are sometimes drawn by headlights and spooked."

Silently we prayed that he was right. It's funny how circumstances can change the whole course of one's life without warning. In the next couple of days, we had planned to be at home bragging about our trip.

"Tell you what,boys," we heard the Sheriff saying, "I don't want your car bothered until you're ready to leave. Your car is now considered temporary evidence until this matter is cleared up. For your own protection, we'll put it up safe and sound for the time being at Luke's place."

"Who's Luke?" Rod asked.

"Luke works on our squad cars when they need fixing," the Sheriff answered. "He has a fenced-in garage just down the road. Sort of like our impounding lot. He's our only mechanic here and will be the one working on your car repairs when the investigation is through."

"Hold on a sec," Sheriff Relliford said as he abruptly left for the back room, leaving Rod and Jeremy to exchange looks of relief.

"I'm feeling better about this whole thing," Rod sighed.

"Yeah, me to," said Jeremy, "The Sheriff is a real pro. I'll bet he's real popular here."

."I feel a lot better about him than that dumb Deputy of his. Couldn't the Sheriff had done better than that?"

We both laughed at the seriousness of Rod's question. We surmised that they were probably old friends, or married into each other's family. Our conversation was interrupted by the Sheriff's return.

"It's all set," he told us, "You boys follow me in your car to Luke's and then I'll take you to Sarah's restaurant for a bite to eat and then we'll get ya put up at the hotel. There's only one, you know."

Somehow we weren't surprised. We left and followed the Sheriff to Luke's Garage about three blocks away. It was an immaculate, well-kept place. The fenced-in yard was huge and contained at least 12 cars including two cruisers. The Sheriff told us that Luke was the only legitimate mechanic in town with papers. Six men worked for him. We were impressed.

"Come on," the Sheriff said as we left Luke's and climbed into the squad car, "Let's get you two something to eat."

We went to a place called Sarah's. It was really more like a huge home trailer made into a restaurant. The eating counter took up most of the space inside, but it was nice and clean with air conditioning to boot.

"Real home-cooked food," the Sheriff said as we sat down.

The Sheriff introduced us to Sarah, a nice, friendly old lady who told us that five minutes later we would have been too late. We ate a hearty meal of pork chops, fried potatoes, green beans and a toss salad. For dessert, we had pumpkin pie. Rod wanted to know if they served sweet potato pie. Sarah just laughed and pointed, "That's served over where the coloreds stay. Never have been able to steal their recipe," she smiled.

Rod thought that was extremely funny. Jeremy laughed too.

The Sheriff slapped Rod on the shoulder.

"Son, that's another thing I was going to talk with you about. I'm not about to apologize for the whole town, but life goes on here the way it does. Always has as long as I can remember. All of the black folks here stay on the other side of the railroad tracks. It's our colored section. Even though I don't like it, I can't change it. I'm elected to just keep law and order."

Rod nodded and said that he understood.

"In Chicago," he replied, "we have our white parts of town and our black parts. Some parts are integrated, but there's always racial problems no matter what part of the city you go to. Here, you just don't pretend. I can deal with honesty whether I agree with it or not."

The Sheriff smiled. "I just don't want any trouble while you're both under my protection. Of course, both of you will stay together here at the hotel, but Rod, if you want to walk around, sight-see, or just hang out while you're here, I suggest that you do it in the colored section. It just works better that way."

Since we were just talking about a couple of days, neither one of us had a quarrel with the Sheriff's advice. In fact, we both told him that we appreciated his candor and honesty. Sheriff Relliford seemed like a genuinely nice person and Rod and I soon felt at ease.

After we left Sarah's, the Sheriff dropped us off at the hotel and told the clerk to give us what we needed, because we were guests of the Sheriff's Department. He explained that we were temporarily side-tracked on our way home. The clerk acknowledged the Sheriff's directives without further question. After seeing us to our room, the Sheriff told us that he would notify the Coroner to have the blood on our car analyzed as a normal procedure, and in a day or so, we should be on our way. We thanked him for everything and then prepared to turn in for the night.

Sheriff Relliford left the hotel and trundled back to his cruiser feeling the effects of a long day. It was now approaching well near midnight and he had put in over 12 hours. He was looking forward to going home and getting a good night's sleep. Jake, the third-shift deputy, should already be on duty so that he and Willie would be relieved. When he arrived back at the station, he was surprised to see that Willie was still there. His car had not been moved.

"Willie, what are you still doing here?" queried Sheriff Relliford.

"How are you doing Jake?"

Both men were seated at the desk busy with the report he had written.

"Fine, Sheriff," said Jake. "Willie and I were just going over your report here."

The Sheriff grunted and moved to the back room. When he returned, he gathered up his report.

"This is official stuff," he scolded them, "until I ask for assistance, this is confidential. Nobody is to be told nothing until I say so. It's only an accident report. Probably nothing."

After gathering up his keys and jacket, the Sheriff instructed Jake to call John Cuthbert, the coroner, and have him examine the boy's car over at the garage.

"Come on, Willie," he said, "let's go home."

As they were leaving the station, Willie wanted to talk about the blood on the boy's car mentioned in the Sheriff's report.

"Jake and I were thinking what if those two were lyin'? Trying to hide something. I don't trust those people from up north. They think they're smarter'n everyone else, and the black boy seemed kinda uppity to me. Yes sir!" Willie rambled.

"Damn it, Willie," the Sheriff spat out, "why are you going on about this whole thing? Nothing has happened, has it?" Willie scratched his head.

"Dunno," he answered, "but we ought to check it out don't you think?"

Sheriff Relliford thought it over for a minute. The only way to shut up Willie was to satisfy his curiosity.

"Okay," the Sheriff responded. "Get in my car and we'll go see for ourselves."

The Sheriff and Willie climbed into the cruiser and headed for the spot where the boys had reported the incident. Upon arriving, both took flashlights and split up checking both sides of the road. After about 15 minutes, they met back at the car.

"Well?" the Sheriff asked Willie, "Where's the body?"

Willie just shook his head and said nothing.

"Now, until we do hear something, I don't want to hear about this anymore. We'll just have to wait for the coroner's report. And Willie, you and Jake keep your lips buttoned up, you hear?" instructed the Sheriff.

Willie consented as the two got back into the car and drove back to the station in Willie's car.

On his way home, Sheriff Relliford was a little uneasy. He should have put the report away before he left with the boys earlier. Jake was all right, he thought, a good deputy. But Willie wasn't always too bright. Talked too much, especially when he drank, and with his dislike, maybe even hatred of the town's blacks, he was making too much over the issue. It was almost as if he wished there was more to it.

As he aimed his car toward home, his thoughts went back to his first arrival in this small town some 12 years and two children ago. Now both are grown and living in California. He had worked hard to put them through college at Georgia Tech in Atlanta, where he grew up and worked as a Police Officer for over 10 years.

Atlanta is full of blacks and he was liked and respected by the black officers who served on the force with him. Sure there were problems between the blacks and whites on the force, mainly because the blacks were often passed over for promotions. Unfortunately, when a handful of black officers were busted by Internal Affairs for taking payoffs from drug dealers and pimps, it made it doubly difficult for all the rest of the black officers, good and dedicated cops. Family men.

Blacks, however, were not by themselves. Many of the white officers were dirty too, yet more than a few who were suspected by Internal Affairs were ever prosecuted. He never quite figured out why the blacks were always caught and most of the whites were not. He guessed that deep down inside, he knew the answer.

Prior to working on the Atlanta Police Force, he had served three years in the U.S. Army as an M.P. at Fort Ord, California. Again, he was friends with many black soldiers there, from all over the country. He had always felt good about being a Southern boy from Atlanta and being accepted by big city blacks from the likes of Cleveland, Chicago and Detroit.

He never raised his children to be prejudiced but made it clear that he did not believe in the mixing of the races. He just couldn't deal with the thought of having mixed blood in his family. He sighed heavily at the thought, and conceded that this was a chink in his own armor. Way down deep, he supposed there was some prejudice after all. He had always defended this position by saying that mixed marriages were always too tough on the children. Well, you have to find something, don't you?

Pulling into the driveway of his home, a nice but modest one-story brick ranch house, he realized that being the Sheriff here was indeed a good alternative to an early retirement. He and Peg led a good quiet life here, and most of all, he was his own boss. He liked that, except at times like this when he would come home at three o'clock in the morning. He knew that Peg would be furious and his dinner would be back in the refrigerator. Peg, however, would still be up. He smiled to himself as he opened the door and heard Peg's voice.

"It's about time, Toby Relliford," she greeted him, "John Cuthbert called a little while ago, and said that he would not be able to check that car your deputy told him about right away. He's got an autopsy to do in the morning. Old man Piersall died suddenly. Said he'd call you tomorrow afternoon."

Toby had taken off his shirt while his wife had been talking, and had made his way into the living room where Peg was curled up on the sofa knitting.

"Why aren't you asleep by now?" Toby asked her.

"After all of these years of being a policeman's wife," she replied, "why do you still have to ask me that? Anyway, I was wondering about John's call.

" What happened?"

Toby finished undressing as he told his wife about what had happened with the two boys. He assured her it was nothing to worry about. Peg put up her knitting and stood up. Her full-bosomed figure failed to go unnoticed by Toby's probing eyes. Her housecoat hung carelessly open and her short gown underneath barely came down to her knees. She always had nice long, shapely legs. She was still quite a dish, Toby was thinking after all these years.

"No way," she said catching the way he was looking at her, "Three in the morning? Forget it! You're not 25 anymore. You're just a dirty old man!" she teased him.

"Yeah," smiled Toby," and like Sanford used to say on TV, I'll be a dirty old man until I'm a dead old man."

They both laughed and headed arm-in-arm to the bedroom. Suddenly Peg stopped.

"Did you forget something?" she asked looking back.

Toby paused for a second and then turned to get his uniform that he had thrown across the living room chair.

"Women," he muttered, as he gathered up his clothes.

"Men," Peg mocked, as she reached behind her to pull up Toby's hand that had strayed too far below her waist. Their snickers could be heard as they disappeared into the darkness and solace of the bedroom.

Jeremy and Rod slept hard through the night. The strain of the long hours of driving, coupled with the stress of everything else that had happened in the past several hours had left them thoroughly worn. They did not awaken until almost noon the next day. After waking up, showering and getting dressed, the boys walked down to Sarah's and had a healthy brunch. They enjoyed the food and the friendly atmosphere at this small country diner and decided that it would be their official dining spot for as long as they were in town. Remembering the Sheriff's advice to be as inconspicuous as possible, the boys returned to their room and decided to just hang loose.

"Well it's been over 12 hours now," Rod said as he turned on the TV.

A soap opera was on.

"Aw, man, I forgot about daytime television," Rod continued, "Even way down here you can't get away from this junk."

The boys looked at ESPN for a while on the cable, but nothing of real interest was on. Rod decided to call Andrea, his girl friend, at home, but Jeremy suggested that they call their parents first and let them know that they would be a couple of days late.

"If your folks are like mine, when Thursday gets here and we're not back, it's worry time," Jeremy was saying.

"Same here," Rod said, "good idea!"

Both of the boys took turns calling their parents. Jeremy mentioned to his mom that there was only one mechanic in town to make repairs to the damage on the front end of the car and asked her to tell his dad to notify the insurance company to have the necessary work done.

"I know he doesn't want to see the car like this," he added.

His mother assured him that she would tell him. After reassuring their parents that they were okay, they settled back to relax awhile. This was destined to be a classic "boring" day they concluded.

Sheriff Relliford dropped by at about three to tell them that the coroner had not checked out their car as of yet, that he would get around to it shortly. Nothing had been reported out of the ordinary he had told them.

Jeremy walked over to the General Store to get a deck of cards for him and Rod to pass the time with. What should have taken 15 minutes, took almost an hour. When he got back, Rod asked him what took so long.

"Man, you ought to see the Sales Clerk over there," Jeremy gushed, "nowhere was there a finer hunk of country female flesh."

He described her figure by making an hour-glass shape with his hands.

"I might have known," rasped Rod, "less than a couple of days after leaving the beach your hormones are out of control already."

Jeremy waved him off.

"I'm not kidding this time, Rod," he said seriously. "She's special! You ever see a girl who knocked you for a loop at first sight? Man she did and I ain't kiddin' you."

Rod thought about Andrea. He knew the feeling all right. To this day, he swears that he fell in love with her the first moment they met in his sophomore year at Waynesville. To top it off, she was even from his home town, but had lived in the Hyde Park area of Chicago while he had lived on the other side of town.

"What happened?" Rod asked excitedly, noticing Jeremy's flushed expression as he mockingly rolled his eyes around.

"Tell me everything. We've got nothing but time, "Rod was saying, putting down the deck of cards.

"Well," Jeremy started, "I went into the General Store after the cards, but couldn't find them anywhere. I didn't see anybody behind the cash register when I first walked in, so I was just looking. Then came this southern accent straight from heaven. Sounded like a chorus of birds singing," Jeremy sighed.

"Damn the voice," Rod interrupted, "What did she look like?"

Jeremy described Beth McCallister as a young woman in her early twenties, about five foot six inches tall and 125 pounds.

"About a size eight," he estimated.

She had long blonde hair that was braided underneath in the back with bangs that spilled across her forehead and curls around the side. A classic Georgia peaches-and-cream-complexion," he added.

"Man, Rod," he said, "she had the most beautiful set of full lips in the w-o-r-l-d," he spelled out. Her cute button nose just fit right in," he added. "She had on a long frock and I couldn't see her legs, but the way that it clung to her waist and the protruding curve of her behind underneath, told me all I needed to know about her figure," he concluded.

"The first thing I looked for when I caught my breath was a ring. I couldn't believe she wasn't married. They must have some lame dudes in this town," he said shaking his head.

Jeremy continued on about how she had teased him about not looking like the gambling type, and had noticed by his appearance that he was not from around here. He explained the situation to her and almost hated to tell her that they would probably be leaving sometime tomorrow.

"I told her that I would stop in to see her tomorrow before we left. Maybe we could write or something," he finished.

He indicated further that it would be early tomorrow morning.

"She sounds like she was all right," Rod responded.

"It was her personality," Jeremy clarified, "as much as anything else. She was so nice. Easy to talk to. Have you noticed how much more open, and less pretentious people in the south seem to be?" he asked Rod.

"Yep," Rod agreed, "strangers will talk to you down here. Back home, if you speak to somebody, you don't know they make you feel foolish by the way they look at you."

Jeremy agreed wholeheartedly. "I don't care what they say," he added, "there is definitely a difference between northerners and southerners. You can feel it in their attitudes and personalities."

After some more small talk, the boys settled down to playing cards. Spades was the popular choice at the moment. They played cards late into the afternoon until it was about time for dinner. They walked to Sarah's and were greeted with a warm "Howdy, fellows, still with us?"

They smiled and told her that they were addicted to her home-cooked food. She smirked, "Ain't nuthin' new. I'm the best cook in town," she said with dancing eyes. "What'll it be this evening?

Rod and Jeremy ordered the special of the day.

"We'll probably do some sight seeing tomorrow before we leave," Rod was explaining, "can you give me some directions to the colored section?"

Sarah gave him the directions using landmarks and physical descriptions as there were no streets between the two places. About a quarter of a mile separated the two areas, connected by only one dirt road crossing the railroad tracks. Thanking Sarah for everything, the two boys left and headed back to the hotel, with anxious anticipation of what tomorrow held in store.

Chapter Three

Second Thoughts

As Jeremy and Rod were sound asleep in their room that night, resting up for an early start the next day, there was quite a bit of activity in the small town. Part of it involved three of the town's local rowdies, Hank Peters, Bobby McCallister and Jimmy Cuthbert. Often loud and boisterous but otherwise harmless; most of the town's night patrons just ignored them. All three were from respected homes and they just had a habit of blowing off steam.

Sheriff Relliford had to confront them about their unruly behavior on more than one occasion. Bobby McCallister's sister, Beth, was always on her brother about doing silly things and not acting his age. He had threatened to flatten her more than once, but had never done so. At 25, he was a well-built man with auburn colored hair, thick and a little long, he was sometimes reminded. He was generally good-natured, but had a propensity for moodiness, especially when things didn't go his way.

Like the time seven years ago as a senior in high school when his football team had lost a close championship game. Bobby got into a post-game fight with two players on the opposing team and was the only one on his team who refused to shake hands with the other players. This act of sportsmanship was mandatory by the league's athletic bylaws. As a result of his actions, all of the college scholarships that were offered to him were withdrawn or substantially reduced.

He became an angry and moodier person from then on. He simply shrugged off the advice of his coach who later had told him that good players were a dime a dozen anymore. He wanted Bobby to understand that coaches today felt that it was just as important to be a good student and have a coachable attitude, as it was to be an outstanding athlete.

"Yeah, a suck ass," Bobby had retorted as he walked away. Now he was 25 and still did not have a steady job while continuing to live at home.

Hank Peters was the bigger of the three and surprisingly the most even in temperament. He was a big, round, burly man with a crew cut to his short red hair. His massiveness was betrayed by a baby face, and he was often teased about it. Many fights had come as a result of careless remarks about his "choir boy" looks. He resented being teased about it. Yet on the whole he was sort of a likeable kind of guy. He just drank too heavily, too often.

His parents were well-liked farmers in the town and much of his muscle was the result of doing the heavy chores on the farm. At 26, he did the heavy work because his father had a chronic back ailment for years. His dad had always told him that one day the farm would be his sole responsibility if he could only keep himself out of trouble and work out his drinking problem.

Jimmy Cuthbert, on the other hand, was the smallest of the three and the meanest. With all of his clothes on and dripping wet, he would have difficulty moving the scales past 150 pounds. He lacked muscle definition but was deceptively strong for his size. He was no pushover by any means.

His dark hair was always well groomed and his small dark eyes had a piercing look to them. Hank and Bobby had nicknamed him "X-ray man" because of it. He was the only college graduate of the three at 27 but had, so far, failed to pass the examination of the state's medical licensing bureau to practice medicine. He secretly believed that there was some kind of conspiracy against him but his father had told him this was hogwash.

"You pass the board, you practice medicine," he had told him.

He was further scolded for not being man enough to handle adversity by his father. He hated his father's preaching but never got over the feeling that he had let him down. Because of his own inadequacies, he was intolerant of people whom he classified as "inferior" or who lacked his "smarts." He didn't need them always comparing him with his dad. His father, John, was the town's Coroner.

It was now about two in the morning and the three were together at the town's main nightclub, "The Silver Dollar", drinking and dancing. Jimmy was arguing rather loudly with another man seated at the bar. He was visibly intoxicated and rude. Hank and Bobby were unsuccessful in the role of peacemakers, partly because they were almost as drunk. Finally, the bartender had to ask them to leave before it went any further. Hank and Bobby offered little resistance but Jimmy was not as cooperative.

"I spend more money in here than any of these stiffs," he said waving his arms around the room.

"I just think you've had enough," the bartender responded. Why don't you go home, Jimmy, and sleep it off?" he asked.

Hank and Bobby both got up rather unsteadily and told Jimmy that it was time to go anyway. They left the bar together with Jimmy still muttering to himself something about not needing those jerks or their booze.

Outside, the cool night air felt good.

"I don't know about you guys but I ain't feelin' no pain," Hank said thickly as they made their way to the parked car.

"Jimmy, you all right?" Bobby asked, "Think you can drive all right?"

Jimmy shook his head. There was no need for concern. "I'm fine. Let's just get out of here. It's almost three o'clock," he sputtered.

The three climbed into Jimmy's car and headed for Hank's farm. As they drove, Hank was saying how hard it was going to be to get up in a few hours and do the early morning chores.

"Aw, you're used to it," Bobby teased, "That ol' rooster of yours'll wake you up."

As they headed out of town, Jimmy was talking about how he was going to pass the Examining Board's test the next time and was not paying attention to the speedometer.

Suddenly the car lurched to the left and skidded as the brakes squealed loudly. There was a sickening thump as the visible body of a person catapulted over the hood of the men's car. Jimmy fought the wheel, skidded the car to a 45° angle and stopped. There was no doubt as to what just had happened. The car had hit someone in the road. Jimmy never saw who it was. It all had happened in the span of a heartbeat.

"Oh, no!" wailed one of the men, "Hell no! I know this didn't happen to us." Another cursed audibly. There was total chaos in the car for several minutes. Cursing and profanities clothed the dark stillness. Panic reigned. One by one, the men stumbled out of the car—dazed and moving on unsteady feet. Off to the side of the road a short distance back, lay a crumpled figure. Jimmy had a flashlight in his hand examining the car. The hood was bent badly and blood covered the grill. He began to cry.

"Shut up," said a voice piercing the night, "that ain't gonna change nothin'." Bobby sprinted to the fallen figure, followed closely by Hank. They called for Jimmy to bring the flashlight. When it came, the light fell upon a man which none of them recognized. There was no other sound to be heard except the heavy breathing of the three men.

Jimmy bent down over the body and examined him for any signs of life.

"Is he . . . Is he dead, Jimmy? Jimmy?!"

Someone squealed in the darkness.

"Yeah," muttered Jimmy fighting back the tears welling in his eyes, "Deader than a door nail," he finished, shaking his head vigorously back and forth.

"Are you sure?" asked Bobby. "damn it, Jimmy are sure?" he demanded thickly.

"Sure I'm sure," Jimmy shot back, "I'm a doctor ain't I? I might be drunk but I know a dead man when I see one."

Hank gagged and said he was going to be sick.

"What the hell are we gonna do?" Bobby asked.

Hank, recovering from his vomiting spell, suggested that they call the Sheriff. After all, it was an accident. The man had come out of nowhere. After some discussion, the others disagreed. They were all half drunk even though this had helped to sober them somewhat. "What do you think the Sheriff would do if he found us like this?

" Ol' Sheriff Relliford ain't no fool, Hank," Bobby was saying, "we'd be up a creek without a paddle."

Jimmy nodded in agreement.

"Bobby's right, Hank. We can't go to the Sheriff. Not like this. Not yet, anyway."

Jimmy suggested that they first talk to his father.

"He has to make a report on all deaths, anyway," he reasoned. "He'll be able to tell us what to do."

The three agreed that this was the best solution. Not taking a chance on moving the car for fear of being seen, Jimmy told Hank and Bobby to stay where they were, out of sight while he went to get his dad. Sprinting out of sight, he disappeared into the blackness.

An eternity passed. No one said a word as the men sat down in the tall grass along the roadside. Hank thought he was dreaming. Bobby wrung his hands in complete exasperation. Both were scared. Now more frightened than drunk. They just waited and prayed.

After what seemed like a week, they heard the sound of a car engine and saw the approaching lights of an oncoming vehicle. They knew it was Jimmy and his dad. They jumped up and bolted down the road toward the oncoming car, waving their arms deliriously. John Cuthbert had to maneuver the car to avoid hitting them. He screeched to a halt and jumped out of the car with his son.

"Okay, okay," he yelled at Hank and Bobby, "just calm down. Calm down!" he repeated. "Jimmy's already told me what happened. Let me check it out."

He had just finished having a time with his son. When Jimmy had burst in the house, he was completely out of control and breath. He had never seen his son so hysterical! He eventually had to give him a mild sedative to calm him down. He was reeking with the smell of alcohol. John was scared almost to death. He hated to see anything wrong with his boy. His whole world revolved around Jimmy, even with all of his faults. That's why times like this were so frustrating and hard to take. He taught his son everything that he knew. No sacrifice was too great. Because of this, he could feel his anger mounting by the second as he surveyed the scene before him. He was emotionally spent.

After an extensive examination of the victim, the Coroner confirmed his son's report. The man had been killed instantly.

"How fast were you goin'?" he barked at Jimmy.

"I don't know, dad," came the reply, "I wasn't paying attention."

John interrupted angrily, "Not paying attention? How in the hell could you have not been paying attention to your speed? That's lunacy," he spat.

"It was in the middle of the night, Dad," Jimmy attempted to explain, "the last thing I expected was to have somebody wandering around on the road."

Bobby and Hank echoed Jimmy's sentiments.

"That's beside the point," rasped John Cuthbert, "none of you boys could pass a sobriety test! You're all soused and a man's dead, damn it!"

He told the boys to take his car home and to sober up. He had to finish his work and told them that he would contact the Sheriff himself. He wanted them out of his way so that he could think what his next move would or could be. The three left unceremoniously as John Cuthbert turned to his work.

John was a man of 58, medium height and built. His light brown hair was now flecked with gray throughout, but his short sideburns were snow white. He had a craggy sort of face with a keen slim nose and small thin lips. His overall appearance was what could be classified as nondescript. He would have made an excellent FBI agent in as much as he had no outstanding features that would cause him to stand out in a crowd. If he were a woman, he would be classified as a "plain jane." His sandy hair was thinning on top and his round horn-rimmed glasses had slid down over his nose.

John's life was a mirror of his appearance. He grew up right here in Midway and went off to college after graduation. He had always wanted to be a doctor and had proceeded right into med school after completing his undergraduate work. He had graduated and received his license to practice medicine well before his 30th birthday. He met and married his wife, Beth, right after graduation! Being one who never cared much for the big city, he returned home and became the town coroner some 25 years ago.

He led a rather comfortable and ordinary life here being one of the town's highest paid officials. He and his wife had only the one child, Jimmy. Often, he had regretted having only the one child because he knew that that was part of the reason why he was so close to his son. Since junior high school, he had not missed one single activity that Jimmy was involved in. He saw every football game at Jimmy's high school because he played in the band. He took him to every 4-H meeting he attended, saw every concert that he played in, and paid his way through eight years of college.

He was confident that Jimmy would pass his Board Exam next year and maybe even become the town's next coroner eventually. Such were the thoughts of this father. It was dark out here alone John noticed. That was good, he decided. No one had seen the accident or the boys leaving. There was really nothing else to do here as far as his work was concerned. The man whoever he was, lay dead. Jimmy had accidently killed him and nothing he could do would change that. Now, his whole life and his future would be affected forever.

Even if Jimmy reported the accident after he sobered up, when the skid marks were measured, it would surely show that he was traveling too fast. He would be charged with vehicular homicide, speeding, and now, leaving the scene of an accident. He would serve a lot of time, John concluded. What would become of all of the expensive schooling that he had paid for? All of the plans he had for his son? Would he ever be allowed to practice medicine at all? It most certainly would be ascertained that he had a drinking problem.

His son's future was in his hands now. No on else knew what had happened except him and the boys. He knew that Hank and

Bobby would never say anything. It was all up to him. Could he let his son down? Jimmy had come to him for help, hadn't he?

As he sat in the car which was covered with blood, he made his decision. He would have to protect his son at any cost. He trembled at the thought of a coverup. He would betray his Hippocratical oath and compromise all of the ethics of his profession if he did. But what could he do? The man was already dead. Turning in his son wouldn't bring him back. His life was over. Why should he also end his son's before it started? Such were the thoughts of this father.

No job was worth the life of his only child. John knew in his heart that what he was thinking was wrong. He would not try to fool himself or rationalize away the truth. Jimmy had killed a man, negligently. He was drunk. Still, John thought, it was his boy. Blood is thicker than water he was always taught.

Then he remembered! The Sheriff was holding the car of two out-of-town strangers at the pound. He had just examined the blood on the car several hours earlier and had not, as yet, made his report to Sheriff Relliford. He had intended to do that first thing this morning, only a few hours from now. The blood on the car, he had determined, was not human blood. The car had struck some sort of animal. He would switch blood samples! No one but he would ever know.

The man was already dead so what harm would be done by protecting his son and his future? After all, these two men were outsiders from up north and he would gladly substitute them for the life of his own boy. Therefore, out of this concern for his son, the web of guilt is now over layered with the gold of love; thus the Gilded Web has now been spun.

It all seemed so clear now. All he had to do was to clean the blood off Jimmy's car, put the dead man's blood on the stranger's car and take the body to the site of the accident and wait. Maybe the dead man's absence would never be reported. What if he had lived alone? John's blood began to race and his pulse quickened. That's it he shouted to himself. The perfect plan! But he had to hurry. There was no time to waste. It would be light soon and he had too much to do.

Hurriedly, and with trembling hands, John went to work. First, he had to clean up Jimmy's car. He started up the engine and drove speedily into town, taking the back roads to his office. Pulling the car into the office garage, he proceeded to clean every trace of blood from the car. He would have to have the grill repaired later in another town. As for now, it would stay right here for a day or two. After cleaning the car, he washed away all traces of blood from the scrub brushes he used and discarded the dirty towels.

Going into the office from the garage, he hurried to the examining room to retrieve a body bag in which to carry the corpse. Borrowing one of the extra cars from the garage, he left the office and sped back to the site of Jimmy's accident. So far, so good. The town was fast asleep. Getting out of the car, he took his black bag and bent over the corpse. Shaking, he took three syringes from his bag and drew three vials of blood. He wrapped them carefully and put them away. He looked at his watch. Four o'clock. He had to hurry. It would be getting light in a few hours. He was thankful that the moon was not overhead. It was a pitch black tonight.

He got the body bag from the car and hurriedly struggled to put the corpse inside. This was not a big man but his dead body weight felt like a load of cement. Opening the trunk to the car, he wrestled the body inside. Closing the trunk, he leaned against the car to catch his breath. He sure missed his assistant's help. But there was no time to rest. He had to find out where to take the body but first, he had to get to the other car and transfer the victim's blood to it.

He drove back to his office and got some soap, brushes, and towels and then sped over to Luke's Garage. As expected, no one was there. Walking up to the fence, he shined a light in the direction of the boy's car. He smiled as he saw it still there. Where else would it be, he mused. Sliding the pan of water and his black bag and cleaning utensils under the chain-link fence, John climbed the six-foot high fence, remembering that he had not climbed fences like this since he was a child.

Dropping over the other side, he gathered up his materials and proceeded to the impounded car. He carefully cleaned away the blood on the fender. There was not a lot of it, unlike what was on Jimmy's car, he thought. After drying the car thoroughly, he extracted the three vials of blood and carefully poured them over the same fender. Since the car was not allowed to be touched, he knew that the blood would have plenty of time to dry. Gathering up all of his stuff, John exited the way he had come in.

Hurrying back to his car, he placed everything inside and checked his watch. Five ten! He was doing fine but time was passing on. As he headed for the Sheriff's office, his car and headlights were the only signs of movement in the velvety night. In his wildest dreams, he would have never imagined himself in such a web of circumstances. His life had always been so predictable, so uneventful. He was often bored by such a bland existence, but now, he wished for it again. He would never complain again about his life's routines because in reality, it was not boring but secure.

Arriving at the Sheriff's office, he parked his car and prepared to get out. It was then that he remembered the body. It was still in the trunk! A chill stole across his back and down his spine. The cold reality of what he was doing struck him as if for the first time. He had been so busy, that he hadn't had much time to think about what he was doing. He cursed Jimmy as he climbed from the car and went into the station. Jake was on duty.

"Howdy Jake," John said stepping inside. "Mr. Coroner," Jake answered, "what are you doing out at five thirty in the morning,?" he asked.

John answered, "Well, I've got a busy day ahead of me and I need to get some things done early. You know, I've got to have that report on that vehicle done for the Sheriff this morning."

Jake nodded, "Yep, he was asking me about it just before he left last night. How can I help you?"

John Cuthbert told Jake that he just wanted to see the report for a minute. "Something I want to check out," he said. Jake went over to the file cabinet, pulled out the report and handed it to the Coroner. John looked it over for a few minutes, scribbled down some notes, thanked Jake and left.

Climbing into his car, he headed in the direction that the Sheriff's report indicated the boys' accident had occurred. He had no misgivings about what he was planning to do. Pinning a homicide on someone else was a serious offense as well as being morally wrong. Not being a particularly religious person, John was bothered more by the violation of professional ethics than he was about the rightness or wrongness of his actions. He was a doctor, not a clergyman.

Still, guilt gnawed at his conscience as he drove. Upon arriving at the location mentioned in the report, John got out of his car, took his flashlight and looked for the exact spot of impact. He found the skid marks that were still visible on the dirt road. He estimated that the hit took place a few feet back, as the car wouldn't have stopped instantly. Backtracking, he estimated the position of the impact. It was only a half hour until daylight. He had to work quickly.

First, he removed the body from the trunk. Taking his black bag from the car, he again drew three vials of blood from the corpse to spread on the ground at the place of impact. Only one thing was left to do. The body had to be disposed of. But where? In the report, it said that no body was found after an initial check. John looked around him. His flashlight searched the roadside. Thick bushes, trees and high weeds lined both sides of the road. He could dump the body anywhere and later, in his report, theorize that the man did not die instantly but was knocked off to the side and had crawled into the bushes before dying.

He took the body from the bag and cut an incision in the lower torso so that blood ran freely and dragged the body through the dust to the clump of bushes where he hid the corpse, leaving a faint trail of blood. Unless someone examined the spot in broad daylight, the blood and the trail would go unnoticed. As the first sign of dawn began to creep into the darkness, he had finished his work of deception. All the pieces were in place, he thought to himself. All he had to do was to go to the office and wait until the body was found.

He breathed a deep sigh of relief now that he had finished the job. As he walked back to his car, the first bird began to chirp in a tree nearby. He had finished just in time. Heading for home, he decided to write up his report that afternoon and give it to the

Sheriff. Of course, it would say that the boy's car was smeared with human blood.

At eight o'clock sharp that same morning, Rod and Jeremy were jolted from their deep night's sleep by the piercing wail of the alarm clock. Such an uninvited intrusion. Jeremy winced as he rolled over and banged the alarm button down. Rod groaned and stirred.

"Too bad you can't arrest alarm clocks for disturbing the peace," Jeremy said.

"You got that right," Rod added. "Man I was out like a light."

"Me too," Jeremy added, "but Rod, my boy, we've got some day ahead. I can't wait to see Beth!!"

"Yeah, you mean you've got an exciting day ahead. Me? I'll have to make some fun," Rod scowled mockingly.

"Why don't you call Andrea before we leave the hotel this morning?" Jeremy suggested hoping to make Rod feel better while at the same time, assuaging his own feeling of guilt. Rod was right, of course, this was really his day.

"That's the best thing you've said all summer," Rod joked, "but until I shower and get dressed, I ain't callin' nobody. I know you're just trying to make me feel better. Don't worry, I'm not gonna interfere with you and Beth. Just pretend I don't exist."

"That's cold-blooded, man. Real cold," Jeremy came back rolling out of bed and stretching.

"Good!" smiled Rod, "just how I wanted you to feel."

After showering and getting dressed, Rod called Andrea. She was still in bed since being back home for the summer vacation. She and Rod had talked about getting married after graduation. Before meeting her, Rod was set on being a bachelor until he was 30. Funny how fast plans can change, he thought. It was good just hearing her voice, though. Jeremy was right about that.

He remembered how dejected he was when he first met her on campus. He had just informed the football coach, Brad Wilson, that he would have to quit football because his grades were suffering. He loved football and the pain of leaving the team was not made any better just because he wasn't on scholarship. The decision to quit was not a hard one to make but giving up something that you love to do is never easy. He was disappointed more in himself and his failure to be a student-athlete than anything else.

He would never forget the look of disappointment on his father's face, who himself was a football player in high school when he told him of his intentions. Dad had never missed a game that he had played in through his entire high school career. He even sat through many of the teams' practice sessions after getting off work.

Hardly any of the other players ever saw their parents at the games on Friday, let alone at practice! Whatever he needed, new shoes, gym bags—whatever—his dad had always found a way to get it for him. When he had a bad game, his dad was always there to offer advice and encouragement. He never pressured him, though, in spite of all the support he gave. It was something special to see his dad jumping up and down, waving the school banner whenever he scored a touchdown or made a spectacular play.

He was not only his father, he was also a friend. However, after quitting the team following his freshman year at State, his dad had told him that it was a wise decision because the bottom line of going to college was to get an education which would help pave the way to a good future. Still, the look on his face . . .

Rod had become very despondent during this period in his life. For the first time in five years, he was not in pads. Something was missing. He felt incomplete. One evening during a spring dance, he was sitting outside the dance hall. He had wanted to just be alone for a while.

"No person is an island, you know," came a friendly voice.

He turned around and saw the world's most beautiful woman looking down at him. With coal black hair cascading down her face, the whitest teeth he had ever seen, and lips that begged to be kissed, he met Andrea. Sheer ebony skin glistened with perspiration from the hot, crowded dance in the Union Hall. The swell of her voluptuous breasts were accentuated by a small waistline and well-rounded hips, a shapely rear end. Her legs, hardly hidden by the shorts she wore, were long and shapely.

Rod swallowed. Hard. Who in the hell was this, Rod had thought instantly. No girl had ever before affected him like this. He thought he was in heaven <u>and, she was speaking to **him**</u>!

"Oh, Hi," he stumbled after catching his breath. "I didn't mean to stare like that, but you caught me completely off guard."

"I'm sorry," she apologized, "I should have sent a messenger first."

They laughed. Rod invited her to sit down on the steps with him and they talked for a while. Although he didn't know her, she knew him from playing football.

"All of the girls know Rodney Blake," she told him. "Don't you know that athletes are the best known people on campus?" He did now.

Man, what a stroke of luck. This girl was gorgeous **and** nice. The two don't always go together. Same with the guys, though. Most of the players on the team were stuck on themselves and felt like they didn't have to do what all the other students did because of who they were. Rod had never shared their egomania. When he quit the team for academic reasons, they had said he was silly. After that night, there was no one else for Rod but Andrea. She was the tonic he needed! Disappointment was no longer his closest friend.

"Hey, man, you okay?" shouted Jeremy from the bathroom as he finished combing his hair. "After you hung up from talking to Andrea, it's like you died or something. What happened, she quit you?"

"You kindin'. She loves me, man. The girl is in love! You hear me?" he added.

" You were right though. I didn't know how much I missed her until I heard her voice. Man, we gotta get out of here and soon," he urged.

"The Sheriff said a couple of days," Jeremy reminded him, "that means that by tomorrow, we should be on our way. In the meantime, I've got to lay down some seeds with Beth so that she remembers me when we leave. I want to grow on her." "Okay Robert Frost," Rod retorted, "let's go eat, poet."

"After breakfast and we split up, when are we going to meet back here? we've only got the one key, you know," Jeremy said.

"Let me have it," said Rod. "If either one of us blows the time, you're better off wandering around the town than me."

"Right." Jeremy agreed." You keep the key and we'll meet back here at nine tonight."

"It's a deal."

As Rod puts the key in his pocket, the boys exchange high fives, closed the door behind them and began the trek to their official dining place down the road with feelings running high.

After eating breakfast, the boys walked back to the Sheriff's office to check with Sheriff Relliford and to tell him of their plans for the day.

"Sounds like you boys are gonna have yourselves some fun today," the Sheriff beamed.

"It ain't exactly New York," Jeremy was saying, "but this place doesn't seem to be all that bad."

"Not an awful lot of young folks here if that's what you mean," the Sheriff responded, "but Jeremy, there's a couple of historic sites that you can visit like the old stone mill down the road and the underground railroad museum.

" Rod, I'll take you to the Jefferson's house in the colored section. They're awfully nice people, friends of mine. Since you don't know anybody there, they'll take you in and introduce you around. I'll pick you up from there about eight thirty or so."

Jeremy and Rod were grateful for all that the Sheriff was doing for them and told him so.

"You've completely changed my opinion of the small-town, southern sheriff," Rod offered, "you're not exactly what the movies portray. You know, the redneck sheriff thing and all."

"Things have changed a little over the years," the Sheriff told him, "but the fact that I'm taking you to the colored section of town just to have some fun, still shows that things aren't quite together yet. Both of you seem to be decent, law-abiding kids and I want you to enjoy our little town while you're here."

"Ever think of working for the local Chamber of Commerce, Sheriff?" Rod teased with a laugh.

"That bunch? They're all stuffed shirts," Sheriff Relliford said with a laugh, "Me? I'm just common people."

The Sheriff then informed the boys that he was expecting the Coroner's report sometime soon.

"Nothing unusual has been reported," he continued. "I would imagine that by tomorrow sometime, we can get your car cleaned up and released and get you on back to school."

"Sounds great to me," Rod said. "I don't know about Jeremy, though," he added, "seems like he's sweet on one of your girls."

Jeremy's face flushed a little.

"That so?" mused the Sheriff, "Anybody I know?" he teased.

Jeremy told him about meeting Beth at the General store yesterday.

"Oh yeah. Roger and Sally McCallister's girl. Hey, that's a looker there for you," he grinned, "kinda cute, huh?"

"She's fabulous," Jeremy corrected.

The Sheriff smiled, patted each boy on the shoulder and said,

"Well, don't let this ol' man hold you up. Rod, we'd better get going. Wait'll you see some of the girls where you're going."

Rod winked at Jeremy. "All right," he exclaimed, "now you're talkin' my language."

After exchanging goodbyes, the boys and the Sheriff got ready to leave the office.

"Willie, hold down the fort," the Sheriff yelled, "I'll be back in an hour or so."

In the Sheriff's car, Rod was curious about his relationship with the blacks on the other side of the tracks.

"How do they feel about you, really?" he wanted to know.

Sheriff Relliford began by recounting the events surrounding his coming to Midway around the mid-seventies.

"Things were pretty much in turmoil like it was in most of the nation then. Racial tensions ran high." He recalled how the blacks were often mistreated and had little or no voice in anything. His predecessor was hated by the blacks and with "just cause."

"He was your typical redneck," the Sheriff chuckled. The blacks had total mistrust in the Sheriff's department back then, he continued, and his experience on the force in Atlanta had told him that he had a tremendous public relations problem to deal with.

So he first began to tour the black neighborhoods, alone, going from door to door and simply introducing himself to the people. Of course, everyone wanted to know what he was up to."

The only time these people ever saw the Sheriff was when there was trouble. Usually when the Sheriff came, it was to settle a domestic quarrel or to arrest someone," the Sheriff added. " this created negative images for the department with the black community. "It was bad," he told Rod, "real bad."

"Did anybody talk to you at all when you knocked on their door?" Rod was asking curiously.

"Not at first," the Sheriff replied, "they probably thought I was spying or something."

Then he told Rod that two things had opened the door for him. First, he met the Jeffersons. They had a nephew who had served with him on the Police Force in Atlanta. When he came home for the family's annual reunion some 10 years ago, he had told them about Toby. Said he was okay. He was introduced to most of the people in the section. "Trust him," he recalled John telling his black friends, "he's good people."

"Damn, that's the only way you could have made it," Rod nodded. "With black folk, somebody's got to speak for you."

"I found that out the hard way," the Sheriff acknowledged. "I was about to give up until the Jefferson's opened up their home and arms to me. But, there was one other thing, though."

He told Rod about the time some 10 years ago when a young black couple had attempted to buy a home for sale in town. Since segregation was technically illegal, they had every right to purchase the property. When they showed up at an open house, the word spread rapidly. In a matter of minutes, a third of the town showed up, surrounded the house, and refused to let the blacks in.

" When I got there, the couple was sitting in their car being bombarded with rocks and eggs and were being called all kinds of nasty names. I had to fire a shot in the air, stand in front of the couple's car and order the crowd to back off."

"That's it," I had yelled, "no one breaks the law here!"

I was called a nigger lover. Anti-black feeling ran high. I had to tell them that I would arrest anyone who started trouble. I was the most unpopular man in the county right then. After a few minutes, the crowd quieted down enough so that I could be heard. My words to them were that they were violating the Federal law. I tried to appease them by appealing to their sense of good citizenship and yelling to them that I understood their concern. I let them know also that my job was to protect all citizens from mob rule and violence no matter what color they were. All I was trying to do at the time was stall until cooler heads prevailed which they did finally.

"I was told later," the Sheriff continued, "that this was the first time that the Sheriff's office had stood up for the rights of colored people in the town."

"What happened after the crowd broke up?" Rod inquired.

"Well, I escorted the couple to my office and we talked. While we were inside, someone threw a brick through the window. When my Deputy and I went outside to investigate, no one was around. I decided to continue our talk at the Jefferson's home. When we pulled up, half of the black people living in the colored section showed up. I told them that I wanted to help but that I was only one person. The young couple came to my defense and told them how I had risked my safety by standing between their car and the mob as they cheered," the Sheriff said in amazement. "I'll never forget that."

Rod listened intently.

The Sheriff then told Rod that the local NAACP had sent the couple in as sort of a trial balloon to test the waters.

"What happened?" Rod asked.

"Same old story," continued the Sheriff. "The local Real Estate agencies, there's only two, put heir heads together and bought the property themselves. All nice and legal. When the NAACP protested, crosses were burned in the colored section and roving white gangs beat up on some of the blacks. I guess they were sending a message."

He explained that ever since then, no other blacks had attempted to purchase property in the town.

"At the next election, I lost a lot of votes," Sheriff Relliford said, "but damn near every black voter in the precinct supported me. I barely made it back in."

"How about now? What do the whites think about what you did?" Rod asked. "You still seem pretty well liked here even now."

"Time cures a lot of ills," the Sheriff replied. "Since the blacks didn't get the home, several of the town's leaders felt that I was only doing my job and threw their support behind me later on."

The Sheriff then admitted that his popularity with the town folks made forgiveness come a little easier.

"Had the NAACP continued to press the issue, I might not be the Sheriff today," added Toby Relliford. "I was determined to uphold the law, no matter what."

The sun was beginning to climb the morning sky as the Sheriff's car wound down the twisting dirt road to the colored section of the town. Rod settled back and drank in the scenery. Tall, thin saplings like telephone poles with leaves formed a picket-like fence along the road side. Thick foliage and wild underbrush was everywhere. The red colored clay-like earth caught Rod's attention.

"That must be the red Georgia clay everybody talks about," he said thoughtfully.

"Uh-huh," said the Sheriff, "pretty ain't it?"

The car bumped slowly over a double set of railroad tracks and soon squeezed its way over a small narrow wooden bridge that spanned a narrow creek.

"Huge mosquito hotel," Rod quipped eying the narrow winding stream.

"Actually there's good catfish in there," the Sheriff remarked. "Down the stream a little bit where it widens, is a hot spot," he said pointing upstream.

As the car rolled into the outskirts of the black district, Rod did not see what he had expected to find. He thought he would find squalor and deep poverty. Instead, small, quaint farms scattered the countryside. They lay serenely nestled in the landscape like little communes. Each plot seemed like an acre or two. The small houses were old wooden frames but most were neatly kept. Each had as few cows, some chickens and hogs.

"Most of these people live off of the land in this part. They own the property passed on from generation to generation," the Sheriff cited.

"They're quiet folk for the most part. More than anything, they just want to be left alone. It's amazing how many of them come back here, even after they finish school. Several of the younger blacks here have college degrees in agriculture on the bigger spreads," he was saying.

"Yeah, it used to be that the blacks would flee the south for up north," Rod replied, "but not so much anymore. They've discovered the north is no panacea and in some ways, the south has come further along in race relations than the north. Boston and Chicago are about as bad as any other place you can find."

"You've got it," the Sheriff agreed.

The car wound its way closer to town. At first sight from a distance, it kind of resembled Midway. Wood frame buildings lined the dirt road. As they drew closer, however, the difference was noticeable. The buildings were much more run down and several were almost unpainted. They had aged so much. They were also crammed closer together. Rows of flats lined the streets. Rod saw a little old gray-haired woman looking intently at them as they passed, sitting in an old rocking chair on the porch and sucking on a corn cob pipe.

"That's ol' Granny Moseby," Toby Relliford said watching Rod's eyes, "Don't nothin' happen here that she doesn't know about."

"How do you know that?" Rod was asking as the Sheriff waved.

"That's who I talk to when the Jefferson's don't know anything," he answered, "Nice old lady, though. Always so polite."

Rod noticed that contrary to Midway, there were a lot more people on the street, many just milling around. The Sheriff explained to him that some of the people worked, but most were on some kind of government assistance and fixed income.

"Some are farm hands on both black and white spreads. Since there is no major industry around here, jobs are scarce," the Sheriff continued. "All of these apartments you see are low income Federal housing."

"The ghetto is the same no matter where you go, huh?" Rod remarked more than he asked.

The Sheriff didn't answer, but instead, waved at a passerby. Even though the town was shabby compared to Midway, Rod had seen worse. Nothing was any worse than the miles of run-down high-rise apartment buildings in Chicago, surrounded by high chain-link fences and windows on practically every store barred up. Front yards were dirt where the grass was worn away by playing children who had no playgrounds to go to. At least, here the people were not stacked on top of each other like cans in a grocery store.

"Not very pretty is it?" said the Sheriff.

"I've seen worse," Rod answered, "at least they probably don't kill each other over crack."

"Not much of a market here for drugs," Toby replied, "but every now and then we have trouble with alcohol-related crimes."

The Sheriff's car rolled to a stop outside of a little carry-out store with a sign advertising barbecued ribs.

"This is Nate and Gloria Jefferson"s little shop," he told Rod, "the one's that I want to introduce you to."

As they got out of the Sheriff's car, several people walking by slowed down with curious looks on their faces. One old fellow in overalls with a big wad of tobacco tucked in his jaw, stopped.

"Howdy Sheriff," he spoke, "how's the missus?"

"Okay," Toby smiled,"everything's okay! Leroy, got somebody here I want you to meet."

He introduced Rod to the old man and told him that Rod was here to look around and spend the day while he waited to have his car fixed in Midway before going home.

"Ain't nuthin' over there is there, son?" he winked at Rod as he shot a stream of tobacco juice jetlike onto the dirt road. Rod bet to himself that he could hit anything with that stream of tobacco.

"No sir, it ain't," Rod replied, "I came to meet Mr. and Mrs. Jefferson."

"You'll like them, yesiree," Leroy said extending his hand to Rod, "have a good time young fellow. Sheriff, tell Deputy Willie Joe we sure miss him around here," he added with a mischievous twinkle in his eyes.

Toby grinned and playfully shoved the gingerly old man.

"Get outta here, Leroy," he said smilingly.

The old man said goodbye cordially and ambled on.

"He'll spread the word that there ain't no trouble," the Sheriff told Rod.

Rod marveled at how easy the Sheriff got along here. He acted as at home as any white person could, Rod thought to himself. It's all in the way you treat people.

"That old man really likes you," Rod said.

"Don't know about that but we respect each other. Anyway, I get along with the older people here a lot better than some of the younger ones. Most of them are not old enough to remember the seventies," he replied.

"Come on, let's go inside."

Rod and the Sheriff were greeted as they came through the door by a portly middle-aged woman with an apron around her thick midriff. She was a handsome medium brown-skinned woman with gray hair neatly folded in a bun on the back of her head. She was full-figured and bosomy with a smiling and friendly face. She had perfect white teeth and wore no makeup. Yet she was an attractive woman, Rod observed. She reminded him a little of his mother.

"Well, if it isn't my favorite Sheriff and his honored guest," Gloria Jefferson greeted them, hugging Toby.

"Hello Gloria," smiled Toby, "How's everything?"

"As you can see, I ain't too busy. Ya'll are my first customers this morning.

You must be Rodney Blake," she said turning to Rod offering her hand.

"Yes ma'am," Rod acknowledged shaking her hand warmly.

"Well, welcome to our little place. Had anything to eat yet?" she asked.

"Yes ma'am," Rod answered.

"How old are you?" she asked Rod.

"Twenty."

"Well, you call me Mrs. Jefferson or Gloria if you want to. You're old enough and polite enough." Rod nodded his acknowledgment.

"Gloria, you don't know how much we appreciated you and Nate doing this for us. By the way, where's Nate?" the Sheriff asked.

"Out in the back, outside, firing up the grill. We specialize in ribs, you know," she answered.

"Yeah, I sure do and sweet potato pie too. Old Sarah in town has been trying to steal your recipe for years now," he joked.

"Aw, she don't need mine. Now that's one white woman who knows how to burn," Gloria said.

They shared a laugh and headed out back to see Mr. Jefferson. He was busy piling coals in the homemade barbecue pit. His bald head glistened with sweat as he worked. When his wife called, he stood up and turned around. Rod noticed that he and his wife looked more like brother and sister than a married couple. They were about the same complexion and build except where Gloria was generous, Nate was massive. Well over six feet tall with huge shoulders and arms, he had the same kind of face his wife had: warm, friendly and handsome. Rod pictured him bending steel rods with his bare hands. He reminded him a little of Otis Sistrunk, the former lineman with the Oakland Raiders NFL pro team. Nobody kicked sand in this man's face.

"Well, if it ain't Toby Relliford, the modern-day Wyatt Earp," he greeted us with a smile. He and Toby shook hands vigorously. "Welcome, son," he said to Rod, "I'm Nate Jefferson."

"Pleased to meet you, Mr. Jefferson," Rod responded, shaking his hand. Nate Jefferson's huge mitt literally swallowed Rod's hand which wasn't small in its own right. It was a firm and friendly handshake. Rod had always hated cold, limp and loose handshakes, especially from men. He liked the Jefferson's immediately.

"Good to see you again Nate," the Sheriff told him, "seems like I can always count on you and Gloria to come through."

"Ain't no problem, Toby," Nate replied, "you can do me a favor though. I need some help puttin'this rack on the pit here," he said pointing to a huge homemade grill made from two oil drums laid side-by-side with piped ventilation and heat control. It was an impressive work of art. The grill was a large six-foot screened-type grill. It had to be awfully heavy, Rod thought. The three men hoisted the grill into place over the charcoal-filled oil drums. Nate explained to Rod that the upper half of the oil drums were hinged doors that closed over the pit to control the temperature.

"We use that especially when we roast whole hogs," he said.

"Man, this ain't nothin' like the little gas grills from the department stores back home," Rod marvelled. "These are made for some serious cookin'!"

The two men laughed.

"That ain't nothin'," Jefferson said, "wait'll you see the ribs down here. They **have** got meat on 'em. Ya'll get cheated up north," he added.

Rod guessed that he was probably right. He couldn't wait to find out. His mouth watered at the thought. The three men walked back inside the store. Gloria watched them coming from inside where she was busy mixing up a batch of her famous sweet potato pie. She and Nate were always glad to see Toby. He was a good sheriff and had always done what he thought was right by the coloreds here in the section. She remembered how he had arrested three drunks from Midway about ten years ago for burning crosses in the section. Even though the men were later set free, Toby had really chastised them. He never shrank from his duties as an officer of the law, even if it got him into trouble. Funny thing though, she smiled, because he didn't take sides when trouble came. He had won the respect of both the blacks and whites in these parts. Like the Bible teaches, she reflected, justice knows no color.

"Well, I've got to be gettin' back," Toby was saying, " can only leave Willie Joe by himself for so long."

"How's Peg?" Gloria asked, "And the children?"

"Peg and the kids are fine," Toby replied. "How's your kids doin' in school?"

"Oh, they'r managin'," she replied.

"Clint's on the track team at Clark State," Nate interjected, "I'm savin' up so that I can go to Atlanta in April to see him run," he beamed.

"Good. Glad everything's okay. I'll be back at eight thirty tonight for Rod," Toby told them. Rod thanked the Sheriff for everything as he and Nate left together for the Sheriff's car.

"Don't you wish that blacks and whites everywhere got along as well as those two and you and Jeremy?" Gloria asked Rod.

"Sure do," he replied nodding, "I don't understand why it's so hard, though. With me and Jeremy, once we ironed out our differences, being friends just naturally happened."

"That's just the point," Gloria added, "Folk have got to eat together, share together and work together. That's the only way to experience the fact that we are all God's children."

"I used to have a thing about forced bussing," Rod said, "until I realized that there has yet to be a better way to make people rub elbows. Nobody likes being bussed, blacks or whites, but until something better comes along it's the lesser of the two evils."

"Is that what they're teaching in college these days?" asked Gloria.

"Nope. Not exactly," replied Rod, "but then college is not so much to teach you what to think but how to think!"

"I like that," Gloria smiled, "you sound like a philosopher."

"Engineering," Rod informed her.

"You came at a good time," she told Rod, "there's a dance down at the skatin' rink this evening if you want to go. In the meantime, let's get some food in that body of yours. It's almost lunch time."

"Great!" Rod replied. He was beginning to get a little hungry. He thought about how Jeremy was making out with Beth and what he was doing right now.

Jeremy was also wondering about Rod. He wished that the two of them could do things together here in town. They had not been separated once during the past two weeks. He resented the fact that it had to happen now. Yet he realized that it was one of the realities of life, even today. In some instances, race still made a difference to some. Still, he was not about to forfeit his plans for the afternoon. Rod was good at finding fun. He had little to do until three, the time that Beth got off work at the store. He would pick her up then, but for now, he decided to pay Toby a visit and check on the progress of the Coroner's report.

Before the Sheriff came out of the back room, Deputy Willie Joe uttered some underhanded racial remarks about how he was now with his own kind of people. Not wanting to ruin his afternoon, Jeremy chose to ignore him. Coming out of the back room, Toby overheard part of his ribbing.

"All right, Willie Joe," he said, "That's enough. Don't you have anything better to do with your time?"

"Aw, I was only pokin' fun, Sheriff," Willie Joe drawled, "didn't mean no harm."

"Not to you, maybe," the Sheriff scowled, "but you're talkin' about his friend. How's it going, Jeremy?" Toby asked.

"Fine, Sheriff," he replied, "just stopped by to see if the Coroner has made his report yet."

"Nope. Not yet. He did call about an hour ago and said that he wouldn't be too much longer. I'll expect to hear something real soon, though."

Willie Joe asked the Sheriff if he wanted him to man the radio in the back.

"Oh, that's all right, Sheriff," Jeremy interrupted, "if you hear anything I'll be down at the old mill this evening with Beth. We're just gonna walk around a little bit and pass the time."

"Okay. Don't worry, I'll find you when I hear something." Jeremy thanked the Sheriff and left.

He walked over to the garage where the car was. He decided to get some tapes that he wanted Beth to hear. After identifying himself, he was taken out back and let into his car as the attendant stood watch. Nothing had been touched inside. He got a few selected tapes from the carrying case on the front seat and prepared to leave. Giving his car a quick once-over, he thought that there was more blood on the car than he remembered. He wasn't sure but it sure seemed like it.

"No one's bothered the car have they?" he asked the attendant.

Not a chance," he replied. "Sheriff Relliford left strict orders that your car was not to be touched."

"It's getting awfully dirty just sitting here in the dust," Jeremy said.

"Well, I'm sorry about that but we don't have enough room inside to store it," came the reply.

"Yeah, I know," Jeremy said. "Well, thanks anyway."

"You bet," said the attendant.

Jeremy left the shop feeling that his imagination must be working over time about the blood. Still, the longer he waited, the more uneasy he was becoming. Time passed slowly but before long, it was time to head for the store. His heart raced a little as he made his way to Beth's shop. First they would go to Sarah's and get a bite to eat. He figured that Beth would be a little hungry. She had been working since seven this morning.

"Hi," Jeremy greeted her coming into the shop.

"Hi yourself," Beth smiled, "I'll be off in a minute as soon as I ring up the register." He watched her as she worked. She moved gracefully around the counter, brushing a blonde strand of hair out of her eye.

Her replacement came in from the storage room, an older woman with thinning red hair and a mousy appearance. She was pencil thin, Jeremy observed, and her voice squeaked when she talked. They exchanged some brief remarks, smiled at each other, and Beth soon emerged from behind the counter.

"Ready?" she beamed showing those white teeth through a smile, "I'm yours for the rest of the afternoon."

"Great! How about something to eat?" Jeremy grinned.

"Best offer I've had all day," she said taking his arm.

Jeremy wondered if all southern girls were so casual. Back home you had to have second thoughts about taking a girl's arm on the first time together. Once in high school, a girl had refused the advance by telling him, "I don't like to be taken for granted." He remembered that they never went out again after that. He didn't want to. Leaving the shop, they walked slowly toward Sarah's, Beth pointing out the various buildings and places of business as they passed.

"How come you're not spoken for?" Jeremy asked her as he felt her warm body close to his, "I mean, with your looks, the guys must be knockin' your door down." She smiled.

"That must be a compliment, I'm sure," she said.

"A crude one, yeah," Jeremy responded.

"Oh, there's been some dates, sure," she told him, "but not lately. I was only real serious about a guy once, four years ago, but it just didn't work out."

"What happened?" Rod asked, "Want to talk about it?"

"Not really," Beth replied. "I was still in high school at the time and my ma had raised me with what could be called old-fashioned values. His were more modern."

"Meaning?"

"He wanted sex without a commitment. I was only 17 at the time and was not ready for a lot of the stuff that my girlfriends were into. They said I was stupid because he was so popular. Big time athlete and all . . . But that didn't impress me. He had little or no morals about him. Still, I was young and swore up and down that I was in love with him."

"Were you?" Jeremy prodded.

"Then, yes. But now that I look back on it, I couldn't have been because I never let him have his way. Eventually, we just broke up. After graduation, he left town to go to college on a track scholarship. I haven't heard from him since."

"How about now? Anybody special?"

"No. I haven't found anyone that interesting until yesterday, that is," she teased squeezing his arm gently. Jeremy blushed slightly.

"I bet you say that to all the guys."

"Huh-uh. I only say what I mean. But hold on a second here," she said coming to a halt, "enough about me. What about you? Tall, handsome college man with a good tan. How many girls are in the black book that you've got hidden some place—s e c r e t?"

"No black book. No secret place," Jeremy winked. "I'll admit, though, that the college scene is pretty wild. At state, there's a lot more girls than guys, so they're out there."

"Meaning?" she mocked him.

"Meaning that I'm not gonna lie to you and tell you that I spent all of my time in the dorm studying. I partied a little."

"A little?"

"Okay, more than a little."

"Why do you sound so much like a parrot? You makin' fun of me?" he said, unable to keep himself from laughing.

"Just the facts, man . . . Just the facts," she smiled.

"No. No one special. Most of the campus girls are mirror images of each other. I never found one that just stood out or who was different. Unique. Until yesterday, that is," he finished.

Their eyes met fully. Jeremy drank in the deep blueness of them which seemed like an ocean washing over him. He was lost for a moment. He felt her stir against his body as she started walking again. She was looking down in front of her as he reached and took her hand in his, entwining their fingers together. She squeezed his hand snugly, indicating her approval.

They walked on for a while, savoring the moment. No words were needed just then. Their eyes had spoken for them. Beth had never felt so comfortable, so soon, with a man before. He had such a nice face and seemed honest and sure of himself. She thought his New York accent was cute and his eyes seemed so full of longing. She was having trouble sorting out her feelings at the moment. All Jeremy knew, just then, was that he couldn't envision never seeing this girl again when it was time for he and Rod to leave. He would have to think of something.

"Will you write me?" he asked quietly.

"If you want."

"I want."

"Then I will," she whispered.

Jeremy took his hand from hers and put his arm around her shoulder, drawing her ever so close. She laid her head on his shoulder as they walked silently, each overwhelmed by the suddenness of the moment. Who can explainthe mystery of moments like this, when nothing makes rational sense, yet everything is completely understood when not more than 24 hours ago, two lives existed autonomously in a universe of isolated, mutual exclusiveness, yet somewhere on a microcosmic scale, they were destined to intersect in a moment when the vastness became minute. Who can fathom the workings of nature? All we know is that its formulas work like a magic of sorts. So, it is and always has been a mystery still unexplained.

"I'm really not very hungry," Beth confessed to Jeremy. "Are you?"

"I thought I was," Jeremy replied, "but not now."

"Good, let's just walk down to the old mill. I want to show you our town's centerpiece," she bubbled.

"Okay. Rod and I don't have much time left here anyway. We'll probably leave in the morning. That doesn't give us a whole lot of time together," he told her pulling her even tighter to him.

"I know," Beth murmured, "I was already thinking about that. It's funny. I almost couldn't sleep last night thinking about you from yesterday."

"I was the same way too," Jeremy confessed. "I told Rod about you and that helped a little. I told him that I had never met anyone quite like you before."

"You two are close, aren't you?" Beth asked.

"Yeah. Pretty close," Jeremy said.

"I'd like to meet him before you leave."

"No sweat. I can't leave without him," he grinned. He kissed her lightly on the forehead as they walked. She tasted like honey.

"I didn't give you permission to do that," she said in mocked surprise.

"I know you didn't."

"You knew it was all right, didn't you?"

"Yes."

John Cuthbert mounted the steps of the Sheriff's office with a pensive and nervous look on his face. He looked tired and worn. His mind momentarily wandered back over the events of the last 15 hours. Had he thought of everthing? Did he cover his tracks? Was something left undone? As he entered the door to the station, he relaxed a little. He was confident that all was taken care of.

"Willie Joe, where's the Sheriff?" he asked the deputy who was getting a drink of water from the fountain in the corner.

"Hold on, Mr. Cuthbert, I'll get 'em," Willie answered. He disappeared in the back room and came back out almost as soon as he had left.

"The Sheriff's on his way out. He's been expectin' you," Willie Joe said looking at the report in the Coroner's hand. "What's the verdict?" he asked.

"I'll wait until your boss comes in," John replied, "It doesn't look good."

"I knew it!" Willie Joe exclaimed excitedly, "that nigger was lyin' as big as you're born. He was covering up somethin'! Done drug that white boy with him too."

"Hold your horses, Willie Joe," John suggested, "Don't jump the gun." As he spoke, he realized that Willie Joe might be useful to him later on. As the thought crossed his mind, the Sheriff came into the room. Willie Joe was squirming excitedly on the edge of his seat but said nothing.

"Better sit down, Toby," John told him, "the report ain't good." A startled look stole over Toby's face.

"What do you mean?" he asked wide-eyed.

"Here," John said handing him the report, "read it yourself."

Willie Joe jumped up and moved behind the Sheriff's chair so that he could look over his shoulder.

"Sit down, Willie Joe," he barked, "I can read it for myself."

Willie Joe did as he was told. As Toby read the report, his face began to fall apart. He read on, turning a page. The corners of his eyes were etched with puzzlement and his forehead furrowed deeply.

"John, there must be some mistake here," he said, turning again to the report in disbelief. "How could there have been someone hit? Willie Joe and me checked out of the place ourselves, didn't we?" he said turning to the Deputy.

"That's right, Coroner," Willie Joe agreed scratching his head in bewilderment, "that's a fact."

"I'm sure you did," John responded, "but this is the result of my tests. The blood is human without a doubt. You can have it double-checked if you want to Sheriff but the results are conclusive." Toby waved his hand.

"No need for that. I trust your work." He reread the report again in disbelief.

"This doesn't necessarily mean that someone's been killed," John advised. "Have you gotten any missing person reports?"

"No. I've been monitoring the radio ever since the boys arrived in town," Toby told him. "Nothing. Absolutely nothing."

"Well, maybe there's nothing to worry about," John said standing. "Let me know if anything turns up."

"Yeah, yeah," Toby muttered never taking his eyes off the report, "Sure will John, thanks."

"Only doin' my job, Sheriff," John said as he left.

Once outside the door, he paused. He could hear the excited squeals inside from Willie Joe and the harsh tones of Toby who told him to sit down and shut up. He heard the Sheriff saying that he needed time to think. John left breathing a sigh of relief. He hated what he had just done. In all of his years as a physician, he had not so much as told a lie about his work. He was always up front and saw himself as a man of honesty and integrity. He didn't relish the realization that all of that was now destroyed forever. The clock could never be turned back now. If only he had a choice. But there was none. It was either his only son or the two strangers. For him, the choice was easy.

Toby sat perplexed and troubled. He had never even imagined that anything like this would happen. He was certain that the boys had struck an animal of some kind. It was not out-of-the-ordinary. Toby instructed Willie Joe to make a fresh pot of coffee.

As he went back over the details of the boys' accident and his search at the scene that night, he realized that it was not much of an investigation. He had checked, spottingly at best, just to satisfy Willie Joe. He could have overlooked hordes of clues in the pitch darkness, he acknowledged grudgingly. In light of John's report, an official investigation would now be necessary.

"Willie Joe," he said, "first thing in the morning, me and you will have to conduct an official and thorough investigation of the boys' accident. We can't take anything for granted anymore. And Willie, read my lips! If you breathe a word of this to anyone before morning, you won't work here or anywhere else ever again. Is that understood?" Willie nodded his head vigorously.

"I understand, Sheriff."

"We don't know anything yet. Absolutely nothing. For all we know, whoever was hit might not even have been hurt bad. Could have just been a drunk or something. Anyway, we'll check it out in the morning. It'll be dark soon, so we don't have enough time today," he concluded.

"What about the two boys?" Willie Joe asked.

"What about them?" snapped Toby.

"Do we need to hold them?"

"On what charges?" Toby asked. "As far as we're concerned, they haven't done anything. Of course, they can't leave town until this is cleared up, if that's what you mean?"

"Yep. That's what I was talkin' 'bout," Willie Joe responded.

"Jeremy's with Beth McCallister somewhere in town and Rodney's over at the Jefferson's place. I'll pick them up at nine tonight and tell them to stay put at the hotel." Toby added.

Coffee's done, Sheriff," Willie Joe informed Toby.

He walked slowly over to the coffee pot and absent-mindedly poured a cup of hot coffee and slumped heavily in a nearby chair.

Night had just begun to fall in the colored district as Rod danced to the beat of a song. He had certainly enjoyed his time in the village and had eaten to his heart's content. Couldn't get much better than this, he thought to himself as he moved to the music. Good food, good party and lots of pretty women, just like the Sheriff had said.

He had met several young ladies who seemed interested in him, especially one named Rosie. She was a light-skinned, black-haired beauty with a terrific body but Rod had decided she was a little too young to talk to. She looked like she was only about 17. Anyway,

Andrea was on his mind. He wished it was her that he was dancing with now. Toby would be coming back pretty soon, so he would have to leave for the Jefferson's before long.

Jeremy and Beth sat quietly on a park bench near the old mill, listening to the water pouring over the huge mill wheel. Beth was curled up beside him as Jeremy stroked her long blonde locks gently.

"I've had a wonderful evening today," she was telling him, "I just wanted you to know that."

"Me too," Jeremy said soothingly. "I wish I had met you ten years ago."

"You wouldn't have liked me then. I was skinny and too quiet."

"I would have liked you," Jeremy assured her.

"What time is it?" she asked.

Jeremy strained his eyes to see his watch in the advancing darkness.

"Eight thirty. Toby is probably on his way to pick up Rod," he said.

"I guess we'd better be getting back. Let's stop at Sarah's on the way and get a sandwich or something. I'm really hungry now," she said.

Jeremy climbed down off the picnic table and reached for Beth. She made no attempt to move. He stepped closer to her and took her face in both of his hands and slowly lowered his mouth to her warm, luscious and eager lips. Her lips parted at the slightest pressure and he kissed her deeply. She groaned softly and melted like butter in his arms. His tongue explored the innermost parts of her willing mouth. Her arms went up around his neck and clutched at him desperately, as she whimpered with joy and excitement.

Jeremy crushed her against his body with powerful arms and they kissed for what seemed an eternity. He trailed his lips over her small nose, her moist eyes, her fragrant hair and down the nape of her neck and back to her eager lips once more. She shuddered as his tongue once again searched for hers. She pulled away kissing him violently all over his face with soft fluttering kisses like the comfort of a gentle breeze. Jeremy's heart was racing out of control and Beth began to breathe heavily as her excitement grew. They kissed. And kissed again.

"Please, please," Beth whispered huskily as she pulled her lips away, "We've got to stop. Jeremy, we have to!"

"I know, baby," he whispered, "I know."

There in the stillness and cover of the dark, they clung to each other furiously, never, ever wanting to let go.

"I'll write you every day," Jeremy promised her kissing her eyes softly tasting salty tears.

"You promise?" she pleaded urgently.

"Count on it," Jeremy said, "that's more than a promise!"

Slowly, reluctantly, but joyfully, the two lovers headed back to town, arm-in-arm, the way they had come.

Toby drove his car carefully and measuredly through the thickness of the night, not saying much at all. Rod had noticed a drastic change in the Sheriff's actions when he had picked him up at the Jefferson's place. He had been cordial and polite enough but he was not his old self. He had left the Jefferson's place unusually somber and uneasy. Rod was thinking that something must have happened at the office but said nothing. If it had, it was certainly none of his business. He wouldn't pry. They rode in uneasy silence into town. Stopping at the old mill, there was no sign of Beth and Jeremy.

"They must have gone back to town," Toby said, breaking the silence, "let's check at Sarah's place. If they're not there, you go on back to the hotel until I find him. Okay?" he asked Rod.

"Okay," Rod replied. "I wish you'd say something, though. I know something's not right. Did I do something wrong back there?"

"No, it's not you, Rod," the Sheriff told him, "I just need to talk with you and Jeremy together, that's all."

"Then something's wrong," Rod said nervously.

Just then they saw Jeremy and Beth coming out of Sarah's restaurant headed toward the hotel. Toby guided the car alongside them and honked his horn softly as he rolled down his window. They were so preoccupied that they didn't see the car drive up.

"Hop in you two," Toby said, "We'll give you a lift. Beth, I need to talk to the boys."

Jeremy and Beth got in the back of the car with puzzled expressions on their faces.

"What's up Sheriff?" Jeremy asked. "Rod, what's wrong? You look funny. Something happen over there," he inquired.

"Naw, Toby just wants to talk with us, that's all," Rod answered.

"About what Sheriff?" Beth asked nervously.

"Police business, Beth," Toby said, "the boys ain't done anything yet that I know of but I have to ask them some things as part of my job. Don't worry. They're all right. Do you need a ride home?"

"No, I drove," Beth answered, "my car's at the store."

The Sheriff stopped at Beth's car and she got out. She told Jeremy to call her at home as soon as they were finished. He promised he would and the Sheriff then sped toward the station. Inside, Toby got the Coroner's report and handed it to them as they headed into the back room, closing the door behind them.

"Sheriff, this can't be right," Jeremy exclaimed after he and Rod had read the report with disbelief.

"We looked around, even listened for any sounds of crying or pain and heard and saw nothing. We told the truth" he pleaded.

"I know you did," said Toby, "but I can't dispute what Doc wrote in his report. Doc Cuthbert is one of the county's most trusted coroners."

"But this means that Jeremy and me hit somebody!" Rod said with a rush.

"I know," the Sheriff said, "but don't jump to conclusions. Nobody's been reported hit. That's what's strange. I should have gotten a hospital report or something by now. It just doesn't add up."

"What does this mean?" Jeremy asked.

"It means that I'm gonna have to ask you boys not to leave town until my deputy and I investigate this thing thoroughly. We'll have to recheck the site, check the hospital and ask around town about somebody being hurt in an auto accident. That sort of stuff. It shouldn't take long. I wouldn't worry too much. It might turn out to be nothing serous at all," he reassured them.

"Let's all go home and get some sleep," the Sheriff said.

"I won't sleep until this is straightened out," Rod was responding in distress. "Man, I can't believe this is happening!"

"We'll get started first thing in the morning," the Sheriff told them. "I'll let you know the minute we're through. I'm sorry fellas but I've got no choice!"

Apprehension engulfed the boys as Toby drove them back to the hotel. Once inside, they both fell across their beds without bothering to turn on the light and lay there with their clothes on staring at the ceiling in the darkness.

Chapter Four

Relationships

"Over here, Sheriff," called Willie Joe, as the morning sun beamed brightly overhead. "I found some blood." It was seven in the morning as Toby and Willie Joe were conducting their investigation of the reported accident site. A couple of things didn't quite fall into place. Toby had found only one set of skid marks in the dust but now Willie's call to him indicated that blood had been found in two different places.

"Okay, Willie," the Sheriff called back, "Give me a second to mark this spot." Marking the spot, Toby hurried over to Willie Joe.

"What have you got?" he asked.

"Look. Lots of blood here and some over there too," Willie Joe said pointing.

Toby examined the spot where Willie was standing and then followed a faint trail of blood toward a clump of thickets near the road.

"It looks like something crawled or drug itself away from this spot," he said following the trail. "We didn't see this the first time because it was too dark," he continued.

The Sheriff and Willie followed the faint trail of blood to a thick clump of bushes. The brush had been flattened by a heavy weight. Pushing through the thicket, they stopped in their tracks at the same time and gasped. There on the ground lay the sprawling figure of a man obviously dead.

"Holy moly," exclaimed Willie Joe, "I'll be damned!"

"Careful, Willie," Toby Relliford directed, "Don't touch anything."

Toby's heart fell into his stomach. He was numb and slightly dazed. It was not the sight of a dead body that affected Toby this way. He had seen his share of them while serving on the Atlanta police force. It was, instead, the immediate realization that this man had been lying here for about two days, assuming that he was the object that the boys had reported hitting. Neither he or Willie recognized the dead man.

"First thing we have to do is get blood samples," the Sheriff told his deputy. "Willie Joe, get the kit from the car," he instructed.

As Willie left, Toby got his notebook and a pen from his breast pocket and took detailed notes about the victim's appearance, position of the body and his clothing. He touched nothing. He noticed that one of the victim's shoes was missing. Willie Joe had returned with the physical evidence gathering kit the Sheriff had asked for.

"While I get some blood samples, I want you to look around and see if you can find anything else," he told Willie. "If you find anything, don't touch it."

"Yes sir," said Willie Joe leaving almost at once. Toby busied himself collecting the blood samples that were found in both spots. Once he had finished his work and Willie Joe had reported that nothing else had been found, the Sheriff turned to his deputy.

"I'm gonna go get Doc Cuthbert and bring him back here. I want you to stay and safeguard the evidence. Nothing is to be touched until we get back."

"I'll guard it with my life, Sheriff," Willie Joe promised sticking out his chest with pride. "I ain't never been a part of a murder investigation before, so I'll do my part—you can count on that!"

"Nobody said anything about a murder," the Sheriff corrected him. "This is a homicide, Willie. A homicide."

Homicide? Murder? What's the difference, Willie thought to himself but said nothing. "Yessir," he answered simply.

Sheriff Relliford climbed into his car and headed for the Coroner's office. breaking the news to Jeremy and Rod was going to be extremely difficult. He would have to tell them that they would now be unable to leave. He knew that they were already planning to head for home. He felt a tinge of anxiety because he was beginning to grow fond of them. He enjoyed their company and knew that both of them were too honest to be lying or trying to hide something from him.

Even though the two incidents still might be unrelated, the chances were growing extremely remote. There was human blood on the boys' car and now they had found the body lying off the road at the spot that the accident had occurred. He would have to confine them to their room without arresting them until the Coroner's inquest was finished. He would talk to them after he and Doc had finished what was left to do. He pulled up to the Coroner's office, got out of his car and pushed through the door carrying his evidence kit with the blood samples.

"Good morning, Sheriff Relliford," John Cuthbert's secretary greeted him.

"Good morning, Marge," he responded to the bespeckled, gray-haired woman seated behind the desk. "John in?"

"Just a moment," she said moving away from her typewriter and pushing the button to the intercom.

"Sheriff Relliford is here to see you," she spoke.

After a brief pause, she pointed behind her.

"He said to go on back."

"Thank you."

"You're welcome."

Toby ambled his way to the back of the outer office and through the door. John was seated at his desk drinking coffee.

"Howdy, Toby. Want a cup?" he asked gesturing to the coffee pot behind him.

"Don't care if I do. I need one this morning," Toby replied, putting his kit down on the floor next to the seat that he would sit in.

Walking over to the coffee table, Toby began. "Willie Joe and I have spent the morning investigating the boys' accident again. We found a body, dead in the bushes just off the road where the boys reported hitting something," he continued walking back to the chair opposite of John's at the front of the desk. He sat down.

"Who was it, anybody we know?" John quizzed.

"We didn't recognize him. We didn't search the body for a wallet or anything," the Sheriff went on. "We'll do that when you go back with me for your examination." Toby asked.

"I don't have anything to hold me up. My assistant called me this morning. His wife is not feeling well and he may have to take her to the family doctor. You and Willie Joe will have to assist me," he said. John said.

"No problem."

"When do you want to leave?"

"Right away," Toby said, "I need you to also check out these blood samples that I took from the scene. We need to see if they match the blood on the boys' car and that of the victim."

"Well, let's get the body here first," John said standing, "the test shouldn't be too hard to do. Here, I'll take those," John volunteered reaching for the two samples that Toby had taken from his kit and held in his hand.

"Oh, dear," Toby said handing them to him, "Strange thing. We found blood in two different spots."

"Oh, really," John said surprised. His eyebrows arched.

"May not be important though," Toby said, noticing the Coroner's apparent surprise. "It just seemed a little odd because one of the samples was not near the spot where the man was hit. I can't figure out why if someone was hurt that bad that he would try and crawl instead of calling for help. The boys said that they didn't hear anything."

"Mystery to me," John answered nervously. "Maybe we can find some answers when I get a chance to do the autopsy."

"Maybe so," Toby said. "Who knows what anybody would do in those circumstances, anyway?" he sighed.

Still, Toby's question had greatly disturbed John. That was one question that never crossed his mind in his haste. Though it was a question that could never be answered—still, it was an indication that he could not take Toby Relliford for granted. He was an outstanding Sheriff, John conceded, and he could not be taken lightly. He would have to be extremely careful.

"You don't mind riding in the hearse, do you Toby?" he asked the Sheriff.

"I'll go in my car, Doc.," the Sheriff responded, "I'm sure Willie Joe won't want to ride back in the hearse."

They both chuckled as they left the room. Stopping at the front desk, Toby asked to use the phone while John went outside to get the hearse.

"Jeremy, you two up yet?" he spoke into the mouthpiece. After a brief pause, he said, "Well, after breakfast, I want you and Rod to stay put until you hear from me. Stay at the hotel, okay?" . . . a pause . . ."Alright, I'll see you in an hour or so. Goodbye."

Hanging up and thanking Marge, Toby headed out the door just as John pulled up in the black shining limousine. Toby leaned into the open window.

"Only time I ever wanted to ride in one of these things was when I didn't know anything about it," he said to John who just smiled. John confessed

"Most people feel that way. It's natural. I didn't like them at first myself.

"But, it comes with the job," he noted. "I'll follow your car out to the site if you're ready to take off."

Shortly, the two men arrived at the scene, got quickly out of their autos and made their way to Willie Joe who was still standing at attention next to the body.

"Good job, Willie," the Sheriff said. "Anybody come by?"

"Not a soul, Sheriff."

"Good! Recognize him, John?" Toby asked the Coroner.

"Nope. Can't say that I do. Never saw him before," John replied, "but I can tell he's been dead awhile, though."

"Well, as soon as you get his belongings to my office, we'll try and get a make on him. How long do you think that'll take." Toby asked.

"I'll try to have my report and everything done in a matter of hours," John replied.

"Good."

John briefly re-examined the body and then asked Willie Joe to help them load the bagged corpse into the hearse.

"Do I have to?" he begged. "I can hold the door open for you?"

"No, we need some muscle," chuckled the Sheriff. The three easily slid the body into the back of the black limousine and Doc shut the door.

"Want to ride back with me?" Doc Cuthbert asked Willie Joe.

"Uh-uh. No way," Willie Joe said retreating defensively.

"Sheriff's car got me here and it's takin' me back."

Everybody laughed heartily. John told Toby he'd call him as soon as he was finished. Then, he drove out of sight. After a brief last check of the area, Toby and Willie Joe proceeded in the direction of town, too, with the Sheriff deep in thought but uneasy about the whole situation.

Back at the office, Toby got himself a cup of coffee, informed Willie Joe to hold his calls and shut himself in the back room to think. Several things were not falling into place. How could the boys fail to hear the cries or agony of someone so badly mutilated, yet, had not died immediately? While the man dragged himself, he must have made some kind of sound. The boys had reported that it was so quiet that night, they would have heard anything for hundreds of feet. Why were there two separate blood trails in the dust?

He decided to talk to Rod and Jeremy again. Maybe he had overlooked a small detail that might be significant. In the boys' hotel room later, they told the Sheriff the exact same story again.

"Nothing else that you can remember? Anything?" Toby asked them.

"Nope. That's it, Sheriff," Jeremy said. Rod agreed.

"Sheriff, there is one thing I ought to mention to you. I mentioned it to Rod a while ago," Jeremy volunteered. Toby scooted to the front of his chair all ears.

"What?"

"It's probably nothing," Jeremy began, "but I swear, Sheriff, when I stopped by the garage yesterday as I waited for Beth to get off work, I'm certain that there was more blood on my car than there was before."

"Oh?"

"Yeah. I could be wrong because Rod and I were both pretty shook up after the accident and it was dark that night. But still, I remembered that when I checked my car with the flashlight, there just didn't seem to be that much blood."

"What are you saying?" Asked Toby.

"I don't know," Jeremy admitted. "The attendant at the garage said that my car had not been disturbed."

"It doesn't sound like much to go on. Luke's place is not patrolled at night and there is no guard dog there either. We can't afford to overlook anything though. Let's take another look. Remember, I saw your car that night too," Toby told them. The three left the hotel together and went over to Luke's. After looking at the car again himself, Toby pulled out his pad and scribbled down some notes.

"We could be wrong, you know," the Sheriff suggested, "but Jeremy, I believe you're correct. There does seem to be more blood on you car. In Police work, sometimes the most trivial observations can be critical. And then, too, we aren't certain about this ourselves."

"But why would anyone tamper with our car?" Rod asked.

"We don't know if they did," Toby added, "We might be way off base. What would be the motive for a tampering? We just need to keep our thoughts to ourselves about this. Let's go."

Back in his office, Toby had decided that no one would be informed about his suspicions. He was convinced that someone had altered the blood on the boys' car. He dared not let the boys know his true feelings but his trained eye, seasoned with more than 20 years of police work had spotted it immediately. The car had been tampered with. But this just didn't make any sense. Why? Who? Toby took a pad and chronologically began to write down all of the events regarding the boys' accident up to the present time. He would make sure that nobody would get their hands on his notes this time.

First, the boys had heard nothing immediately after hitting something. They found no body. He himself had found no body. Secondly, no missing person report had been filed. Thirdly, there were two isolated patches of blood at the site. Fourth, the victim was missing a shoe that he, himself, had secretly looked for during the investigation this morning. At the time, it didn't seem important enough to mention. And finally, he was convinced that someone had messed with the boys' car. As he pondered over his notes again and again, he searched his trained mind for some connection—some link that would make sense. He found none. He slumped in his chair as a worried look stole across his face.

John Cutbert was on the phone in his office talking long distance to a body shop in nearby Chattanooga which was the closest big city to Midway. He was making arrangements to have the front-end of his son's car repaired. John explained that he didn't have enough confidence in the local shops here and that he was willing to pay extra to have the car fixed immediately. He made a deal with whomever was on the other end of the line and hung up breathing a sigh of relief. He had to get Jimmy's car out of the back garage before anything else happened. He picked up the phone again.

"Jimmy?"

"Yes, Dad."

"I've made an appointment for you in Chattanooga to have your car fixed this afternoon. Get over here as soon as you can and take off. They'll fix it as soon as you arrive. You're supposed to be on your way back to school if they ask."

"All right," Jimmy responded, "be right over."

Hanging up, John now contemplated his next move. Once his son was gone, he would get his autopsy report and lab findings to Sheriff Relliford. He had bagged up the dead man's belongings to drop off at the Sheriff's office as well. Was there anything else?

Any details left undone? He made a careful mental check. Once Jimmy's car was fixed, there would be no way to connect him to the homicide.

He relaxed a little and smoked a cigarette. Picking up his report for the Sheriff, he went over it slowly and carefully once again, looking for any possible mistakes. He was convinced it was fine as he laid it down once more on his desk. The blood samples on the car, that of the victim and one of the samples taken from the road, all matched. The fourth blood sample was from an animal of some kind, totally unrelated to the accident.

What troubled him somewhat was the discovery that the animal's blood found near the scene was about a day older than the blood of the dead man. Of course no one knew this but him and it was not noted in his report. Since it was not human blood, nobody would question how old it was. Animals are hit around these parts all the time. Still he wished that Toby had not found it. He was interrupted from his thoughts by the buzzing of his intercom.

"Yes?"

"Your son is here to see you, Doctor," his secretary informed him.

"Good. Send him right in." Moments later, the door swung open and Jimmy strode in, smiling confidently.

"Thanks Dad, for everything. I owe you one."

"Yeah," John muttered to himself. "Just get the damn car outta here and take the back roads out. Here's the name and address of the place in Chattanooga and some extra money in case you have to stay overnight," he said, handing his son a piece of paper and a handful of money.

"I don't want any receipts either. Tear it up and throw it away when you get it. We don't want any evidence left around of you getting this work done."

"Okay. Can I take Bobby and Hank along?"

Hell, no, "John snorted, "You've had enough trouble with them two. Jeez, you never learn, do you?"

"Sorry. I didn't mean anything. They're just my friends," Jimmy said apologetically.

"What're they doin' anyway?" John asked his son.

"Nothin'. They've been too scared. I told them that they didn't have to worry. That everything's being taken care of."

John shot up from his chair and slapped both of his hands into his son's chest, knocking him off balance and a couple steps backward.

"Don't come in here with that lighthearted , easy-going shit! As long as your butt stinks, don't you ever again, in you whole damn life, do something to me like this again. All I've ever wanted was a son to be proud of. A boy that made something out of himself. Instead, you've been one big headache. This is the last straw." John rasped.

Jimmy was startled at first. This was the first time that he could remember feeling that his father really wanted to hit him. He knew his dad was upset over what had happened these last two days but he had never acted this violently before. He was always so rational and in control. Tears began to well up in his eyes.

"I didn't mean it that way," he choked.

"I hope not, damn it! A future physician must have more of a regard for human life than what you just showed me." John retorted.

Jimmy explained that what he had said was meant to be out of a sense of confidence that he had in his father, instead of a lack of concern over what he had done. John apologized and said that he overreacted. The two embraced. John got the car keys out of his desk drawer and gave them to Jimmy.

"This time, pay attention to your driving," he said.

"I will."

"Call me when everything's done."

"Yes sir," Jimmy said. The door opened and closed quietly behind him as he left the room. John now turned his attention to other matters. Gathering up his report, he left his office and stopped at his secretary's desk.

"I'll be gone for awhile. Be back in an hour or so," he told her and left. Going into the back garage, he rounded up the victim's belongings, got into his automobile and headed for the Sheriff's office. Toby was in the front office as he stepped inside.

"John," he exclaimed excitedly, " I was wondering how long you'd be. Willie, we'll be in the back room," he said to his deputy as the two men disappeared closing the door behind them.

Willie strained his ears to hear the muffled conversation going on in the back room. Curiosity had been eating at him these last couple of days. Especially since the Sheriff had demanded that he say nothing to nobody about what was going on. He hated keeping secrets. Nothing exciting had happened around here for the longest time. He relished the thought of getting first-hand information to his buddies. It gave him a sense of importance . . . of power. He only heard a few words here and there. Not enough to know what was really going on except that he could tell that Sheriff Relliford was not pleased. He gave up trying to listen and went back to his desk. He would find out soon enough.

After what seemed like an hour, the Sheriff and the Coroner emerged from behind closed doors. They were saying their goodbyes and shaking hands. The Sheriff's face was grim and etched with worry. John walked away, looking down at the floor. Before Willie could say anything, the Sheriff turned abruptly and strode back into the rear office, slamming the door behind him. He knew enough about the Sheriff not to bother him at times like this. All he could do was wait. He was ready to explode. What was happening? What had Doc said? He had not seen the Sheriff so visibly upset in a long, long time. He bit his lip and waited.

The Sheriff finally came out of the back room walking as if the weight of the world was slung on his back. He was drained and his proud shoulders drooped noticeably. He spoke in almost a hush.

"Willie, I'm gonna have to pick up the boys."

"For what, Sheriff," Willie said wide-eyed.

"I'm forced to take them into custody."

"You mean arrest 'em?"

"That's right."

"On what charge, Sheriff?"

"Vehicular homicide."

"Sure nuff, Sheriff?" Willie asked again. "Now if that don't beat all. What'd Doc say?"

"The victim's blood matches the blood on the boys' car. He said there's no mistake. They're the same."

"What about the blood on the road?"

"The same."

"Holy moly," mumbled Willie Joe, scratching his head.

"Get one thing straight, Willie Joe. The boys are innocent until proven guilty. There is definitely going to be a thorough investigation. I'm going for the boys. Say nothing to no one about this. I'll be right back."

The sheriff left the room as Willie Joe sat down trembling with excitement. Man, what a scoop, he thought to himself excitedly.

Toby knocked on the door of Rod and Jeremy's room. After a brief pause, it flew open and Rod invited the Sheriff inside.

"I can tell by your face it's bad news, isn't it?" Rod asked.

Jeremy came out of the bathroom still half-shaven. He wiped his face with a towel as he sat down.

"I've got bad news," Toby began, "you're right Rod. We've got a problem." Toby shared with the boys his meeting with the Corner and his report. Jeremy and Rod were devastated. Their mouths dropped open and their eyes widened in disbelief as the Sheriff spoke. They sat and stared at each other in shock.

"Sheriff, there couldn't have been a dead man there that night," Jeremy spoke up. "We checked and we listened. We didn't hear a sound. Nothing."

"I believe you," Toby responded, "but even though you looked, you wouldn't have seen the body anyway. It was too dark. Willie Joe and myself missed it too."

"Yeah, if it was there," Rod retorted. "I believe Jeremy. Somebody's trying to set us up."

"But why? And who?," Toby asked.

"I don't know," Rod admitted.

"Does this mean we're under arrest?" Jeremy asked.

"I have to take you in if that's what you're asking," Toby answered.

"I'll have to hold you until bail is posted and after that you'll have to stay in town until your hearing. I hate to have to do this boys but I have no other choice."

"Aw, man," Rod moaned, standing up and starting to pace the floor.

Jeremy just sat in stunned silence staring at the floor. Toby said nothing. Silence hung in the air like a thick cloud. Jeremy finally stood up.

"Well, we might as well go," he said hesitantly. "We've got no choice."

Rod stopped pacing. His eyes pleaded with the Sheriff but he remained silent.

"You'll need to pack your stuff," Toby told them. "We'll load it in my car." Jeremy and Rod nodded and began to move robotically about the room gathering up their belongings, slowly, methodically. After several minutes had passed, they finally indicated that they were ready to go. Toby grabbed an armful of luggage and the three left the room and headed down the hall. They stopped at the desk and paid the clerk for the room.

"You boys come back," the clerk told them. "Fine kids," he said to Toby as they picked up their belongings. Toby nodded as they left. Arriving at the station, the Sheriff and the boys unloaded the squad car and began to carry the gear up the steps to the front door. Willie Joe met him at the door and took Toby's load himself. The four men went inside and closed the door.

"Where do you want this stuff, Sheriff?" willie Joe asked putting his load down.

"Lock it up in the back," Toby instructed. "Rod and Jeremy, you come with me."

Sheriff Relliford took the boys into a back room that was behind the room where the radio monitoring equipment was located. Stepping inside the small dark room, Toby hit the switch and flooded the room with light. There was a corner with photographic equipment set up complete with a cloth background on the wall. On a desk in the middle of the room was finger-printing equipment. A stencil machine and a desktop copier filled the table top. There were two stools with long legs in a corner for picture taking. There was not a lot of space for idle movement. The boys knew what the room was used for.

"So, this is the mugshot and finger-printing room," Rod said sarcastically, "always wondered what they looked like."

"Now we know first-hand," Jeremy added.

"This is just procedure," Toby said. "We have to get a make on everybody we hold. It's just a formality."

Being photographed and finger printed was one of the most humiliating experiences that Jeremy and Rod had ever had happen to them. As far as they were concerned, it was a one-time experience.

"I don't see how anyone could go through this time after time," Rod said looking at the black ink that covered his finger tips.

"It comes off pretty easy with this," Toby said, handing the boys a jar of a gooey-looking substance. Cleaning up and turning off the light, the three made their way back to the front office. Willie Joe hung up the phone as they entered the room. He stared icily at Rod without blinking.

"You'd better get a cell ready," Toby told him.

"A cell? You mean two cells, don't you Sheriff. We don't lock up the colored with the whites, remember?"

"I said a cell," the Sheriff repeated with the emphasis on "A."

Willie Joe quickly got the point. As he left, Toby told the boys that they should call their folks.

"Tell them to come down as soon as possible. You'll need to have someone post bond and seek legal council. Since this is a homicide, I can't get bail waived."

"Is this our **one** call?" Jeremy asked.

"Make as many as you need."

"Thanks Sheriff."

"No thanks are necessary. I'll leave you alone for ten minutes. Take your time," Toby said as he left the room to join Willie Joe in the back.

Jeremy called first because his father worked with a battery of New York's finest attorneys. He called his father's office. After dialing, he paused.

"John McCutchin, please." pause

"This is his son, Jeremy." another pause.

"Dad?"

"Jeremy? Where are you calling from?" said the voice on the other end. "You in town?"

"No, Dad. I'm in Midway."

"Where the hell is Midway, son?" John said with agitation.

"In Georgia, near the Tennessee border. Rod and I are in trouble. We need your help."

There was a long pause. Then, John McCutchin spoke again.

"Sorry son, I had to push the mute button. Are you all right?" he asked.

"Yes, we're fine, I guess. We're in jail."

Rod heard Mr. McCutchin's explosive reaction from where he was sitting. Jeremy told his father to take it easy and give him a chance to talk.

"No, we didn't do anything. There was an auto accident a couple of nights ago. Rod and I hit something in the road. We've been here since I talked with Mom the other day. There's been a dead body found where we reported our accident."

"When?"

"This morning."

"By whom?"

"The Sheriff."

"Let me speak with him, Jeremy. Right now, son."

"Yessir."

Jeremy put the phone down and went to the back room where the Sheriff and Willie Joe were. Rodney picked up the phone.

"Mr. McCutchin?"

"Yes, Rodney. You okay?"

"I'm fine. So's Jeremy. I just wanted you to know that the Sheriff's alright. He's trying to help us."

"How are they treating you down there?"

"Except for one deputy, fine."

Just then, Jeremy returned with Toby Relliford and Rod handed the phone to the Sheriff. Sheriff Relliford and Jeremy's Dad talked for several minutes. The Sheriff reassured him that nothing would happen to either of them. A moment later, he handed the phone back to Jeremy. "One more minute," he told him, "Rod has to call his folks."

Jeremy talked quickly and also asked Rod for his parent's address and phone number. After giving them to his father, he hung up.

"Dad and Mom will be here tomorrow," he said to Rod. "They're flying to Chicago to pick up your parents and they're all coming together." Jeremy and Rodney embraced warmly.

"That's fantastic," Rod said exuberantly, "I'm gonna tell them to bring Andrea along if she can afford to come."

Rodney then called his mom at home. At first she was hysterical but Rod was successful in calming her down. After several minutes of talking, Rod told his mother that he wanted Andrea to come down with them if she could.

"Sure, son, anything," she promised.

"Mom, I want you to talk to the Sheriff for a minute," he told her, "and don't worry, we're okay. Here's the Sheriff," he finished, handing the phone to Toby Relliford. The Sheriff spoke in soft, reassuring tones to Rod's distraught mother. He reassured her that Jeremy and Rod would be well taken care of. Finally, he hung up. Just then, Willie Joe returned.

"Cell's ready, Sheriff," Willie Joe reported rather matter-of-factly. Toby nodded.

"Ready boys?" he asked.

Rod and Jeremy nodded and followed the Sheriff from the small room and into the back room. The radio was registering an incoming call.

"Willie Joe, take care of that for me," the Sheriff said as he and the boys headed for the outer office.

Following the Sheriff across the main lobby, they entered the other side of the building through a locked, heavy metal door. Inside were a cluster of small cells. The lighting was poor and the air was stale and rancid. There were no other prisoners in the room. Approaching the cell that Willie had prepared, the faint smell of a pine scented cleaner mingled with the stale aroma of the cell block.

Two beds, more like cots, sat along two walls. The cell was complete with a commode and a wash basin. Two towels, wash cloths and soap completed the furnishings.

"Not exactly the Waldorf-Astoria," Jeremy made light as he and Rod went inside. Toby Relliford, leaving the cell door open, sat down on one of the newly-made beds and sighed audibly.

"I hate this boys," he whispered. "I know that neither of you deserve to be behind bars. I won't rest until all of this is cleared up. I want you to trust me. If you want to take a shower from time to time, let me know. You can use the employee's shower in the other wing since we're not overcrowded."

"Thanks, Sheriff," Rod acknowledged. Jeremy expressed his appreciation as well.

"You won't be crazy about the food but you can live with it," he continued. "I'll slip over to the restaurant every now and then and get you some real food but no one is to know about it."

"Something's just all fouled up, Sheriff," Jeremy said. "I wish I could put my finger on it."

"Whatever it is," the Sheriff said standing up, "I'll find out. There's some questions that still have to be answered."

Toby strode from the cell, closing the iron bars behind him. Turning the key in the lock was one of the hardest things that he had to do in a long while. The click seemed to echo around the entire cell block. He stood silently for a moment watching the two boys. A feeling of foreboding crept over him for an instant. This would be big news in this small town when word got out. Excitement was measured around here by who bowled the highest score in the local bowling tournament. The fact that Rodney was a black outsider would certainly not help matters either. He knew deep down that some rough times were ahead.

It would help a little that the victim was not from Midway but he was white and Toby knew that that fact alone would be a problem. He hoped that times had changed some things. Dulled some emotions. He couldn't be sure, though—only time would tell. Making his way back to the office, Willie Joe handed him a message.

"John Stearns wants you to call him right away."

"The prosecutor's office?" Asked Toby.

"Uh-huh. I called while you were in the back," Willie Joe said.

"You shouldn't have done that," the Sheriff told him, irritation obviously in his voice. "I haven't talked with Doc yet about notifying the victim's family and I haven't gone through his things yet. There's still work to be done. Don't become a pain, Willie Joe," he warned.

Willie resented the Sheriff's reprimand. He didn't like being treated like a child. He acted like he was more concerned about that city boy and his nigger friend than he was about his own deputy. Toby picked up the phone and dialed.

"Attorney John H. Stearns, please. This is Sheriff Toby Relliford." After a pause, Toby spoke again.

"John? Toby."

"Yeah, Toby. Willie Joe called a while ago. What's the score?" John inquired.

"I'm holding two college boys in connection with a possible vehicular homicide. Formal charges have not been filed yet, but I'll be getting you a detailed report in the morning so that an inquest can be scheduled. I'll let you know when the boys' legal counsel gets to town. Their folks are on the way down. Should be here sometime tomorrow."

"That Deputy of your's is sure quick on the trigger," John told Toby, "I thought all of that was already done."

"I just chewed his butt," Toby said, "Doc Cuthbert just gave me the autopsy report an hour ago. I'll get back with you."

"Okay. I'll wait until I hear from you."

"Right," said Toby as he hung up the phone.

"That's how business is done around here," Toby told his Deputy. "Due process!"

Toby hurried off to the back office where the dead man's belongings were left by the Coroner. Opening the small bag that contained his personal belongings, he began to examine its contents. Maybe he could find out why he was in Midway walking in the street in the middle of the night. He knew that it would not be long before the Coroner's report would make the local newspaper and everything would soon become more complicated. First, there would be the news reports, curious inquiries by town folks and just plain excitement that always surround the out-of-ordinary happenings in a small town.

In the plastic bag that held the victim's personal belongings, Toby found a Tourist's Guide from the Elkhill Resort Lodge for hunting and fishing some 30 miles outside of Midway. He also found some receipts from the lodge dated two days ago. He decided that the Lodge would become the first stop in his investigation. The dead man from Mississippi was Arnold Detmer, an insurance salesman. Toby theorized that he was probably at the lodge while on vacation. Informing Willie Joe of his plans for the next couple of hours, the Sheriff left the office headed for Elkhill. The drive to the lodge took him about 45 minutes.

Elkhill was an absolutely beautiful place. Nestled in the rolling hills of the countryside, it reminded Toby of his first sight of Palm Springs. You drive for miles with no sight of civilization, winding through foothills in complete isolation. Then, from out of nowhere, appears this dreamlike resort, complete with a huge lake for fishing, surrounded by a cluster of log cabins, a sprawling lodge, and a nine-hole golf course.

As he headed down the hill toward the resort, it was like an oasis in the desert. Money, thought Toby, you had to have lots of it to spend time here or plenty of plastic. Since he didn't hunt, and what little fishing he did was down at the catfish hole, he had never visited Elkhill. Eyeing its breathtaking serenity, he instantly wished he had. He and Peg needed a couple of days together in a place like this, just to get away.

Pulling up to the lodge, Toby got out of the car and headed for the door. He realized that he still had on his uniform. He wished that he had gone home first and changed clothes so as to minimize his presence. Well, no matter. He was on official business. Going inside, he identified himself to the clerk at the front desk. Several guests were shooting pool at three tables across the room. They paid him little attention as he talked. The clerk behind the counter checked the guest list and confirmed that the man was indeed a registered patron.

"Two of those guys over there shooting pool have been looking for him since yesterday," he said pointing. "They figured he must have went off somewhere to a secret deer trail. None of them have had any luck so far."

"Thanks," Toby replied.

He made his way over to the pool table and asked who was there with Arnold Detmer. One big fellow with a thick craggy mustache, overalls and a red and black wool shirt nodded.

"Me and Ted here, Sheriff," he said gruffly pointing to his partner who was about to shoot.

"Where's Arn anyway?'

"I'm afraid I've got bad news," Toby began. "Mr. Detmer was killed accidentally in an auto accident a couple of days ago just outside of my town. His body is at the morgue in the Coroner's office, pending notification of the next of kin."

Excited conversation ensued. Soon the other pool shooters surrounded the table.

"I just can't figure out why he would be walking or running in the road in the middle of nowhere at midnight," the Sheriff was saying.

"The only thing that I can think of," said the big man with the mustache, "was that he went off by himself after deer. Arn was always doing strange things like that. I never dreamed, though, that something like this would happen."

"He probably drove off and set up camp somewhere," a tall thin man in hunting clothes said. "He was an expert camper. I'll bet anything that he was hunting on his own."

"We didn't see a car at the scene," Toby said.

"He drove a new Caprice," the big man said. "It was a rust colored sedan. Nice car."

Toby jotted the information in his notebook and informed the men that they should go to the Corner's office to make a positive identification as soon as possible. Before leaving, he thanked them all and told them how helpful they had been. As he left and headed back to town, he decided that his next move was to find the victim's car. He figured that shouldn't be too hard. As he drove, something was knawing at the back of his mind but he couldn't put his finger on it. Something that someone had said. Oh well, it was probably nothing important, he decided.

After arriving back at his office, he told Willie Joe to get in touch with Jake and for them to take the Jeep immediately and comb all of the deer trails and camp sites between Midway and the lodge for the victim's car before it got dark. Next, he called Doc Cuthbert and asked him to call back as soon as positive identification of the deceased was made so that he could notify the man's family. Pausing to catch his breath for a moment, he decided to check in on Rod and Jeremy. They greeted him anxiously.

"Anything turn up?" Jeremy asked.

"Not yet," Toby responded, "still asking around. Something bothers me though! The dead man was driving a car when he left a lodge that he was staying at. At the scene of the accident, we didn't find one. I've got Jake and Willie Joe out looking right now. The car should be at least within a few miles of the accident you would think."

"Sounds reasonable to me," Rod was saying as Toby pulled up a chair and sat down.

"You boys eat yet?" Toby asked.

"Yeah, if that's what you call it," Rod said sarcastically.

"Who cooks for you, anyway?" Jeremy quizzed, shaking his head back and forth.

"You two have just been spoiled by Sarah's home-cooked meals," Toby came back.

"We've got money in our wallets . . ." Jeremy started but was interrupted by the Sheriff in mid-sentence.

"Okay, okay. I'll have Sarah send something over this time," Toby said standing up. "This one's on me but I can't make this a habit. We pay folks down at the county building to provide food for us here. So, you'll have to eat the food sometime. Okay?"

Rod and Jeremy nodded their heads vigorously while winking coyly at each other.

"Be right back," Toby said standing up and heading for the door. Looking back, he told the boys, "I just want you to know that I'll be working overtime to bust this case open. You can take that to the bank." He closed the door behind him.

While waiting for the Coroner's call, the food to be delivered from Sarah's and the return of Jake and Willie Joe, Toby sat down at his desk to try and put some pieces of this puzzle together. He was just not feeling easy about many of the bizarre circumstances surrounding this case. Something was not ringing true but he didn't know what it was.

He pulled out the note pad from his visit to the lodge, the notes from his previous investigation, and placed them together in front of him along with Doc Cuthbert's autopsy report. He poured over them again. First, they had initially found nobody at the site. Then they did. This didn't bother him so much since the initial investigation was hastily conducted in pitch blackness. But, the boys' car was definitely tampered with—of that, he was certain. But why? By whom? That didn't make any sense at all. But above all else, it mystified him as to why someone would run in front of a car on a dirt road outside of town at midnight. Even if he was camping on his own, why would an experienced camper and hunter run into the path of oncoming headlights? An experienced deer hunter certainly would not track at night, would he?

Toby stood up and paced in a small circle thinking. He was missing something. Then it hit him. What had been eating at his subconscious was something that one of the men at the lodge had said. Mr. Detmer had been missing since yesterday! Jeremy and Rod's accident had happened two days ago. Did one have anything to do with the other? Could the big man be mistaken about the time? He had to find out. His pulse quickened at the thought. Just then the buzzer at the front door rang. Toby was jerked from his train of thought. He hurried to the door and let in the delivery boy from Sarah's who was loaded down with two trays of food.

"Here, let me give you a hand," he told the delivery boy, holding open the door and taking one of the trays.

"Thanks, Sheriff," said the grateful lad.

"Put you tray over on the desk and tell Sarah I said thanks for everything. Here's the money for the food."

"Yessir, I'll tell her. Thanks again, Sheriff." Toby reached into his pocket again and pulled out another dollar bill.

"This is for you."

"All right!" exclaimed the beaming youth, his eyes aglow. "Thanks again. See ya's later, Sheriff."

He tore off down the street in the direction of McCallister's candy store. Toby smiled to himself as he picked up the two trays and headed to the cell block.

Rod and Jeremy welcomed the food with open arms and voices of excitement. Sarah had fixed mouth-watering meals that instantly reminded him of how hungry he was himself. The boys devoured their meals much like a pack of thin wolves would gulp down a fallen prey after a hard, lean winter. You would think that they had not eaten in a month. He knew that a lot of their actions were due to anxiety and some depression. Many people eat excessively when depressed or at least, develop huge appetites. He sat and watched them. Just then the phone rang. He moved quickly to the outer office and picked up the receiver.

"Sheriff Relliford speaking."

"Toby, this is John. I've got thee fellows here from Elkhill who have identified the body. They say that you talked to them about two hours ago."

"Yeah, John. That's right. Do me a favor, will you? Tell them to stop by my office before they go back to the lodge."

"All right. I guess it's okay now to notify the next of kin. I'll be giving the information about the death to the newspaper. It'll be in tomorrow's issue."

"Right," Toby replied, "Thanks, John."

"You bet." Both men hung up.

Toby sat down at the desk to regroup his thoughts again but before he had barely sat down, he heard Jeremy calling him from the cell block. Hurrying to the back room, he discovered that he had not given them anything to drink with their food. He went back to the water cooler in the front office, got a couple of large paper cups and filled them with fresh cold water. He entered the cell through the open door which he purposely had not locked and handed the water to Jeremy and Rod.

"I'll be out front if you need anything else. I'm waiting on three fellows who I need to talk to."

Jeremy and Rod both thanked him and he left, closing the door behind him. A few minutes later, the three men came into his office, eating sandwiches and drinking from paper cups.

"Sit down, Gentlemen," Toby said. "Thanks for stopping by. This'll only take a minute."

"That was old Arn all right," said the big fellow with the mustache. "Man, he was messed up."

"I'm sorry that you all had to do that but it was necessary," Toby was saying, "the undertakers will do a good job with him. I just wanted to be doubly sure about exactly when it was that Mr. Detmer was first noticed to be missing."

"A little over a day ago. Yesterday morning we couldn't find him," the thin man said. "He might have snuck out that night sometime."

"Are you positive?" Toby asked.

"Absolutely."

"I'd like for you fellows to make a sworn affidavit to that effect. It's very important. All it means is that there will be an established time on Mr. Detmer's disappearance."

The men agreed and Toby gave them official forms to fill out. After they completed and signed the affidavit, Toby stood up and shook each man's hand.

"This is a very important thing that you've done, Gentlemen. Thanks. If it is necessary for you to testify at the trial, we'll have to issue subpoenas, of course. I don't know if that will be necessary though," Toby concluded.

"Glad to help out, Sheriff," the big one said. At that, the three men left and Toby sat down at the desk once again.

This was significant, he thought to himself. If the men were correct, the dead man couldn't have been killed by Rod and Jeremy! They had reported their accident a day earlier. But, the key word was if. Toby scribbled some notes in his pad and paused again deep in thought. If the dead man was not who the boys had hit in the road, maybe Willie Joe and Jake were on a "wild goose chase." The car might well be somewhere else. Well, he would know soon enough. It was beginning to get dark and his deputies would be returning soon. He decided to talk to Jeremy and Rod. He had nothing to go on, really, but something was beginning to smell fishy.

After detailing the latest chain of events to Jeremy and Rod, he was pleased to notice a sense of the slightest signs of relief steal across their faces. He gathered up their dirty dishes, locked the cell door and headed for the office. Just then, Jake and Willie burst in.

"Nothin'! Plain zero," Willie Joe exclaimed, wiping sweat and dust from his face. Jake pounded his hand against his thigh amid a cloud of road dust.

"We didn't see a thing," he started. "We covered every deer trail and back road in the county."

"Thanks, boys," Toby said smiling. "Willie Joe, your shift is over. You can go on home. Jake, I know we got you here early today, so after you get settled down, pull out the cot in the back and take a nap if you get sleepy. The boys have already had their dinner."

"Okay," Jake responded, "Right now I'm gonna wash off some of this dirt and dust. Thank heaven for paved roads."

While Toby busied himself with the task of notifying the deceased man's family, Willie Joe ambled outside and made his way to his car. This had been the hardest day's work that he had put in for some time. He needed a drink to settle his nerves and calm him down. As usual, his watering hole was The Silver Dollar.

After finishing the necessary calls to the deceased man's family, Toby pushed back from his desk and lit his pipe. He inhaled deeply as he contemplated his next move. He decided to play a hunch. Since his deputies had failed to find the victim's car, and since he was reported missing only yesterday, maybe he wasn't out hunting like his friends at the lodge had thought. Maybe he was doing something else. If his car was not found where it should have been, it must be somewhere that they hadn't looked. Toby got up, cleaned off his desk, locked his notes in the safe and called Jake.

"Jake, I'm leaving now. I'm gonna go look for Mr. Detmer's car myself. I've got a hunch as to where it might be."

"Everything's under control, Sheriff," Jake said toweling his face. "Good luck. See ya in the morning."

Toby left and climbed into his car. Midway was, by far, the closest thing to civilization to the lodge. So, if the man wasn't hunting, Toby was sure he must have been in town. Driving slowly down the streets of Midway, he beamed his floodlight on the parked cars looking for the tan Caprice with the Mississippi license tags. First down one street and up another. Nothing! If anyone was visiting town in the middle of the night, he must have been at The Silver Dollar. That's it!

Excitedly, Toby turned his car around and headed in the direction of the night club. He pulled up outside of the club and slowly and methodically checked vehicles along the front and on the sides of the bar. There was no car to be found with the description that he was looking for. Disappointment etched across his face. He slumped in his seat. His hunch had been wrong! All of the streets in the heart of town had been checked. Where else was there to look?

Toby reluctantly pointed his car toward home. He rolled slowly past the deserted buildings on the outskirts of the town—first, the old post office and then the General Store. Something glistened for an instant in his headlights. It looked like a rear light reflector. Toby stopped his car and backed up. He shined his floodlight at the deserted, dark figure of the old building. There, pulled up alongside the store, in the grass, was a car. Toby caught his breath. He drove up closer, keeping his light trained on the vehicle. Sure enough, there it was. Mississippi tags!

His heart caught in his throat. He was right! The man had been to Midway after all. Toby grabbed his flashlight and sprang from his car. The car had a flat right front tire. The trunk was partially opened and the doors were unlocked. Toby opened the front door on the passenger's side and shined his light inside. It was littered with various types of hunting equipment, even a crossbow. The man must have been some kind of hunter, he thought to himself. On the from seat was a half empty bottle of whiskey and an open pack of cigarettes. Climbing back into his car, he sped back to his office. He rushed inside.

"Jake. Jake. I found it! I found the car!"

Jake sat up bleary-eyed. He had dozed off at the desk.

"Huh? What? Oh, Sheriff, it's you. I must have fallen asleep."

"I found the car," Toby repeated.

"You did? Where? We looked all over the place."

"Yes, but you didn't look here in town. He was right here in Midway! Before we knew what we were looking for, we must have passed right by it and never paid it any attention."

"Where is it?" Jake asked.

"Alongside the old general store off in the grass. The guy must have blown a tire." Toby said.

"That's no big deal. You can fix a flat in five minutes." Jake replied.

"Yeah, I know. I haven't figured that out yet. I'm gonna get his keys, lock up the car and tag it. First thing in the morning, we'll take some photos and then have it towed to the pound as evidence for further investigation." Toby finished.

He hurried into the back office and retrieved the keys to the car. He picked up a tag marked "Do not touch. Official Police Business."

"You've got a cot in the back, Jake. If you fall asleep, make sure the front door's locked," he said leaving the room.

"See you early in the morning," he called back, closing the door behind him. As he climbed back into his car, he was exhilarated. For the first time, he felt that he was getting somewhere. He didn't know where, but at least his hunch was right. As he drove, it struck him. The man's car was at least two miles closer to town than where the boys had reported their accident. Why would he have walked away from town if he was in trouble? Or better still, why didn't he fix the flat tire himself? Toby shook his head. Obviously the man had been drinking. The bottle was half empty. He could have just been drunk. A half a bottle of whiskey would put out a lot of lights.

Having arrived back at the General Store, Toby locked the car and put the tag on the rear window facing the road. It was now time to go home and get some sleep. He would have to get an early start tomorrow. Driving home, he was now more confused than ever. The whole thing didn't make any sense. Maybe after they've had a chance to go over the man's car thoroughly tomorrow, some questions might be answered. But right now he was exhausted. This had been one long day.

Willie Joe was soused. For the last three hours, he had been pouring down one drink after another. He and four others were at the bar, talking loudly over the music. Willie Joe's voice was tinged with anger as he recounted being put down by Sheriff Relliford earlier.

"You'd think that I committed a crime or somethin by calling the Prosecutor's office" he scowled. "It'll all be in tomorrow's paper, wait and see."

"Why would he be so touchy?" one of the men asked.

"I don't know," Willie Joe answered, "but I can just look at that Chicago nigger and tell he's hidin' something. You know how they get that funny look when they've been caught doin' something."

"What about the white boy, Willie?" another asked.

"One of those bleeding heart liberals from New York. His father's a big shot in New York City. Some kind of broker or somethin'. Doc Cuthbert has already told the Sheriff that the blood on their car matches the blood of the dead man. To me, that's as clear as it gets." He tossed down another shot.

"Ol' Toby has always had a soft spot for the coloreds ever since he came here," somebody chimed in. "Remember how he used to brag about serving with them in Atlanta? Then he arrested Joe and Billy for burning crosses when those niggers tried to buy old man Clayton's House years ago."

"Yeah, sure did," mumbled another. "And that ain't all. Look at how he pals around in the colored section. They think he's some kind of hero."

One man sitting close by who overheard the conversation spoke up.

"Wait a minute, Deputy Biven, you were just a kid when all of that happened. Everybody in town knew that Joe and Billy were just plain troublemakers. What they did was uncalled for. Toby Relliford is the best Sheriff we've ever had here. Just because he tries to be fair to . . ."

"Hold on," one of the men sitting with Willie Joe interrupted, "the deputy is talking about what is happening now! Two boys from up north done run over and kilt a white man from Mississippi and the Sheriff is puttin' down his own Deputy for tellin' the Prosecutor about it. Now that don't sound right to me."

Several bystanders who had now gathered around the bar agreed.

"Seems like somebody should have been told something," one bleary-eyed blonde who had one too many was saying. "When did this happen?"

"Couple of days ago," Willie Joe answered. "The Sheriff told me not to say anything."

"See what I mean? A man's been dead for over two days, right here in town and no one knows anything about it. I think some questions need to be answered."

"I'm sure the Sheriff has his reason."

"Oh, yeah? What?"

The crowd around the bar had grown much larger by now. Many of the people were trying to talk at once. Even in his inebriated state, Willie Joe realized that things were getting out of control. Old memories were rekindled that had been dormant for years as the conversations went on. He now wished that he had said nothing. He had let his anger come out at the wrong time and the wrong place. Many of the people around him, like himself, were drunk or well on their way. He had to do something quick. He stood up and motioned for silence, shouting above the noise.

"Just a minute, folks. Take it easy now. You'll be able to read about everything in the paper tomorrow. The Sheriff has already arrested the two and charges will be made at the right time. This is Sheriff's business and we'll handle it. There's no cause for alarm. The prisoner's ain't goin' nowhere! Now go on back to your dancin'!" He directed.

Slowly, the crowd quieted and began to disburse. Music began to once again drown out the buzzing of continued conversation. In five minutes, The Silver Dollar was almost back to normal. Willie Joe had succeeded. They had responded to him! A sense of euphoria filled his whole being intoxicating him even more. For the first time in his life, he felt a true sense of power. And, he loved it.

"You sure handled that Deputy," the bartender grinned. "I was beginning to get a little nervous."

"Aw, it wasn't nothin'!" Willie Joe said proudly.

He sat at the bar for another half hour or so until he felt sure that everything was under control. He smiled to himself because he felt that he had done the right thing. These people had a right to know what was going on around them. After all, he was a public servant only doing his job. Looking around him, he couldn't see where any harm had been done. Everybody was back to dancing and having fun now as if nothing had ever happened. Looking at his watch, he decided that it was time to go home. He stood unsteadily on his feet and pulled out his wallet to pay his tab.

"It's on me this time, Willie Joe," the bartender told him refusing to take his money.

"Thanks, Joe," he said standing even straighter than before. "See ya tomorrow."

As he left The Silver Dollar heading toward his car, he passed by John Cuthbert on his way up the steps headed inside.

"Calling it a day, Deputy?" he asked Willie Joe stopping next to him.

"Oh, hi Doc," he answered. "Yeah, I'm headin' in. Been a long day. Things will be movin' in the morning when everybody reads the paper. They sure enough got excited a little while ago when I told them what had happened."

"You talked about that tonight?" John asked in surprise looking in the direction of the bar.

"Just for a minute. I calmed things down real quick though," Willie Joe said sticking out his chest.

"Oh." John responded. Good old Willie Joe. He knew things were working out better than expected.

"Be careful driving home, Deputy," he added making his way up the steps. "We've already had enough excitement around here today." With that, he disappeared inside The Silver Dollar.

Willie Joe made his way to his parked car and climbed inside. As he turned the key in the ignition and slowly rolled down the street past the nightclub, he could have sworn that he heard the music inside stop again.

Toby pushed through the door of his office at seven thirty sharp the next morning. He had slept comfortably last night for the first time in days and was ready to tackle the world. His first task was to put in a call to Luke and have him send out a tow truck to pick up Mr. Detmer's car.

"Good morning, Sheriff," Jake greeted him coming from out of the back. "I've just finished giving the two their breakfast. Anything you want me to do before I leave?"

"Not really. Anything happen last night?" Toby asked.

"Nothing unusual. Just a routine night." was his reply.

"Okay. See you tomorrow."

"Right," Jake replied putting on his hat and picking up his keys. "Coffee's on."

After exchanging goodbyes, Toby checked in on Rod and Jeremy. They were gingerly picking over their food but at least they were eating. He reminded them that their parents should arrive sometime during the day.

"I know you'll both be glad of that," he said.

They both agreed in unison. Toby smiled and told them that he was going after the morning paper and asked if they needed anything. When they answered they did not, he left and headed across the street to the newsstand. Returning with his paper, he noticed several people milling around outside the office. He shrugged it off, went inside and sat down at his desk with a cup of coffee. He opened up the paper and turned immediately to the obituary section. There it was in bold print!

Detmer, Arnold AGE: 53
Meridian, Mississippi
Insurance Salesman

Cause of Death: Vehicular Homicide
Tuesday, August 16 2:30 a.m.
Notification of next of kin pending

It leaped out at Toby like a bobcat springing on an unsuspecting prey. It was now officially news. Just then, Willie Joe came hurrying through the door hollering excitedly.

"Sheriff, Sheriff, there's a group of people starting to pile up outside. Right now they're just standing around talking but I don't like it. I can't remember . . ."

Before he could finish, Toby waved his hand in front of Willie's face.

"Calm down, Willie Joe. I saw them a few minutes ago. They've read the morning paper, it seems," Toby said walking over to the window and looking out. He noticed that quite a few more had assembled since he had gone after his paper.

"I can't figure out what all the excitement is about," he said, rubbing his chin. "It's not like something like this has never happened before. Not very often, I admit, but we've had accidental deaths before."

"Maybe it's because one of them boys is a black," Willie said before he thought. Instantly he knew that he had made a mistake and he fidgeted nervously.

"How would they know that?" Toby asked curiously, looking square at Willie Joe.

"It was last night, Sheriff. Me and some friends were at The Silver Dollar and I accidentally let it slip out. I didn't mean nothin' by it," he said apologetically, almost childlike.

"Well, don't worry about it now. They were bound to find out sooner or later, anyway. I'll go out and talk to them. You stay inside with the prisoners." Toby directed. Stepping outside onto the steps, he was immediately aware of a growing carnival- like atmosphere. These people were restless, like cattle on the verge of a stampede. Their numbers continued to swell. Toby guessed that there were about 30 people by now. In some ways, it was reminiscent of the days in the seventies but not as volatile. At least, not yet.

"What can I do for you people," Toby spoke with an air of authority. This was something that he had learned at the academy in dealing with a crowd.

Someone in the crowd spoke.

"Which one of them two was driving?

"It doesn't matter. I'm holding both of them," Toby answered.

"They were not drinking or under the influence of any substances. What happened was an accident, pure and simple. It's under investigation." Toby responded.

"Was the nigger drivin'?" somebody shouted.

"That question will be answered at the inquisition as part of due process," Toby replied stonily. "And I don't have a nigger in my jail. I've got a black. An American just like you over there," he said pointing in the direction of the man who had spoken.

"What are you hidin' Sheriff," a woman yelled. "We know that the man in the paper has been dead for almost three days and we're just now hearing about it."

"Yeah," somebody else chimed in.

"What about that, Sheriff? What are you covering up?"

Toby's patience was beginning to wear thin. He was aggravated by the fact that now he knew that Willie Joe had spilled more than he had let on a while ago.

"There's an investigation going on to determine some unusual circumstances. That's all I'm going to say. I'll be making a statement to the newspaper soon and you can all read about it then. Now, I want all of you to clear the street immediately. I don't want to have my deputies arrest anybody."

Toby waited. He stepped forward in a defiant gesture. It was now very important that he act from a position of strength and authority. The crowd began to murmur among themselves. They milled around each other.

"Come on," one man yelled, "let's go like the Sheriff said. Are we gonna act like we did once before? You all remember don't you?"

Several of the people in the crowd nodded their heads. Just as they were about to disperse, one man turned back and shouted angrily.

"If the black fella did it, he's dead meat."

His words seem to gain support from some of the others.

"Go on. Break it up," Toby ordered again.

Soon the street was empty again and Toby strode angrily back into his office, slamming the door behind him.

"Willie Joe, come in here right now," he yelled toward the back room.

Willie Joe appeared almost at once looking like a fox that was caught in a chicken coop. Toby scowled at him and slammed his fist down on the desk.

"What the hell do you think you're doing, giving out confidential information about police business to a bunch of drunks at The Silver Dollar? Only you, Jake and myself knew that the body was not found for a day or so. You leaked information that could very well jeopardize this whole matter."

Willie Joe said nothing. What could he say? He knew that Toby had him dead to rights.

"All of this happened because you couldn't keep your mouth shut for a little while. I gave you orders to remain silent. I have no choice but to ask for your badge. As of now, you're under suspension pending an investigation by the Review Board. "

Tears welled in Willie Joe's eyes. Only last night, he was at his zenith—now, a mere eight hours later, his world was being shattered. Torn apart. Being a Deputy Sheriff was the one thing in his life that had any meaning.

"You need to learn how to control your emotions, Willie Joe, if you ever want to go places in this business. If both of those boys were white, you'd have been okay. You would have gone about business as usual. But no, you kept needling Rod every chance you got. You couldn't stand that I was treating him like a human being. That ate at you until your own racial hatred made you resent me as well. That's it, isn't it?" Toby asked.

With tears streaming down his face, Willie Joe dropped his head and nodded in agreement. Toby ambled over to him slowly and put his arm around his shoulder.

"Willie, you're a good Deputy but because of your prejudice, I can't risk having you around. Not now. I can't afford another slip up. Maybe when this is over, we'll review your suspension."

Toby knew full well that this job was Willie Joe's life. He couldn't leave him without any hope at all. All through high school, Willie Joe was teased by the other kids because he was a little slow. Not mentally retarded but slightly learning-impaired. He graduated from high school but it had been more of a social promotion than a graduation. When he had applied for the Deputy's job, he was one of the most eager and willing applicants that Toby had ever seen. He was willing to do anything asked of him. Toby had liked that.

He valued attitude as much as competence. So, he took a chance with him. He was really quite fond of his Deputy and now that he had been forced to relieve him of his responsibilities, he could feel anger beginning to surface from deep within. A society which harbors racial prejudice without cause and teaches its citizens to practice discrimination, is as much to blame for Willie's condition as he is himself. He had been taught these things since childhood. And he was not alone. Most of the people that had gathered outside of his office a little while ago came because Rod was black.

"You go on home now," Toby told him. "You've got about a month's pay coming. As soon as I file my report with the Review Board, I'll get your check. In the meantime, we'll see if we can get you some temporary work somewhere. Alright?"

Willie Joe nodded his head and walked over to his desk taking off his badge and laying it down.

"I know you're right, Sheriff. I don't blame you for having to suspend me. I didn't know that I would cause this much trouble. I shouldda guessed it, though. I'm sorry."

Toby suggested that he tell the boys goodbye before he left. Willie Joe obliged him by doing so. Jeremy and Rod both felt sorry for him as he said his goodbye.

"I hope this'll help him grow up and become his own man," Toby told the boys later as they talked.

"Yeah, me too," replied Rod, "but I can't help but think that he reflects the mindset of most of the people in this town."

"Unfortunately, you're probably right," Toby conceded.

Just then, the phone rang in the outer office.

"See you boys later," Toby said standing up and striding from the room to answer it.

"Sheriff Relliford?" a voice asked.

"Yes."

"This is John McCutchin, Jeremy's father. We're here in town. Just arrived. I'm on my car phone and we're headed in your direction. Is this a good time to stop by?"

"Absolutely," Toby said excitedly, "the door's open."

"Be there in a minute."

"Fine." The line went dead.

Toby rushed back into the cell block to give Rod and Jeremy the news. The boys greeted the message with shouts of joy. Rod danced and pumped his right fist back and forth. "Cha-ching!"

Jeremy hooped and the two exchanged high fives.

"Yeah! Yeah!" They both shouted simultaneously. You would think a basketball game was in progress. Toby grinned from ear to ear. He felt tremendously relieved. There's nothing quite like hearing from home.

"They'll be here any minute, "Toby told them. "As soon as I talk to them, they'll be in to visit you." He left the cell block, closing the door behind him. Even the three inches of the steel door did not muffle the sounds of jubilation coming from the other side. Toby himself was exhilarated.

Within minutes, the office door opened and six well-dressed people entered his office. Toby guessed who they were by observation. Jeremy was the spitting image of his father and the woman holding his arm would be Jeremy's mother. The black couple had to be Rod's parents and the beautiful young black woman, he guessed, was Rod's girl. The other distinguished looking and well-groomed man had to be their attorney. He was right on every count! Jeremy's dad introduced everybody. Their handshakes were warm and firm. Their eyes Friendly but worried.

"How's our boys?" Rod's father asked in a deep baritone voice.

"Oh, the boys are fine," Toby responded with a slight gesture of his hand. "In fact, when I told them that you were here, you'd think that I had just given them two Superbowl tickets."

They all laughed.

"Can I see Rodney?" asked the young lady excitedly.

"Sure, but first we have to talk. Come on over here," he instructed them as he walked toward a table surrounded by chairs on one side of the room.

Everyone pulled up a seat and sat down. Rod's mother wrung her hands anxiously. Toby took his time and related to them the circumstances surrounding the boys accident. Harold Steinmetz, the family's attorney, spoke first when Toby had finished.

"I certainly can understand your situation, Sheriff, in having to hold Rod and Jeremy especially in light of the Coroner's report. However, formal charges have not been filed, am I correct?"

"That's right. First there will have to be an inquest. That's why I was waiting until you all got here. Rod and Jeremy can be released on bail but must remain in custody."

"How soon can we arrange that to happen?" Asked Mr. Blake.

"Whenever you want." Answered Harold.

"How about tomorrow?" Asked Mr. McCutchin.

"I'll get in touch with the Prosecutor's office and the Coroner's office first thing in the morning. In the meantime, you all can visit with the boys while I call a bail bondsman." Replied Harold.

Toby stood up and shook hands with everyone again.

"Wait here."

The Sheriff left disappearing into the back. In a matter of seconds, Rod and Jeremy burst into the room. Emotions ran amuck. There was momentary chaos as everyone attempted to talk at the same time. The boys hugged and kissed their parents, tears running unashamedly. Both mothers wept openly. Fathers and sons enjoined in long, firm embraces. First and foremost, this was a family reunion. It had been almost a year since parents and children had been together. Rod's girlfriend, Andrea, waiting silently in the background, sobbed. Toby and Attorney Steinmetz simply looked on. Toby motioned to him to join him in the back room. Once inside, they closed the door. Toby spoke first.

"Tell me the procedures from here on in."

"Well, first we'll have the inquest tomorrow and if, in fact, there is enough evidence to warrant formal charges, the boys would then be arraigned. If the arraignment rules against Jeremy and Rod, an indictment will follow along with, of course, a subsequent trial-by-jury." Added Harold.

"Even though the Coroner's report seems pretty conclusive," Toby said, "my investigation up to this point has raised some significant questions in my mind about the boys' innocence. There are just too many loose-ends for my comfort."

"If formal charges are made, I'll need all the help from you I can get, then," Harold told him. "I may have to ask you to do some investigative work for me during the trial."

"I'll certainly do what I can. You can be assured or that. I'll call you early tomorrow morning as soon as I have made arrangements for the inquest."

"Fine."

"The hotel where Rod and Jeremy originally stayed is just down the street. I'll call and make arrangements for all of you." Toby said.

"We'd all appreciate that," Harold replied, "and thanks again for everything." The two men shook hands again and went back through the door to the front office where everybody was now seated at the conference table. Rod and Andrea sat close together, hugging. Just then the office door opened and a man in a dark suit slipped quietly inside.

"That's Bert, the bail bondsman," Toby whispered to Harold.

The two crossed the room and greeted the man. They talked for several minutes and then joined the others. Toby motioned for silence.

"Everybody, this is Bert Sallenger, the town's bail bondsman. Mr. McCutchin and Mr. Blake, if you'll join us in the back, we'll make arrangements for Rod and Jeremy's release." Harold finished. It grew suddenly quiet and sighs of relief were audible. The four men slipped silently from the room and the noise began to build once more. After several minutes they reappeared.

"Everything's been taken care of," Toby announced.

"Jeremy, you and Rod are free to go but you cannot leave town. I must be informed of your whereabouts at all times. Okay?"

"You bet, Sheriff," Rod exclaimed. "We ain't goin' nowhere until this mess is cleaned up."

"Count on it," Jeremy added as both jumped up out of their chairs. They both walked over to him and shook his hand. Rod turned to his parents.

"Mom, Dad, Sheriff Relliford here has been the only friend that Jeremy and I have had through all of this. I think that it's important for me to tell you that I trust him because you know how I feel about being in this situation in a small, southern town. Dad, he's good people."

James Blake stood up.

"Then, son, that's good enough for me."

Toby thanked Rod and then cautioned the families about the town of Midway.

"People here are just simple country folk but like most small towns in the south, racial prejudice and suspicion of outsiders is as much at home as everything else. I'd advise you to stay put at the hotel as much as possible, especially now, until this thing blows over. If you have any problems at all, call me at once. Believe me, the town knows you're here. It might be best for me to arrange to have Sarah send food to your rooms, just to keep your profile as low as possible. Of course, that's your decision."

Mr. Blake objected, saying that the boys had done nothing wrong.

"Because I'm black, I'm not hiding from anybody."

Rod then explained to his father about the makeup of Midway and the colored section across the tracks down the road.

"Dad, that's just how it is here."

His father grunted but said nothing else.

"Okay Sheriff," said Mr. McCutchin, " what do you think is best? In the meantime, I'm going to the hotel and shower."

Everyone else expressed the same sentiment as the parties headed toward the door, weary and tired now that emotions had ebbed. One by one they filed out of the Sheriff's office and boarded a luxurious and crafted minivan that the parents had rented after flying into Memphis. Toby watched at the door as they slowly drove in the direction of the hotel.

For the first night, Toby slept soundly. When the alarm clock screamed as six thirty that morning, Toby was literally startled. For several moments, he was disoriented. However, he had slept deeply and felt well rested. He glanced over at his still-sleeping wife and decided to ease himself slowly out of bed so as not to awaken her. He showered, made himself a pot of coffee and poured a cup. Today would be a long one so he decided to write Peg a note and tell her that he'd be later than usual getting home. Scratching the note on the pad next to the wall phone in the kitchen, he opened up the back door and slipped outside. The early morning air was refreshing and the birds were just beginning to announce the start of day.

Andrea was awake in her room, alone. Mr. and Mrs. Blake and the McCutchin's were all in separate rooms. She hated being alone at a time like this because she didn't have anyone to share her feelings with. She realized, however, that being the odd person out had made it necessary for her to sleep alone. It was especially hard with Rodney just down the hall. It had been over a month since they had been together and she missed him so much. To make matters even worse, she was afraid. Jeremy and Rodney were in serious trouble! What if they were found guilty? She shuddered at the very thought. There was never any doubt in her mind that Rodney was the guy for her from the first moment she met him. Marriage was to come immediately after school.

They would have three children and their very own home. Their plans were already made and they had decided to stay in New York after graduation. Rodney was obsessed with the New York Giants and ready to settle down . . . now this! She felt her world coming apart at the seams. She was petrified at the thought of a southern judge and jury holding the fate of the future of the man she loved. She had seen so many movies, read so many books . . . tears began to cloud her vision and in spite of an effort to fight them back, they spilled down her cheeks in a steady stream, glistening like icicles against her ebony skin. She wiped them away but they just came back again. Why was life picking on them? It all seemed so unfair. What had she done wrong?

She prayed to God silently as she lay. He was always a pillar of strength for her in times like these. She and Rod went to church at school together most of the time, unlike many of their classmates. They shared so many things in common and now it was all threatened. So, as she continued to pray, she felt the familiar surge of an inner peace beginning to take hold of her. Maybe she was overreacting? Where was her faith? She brushed away at the tears again and this time she won.

Jeremy and Rod were out cold. They had not slept like this in ages. Well, at least in days. They were not disturbed when breakfast rolled around that morning.

"Poor dears," Mrs McCutchin said when no one answered the knock on the door.

"Let 'em sleep," Mr. Blake advised, "but that won't stop me. Come on." They all laughed as they headed down the hall towards Sarah's.

Sheriff Relliford, Doc Cuthbert, John Stearns, The County Prosecutor, Harold Steinmetz and The Defense Attorney spent the entire morning pouring over every detail of the case. Toby purposely did not mention the victim's missing shoe. He decided that he would make that a part of his own secret investigation. It wouldn't shed any light on the situation anyway. After hours of deliberation, it was agreed that the Coroner's report carried just too much weight to be dismissed. Formal charges would have to be filed by the state.

"We have to go public at this point," the Prosecutor was saying, "Rod and Jeremy will have to be arraigned.

"Because of the potential for racial unrest in this situation, I would strongly suggest that the arraignment proceeding be before the District Judge T. Howard McGill," Harold Steinmetz replied. "We want to keep this as low key as we can. It will probably escalate on its own enough as it is and I hear that this Judge is very good at maintaining order in his court."

"That's fine with me," replied John Stearns. He continued, "Let me make arrangements for the pretrial date first and then we'll make a statement to the press. How's that?"

No one disagreed.

Harold suggested that he break the news to Rod and Jeremy along with Sheriff Relliford. He shook hands with John Stearns and thanked him for his cooperation. The Sheriff and Attorney Steinmetz left together.

The boys woke up about noon and showered and dressed. They planned to have a good lunch and then spend some liesure time with Andrea and Beth. Checking their parent's rooms, they found them empty but later, found everyone in the hotel lobby sitting together. Attorney Steinmetz was talking as they approached. The boys noticed the somber expressions on their fathers' faces and the tears in the eyes of their mothers and Andrea.

"Hey, what's up?" asked Rod wide-eyed, walking over to Andrea and putting his arm around her.

"There's been an arraignment requested by the County Prosecutor," Steinmetz replied. "That means that formal charges will be filed on both of you involving the death of Mr. Detmer."

What followed was stunned silence. Jeremy groped for a seat, dazed and muttered a weak, "Wow" he sighed as he sat down next to his father.

"This is heavy," Rod mumbled squeezing Andrea closer to him. She put her hand over his in a gesture of reassurance.

"Exactly what does this mean?" Mr. Blake asked Harold turning to him expectantly.

"The boys will continue to be free on bail until after the pretrial hearing with a district judge. If the case is dismissed, they're free. If not, an indictment will be handed down and a trial date will be set," he responded.

"What about Jeremy and Rod during all of this?" asked Mr. McCutchin.

"If there is an indictment and subsequent trial, both will have to be confined by Sheriff Relliford until its conclusion."

Toby simply nodded soberly.

Harold Steinmetz then told everybody that as soon as he heard from Stearns, he would call another session of everyone together. He suggested that, in the meantime, the boys go and eat and try to relax as much as possible.

"There's nothing more we can do at this point," he finished. Toby stood up.

"I'm sorry boys," he said. "I never thought it would come to this. Attorney Steinmetz, I'll be in my office when you need me. Goodbye all." With that, the Sheriff left the room.

"I'm going to my room and lie down for a while," said Mrs. Blake tearfully. She was joined by Mrs. McCutchin. Mr. Blake and Mr. McCutchin remained glued to their seats. Andrea clung to Rodney as Jeremy got up.

"See you later Dad. We'd better go get some lunch."

"Okay son."

"Rod," his father said, "I'll see you later too. Don't worry, I believe everything will somehow work its way out."

"Yeah," replied Rod, "me too."

Rod, Jeremy and Andrea left while the two fathers simply sat looking at each other in disbelief.

Before heading for Sarah's, the three made their way to Beth's shop to break the news. Needless to say, she was floored and immediately broke into tears. Rod and Andrea stood helplessly by as Jeremy attempted to console her. Beth requested the afternoon off and was given permission to leave. They left together, each couple clinging to the other in quiet desperation.

Sarah greeted them warmly as she gave them all menus. Several customers had turned around and looked up at them when they had entered. Soon undercurrents of hushed conversations were audible along with sidelong glances and some stares.

"Beth McCallister, what are you doin' here?" said one bespeckeled, portly man dressed in a white shirt with the sleeves rolled up and brown trousers.

"I've got the afternoon off, Mr. Robinson," she replied.

"Well, what are you doin' with them?" he asked pointing to Jeremy and Rod.

"They're my friends."

"They're murderers, Girl! They've killed a man. Your parents are gonna skin you alive, just wait."

"I'm grown, Mr. Robinson. I choose my own company."

"Not yet you ain't. You still livin' at home ain't you? Anyway, you seem to be a mighty poor judge of character by the looks of things."

"Mister, why don't you back off?" Jeremy said in a voice tinged with impatience.

"Don't you talk to me like that nigger lover! Look what you got yourself into. Your ass is in the fryin' pan now."

"Okay, Ben. That's enough of that kind of talk in my place," Sarah said dropping the dishcloth she was using to clean the counter."

These boys haven't been convicted of anything. Just leave 'em be. What'll it be boys?" she asked turning her attention to Rod and Jeremy.

They all ordered lunch and ate in silence. Mr. Robinson and his friends left during their meal telling Sarah their money was on the tables.

"And there ain't no tips," retorted Ben Robinson.

"Fine," shot Sarah. She shook her head.

"You'll get used to that around here," she said to Andrea who sat in disbelief. "We've got a town full of folks like 'ol Ben."

* * *

The quiet roar and gurgle of the rushing water down at the old mill was soothing to the ear as Jeremy and Beth lay together in the grass by the creek. It was peaceful and quiet. Rod and Andea sat arm-in-arm on a stone picnic table nearby.

"They're sitting on our spot," Beth whispered to Jeremy looking in Rod and Andrea's direction. Jeremy nodded. It was there only a couple of days ago that he began to fall for Beth in a big way. He smiled faintly to himself.

"Ever think we'll be like them one day?" he asked her teasingly.

"Like what?"

"Planning their future together."

"That's not in my hands," she said softly, "but this is." She pulled Jeremy's face down to her's and crushed his mouth to her waiting, moist and parted lips. her tongue darted swiftly inside, exploring. Jeremy devoured her sweetness. Beth moaned deep in her throat as his tongue invaded all regions of her eager mouth.

"Hey, man! Cut that out!" Rod's voice pierced the stillness. "Ya'll have to get a room somewhere if you keep that up!! Andrea laughed lustily. Beth blushed beet red.

"I'm sorry," she stumbled trying to straighten her hair.

"Don't apologize to him," Jeremy said pulling her to him. "Why don't we try that again?"

This time his lips met hers fully. Rod chuckled softly.

"He really has flipped for her," he told Andrea.

"At least he shows her how he feels," she quipped.

"Meaning?"

"I love you, Rodney."

"I love you, too baby. Very much."

Tears filled her eyes as she looked at the man she loved.

"Don't do that," he said softly brushing back a lock of hair near her eyes. "Ill never leave you. Ever."

Their lips met in a tender, loving and familiar way. Andrea covered his face with soft kisses. Suddenly Rod pulled back.

"Uh, uh. You know what that does to me, don't you?"

"Yes." she smiled coyly looking down at the growing bulge beneath his pants. "I know exactly what I'm doing."

"You sure as hell do and you'd better stop while you can." They laughed and embraced warmly, lovingly. The hour slipped away in serene peacefulness as Jeremy and Beth lay hand-in-hand in the grass and Rod and Andrea sat huddled together as one.

Harold Steinmetz answered the telephone in his room on the first ring. It was John Stearns. The hearing was set with Judge McGill in one week.

"Even though we can't exclude interested citizens from attending the hearing, we can to some degree limit the volition," John was saying.

"Of course, my clients will plead 'not guilty'." John added.

"The evidence is strong against them, Harold. How about a plea bargain? I'll settle for accidental homicide without negligence. The boys could get off light."

"No way," Harold responded. "A plea bargain is like admitting guilt. Jeremy and Rod are innocent but thanks anyway for your offer."

"All right. See you in court. Goodbye."

"Goodbye."

Hanging up the phone, Harold briefly wondered if accepting a plea bargain would not be something to consider. At the inquest, the evidence certainly was very strong, if not overwhelming. The boys and the Sheriff could easily have missed the body in the middle of the night. The blood on their car was the real incriminating evidence. He wasn't sure how he could get around that.

The Sheriff's apprehensions, though, gave him reason for hope. They would have to launch a thorough investigation between now and the trial if an indictment was handed down. He would ask for as much time as he could get to conduct one. But from where he sat now, it didn't look too good. All of his skills would be severely tested. He had fought and won many criminal trials cases during his 20-year career as a trial lawyer but none were anymore challenging than this one. This was going to be uphill all the way. A meticulous investigation would be essential and he was not optimistic about the kind of cooperation that outsiders would get in this small town. One thing was certain. He would have to find an office to rent as soon as possible, one with adequate security for sure. He would check with the Sheriff about that right away. But first, he needed to call his office and make arrangements for an extended stay here in Midway.

The boy's fathers had already paid him a retainer and had told him to spare no expenses. Now all he had to do was go to work and free their sons.

That night, Harold gathered the families together and shared with them his conversation with the County Prosecutor. Both boys agreed that a plea bargain was out of the question.

"You know that if we lose, and that's always a possibility, you could be looking at seven to 20 years depending upon the circumstances," he advised.

"We won't lose because we're innocent," Jeremy said. "I was driving and if I had hit someone, I sure as hell would have seen him. I wasn't asleep at the wheel."

"Neither was I," Rod added.

"I believe both of you," Harold replied, "but all we have at this point is your side of the story. They have all of the evidence. The body, the matching blood samples. The whole ball of wax. I'm sure we can beat this thing but I just want everybody to know what we're up against. It's gonna be tough. Get yourselves mentally ready to tough it out."

"What do you want us to do?" they asked.

"Nothing to do right now until the hearing except remain as inconspicuous as possible."

"Meaning?"

"Stay off the streets and out of sight as much as possible. What happened at the restaurant this afternoon can't help us any."

"He's right son," Jeremy's Dad told him.

"You should have seen them in there," Andrea exclaimed, her voice choked with emotion. "They were awful. I was terrified."

"I wouldn't worry about 'ol man Robinson," Beth volunteered. "He's harmless. Just talks a lot. What concerns me is the way the others listened and left when he left."

"Yeah. We're gonna have to be careful all right," Mr. Blake noted.

"Well, we've got a week to just wait it out," Harold concluded. "Let's wrap up this session for now."

Just then Sheriff Relliford appeared in the lobby. He spotted them and hurriedly walked over to where they were seated.

"Sarah called me earlier," he began. "She told me what happened this afternoon. Rod! Jeremy! Why didn't you let me know?"

"Aw, it wasn't anyting , Sheriff," Rod answered.

"Just some of the town folk blowing off some steam is what we decided," Jeremy added.

"It might appear that way right now," Toby observed, "but I don't like the implications. That's the way it started 15 years ago, just blowing off steam. Then it escalated. Got ugly. I won't allow the same thing to happen all over again. We'll have to take some precautions."

"Like what?" asked Jeremy's father.

"I'm not sure. But Harold will agree with me that the last thing we need is to get the people all worked up before the arraignment proceedings a week from now. We don't need any more obstacles to overcome than we already have," Toby advised.

Everyone looked at Attorney Steinmetz who simply nodded his head in agreement. Toby sat down with a worried look on his face. He paused thoughtfully for a moment.

"I've got an idea. There's a hotel over in the colored section of town. Rod has met many of the people over there and really enjoyed his stay. I could call the Jefferson's and make the necessary arrangements. You would be much better off there than here in Midway. Freer and safer."

Rod's eyes sparkled with excitement.

"Yeah! Dad, Mom, you'd love it over there," he beamed.

"Well, I don't know," his father mumbled. "What about John and Harriet," he added casting an intense look in the direction of Jeremy's parents.

"They'd be fine," Toby assured him. "Of course, they would have to adjust to the soul food," he smiled.

"Right on!" John and Harriet chimed together jumping up and exchanging high fives. Everyone burst into hearty laughter as the tension that hung over the room like a thick cloud was broken.

"Good! I'll make the necessary arrangements. When you get everything packed into the van and ready to go, call me at the office. You can eat your dinner in peace after we get there! With that, Toby left the families to celebrate the moment.

Chapter Five

Searchings

Beth McCallister busied herself restocking and rearranging the inventory on the store's shelves. She was glad that Jeremy and his family had taken Sheriff Relliford's advice and moved into the colored section of town last night. Even though it meant that Jeremy would be a few miles away from her, she had breathed a sigh of relief as they left. They had kissed goodbye and she told Jeremy that she would drive over every day after work. It had now been over a week since they had first met and he was beginning to occupy most of her thoughts. She was so comfortable with him and missed him terribly when they were apart.

She wondered if she was not in love with him but dismissed the thought with a faint smile. Love takes time. Two people had to experience things together, share things as one and in time, loves just grows. This is what she reasoned but she was being led by her heart. It was telling her that there is such a thing as love at first sight. Or, at least, a feeling of love that happens instantly which defies explanation.

She was at a loss to articulate the instantaneous leap of her heart and the total captivation of her mind by Jeremy the first time they met. He seemed to swallow up the world around her. She was very simply, overwhelmed, and it was a total mystery to her as to how it could happen. But then, her mother had told her years ago that that's how it happened with her and her father.

She sighed as she finished her inventory. Maybe love just cannot be explained in simple terms. Could it be fate or maybe some kind of complex chemical reaction between a man and a woman? All she knew for sure, was that it was totally unexpected and unplanned. Perhaps it was a mutual attraction of some kind, sort of like meeting a stranger and having feelings of instant dislike or mistrust without even really knowing them. She was, however, very sure of two things; she couldn't wait to see him again and she knew that he and Rod were innocent of any crime. If there was any basis for guilt,they would not have hung around like they did to find out.

Somehow, she had to find a way to help them. But what could she do? She vowed to herself that no matter what it took, she would not allow anything to happen to Jeremy, not if she could help it. She knew practically everyone in town. Maybe she could find out something from somebody if she stayed alert. She certainly was not going to stand idly by and do nothing.

Down the street a short distance, Harold Steinmetz was setting up office in a vacant room in the rear of the old Post Office Building. It would do as temporary quarters, he thought to himself. It had adequate security but the cluttered room was badly in need of a good housecleaning. The desk was full of old papers and the two file cabinets were unlocked with folders and papers jutting out in all directions.

The room was small and cramped, mainly used now for storage. Instead of throwing anything away, he simply was putting all of the documents into a huge cedar chest. He would ask the Postmaster to have someone take it to the garage in the back when he finished. This was a long way from the plush surroundings of his luxurious New York office but he felt a twinge of excitement and anticipation as he cleaned off the old desk. It reminded him a little of the earlier days right after graduation from law school. This was a little like starting all over again. He felt somewhat out of place here in this small southern town and it reminded him of the old television series, "Green Acres."

Toby sat behind his desk, sipping on a fresh cup of coffee while musing over the article in the paper about the upcoming arraignment hearing of Jeremy and Rod. He had helped Attorney Steinmetz find a temporary office room to work in, and was now waiting until he called him for the two of them to get together so that he could begin to prepare his case.

Toby knew that his notes and reports carried vital information that Harold would need. He wondered if professional ethics dictated that he share them also with the County Prosecutor, seeing that he was supposed to be a neutral party. No way, Toby told himself, could he be neutral in this case. The prosecution was already well ahead. The inquest had clearly demonstrated this. They would have to subpoena his files first he decided.

The Jefferson's had taken care of everything yesterday, just as he had expected. Hotel rooms were available when they had arrived. They ate a hearty meal of sweet potatoes, collard greens, roast beef, cornbread and sweet potato pie. Toby smiled to himself as he remembered how much Rod and Jeremy's parents had enjoyed themselves. He relaxed a little and even gave himself a mental pat on the back for thinking any troublemakers from Midway would venture into the black section, at least not now.

Pushing back from his desk, Toby stood up and began cleaning off his desk. It was Friday and he was planning to do some fishing this weekend to relax. A new deputy was hired several days ago and so the weekend was covered.

"Jake!" he called to his deputy who was in the back. Jake poked his head into the room. "I'm fixing to leave," Toby told his deputy. "I'm gonna do some fishing tomorrow. Tell the new deputy to call Peg if anything comes up. If it's an emergency, you know where to find me."

"Sure thing," responded Jake. Just then the phone rang. "I'll get it," Toby said, picking up the phone. It was Harold Steinmetz.After a brief conversation, the two men had agreed to meet first thing Monday morning to collaborate about the case.

"I'm anxious to go over your notes," Harold told him. "You got it," Toby responded adding, "if you need me before then, you can reach me at home. See you Monday." They hung up and Toby wasted little time getting out of the office.

Beth locked the door to the store, put the keys in her purse and headed for her car. She was glad the weekend was finally here. She planned to spend it with Jeremy, showing him the countryside and just spending some time together. She would pack a picnic basket tonight to take with her tomorrow to the other side of town.

Pushing open the screen to the front door, she quietly let herself into her house. Mom and Dad were not in, probably at the grocery store. They had shopped every Friday evening for as long as she could remember. She wondered if all married couples fell into predictable patterns of behavior like her parents had as she headed toward her room. She heard her brother's voice coming from his room. He was talking on the telephone and there was an unusual urgency in his voice. She stopped, listening. It was not customary for her to eavesdrop on her brother's conversations but something about the tone in his voice caught her attention.

"There's nothing to worry about, Hank," she heard Bobby saying, "Doc Cuthbert took care of everything. Jimmy told me!" There was a pause. Why was Bobby talking about Doc Cuthbert? What did Jimmy tell him that was so important? Bobby spoke again.

"All we have to do is lay low until everything blows over. Nobody will connect us with anything," Another pause. "Alright," Bobby said after a while. "We'll talk with Jimmy tomorrow. The hearing comes up next week and after charges are made, you can relax."

Pause.

What hearing? What was Bobby talking about? . . . Beth wondered.

"Nah. Mom and Dad are gone. Beth'll be home in a minute so I've got to go. See ya tomorrow," she heard him finish. Beth crept back down the hall, retracing her footsteps to the living room. Just as she got there, Bobby came out of his room and saw her.

"Oh,sis. When did you get in?" he asked walking casually through the room toward the kitchen.

"Just now," Beth stammered.

"Mom and Dad went to the store. I'm getting ready to leave but tell them I'll be home for dinner in a couple of hours." He paused. "Jeez! What's wrong with you? You're as pale as a sheet"

Beth tried to compose herself.

"Just tired. I work you know," she answered.

"That's right. Rub it in, Bobby retorted, "I'll find a job soon and then you can get off my back"

"I'm not on your back," she quipped. "It's called a guilty conscience. You haven't been really looking and you know it. All you ever do is hang out with Jimmy and Hank."

"Hey, they're my friends. Okay?"

"Yeah. Right," Beth mumbled heading toward her room. She needed some time to think.

"See ya later," Bobby called out as he closed the door behind him.

Beth, confused and tired, stumbled to her room and fell across the bed. She thought again about what she had heard. Bobby had been talking to Hank about something that they were involved in. Something concerning Doc Cuthbert, Jimmy and the need to stay out of sight. What could it possibly be? Was somebody sick? Doc Cuthbert was the town coroner for heaven's sake, not afamily doctor. And why would Jimmy Cuthbert tell Bobby that his father would take care of everything? Of what? And why would Bobby tell Hank that after the hearing was over, he could relax? What hearing?

Beth pondered these things over and over. They didn't make any sense to her. Bobby must have been drinking. Yes, that's it. Those three must have gotten into some kind of trouble again and Jimmy's dad was going to come to their rescue as he had done several times in the past. She would talk to Bobby about it later. Right now all she craved was a hot shower and some of Mom's home cooking when dinner would be ready.

The boys kicked up clouds of dust dragging their feet through the back country road as they walked. They had just tried their hand at some catfish fishing at the creek and were now headed back to town.

"We just didn't hit the right spot," Rod was saying.

"You couldn't catch a fish if somebody was in the water throwing them up on the bank," Jeremy laughed.

"Oh, yeah? How many did you catch, Bill Dance?" quipped Rod.

"Who's Bill Dance?" "Nobody but one of America's Top fisherman. Didn't you ever see his program on TV?"

"Next time I'll ask Mr. Jefferson to tell us where to go," Jeremy countered.

"Say, isn't Beth coming tomorrow?" Rod asked.

"Uh huh," Jeremy replied." Won't be no fishing tomorrow, buddy, you can count on that. I called her at the store this morning and she's gonna pack us a picnic basket. Hey, why don't you and Andrea join us?"

"Just might do that," Rod added with a nod of his head. "I'll ask Mrs.Jefferson to fry up some chicken wings. Black folks don't eat ham salad sandwiches you know," joked Rod.

"And what's wrong with ham salad.?" joked Jeremy.

"Don't taste like nothing."

"I guess turnip green sandwiches do?"

"Now you're learning. Man, for a white boy, you catch on fast."

"And for a black dude, you're full of it."

They laughed heartily together throwing their arms around each other's shoulders, strolling toward town as the first signs of dusk began to peek over the horizon.

Beth was up bright and early the next morning. Everyone else was fast asleep. Last night her mother had helped her with the food she was taking with her. She had fixed a big bowl of her famous potato salad. After she had dressed and had a cup of coffee, she began packing the basket. Glancing out of the kitchen window, she noticed some dark clouds. Oh, no! Not rain! She turned on the TV to the weather channel. The forecast was for partly cloudy and occasional sunshine but no rain. She breathed a sigh of relief. She was dressed for a picnic.

Her long blonde hair was pulled back in a ponytail and tied with a flower printed scarf which matched her summer dress. She went to the closet and got her umbrella, just in case. She decided to go by the store on her way and pick up some paper plates, plastic forks, spoons and cups. She was early so there was no need to rush. She was humming softly to herself as she loaded the car and slowly drove off. Arriving in town, she pulled up outside the shop, walked across the street to get a copy of the morning paper and went in the store. She was greeted by her boss.

"Oh, you decided to work today?" he chuckled. Beth grinned shaking her head.

"I'm going on a picnic. Had to come in and get some supplies."

"Family outing?"

"No. Jeremy and I have planned a picnic together."

"That new kid?" he continued.

"Uh huh." "Kinda sweet on him, ain't ya?"

"He's nice. I like him a lot."

"Sure hope things work out for him and his friend. Seen the paperthis morning? Seems like quite a bit of excitement has been stirred up by the cover story."

Beth opened up the paper that was folded in her hand. She gazed unbelievingly at the front page. The Sheriff had been accused of harboring criminals in the colored section. The article went on to say that there was no reason to move the boys out of town and it criticized the Sheriff for abusing his authority and office.

"Are they kidding?" Beth asked. "They haven't even been indicted yet."

"People have already been in and out of here this morning. Some of them were highly upset, talking about impeaching 'ol Toby," her boss said ruefully

Where's the Sheriff now?" Beth asked.

"Dunno. His deputy is in though."

Beth folded the paper and got a shopping cart. As she wheeled around the store, she wondered what the big deal was anyway. Some of the people she knew didn't want Rod in town anyway because he was black. What was the protest all about? Because of this, she was convinced that Sheriff Relliford had acted wisely.

"You know, Mr. Radcliff, sometimes I wonder why I even stay here. This town is so narrow minded," she said.

"I know how you feel. A couple of people wanted to know why I didn't fire you for seein' that Jeremy fellow. It's the talk of the town."

"Well let them talk," Beth retorted. "I just don't want to hurt your business."

"Pooh. I told them that you were the best worker I've got. No boss fires his top employee," he answered.

"Thanks, Mr. Radcliff."

Beth finished her shopping, said goodbye, got into her car and drove quickly out of town.

It was about 10:30 a.m. when she pulled up to the hotel where Jeremy and Rod stayed. She went inside and had the desk clerk ring Jeremy's room. She sat down in the lobby and began reading the morning news again. Almost as soon as she began, Jeremy and Rod walked in. They wore short sleeved knit sweaters and shorts.

"Picnic clothes," Jeremy gleamed. "Mmm," he added giving her the once over. "You look delicious."

"Stop teasing. Hi Rod. How's Andrea?"

"Oh, she's okay. Jeremy invited us along if that's alright with you."

"Oh, sure, no problem. I want both of you to take a look at this," she exclaimed, shoving the paper in their direction.

Rod and Jeremy read the front page article together in silence. Then looked at each other.

"You'd think we were already convicted," Jeremy said sarcastically.

"Doesn't surprise me at all," Rod countered. Jeremy tossed the newspaper in the trash basket nearby.

"Picking on the Sheriff is a big mistake," he added.

The three exchanged a brief conversation and Rod left to get Andrea. Beth and Jeremy embraced warmly for a long moment, then sat down.

"I feel so isolated over here," Jeremy began. "I'm glad we're here instead of in Midway but you can't feel the pulse of the town. Not that we could do anything anyway. But this has caught me by surprise. I had no idea!"

"Well, I live here and it surprised me," Beth answered.

"That's the media for you," Jeremy observed.

"Honey, I know you feel helpless here," Beth sympathized, "but let me help. I can be your eyes and ears. Everybody at one time or another comes to the store. I can hear things. Let me do some asking around."

"Beth, you've got to promise me that you will not get involved in this thing. I've got enough to worry about already."

"Okay, I promise. But at least I can keep my ears open."

Just then Rod and Andrea appeared, glued together as if for security. Beth was envious of Andrea's full figure and shapely legs that were amply displayed by the shorts she wore which matched Rod's. She wished that she had worn hers. She has nice legs too.

"Ready?" Rod called out.

"Yep, let's hit the road. We'll have to stop by the Jefferson's and pick up the rest of the food, then we'll be on our way," Jeremy said as they all headed for the door.

Mrs. Jefferson greeted them with a warm smile when they arrived and had their food already packed in a basket. Thanking her, they drove off for the open countryside. They drove until they came to a perfect spot surrounded by an abundance of shade trees.

"This is it," Beth said, "perfect."

They all agreed, got out of the car and began unloading. Spreading two large blankets on the grass, the couples immediately paired off with their partners in peaceful relaxation and conversation. After a while, the suggestion was made to eat and listen to some music on the radio that Andrea had brought along. They ate leisurely and exchanged spirited conversations about a host of topics.

Beth had picked up some beer at the store and they drank it with their meal. Rod complained that he had eaten too much and wanted to dance some of it off. Soon Jeremy and Beth joined them and the four danced, ate and drank away the hours. When they had settled down again, Jeremy said that this was the most fun that he'd had all summer.

"Must be the company," he added gazing lovingly at Beth.

"For once I've got to agree with you Jer," Rod added.

Andrea noted that neither Rod nor Jeremy had shared any of the details about the case with her or Beth.

"All we know is what the Sheriff and the Attorney have told us which isn't much." Jeremy acknowledged.

"You know, she's right," Beth added looking at Jeremy. "How can we help if we don't know anything?"

The boys then related their feelings about what had happened. They shared their apprehensions, unanswered questions and conversations with Sheriff Relliford.

"The Sheriff said that too many things didn't add up but that he doesn't know what to make of it at this point," Rodney was saying.

"One thing he did say that he was sure of is that the blood on our car had been altered," Jeremy added.

"What do you mean altered?" Beth asked.

"Well, isn't that proof enough?" asked Andrea.

"Unfortunately, no. No one measured with instruments and recorded scientifically the exact pattern of the initial blood pattern. That was an oversight. You can't blame the Sheriff. He's not FBI. Anyway, nobody would've ever guessed that something like that would have happened," Jeremy finished.

"So there we are. No real proof but we know something's not right about the whole thing," Rod concluded.

"And that's not all. The Sheriff doesn't believe that the dead man was who or what we hit that night based upon his investigation at the lodge where the man was staying. But again, no proof. His blood matched the blood on our car," Jeremy said.

"Wait a minute. Let's back up," said Beth. "You're suggesting that the original blood was removed and the victim's blood replaced it?"

"We don't know for sure. These are some of the unanswered questions we have to deal with," Rod pointed out.

"All we know is that the Coroner's Report is the cornerstone of the case against us," added Jeremy.

"Who's the Coroner?" Andrea asked.

"Doc Cuthbert," answered Beth. As soon as she said his name, a sick sinking feeling engulfed her. She gasped and let out a startled, "Oh my God. My God!"

"Beth! Beth! What in the world is wrong?" Jeremy cried hugging her to him. She had no blood in her face. Her eyes were glazed.

"I'll get some water," Andrea volunteered jumping to her feet and running to the cooler. In a matter of seconds, she returned and handed it to Beth who gulped down the entire contents.

"Baby, Baby," Jeremy repeated over and over while stroking her long blonde locks.

In a moment, she gathered herself enough to speak. She began slowly.

"Yesterday when I came home from work, my brother, Bobby, was talking on the phone to Hank, one of the guys he hangs around with. They're always getting into something or the other. Anyway, Bobby sounded scared and that caught my attention. He was talking about . . ." she began to cry softly.

Andrea hugged her. "It's alright. Just take your time, honey," she reassured her.

"Well . . . Bobby was telling Hank not to worry. That Doc Cuthbert had taken care of everything and that after the hearing was over and charges filed, they could relax. He told him that all they had to do was lay low. I had no idea what he was talking about at the time but after hearing what you two just told me and Andrea, it all came together at once. My brother somehow knows about what really went on. Oh God, I'm scared. Jeremy please hold me . . . please," she pleaded as she broke into uncontrollable sobbing.

Her whole body shook violently. Jeremy let her cry. Andrea then broke into tears and Rod held her close to him. Both men looked at each other with blank expressions. They were too numb to feel anything. Everyone agreed that maybe they should talk with their parents and Mr. Steinmetz about Beth's experience with Bobby. Maybe Beth would be less upset and reassured that everything would be fine.

"Beth, are you sure? Positive? " Mr. McCutchin asked her when they were all together.

"Yes. I'm positive. Bobby talked about Doc Cuthbert, the upcoming hearing and laying low all in the same breath."

"Of course we can't go to court with this. It was only a telephone conversation with no witnesses. But it does give us something to work with. We don't know if your brother is a part of this whole thing or not, Beth, but I'll bet he knows something," Mr. Blake surmised.

Mary Blake got up and walked over to Beth cradling her head to her bosom.

"Poor child," she soothed. "This must be terrible for her to go through."

Beth held Jeremy's hand tightly.

"We've got to tell Sheriff Relliford and Harold about this," Mr. McCutchin said soberly. "They'll need every scrap of information they can get their hands on."

They all asked Beth to keep this to herself and not to breathe a word to anyone. She promised she would not.

It was now about eight in the evening and they decided that it was still early enough to call the Attorney and the Sheriff. Harold Steinmetz said that he would be right over and the deputy at the Sheriff's office said that he would contact the Sheriff immediately. Beth called her mother and told her where she was and that she would be a little late coming home. After the calls were made, they all got a cup of coffee from the pot in the lobby and sat quietly together, each wrapped up in their thoughts. You could literally hear a pin drop as they waited.

After a half hour or so, Harold Steinmetz came into the lobby. He joined them. As they waited for Toby Relliford, they briefed Harold about what Beth had told them.

"Toby and I were scheduled to meet first thing Monday morning and I'm sure that he was going to tell me what the boys have just talked about. He'll certainly be interested in this," Harold remarked. He got up and went over and poured himself a cup of coffee. He turned to Beth.

"If I can help it, you won't have to testify against your own brother at this point, because there was no other witness to the telephone call. Your testimony would not be admissible as evidence. It would have to be corroborated in some way in order to be introduced."

Beth breathed a sigh of relief.

"Thanks, Mr. Steinmetz. You'll never know how much you've just helped me. Bobby and I are not very close but he's still my brother and I love him."

At that moment Toby appeared, still wearing his fishing gear. He quickly joined them.

"Sorry to take so long but Peg had to come and get me. You fish for catfish at night if you're serious."

Rod and Jeremy looked at each other and shrugged.

"What's up?" Toby asked.

"Looks like that Monday meeting we were supposed to have will start now," Harold told him.

They took turns bringing Toby up to date about what had transpired during the evening. He listened intently but said nothing. After being briefed thoroughly, Toby then began to tell Harold about what his investigation had uncovered so far and the questions that were raised in his own mind.

"I also found the victim's car at least a mile or so from where the man was supposed to have been hit. I think when we look at the car and its condition, you'll agree that it's highly improbable that he could have been out on the road where the boys had their accident."

"What's the most quiet time in Midway?" Harold asked Toby.

"About ten tomorrow morning," he answered. "Most of the people will be in church and those who aren't are still asleep."

"That's the time we need to take a look at that car. You don't want anyone to see you doing any investigative work because it might scare someone off or make them even more cautious. We want them to relax as much as possible. Sometimes overconfidence can make a person careless like Beth's brother. Those are the kinds of things that we need to have happen.

"I've got the car impounded right near Rod and Jeremy's car, so we can work without drawing undue notice." Toby added.

"Good!" Added Harold.

"We also need to take a look at where the car was originally found. Tomorrow, I'll give you a theory about what the victim was doing the night he was killed by what I didn't find in his trunk and why I believe that Rod and Jeremy didn't kill him." Added Toby.

Harold paused for a moment, took a sip of coffee and spoke slowly and deliberately.

"I want everybody to hear me clearly. Everything that we have discussed up to this point is purely circumstantial and conjecture. We don't have one shred of evidence. None at all. In court, opinions and theories don't pay the metermaid. We need real hard physical evidence. Up to this point all we have are ideas. If this case were to come to trial tomorrow, it wouldn't last one day. They have all of the evidence on their side. I want us to be realistic about this situation. So, I'm going to drag this out as long as I can. I'll slow down the jury selection process and stall for as much of a delay as I can get in order to prepare my case, because we will lose the arraignment next week. But that's okay. That's just the beginning. We'll win the war but we'll also lose some early battles."

No one responded there was dead silence.

Harold continued, "Toby, your work has been tremendously effective. You have convinced me beyond a doubt that the boys here have been framed. By we don't know. Maybe our look at the victim's car tomorrow will shed some more light on the case. But unfortunately, you're an enigma. In a small town like this, people will be watching your every move. Especially the wrong ones. You will be under a microscope. You'll scare the socks off of anyone you talk to."

Toby nodded his head. He had to agree, although reluctantly. "From what I hear you saying, what we need is some good old fashioned undercover work," he queried.

"Exactly. Somebody or 'bodies who can operate without drawing the slightest amount of suspicion."

"But who?" Toby asked. "We have just two private investigators in Midway and everybody knows who they are. That eliminates us."

"I have some investigators in New York who might work. Problem is they're older men and would stand out in this small town like a sore thumb. Especially when they start asking question. Of course, I could do some of the investigation myself but it's too time consuming and people wouldn't tell me anything anyhow. No, what we need is someone who the town folks would not be suspicious of." Mr. McCuthcin suggests.

"I've got good ears," Beth volunteered.

"And we can use you," Toby said, "by keeping your eyes and ears open just like you did yesterday. But when this thing starts, your relationship with Jeremy will eliminate you as well. Our problem is the visibility in this little damn town."

They all put their collective heads together trying to figure out a solution to the problem. After a while, they gave up.

"Let's sleep on it. I've always found that works for me," John McCutchin remarked.

"Good idea. Jeremy and Rod, see what you can come up with," Harold suggested.

"Toby, I'll meet you at Stan's at 9:30 in the morning if that's okay with you?"

"That's fine, Harold. Good night everybody. I'm history," Toby said heading toward the door.

Beth told Jeremy that she had to go as well. She said that she would call his room to let him know that she made it home alright. They kissed, she said goodnight and left. Rod and Andrea kissed goodnight and everyone headed toward their rooms. Jeremy was wide awake until Beth called.

The town was practically a ghost town the next morning as Toby and Harold headed for Stan's place. Unlocking the back fence to the yard, they let themselves inside. They made their way over to the victim's car.

"First notice the flat tire," Toby told Harold. Then he took out the car keys and unlocked the front door. He pointed to the half empty whiskey bottle.

"He had been drinking that night and was probably pretty intoxicated. We checked the fingerprints on the bottle and found only his, so he was alone. Now, look at this," he said moving around to the back of the car and opening the trunk.

"No flashlight. We found no flashlight in the trunk or inside the car."

"So?"

"That's significant," Toby pointed out.

"On the way over to where I found the car, I'll explain," he added.

They locked up the car and made their way back to Toby's. As they drove, the Sheriff explained.

"If you have a flat tire during the daytime, changing a flat is no problem if you have the tools. Everything to change the flat was in his trunk. Even if you're drinking, you can fix a flat tire. Right?"

"Right. What's the point?"

"Well, I believe that the reason the flat was never fixed was because it happened at night, in total darkness and the man didn't have a flashlight."

Just then, they pulled up at the old general store where Toby had first found the man's car. He killed the engine.

"Here's where he had his flat. I found the car over there," he said pointing alongside the building.

"See any lights anywhere?" he asked Harold. Harold shook his head.

"It's pitch black out here at night. There's no way to see to change a flat. So here's what I think happened. The man was walking toward the lights of the town to borrow a flashlight to fix his car. He was probably a little drunk and was walking in the middle of the road. Somewhere between here and town, he was hit by somebody driving."

Harold noticed, however, that the closer you got to town, the more houses you saw.

"How do you know that he wasn't going to somebody's house instead of going into town. There's several directions he could've taken."

"True. I don't know exactly where he was going but I do know where he wasn't going— that way," Toby said pointing away from town.

"That's where Jeremy and Rod had their accident. About a mile or so back down the road. They never made it this far. And if the man was going to borrow a flashlight, he certainly wouldn't walk a mile away from town and the lights he saw in the distance."

"Damn it, Toby, I think you're right," Harold exclaimed snapping his fingers. "It makes all the sense in the world. But still, there's the possibility that he could have been disoriented because of his drinking and went the wrong way."

"Hell, anything's possible, Harold. But you know and I know that's pretty slim."

"Where does this leave us?" Harold asked.

"I don't know. But we've got a lot of loose ends to tie up."

"Harold . . . Harold!"

"Yeah, Toby? What's wrong?"

"Damn it, Harold. I've got it. I've got it!" he was shouting, grinning from ear to ear, "but we've got to move fast. If my hunch is right, we can't lose any more time! The boys are college students. Right?"

"Right."

"The only investigators that would not draw attention here would be boys around Jeremy and Rod's age. They could simply be identified as concerned classmates who came down to support their buddies. They could move all around Midway without creating suspicion as they carried out their work. Who would suspect college criminology students? That's the only outside age group that could slip through the cracks."

Harold pondered Toby's idea. It seemed plausible enough. No, it was down right genius. They laughed aloud and clapped his hands together. Once. Twice. On the third clap he clenched his fist.

"Now we're getting somewhere," he said jubilantly.

"But we need to move fast. If my guess is right, we need investigators to cover every inch of the road between here and town looking for anything. The longer we wait, the less our chances become of finding clues."

"We'll talk to the boys right now," Harold told Toby. "I can arrange through my office to fly the students and their equipment here immediately. They can also arrange all the details with the schools admissions office to have the students involved released."

The two jumped into their car and sped back to the hotel to meet with the boys and their parents. They talked excitedly as they drove. At the hotel, a quick meeting was held in the Blake's room. Toby and Harold explained what their plans were and how they wanted to carry it out. Rod and Jeremy grew more excited by the minute. Harold cautioned everyone that they were merely working on the Sheriff's hunch.

"If he's wrong, we're back to square one." Rod and Jeremy put their heads together whispering frantically. A faint smile crept across Beth's face as she and Andrea crossed their fingers in a hopeful sign of good luck. The boys abruptly broke up their private conference.

Rod made the first announcement.

"We've got our guys, Sheriff. A buddy of mine named Dick Wingate is a Senior Criminal Justice major at The University and has already interviewed for work with the FBI. I know for a fact that Federal Agents interviewed him for over an hour."

It was now Jeremy's turn. "Ralph Simon is a close friend of mine at school. He's a Med student in his second year of Graduate School majoring I think, in Microbiology. Together, they could crack anything."

"But they're just college students. How do we know that their work wouldn't be challenged by experts in court?" Mr. Blake asked.

"That's right," agreed Mr. McCutchin." "We'd be taking one big chance."

Jeremy was quick to disagree.

"Dad, at that level of education, some students begin to develop their own methods. Here, maybe this will help."

He got up and went quickly to his book bag and brought back a copy of the University Bulletin which contained all the course listings. He thumbed through the pages briefly and stopped.

"Look here. Criminal Justice major. Listen to some of the courses that Rod's friend has already taken: Criminalistic Laboratory; Criminology; Criminal Investigation. Dad, the same thing the experts take." he began scanning the book further, Toby remarked that even he never had courses or training like that.

"Sounds awfully impressive to me."

"And Dad, listen to what Ralph is specializing in: Pathogenic Microbiology and Tissue Culture. He could look at blood and tell you if it came from a mosquito or an elephant."

Everyone broke into laughter.

"How soon can we get them here?" Harold asked.

"Well, school hasn't started yet. So that's a plus," Rod said.

"I'll get my office on it right away. Once they notify the school about both of your situations and our needs, there won't be a problem. I'll need their addresses and phone numbers so that my people can begin to work as of yesterday. We'll take care of their travel. We've got our own private plane. They can bring whatever equipment they need. I'll instruct my office to underwrite the costs of equipment rental or lease if we have to." Added Mr. McCutchin.

"Mr. Blake. Mr. McCutchin?" Asked Harold.

"We told you to spare no expense. That still goes," said Mr.McCutchin. Rod's father agreed and added, "No expense is too great for my boy."

"Then let's do it," Harold responded standing up.

"I'll try to have them here by Tuesday. The Sheriff believes that every day we waste lessens our chances to gather evidence. They can set up their equipment in my office. It'll be cramped but we'll manage somehow."

"This calls for a celebration," Rod said jumping up, "and I know just where we can go.

Flossie's."

"Flossie's?" his mother said.

"That's right. They have dancing, soul food and a TV bar. It's just right down the street."

"Son," his mother scolded, "don't forget this is still Sunday."

Rod slowed to a crawl.

"Aw man, that's right. Sorry folks."

Andrea smiled and just shook her head.

"Rodney"_always the party animal," she teased.

Mrs. McCutchin popped up.

"I'm with Rodney. If we can't party, let's gorge ourselves on some of this beautiful food. Let's all have dinner together. John always brings along his own special imported wine in his briefcase. Right John?"

Her husband looked slightly embarrassed.

"Well, yes, but . . ." his voice trailed off.

"Give me a few minutes to make some phone calls," Harold was saying, "and then we can all go and have some fun."

Everyone began to move in different directions. Toby smiled to himself. What the heck.

He wasn't on duty officially and he wasn't about to pass up this opportunity. After all of the stress of these past few days, this is just what he needed. He just wished that Peg was here to share this time with him.

Beth tried to pick Bobby's brain the next morning after breakfast. She was planning to see Jeremy that afternoon and wanted to see if she could uncover any additional information about the accident. She asked him subtlely when they were alone if he, Jimmy and Hank had gotten into any trouble lately. He became very defensive and a little angry at her probing. He never looked at her while they talked, instead he fidgeted nervously around the room, demanding to know why she was giving him the third degree.

"You three have been awfully quiet lately. Usually you're out getting into something," she told him.

"What we do is our business," he snapped. "I didn't ask you what you were doing everyday with that McCutchin fellow."

He accused her of being nosey and refused to discuss his activities with her any further.

"Okay. Just thought I'd ask," she answered.

Beth knew that he was hiding something and anger began to well inside of her as she thought about Jeremy and Rod. Here her own brother was obviously covering up for somebody while the man she loved was going on trial for his life. She felt bitterness begin to take hold of her as she watched him walk casually around the house as if nothing was wrong.

Just then, she heard a horn blow outside. Bobby went over to the window, pulled back the curtain and looked out. He waved at somebody and then hurried up to his room. Beth peeped outside. It was Jimmy Cuthbert. Suddenly Beth had an urge to play detective. She knew that she had promised Jeremy not to get involved but now she had an opportunity to maybe do something to help him where nobody else could. Her heart raced as she contemplated her next move.

Bobby came down from his room and went out the door pulling on his jacket as Beth pretended to be busy in the kitchen. When they drove off, Beth sprinted outside to her car and followed them at a long distance. Soon they were headed in the direction of Hank's farm and Beth let them get out of sight so that they wouldn't spot her. She knew where they were headed, so she drove to Hank's place leisurely. She parked her car next to the roadside and got out. She was surrounded by a thicket of trees and walked close to the dirt road leading up to the Peter's farm near the end of the thickets.

She paused behind a big tree. Hank, Jimmy and Bobby were sitting on the front porch talking excitedly and gesturing with their arms. They were some thirty yards or so away and she could not hear what they were saying. She watched for about five minutes from her hiding place. She never liked those two. She and Bobby had many arguments about them. They were always drinking and had nasty mouths. They were known as carousers and chased every loose skirt in town. As they talked, Beth was sure they were up to no good. Probably discussing what Bobby was talking with Hank about on the phone yesterday. She watched them with disgust.

After several long moments Beth stole back to her car, climbed inside and sat trembling in anger behind the wheel. She was tempted to drive up to the house and confront all three of them but thought better of it. She would deal with Bobby herself, later. She drove directly to Jeremy's hotel and had the desk clerk ring his room. About 20 minutes later, he met her in the lobby. Rod was still in bed as he and Andrea were going to shop for some new record albums later in the day. Jeremy and Beth decided to go to the restaurant down the street and get Jeremy something to eat and then go off by themselves somewhere in the countryside. Beth yearned desperately for a quiet time alone with him.

After breakfast, Beth did not mention what had happened earlier. She knew that Jeremy would be angry with her for breaking her promise. As they rode, she held his hand with her free hand driving comfortably with the other. Her stomach fluttered as he locked his fingers between her's and kissed each one of her entwined fingertips. She was becoming aroused and excited.

"I've missed you," she said nervously, not trusting herself to say more.

"I know. I've felt the same way," he said softly, loosening his grip and pressing his lips to her now upturned palm. She thrilled at the sensation.

"Let's stop here," he told her.

Beth pulled the car to the side of the road and came to a stop in two inches of thick grass carpet. All was quiet and still. Beth laid her head back in the seat, her long hair spilling over the headrest. She closed her eyes and relaxed. She felt Jeremy move closer to her and she shuddered. His lips closed softly over her's and they parted willingly to invite his probing tongue inside. Her body suddenly came alive with pent up passion as he pulled her tightly to him. Her own tongue was moving with a mind of its own. They kissed long and deep. Desperately.

Jeremy's fingers sifted slowly through her fragrant hair as she clutched passionately to the back of his neck with both hands.

Her breasts heaved heavily against his steeled chest as he ground her body against his.

She moaned against his lips. His hand made its way to her knees and under the frock she wore.

It was then she remembered that she had left home purposely without putting on panties. This only served to heighten her desire. She closed her thighs together but not before Jeremy discovered that he felt no panty line beneath his fingers. He groaned as desire washed over him.

Pulling Beth on top of him, he forced her dress up over her thighs and straddled her atop him still kissing her wildly. She clung desperately to him, her breathing now labored and panting.

He pushed her gently upright and slightly away so that he could kiss her neck and carry his mouth down between the cleavage of her dress. She threw her head back and moaned audibly as his lips traced the top of one breast, partially hidden by the black laced bikini bra.

His hand slipped between her open legs and traced the shape of her long thighs as she lost herself in sexual longing.

She gasped loudly and crushed her mouth against his in total abandon as his finger slipped easily into her eager love canal. She was sopping wet and completely open to his touch. She cried in ecstasy as he probed the secret insides of her treasure, slowly . . . but knowingly. A second finger entered her eager vagina and was soaked with the hot juices of her love as she rocked slowly back and forth, grinding wildly against his manual invasion. He was astonished at the extreme wetness of her canal and became overwhelmingly aroused.

Jeremy was beside himself with excitement. He was shocked and totally aroused by the wetness and wonder of the woman he held and loved so dearly. He was so hard and erect that he was hurting himself in the cramped position that he was in. He had to have freedom. Beth feeling his hardness with deft fingers, suddenly broke off their kiss and sat up in his lap . . . her breasts heaving up and down as she gasped for air. Damn she was beautiful, Jeremy said to himself reaching for her again. He changed his position, though, to relieve the pressure that was torturing him. He felt as though he was ready to explode. Beth thwarted his advance, reluctantly.

"We've got to stop, Jeremy. I mean it," she panted. "I'd never let you take me in the front seat of a car!" she said emphatically. "Not our first time, anyway. I want that to be special. Don't you?"

"Well . . . me too, but when?" Jeremy protested. "I can't stay like this forever without getting some help." Beth climbed off of his lap eyeing the huge lump between his legs and pulling her dress down at the same time.

"Oh, he'll be fine," she said with a gleam in her eyes and a smile playing across her lips.

Her forehead wrinkled in a thoughtful way.

"Would you have really done it to me in a car?" she asked, suddenly serious.

Jeremy thought for the first time in 15 minutes. This was certainly not the way that he wanted to make love to Beth. Not hardly. This was the way that all the fellas joked about including himself. It was the height of a cheap thrill. This is what you did to someone that you cared little about and heaven knew that he didn't feel that way bout her.

"No . . . at least I hope I wouldn't have," he admitted.

"You seemed so persistent, though," she pointed out.

"Hey, you weren't exactly fighting me off! And besides, you came out here without panties on. What was I supposed to do? Man!" he exclaimed. "I just couldn't stop, Beth. I'm sorry."

"No, it's not your fault. It's mine. You only did what any man would do. I just couldn't stop you. I want you so much. I'm not a tease, Jeremy. I don't usually act like this. Do you believe me?" she pleaded.

Jeremy pulled her tenderly to him and kissed her eyes which were brimming with tears.

"I believe you, sweetheart. Don't cry. I think . . ."

"You think what?" she asked softly as he looked deep into the blueness of her eyes.

"I love you" he said simply. The tears came down unashamedly.

"I love you too, Jeremy. And I want you to have me. It's just that I want it to be right with us. I don't want to repeat past mistakes."

He pulled her closer to him and put her head on his shoulder.

"Tell me about it?" he whispered.

"About six years ago when I was still in high school, I was going with this guy, a star athlete. I thought I was in love, at least as much as a 16 year old could be. My girlfriends all told me that I would not keep him unless I let him do things with me. You know. Well, one night after a game, he pressured me . . . and . . ."

"I know," Jeremy reassured her, "we've all had that first time."

"I thought it was something that I was supposed to do. Afterwards, I hated myself for it. I told Mom about it and she promised not to tell Dad. She helped me a lot. She explained about peer pressure and making your own decisions. She taught me about self respect and morality. After about six months, he and I broke up anyway. He just found himself another girlfriend like nothing had ever happened. I was crushed, totally. Not because I was so much in love but because I had given away a part of me that I could never take back again. Never!"

Jeremy had often thought about the predicament that girls found themselves in after giving up their virginity. With boys, it was completely different. They didn't give up anything. There was no sense of loss at all. After his first time he experienced a sense of gain! He had become a man. Or so he thought. Maybe, just maybe, he continued thoughts, that the wisdom of the Bible's teaching about casual and premarital sex as being wrong is so important. It recognizes the inequality of the sexes that society creates and the stigmas attached to it.

" I believe that God intended sex to be a sacred trust between a man and a woman that goes beyond social practices and abuse. That's the way I want it to be between us," he told her.

"Thank you," she sobbed softly, squeezing his hand tightly. They sat like that for several minutes. Not needing to say anything else. Finally, Jeremy suggested that they go for a walk together.

"It'll help me work off some steam."

"Yes, let's do that before I change my mind," Beth agreed.

They got out of the car and walked together, arm in arm. Time stood still for the both of them. Nothing else in the world seemed to matter except their being together.

Down by the creek, he taught her how to skip stones across the water. She learned quickly, often outdistancing him. He claimed that it was beginners luck. She told him the names of some native birds that winged overhead and serenaded them from the tree tops. They stopped to kiss frequently. Jeremy had never experienced such completeness before with a woman than what he was feeling right now.

It was as if the world was made for them to share at this moment. Beth wanted nor needed anything else but the man she was with. They were truly happy together. Soon tired and exhausted, they headed back toward the car exhilarated, hand in hand.

They drove back to the village and to the hotel. They ran smack into Rod in the lobby.

"Man, where in the world have you been?" he demanded. "Your mother is worried."

Jeremy remembered that he had failed to say anything to his folks before he left.

"Me and Beth just went for a ride. Jeez, I forgot to mention it. Where's everybody?"

"Your folks are up in their room. Me and Andrea picked up some sweet jams down at the shop. Wait'll you hear 'em," Rod said.

"I'd better go up and let them know I'm back. You and Andrea had dinner?"

"Yeah. We're gettin' ready to get lost for a while ourselves," Rod said with a wink.

"See you guys later."

"Bye, Rod. Tell Andrea 'Hello' for me, will you?" Beth asked.

"Sure thing. Later."he replied.

After Rod left, Jeremy and Beth went up to his parent's room to let them know that they were back and everything was fine. Jeremy apologized to his mother.

"Harold called this morning. His office talked with your classmates yesterday and they're all going to the university first thing in the morning to arrange for them to be flown down here as early as tomorrow night if they can," his father told him.

"Good. Beth and I are just going to cool it for a while around town," he replied. "See you after a while."

The evening passed by quickly and soon Beth decided that it was time for her to head home as well. She called her mother to let her know where she had been and that she would be home soon. She, too, had to apologize because in her rush to leave home this morning to follow Bobby and Jimmy, she had forgotten to say goodbye to her mother.

Monday was inventory day at the store and she would have to go in early. She was tired and hungry anyway. It had been a long but exciting day for her. Jeremy walked her to the car and after promising to see him again tomorrow evening, she drove toward home.

After dinner, Beth was planning to take a shower and go to bed when Bobby came home drunk. He entered the front door noisily and stumbled into the kitchen looking for something to eat as Beth was cleaning off the table.

"Fix me a plate, sis, before you put everything away," he demanded.

"You ask me, Bobby. Don't tell me," she said irritated. "Anyway, you smell like a still

" He mumbled something inaudible and sat down.

"When are you going to do something about your life, Bobby? I hate what you're doing to yourself."

"Don't worry, Beth. I'm okay."

She finished preparing her brother's plate and set it in front of him before going over to load the dishwasher."

"I overheard you on the telephone yesterday talking to Hank. What kind of trouble are you in, Bobby?"

"Mind your own business, girl," Bobby said harshly, "and don't listen in on my conversations. You're too nosey!"

Beth was starting to get angry and she pursued the conversation.

"I won't shut up, Bobby. I heard you telling Hank that Doc Cuthbert would take care of everything and to lay low. You wouldn't talk like that unless something was wrong."

"I told you to shut up," he shouted.

"Well, what are you covering up?" she pressed further.

"I also followed you and Jimmy this morning over to Hank's place. I saw you all talking.

Were you talking about that telephone call? Well, were you?" she insisted, turning Bobby around by one shoulder in his chair to face her.

"You followed us? Why you bitch . . ." He yelled springing from his chair.

His fist landed with a sickening thud against Beth's face. She screamed with a shrieking cry of anguish and pain and fell to the floor as if shot, writhing. Her awful screams penetrated the walls. Bobby thought she was dying. He panicked as his parents flew down the steps.

"What in the hell is going on?" bellowed his father in a deep baritone as he and his wife burst into the room.

"Oh my God, my God," cried Beth's mother, streaking over to where her fallen daughter lay, rolling on the floor in pain while clutching her face with both hands. Mrs. McCallister pried Beth's hands from her face while her husband held her still. Beth cried out in agony. The left side of her face near the cheekbone was swelling by the second and her eye was closing as well.

"Jethro, get some ice, quick," said Mrs. McCallister to her husband. "Put some cubes in a towel or something." As her husband hurried over to the refrigerator, she cradled Beth in her arms while her daughter sobbed.

"You'll be all right, baby," she said over and over to Beth. Jethro yelled at his motionless son as he dumped ice cubes into a dishcloth.

"What the hell is wrong with you? If your sister is hurt bad, your ass is mine," he threatened as he rushed over and handed the ice back to his wife. Mrs. McCallister applied the ice to Beth's swollen face and soon she began to quiet down.

"Here, let me see," her father said, moving the ice bag for a second.

"That will stop the swelling. The eye seems to be alright but she's gonna have quite a shiner. Heaven knows I've had enough of 'em. Bobby, have you lost your damn mind? How in the hell could you hit your own sister like that?" he shouted, shoving his son against the wall.

"Dad, it was an accident. I didn't mean to hit her. Not like that. I just wanted to shut her up."

"Not like that, you don't. I've never trusted a man who would hit a woman," he said pointedly. "I don't care what she's done or said. It ain't right. It must have been something awfully bad for you to do that. What'd she say?"

"Aw, it was no big deal, Dad. It's over," Bobby answered.

"Tell him! Tell him!" yelled Beth, now standing and holding the ice bag to her face.

"Tell him what you, Hank and Jimmy are involved in," she cried angrily.

Bobby fidgeted wringing his hands.

"See Dad. That's what made me hit her. She kept on and kept on accusing me of things."

"What things?" his father probed.

Bobby hesitated. He walked over to the couch and slouched down.

"I'll tell you what things, Dad," Beth began. "You Know the two men from out of town that are accused of running over that man from the lodge? Well, I overheard Bobby talking to Hank on the phone yesterday about the accident. I heard him when I came home from work.

I don't eavesdrop on his conversations but he sounded scared. Weird. At first, I thought he had been drinking because he was talking about the arraignment of those two men coming up Thursday and how he,Jimmy and Hank had to lay low for awhile. He told Hank that Doc Cuthbert would take care of everything, so they could relax."

Her Father nodded and told her to go on.

"Well, the next morning, Jimmy Came by and picked up Bobby. They drove over to Hank's and I followed them. They were scheming about something, I know it."

"Did you hear what they were talking about?" her father continued. Beth paused and repositioned the ice pack on her face. "Well . . . no, not really. But Dad, Mom, when you put it all together, those three have to know something about what's going on."

"Well,Son," Jethro asked, "what about it?"

Bobby stood up abruptly.

"All she's talking about is speculation on her part. We don't know nothin'. I was talking about something else."

"Like what?" asked his mother.

"Mom, that's private business. Nobody has the right to pry into my personal affairs."

"It's not your business when it involves the life of somebody else," Beth shouted.

"Now Honey, Bobby said it didn't," her mother said.

"Well, he's lying," Beth shot back.

"Aw, Mom, she's all hung up on that outsider that's involved. You know how she's been running around with him. The whole town's talkin' about it. She cares more about him than she does her own brother," Bobby complained.

Beth sat down and began to cry.

"That's not true . . . that's not true," she sobbed.

"Well, Beth. Unless you know for sure what's going on, I don't want you accusing your own brother of something that critical. He's your own flesh and blood, Beth. Don't let your feelings about this boy turn you against your own brother."

Beth jumped up and ran from the room crying hysterically.

When she left, her father told Bobby.

"You'd better not be lyin' in this house, Bobby! If you do know something, you'd better spit it out."

"I don't know anything about what Beth is talking about," he lied.

After several more moments of discussion, the conversation ended. Beth's father then went up to her room and knocked on the door. Beth told him to come in.

"Beth, you'd better call your boss and tell him that you're sick and need a couple of days off. You can't go to work like that."

"Okay," she muttered, turning over and burying her head in her pillow. Her father gently closed the door behind him.

About noon that Monday morning, Toby called the boy's room and told them that Harold Steinmetz wanted to meet with them briefly about going over the procedures for the arraignment on Thursday. He told them that he would pick them up in about an hour. Jeremy then called the store to tell Beth that, when the meeting was over, he would wait for her to get off work.

He was told by her boss that she wouldn't be in for a day or two because she was sick. He decided to stop by her house and check on her before coming back that afternoon.

At the meeting, Harold told them that the two students from school had been cleared by Admissions to come down. They should be in Midway sometime in the morning and were being flown down by his corporation's private plane. After the briefing concluded, Toby dropped Jeremy by Beth's house.

"Sheriff, I'll only be a minute. I just want to make sure she's alright. You can wait here. I'll be back in a minute."

"Okay, I'll keep the engine running," Toby told him.

Jeremy hopped out and hurried up the walk to the house and rang the doorbell. Beth's mother answered the door and spoke to him through the screen.

"Hello Mrs. McCallister. I'm Jeremy. I was supposed to see Beth this afternoon but I understand that she's sick. I just stopped by to see her for a sec."

"I'd rather you not," she replied. "She's not feeling too well at the present time."

"I'll only stay a minute, I promise."

"Young man, I said that she's not up to seeing company," she responded with an icy tone.

"Mom, you havin' trouble?" came a voice from inside.

Bobby McCallister appeared inside behind his mother.

"No trouble," Jeremy said. "I just asked to see Beth."

"Well, Beth ain't seein' nobody," Bobby said harshly.

"I can speak for myself," came Beth's voice. She wedged herself between her mother and brother. Jeremy couldn't believe what he saw. Beth's eye was swollen badly and had turned black and blue.

"Holy cow," exclaimed Jeremy, "what happened to you, Beth?"

"Bobby hit me yesterday after I questioned him about his phone conversation with Hank," she answered.

Jeremy momentarily lost control of himself. Before he came to his senses, he had burst into the house and tackled Bobby. As they fell to the floor, Jeremy was punching Bobby repeatedly in the face. They rolled over several times in the struggle. Bobby swore profusely as he fought back but Jeremy was too strong for him. Powered by rage, Jeremy drove his fist time and time again into Bobby. Blood ran from Bobby's nose and mouth. Beth and her mother were screaming for them to stop, trying in vain to separate the two combatants.

Finally, Sheriff Relliford who heard the ruckus from outside, burst into the room and pulled Jeremy off of Bobby.

"What the hell is going on?" he shouted. "Jeremy what's the meaning of this?"

"The bastard punched Beth. Look at her face, Sheriff." Toby looked at Beth and whistled.

"That's quite a shiner. You do that Bobby?"

"Yeah, but I didn't mean to hurt her," he said wiping the blood from his face.

"Beth, you want to press charges against Bobby?"

She simply shook her head. Mrs. McCallister was beside herself. She raged angrily at Toby. He had no right busting into my house like that and jumping on her boy. He's not a part of this family.

"You get him out of here right now, Sheriff. I'll be right down to your office.

I'm the one who's gonna press charges. You had no right bringing this criminal to my house in the first place. You hold him until I get down there."

"Mrs. McCallister, I don't think that will be necessary. He just lost his temper," reasoned Toby.

"I don't care," she yelled, "look at my son. He's going to pay for this. Now get him out of here. Now!" she screamed.

Toby and Jeremy left immediately with Beth running behind them. Her mother yelled for her to get back in the house. Toby told her to do as her mother asked.

"We've got enough trouble as it is. You can see Jeremy tomorrow." With that Toby and Jeremy faded in the distance.

Later that evening, Toby was on the phone with Harold Steinmetz.

"This really changes things now," Harold was saying. "With all that we have against us already, this only makes it doubly difficult. From what I understand, the McCallisters are pretty well liked around here."

"Yep. I'm afraid you're right. When this hits the paper tomorrow, all hell's gonna break loose. I'm already in hot water for taking him by the house in the first place. From here on out, I'm gonna have to drop my involvement with this case in order not to jeopardize it any further.

Everything's gonna depend on the kids when they get in tomorrow."

"I think that's wise, Toby. By the way, the Judge refuses to allow bail for Jeremy this time. He claims that it's too risky to let him go at this juncture . . . might cause too much trouble.

I'm inclined to agree. You'll have to hold him until after the arraignment.

Yeah, I was afraid of that," Toby admitted.

"Well, call me when the boys' get to town. In the meantime, I'll talk with Jeremy's folks."

After hanging up, Toby pounded his fist into the desk. Things just weren't working out at all. Of all the rotten luck. He didn't blame Jeremy at all for what he did. If somebody punched Peg like that he'd do the same. The damn timing was just lousy. Beth should not have

Hey, wait a minute! Maybe . . . just maybe . . . this whole thing might work in their favor.

If the other three were involved somehow in this whole thing, they just might start to get a little nervous now. They just might try to be a little too careful. Somehow ol' Doc Cuthbert fit into this puzzle in someway if Beth was right in what she said she overheard. He would not forget that. After all, the Coroner's report was the whole case against the boys.

Harold's phone rang loudly at 4:00 a.m. Tuesday morning. It was Jeff Hodges, his law firm's private pilot. He was at the airport in nearby Chattanooga with Dick Wingate and Ralph Simon.

"The boys have some equipment with them. You'll have to make some kind of arrangements to pick them up. I've got to fly back to New York tonight. I'll stay with them until you arrive. We're at Gate 107."

"Fine, Jeff. Hey, great job! Tell the boys to stay put. We'll get them in a couple of hours."

Harold hung up and called Toby. Toby would pick up the two investigators and their equipment in the Sheriff's van. He thought that it would be a good idea if Harold went along too, so that the two of them could brief the boys together on the return trip. Harold consented.

"Pick you up in a half hour," Toby said hanging up.

The Sheriff's van literally ate up the road between Midway and Chattanooga. At 4:30 in the morning, there were no other vehicles on the road.

"Anyway, the Sheriff isn't likely to get a ticket, do you think?" he joked.

Harold just grinned and nervously kept looking out his side window as the road markings became one continuous blur. While he drove, Toby explained his urgency.

"We may have some more bad luck. The weather forecast calls for rain by thursday. That just gives us a couple of days for the boys to comb the area that we talked about. Rain more than anything else can mess up the search. I'd like to get the boys out there this mornin to get started if I can."

He pressed the pedal down again, just slightly.

Harold cleared his throat. Toby chuckled.

"You're enjoying this, aren't you?" Harold asked timorously.

"Relax a little, Hal. I do this more than you think."

"How long will it take us?"

"At this speed, an hour."

"That would put us back in Midway around seven or so," Harold noted. "If it's not going to rain for a couple of days, why the hurry now?"

"Midway comes to life at about nine or ten. Only a few people are moving about before that time. I want the boys to work as inconspicuously as possible. The less attention they draw, the more effective they'll be." Replied Toby.

"Makes sense to me," Harold remarked.

It wasn't long before the van pulled into the airport. Toby and Harold went directly to Gate 107 after receiving permission to drive around to the loading area. There they met the two men with their gear ready to go. It was just a matter of minutes before the Sheriff's van was loaded and headed back to Midway. Toby introduced himself and Harold to the two college students as they drove.

"I apologize for the rush back there at the loading dock but it's very important that we get back to town as soon as possible. How about introducing yourselves and telling us who will be doing what?"

The boys glanced at each other and Ralph Simon spoke up first since he was the upper classman.

"I'm Ralph Simon, a graduate medical student at the University, majoring in microbiology

I'll be handling the analysis or physical evidence such as hairs, blood, tissues or anything like that," he said.

"Good," replied Toby casting a sidelong glance at him as he spoke. He was certainly an articulate young man who spoke with a measured and confident tone. He was the studious type,

Toby observed, probably a straight "A" student. His dark thick brown hair was curly and well cut. He had a thick but well trimmed mustache and his eyes were framed with expensive black rimmed glasses. He was of average height Toby had observed as they loaded the van but very strong and well built. He loaded a piece of his equipment into the van by himself that Toby was sure needed two people.

After as brief pause, Dick Wingate introduced himself. He was very different in stature and looks from Ralph. He was much taller about Toby's height and his hair was blonde, long and thinner than Ralph's. He was clean shaven in sort of a fresh-scrubbed way. He had a boyish looking face which belonged to that of an altar or a choir boy, Toby speculated to himself. His manner was less reserved and studious than Ralph's. He seemed a bit more relaxed and at ease.

"I'm Dick Wingate, an undergraduate student at the University majoring in Criminal Justice. I'll be responsible for gathering the evidence for Ralph to analyze, I hope," he grinned. Toby liked them both right off.

"Boys, you're part of the team that will eventually help free Rod and Jeremy. All four of us will work together as one. I'll help out behind the scenes but not directly. Attorney Steinmetz here, will be much more visible. From here on out, you will both be treated by Harold and myself as professional investigators and not college students if that's okay with you two," Toby stated.

"Yes sir," they both answered simultaneously.

"The sirs won't be necessary fellas," Harold responded. "I'm Harold and the Sheriff is Toby." The boys nodded together as Harold continued.

"Let me lay it on the line Ralph and Dick. Your friends are in big trouble and the State is well ahead of us at this point. The autopsy and the Coroner's report has Jeremy and Rod in a stranglehold. We know they're innocent but we don't have a shred of evidence. We're all they've got. As their attorney, I'm going to have to depend solely upon the both of you to furnish me with the evidence to build a strong defense."

"Sounds pretty serious," Ralph said.

"Believe me it is," Harold reassured them both.

"However, the picture is not as dark as it appears, thanks to Toby. His preliminary investigation and work has led us to theorize that Rod and Jeremy were framed. We have some suspects to work with but only from hearsay. We can only hope and pray that Toby's hunch is right because you will begin your investigation from that premise. Toby will explain."

The van virtually "flew" over the highway as Toby sped through the night. He conveyed the bulk of his investigative work to the two boys, complete with the questionable circumstances surrounding the case and the loose ends. Dick was highly impressed and told Toby so.

"We'll get started with the search as soon as we hit town," Dick said.

"The two of us can work together combing the area initially," Ralph noted with the acknowledgment that two could cover twice the area better and faster than one.

"Look," Toby responded. "You two are calling the shots from here on in. We're just here to help out. Handle the investigation as you see fit. You know our plan and the suspects that we have. You guys take it from here. We have all of the confidence in the world in your skills.

Why heck, when Rod and Jeremy showed us the course of study that you two are involved in at school from a technical standpoint, we couldn't tell you anything anyway."

Both boys beamed with pride and reclined in their seats in a relaxing fashion. Toby and Harold exchanged a brief glance as faint smiles etched their faces.

Ralph and Dick covered every square inch of ground from the old general store to about a half a mile down the road. Each man covering a side of the dirt road about five yards deep. They didn't look further than five yards off the road because that would mean that the driver of the car would have been driving in the grass and not on the road which didn't make any sense. Anyway, it would be too much for just two people if they searched any more ground than they did. While the boys were conducting their search, Toby and Harold unloaded their equipment from the van into Harold's temporary office. They worked quickly to avoid being seen and having to answer questions about what was going on. They finished their work totally undetected. Once the equipment was situated in the office, what was once cramped was now crammed.

"Don't ever enter this room without turning on the light," Toby joked.

"Well, we did leave room for air," Harold conceded with a smirk.

"We've accomplished a lot though. We have now moved in an investigation team and no one even knows they're here," Toby pointed out.

"Let's go see. They've been at it for a couple of hours now. It's almost ten and folks will be scurrying around before long." Added Toby.

" Driving back down the road, they spotted the boys busy at work.

"Man," Toby said raising an eyebrow, "They're almost half way already."

Seeing the van coming in the distance, Ralph instructed Dick to mark where they stopped. They both stuck a wooden stake in the grass.

"Any luck?" Toby called out as they drove up.

"Nothing yet," Ralph answered.

"We haven't found a trace of blood anywhere."

"This stretch of territory was pretty easy to cover thoroughly because it's pretty open," Dick was saying.

"But from here to town, there's a lot of bushes and trees close to the road so the search will be more difficult." Dick continued.

"We'll tackle that first thing in the morning," Toby instructed them. "Good job."

"Where does that little stream lead to?" Ralph asked, pointing back over behind him to the water down over the side of a little rise running parallel with the road.

"Winds all the way around town and empties into a river about five miles on the other side. It widens quite a bit the closer you get to the black section of Midway. People fish the upper half a lot including myself. Here, it's no deeper than a foot or so," Toby told him.

Harold told them that their equipment was safe and sound in his office. He gave them each a key to the office.

"What was mine is now yours," he added.

"Toby, here's what I think we ought to do first thing in the morning," Dick suggested.

"We'll begin our search just outside of town and work our way back toward these markers here. That way, the later it gets, the further away from town we'll be."

"I see why the FBI is interested in you," said Toby nodding his head in agreement.

"Ralph, what are your plans following graduation?" asked Harold.

"I'm leaning toward medical research in tissue culture but I'm having so much fun here, I might consider police lab work. I never thought about that before until your firm called me.

This seems so much more exciting."

"Well, if you do and choose to work in New York City, I'm certain you'll get other calls from us periodically," he concluded.

"Let's get you both checked in at the hotel and something to eat," Toby said.

"I know you're hungry and Sarah fixes the best food in town. By the way, nobody knows why you're here. So, let's keep it that way. If anyone starts to ask questions, just tell them you're assistants to Harold. You know, legal aides. They will never suspect you to be investigators under cover." Tobi finished.

As the first rays of sunlight began to wake up the night, Ralph and Dick rolled out of bed. They showered and dressed quickly. By seven, it was light enough to go to work and they hit the dirt road soon after. A dew had settled overnight and even the early birds' chirping seemed lackluster. The boys breathed deeply. There was nothing quite like the fresh, cool early morning air.

"We'll start over there by that tree," Dick said pointing.

"We won't get too far off the road for a while because of all the foliage, so we can make good time for the first 100 yards or so. When we reach that clearing down there, we'll stop for a second and rendezvous." Dick finished.

"Okay. Let's go." Ralph complied.

The search began with renewed vitality. Only youth could be so exuberant at such an ungodly hour. The boys searched diligently and patiently until they reached the clearing. They met briefly to confer before going on. Shortly after passing the clearing, they rounded a slight curve in the road and could see their stakes in the ground about a quarter of a mile ahead. Dick called over to Ralph.

"In about an hour we'll be through," he said pointing.

"We must find something between here and our stakes. Let's check very carefully as we go around this bend. Of all the places along this road, this is the most logical point for an accident to happen." Dick cited.

As they worked the curve meticulously, suddenly Ralph cried out.

"Over here, Dick. I think I've found something in front of these bushes!"

Dick hurried across the road and knelt at the spot where Ralph stood.

"That's definitely blood stains in the grass," Ralph said. "Quite a bit of it as a matter of fact. Look here," he added pointing to several areas where there was blood spattered.

"We've done it! We've done it!" Dick shouted jubilantly.

"'Ol Toby was dead on target," he added.

"It certainly looks that way," Ralph added excitedly. "From the amount of blood in the grass, an automobile accident is a distinct possibility. I need to gather some samples," he said, pulling the shoulder strap of the black bag that he was carrying over his head. He sat the bag in front of him and began unzipping it.

"Wait!" Dick cautioned him.

"Before you touch anything, I need to photograph and mark the scene. Let me get a picture before and after you remove your samples." Dick explained.

Dick busied himself taking several pictures of the scene, while Ralph looked up and down the road to see if anyone was in the vicinity. The coast was clear. Marking the spot with a branch from a nearby bush, Dick retreated to allow Ralph to collect as many specimens as he needed and to store them in several containers that he carried in his bag. Aroused to a near fever pitch of jubilation, the boys practically sprinted back to town and the hotel. As they drew nearer to the village they forced themselves to subdue their excitement and walk as casually as they could even though their hearts were ready to explode.

In their room, Dick immediately called Toby. Toby was in the cell block talking with Jeremy when the deputy poked his head inside.

"Telephone, Sheriff," he said.

Toby told Jeremy he'd be right back. When he left he did not close the door. Little things like that made Jeremy appreciate him that much more. He knew he was a prisoner but somehow Toby didn't make him feel like one. The shout from outside that followed startled Jeremy. At first he thought something had happened until the yell was followed by a series of hoops and celebration. The voice was Toby's. Jeremy heard the Deputy ask him if he was alright and what had happened. He told his Deputy that he'd explain later. In a flash he was gone. He had simply just run out of the office. Jeremy had never seen the Sheriff display emotion that even resembled what he had just witnessed. One thing was for sure. You didn't act like that over bad news. Toby was ecstatic.

"Hot damn," Toby exclaimed bursting into the boys room at the hotel. "You aren't kiddin' me, are you?" he guessed as if afraid to ask.

"No way! Toby it's the real thing. Blood and lots of it," Ralph said holding one of the containers in trembling fingers. Toby stared unbelievingly at the blood stained blades of grass before his eyes. He took the container from Ralph's hand and sat down in a chair and just stared at it for as full minute. Then as if awakened from a dream, he jumped up and headed to the phone.

"Harold, get over here quick," he barked.

"We've found it!"

He hung up before Harold could have possibly responded. In less than a minute, Harold Steinmetz charged into the room. Toby showed him the blood covered grass in the container "evidence, pal!" he said triumphantly.

Harold's eyes lit up like a child's at Christmas time. The four celebrated together hugging each other like long lost friends.

" We're on our way, boys," Harold said profusely.

"If the analysis of these samples match those of the autopsy we are on our way. Ralph, how long will it take to get us a report of this?" he asked.

"About an hour or so."

"The office is all yours. I'll stay here with Dick and Toby. I don't want to get in your way or pester you with a dozen questions." Harold said.

"I'll be back as soon as I finish" he concluded.

"With that he left the room. Toby, Harold and Dick sat down together on the couch to begin planning their next move.

"The arraignment hearing's tomorrow," Harold reminded them. "I sure hope those blood samples are a match."

Dick snapped his fingers.

"Sheriff, I mean—Toby," he corrected himself, "we're gonna need to have a look at the Corner's report to check the results of Ralph's lab work. I want to go over it as well. Could you go to the office while we're waiting and bring over your copy? While you're at it, let me see your report too."

"Sure thing," Toby said standing up.

"I'll be right back." He left immediately for his office.

Moments later he reappeared with the documents and handed them to Dick. For 15 minutes, Dick poured over the reports. After finishing his study, he handed them back to Toby.

He had found nothing of value. They waited. A half hour later, Ralph joined them.

"Here's the results, gentlemen. Blood type, DNA information, Time of Death"—the whole ball of wax."

Toby then handed Ralph the Coroner's report. Everybody peered pensively at each other as Ralph settled down on the couch and examined the documents in his hands. His forehead furrowed and he lifted an eyebrow beneath his spectacles. "

"Hey, take a look at this," he said"

Everybody hurriedly joined Ralph.

"From the coroner's report and my analysis, everything matches but one thing."

"What's that?" Harold asked in a hushed voice.

Toby sat on the edge of his seat and Dick looked over Ralph's shoulder.

"The times of death don't agree. My analysis shows that the victim died at least 26 hours later than Doc Cuthbert's report. Here, see for yourself."

He handed the reports to Toby. The three scrutinized every tidbit of information. Dick whistled. Toby drew a sharp breath and Harold just stared.

"There must be a mistake somewhere," Toby muttered.

"If there is, I didn't make it," Ralph said confidently. "This is an elementary procedure.

I learned how to do this in pre-med classes. Somehow the Coroner made a mistake."

There was dead silence for what seemed like an eternity. Dick broke the silence.

"Laying aside the differences in the times of death, how can the same blood from a single accident be found in two different places over two miles apart when death was ruled as instantaneous?" he queried.

Everyone looked at each other completely baffled.

"That leaves us with two unanswered questions. He added.

Wow!" Harold exclaimed. "The jury would love this one."

"The real question is why?" Dick commented.

"This whole thing doesn't make sense, or it makes all the sense in the world if Ralph is right which I believe he is." Concluded Dick.

"What are you suggesting, Dick?" Harold asked.

"Toby was right all along. Rod and Jeremy are the victims of a frameup and the real killer is loose somewhere. Let's add it all up. The man couldn't have crawled two miles if he did when he was hit. Right?" Dick asked.

"Right." Added Harold.

"Which leaves only one explanation. Based upon where Toby found the victim's car with a flat tire and no flashlight at night, he was headed toward town when he was run over right where we found the blood this morning. He was later moved to the spot where Rod and Jeremy hit whatever it was they hit and it was made to look as if he died there."

"That's an interesting theory," Harold remarked, "but where's the proof? We can't prove which site was the original one. So far, that's conjecture."

"I have to agree with Harold," Toby said. "That's the way I see it too but this whole case is loaded with speculations."

"That's true," Dick admitted, "but we've hit a tremendous breakthrough. We do have a real clue that throws this whole case wide open. Doc, let's go after our second clue."

"Second clue?" Ralph queried.

"Yes. I want you to retrieve a blood sample from Jeremy's car and analyze it just as you did the other," Dick directed.

"But why? It's already been analyzed," Ralph objected. Toby sprang to his feet.

"No! Dick is right. Damn it, boy. You're sharp," he shot at Dick." Look! If the blood sample that you analyze from Jeremy's car matches what you just analyzed earlier, that means that somebody put it on the car after the boys first reported their accident. This would solve the problem of the differences in the two times of death. Or it could simply mean that either the Coroner or Ralph is wrong in establishing the time of death," Harold cautioned.

This stumped them all for a moment until Dick came to the rescue.

"We can solve that riddle easily. We need to bring in a third opinion undercover an outside medical examiner who knows absolutely nothing about this case, to do an independent analysis of both blood cultures. He will prove that either Ralph is correct or the Coroner is. One thing is certain. We need the second opinion. Not Doc Cuthbert."

"Wow, Dick, nice shot," Ralph grunted.

"No, he's right Ralph. No one is questioning your abilities but in a court of law, a student's opinion will never fly in the face of a proven professional," Harold advised.

"Well, what if this third party agrees with Ralph? What then?" Toby asked. Before anyone spoke, he answered his own question. "It means Doc either made a mistake or he lied about the time of death."

"Bingo," said Dick.

"I'll have another Coroner here by tomorrow morning. Let me work on it. While everyone is focused on the arraignment, our man can get his work done unnoticed." Finished Toby.

They all agreed. After planning to meet in Harold's office when the hearing ended tomorrow everyone called it a day. Euphoria was the mood of the moment, or at least, cautious optimism.

The tiny courtroom was packed the next morning and buzzing with excitement. It had been a long time since anything as big as this had hit town. Jeremy and Rod were seated with Harold opposite the room from John. Toby noted that the Blakes and McCutchins looked rather pensive and reserved. The boys seemed pretty relaxed. Standing along the back wall were Jimmy Cuthbert, Bobby McCallister and Hank Peters. They had arrived late. Toby glanced about nervously, then relaxed as he spotted John Cuthbert tucked away in the crowd.

At this very moment, no one knew that a Coroner from nearby Chattanooga, Stan Williams, an old friend of Toby's was over at Stan's Garage with Jake taking his own samples for analysis from Jeremy's car. They had purposely not told the boys or their parents what was taking place because they wanted to take no chances of any kind of a slip up or changes of attitudes. People are sometimes unpredictable, they had reasoned.

"There was a delay" the court clerk told everyone as they waited on Judge McGill. This only fueled the already tense sense of anticipation that hung over the crowd. Toby noticed John Cuthbert getting a little restless and fidgety. This was all working to his advantage and Doc Williams' as well. After several more minutes of delay, the clerk's voice resounded.

"All rise, please," he announced as the Judge came into the room.

"The Honorable T. Howard McGill presiding.."

When the Judge was seated, everybody sat down and he pounded the court podium.

"This hearing is now in session. This is not a trial," the judge instructed the room noticing the unusual number of people gathered.

"The defendants are simply here to answer the charge against them pleading their guilt, innocent or no contest. I will explain this momentarily. Are the attorneys here and present?"

When both stood, the arraignment began. Meanwhile, the visiting Coroner had completed taking his blood sample from Jeremy's car and was back in Harold's office with Ralph analyzing the evidence. As expected, Rod and Jeremy pleaded innocent to all charges. The Judge then instructed all present that the next step would be up to the assignment clerk to set a date for the pretrial in which presentations would be examined to ascertain whether or not there is sufficient evidence to warrant handing down an indictment. This concluded the arraignment proceedings. Within minutes, the courtroom was deserted.

Outside, a large gathering of people had surrounded Bobby McCallister and were talking to him about the additional charge brought against Jeremy by his mother of assault and battery.

Beth stood with the boys' parents watching her brother tell his story. She knew that he would make Jeremy appear like a wild man totally out of control. Someone in the crowd surrounding her brother saw her with Rod and Jeremy's parents and pointed in her direction, yelling.

"There she is now, with them!"

"What about your own brother?" somebody yelled at her.

"Traitor!" one woman cried. "You've even turned against your own family and all of your friends," she said throwing an orange she was eating at Beth. It didn't come close to hitting her but it was enough to bring Toby to the scene.

"I want everybody out of here right now, before I fill up that courtroom again with those disturbing the peace," he remarked.

"You haven't heard the last of this," a voice yelled from somewhere in the park.

Beth, Andrea and the parents were the whisked swiftly away by the Sheriff. Toby told the boys' parents to go back to the hotel until things died down a bit. He would call them soon. He waited until they loaded the van and left, and then, he took Beth with him to the station to visit with Jeremy.

As they walked down the street, Toby talked.

"This is going to be ugly, I'm afraid. It seems as though the people believe Jeremy and Rod are guilty already. Looks like another case of small town justice. Selecting an unbiased jury for this one will be very difficult."

"I can only visit Jeremy for a minute or so before I have to go to work," she told him.

Toby nodded.

"Looks like you're becoming mighty unpopular real quick around here," he said with a chuckle.

"For real," Beth replied.

Inside the cell block, Toby unlocked Jeremy's cell and let him into the larger room with Beth.

"I'm not gonna make you talk through bars," he decided leaving the cell block and this time closing the door behind him.

"That about does it," Doc Williams said closing up the examination equipment. Ralph waited impatiently as the visiting Coroner filled out his report.

"You've got quite a little laboratory tucked in here," he said to Ralph as he wrote.

"I was lucky. The University told me to take whatever I needed," he replied.

"Well, you didn't miss much. I'll be finished in a few minutes."

Ralph began to clean up after the Coroner, finding it impossible to just stand there waiting. Finally, Doc Williams finished writing. He handed Ralph his report and shook his hand.

"Tell Sheriff Relliford to call me if he needs anything else. And oh . . . by the way, tell him we're even now." With that, he left.

Ralph anxiously scanned the Coroner's report, his heart racing and his pulse pounding. There it was in black and white, staring him in the face. The coroner's report that he held in trembling hands matched his findings exactly! Ralph screamed in ecstasy. He was beside himself with delirious joy. He couldn't stand still and danced with excitement.

That evening, Toby, Dick, Harold and Ralph met secretly together, plotting their next move. They still had yet to gather proof of where the accident had originally taken place. All they knew was that the same blood had been found in two different locations and both matched the blood on Jeremy's car. One thing was known for sure, though. John Cuthbert was now a prime suspect and his son, Jimmy, along with Bobby and Hank were suspects as well. This changed the feeling of pessimism that Harold initially had felt about this case. Rays of hope were now beginning to emerge. With Coroners' reports, investigation notes and unanswered questions all a part of the mix, the four labored far into the night pouring over every detail of the search for what really happened

Finally Dick asked Toby, "We have everything about the victim accounted for, even down to a half empty bottle of whiskey in his car. But, there's one thing still missing. Toby, what about the shoe?"

"I noticed that awhile back but it didn't seem critical then," Toby told him. "I didn't mention it to Doc Cuthbert when I suspected that the car had been tampered with. Intuition told me not to share anything else about the case with anyone."

"It just might be significant," Dick cautioned. "One of the first things they teach you in Criminal Investigation is that sometimes the most seemingly insignificant matter turns out to be the difference. Ask the Coroner about it tomorrow for me," he asked Toby.

"I will. First thing in the morning," he replied.

"Two things I'll need right away. I've got a plan. Toby, I'll need a two way radio to maintain contact with you night and day. Second, I need you to show me where Jimmy Cuthbert lives and point his car out to me." Requested Dick.

"No problem. We'll get the radio tonight and I'll show you where Jimmy and his car is at the same time." Toby replied.

"What have you got in mind, Dick?" Harold asked.

"If I'm right, like Toby was earlier about his hunch, I'll have you the evidence you need within a week."

"Before the pre-trial?" Harold asked.

"If I'm lucky."

Toby walked over to where he sat and shook the young man's hand.

"Ralph, without your work in the laboratory all of this wouldn't have been possible. Your finding turned this whole thing around for us."

All the men in the room readily agreed and joined Toby with their own congratulatory responses."

"Oh, it wasn't much," he acknowledged.

"I felt all along that the Coroner could not have made an error on such a procedure."

"Then in your mind, it was done deliberately?" Harold asked.

"Absolutely."

"But why? Why would Doc do a thing like that?" Toby asked.

"I don't know," Dick said, "but I'm sure gonna find out."

Toby and Dick drove slowly through the darkened town that night toward John Cuthbert's house on the outskirts. Toby never pressed Dick any further about his plans because he was going to stick to his decision about staying out of the way. He was gaining new respect every day for these two college trained investigators and was confident they could handle every part of the work they were doing. They pulled up to a curve in the road and Toby turned out his lights.

"That's Doc's house right over there and that's Jimmy's car parked out front. Doc always keeps his Mercedes in the garage." Added Toby.

"Wait here for a minute," Dick told him, reaching into the bag he had placed on the front seat between them. He brought out a small gadget of some kind and climbed out of the car. He walked across the street to Jimmy's auto and knelt down. Then he laid down on the ground and crawled underneath the car. In a matter of seconds he was heading back to Toby. He climbed inside and briskly rubbed his hands together.

"What'd you do?" Toby asked him puzzled.

"Tracking device. Jimmy's gonna have a shadow for a while. Only one problem." Dick said.

"What's that?" Asked Toby.

"I don't have anything to track him in."

"Pick it up in front of my office in the morning," Toby said.

"The keys will be in the ignition."

Toby strolled into the office early the next morning. He fixed himself a cup of coffee and walked into the back room where his new deputy sat at the desk reading the morning paper.

"Morning Chad. How's it going?"

The new man dropped the paper he was reading and immediately stood up.

"Good morning, Sheriff," he said hastily.

"Real quiet last night. Just routine stuff."

"Okay. I'm here now and Jake's on his way. You can knock off until tonight. See you then and thanks."

"You're welcome, sir," Chad responded putting on his jacket.

Nice kid, Toby thought silently. Even though he had hired him only temporarily, it would be tough to lay him off if and when he brought Willie Joe back. He had run into his former Deputy the other day working in the local hardware store. They talked for a few minutes and he had said that he hopes everything works out for Jeremy and Rod. He apologized again for what he had done.

Toby walked back to the front desk and picked up the phone. He called John Cuthbert.

"John Cuthbert speaking," he answered."John? Toby here."

"Howdy Toby," he replied. "How's the investigation going?"

"Well, that's what I called you about. The boy's attorney is asking about a missing shoe from the victim that was never found. Know anything about it?" Toby asked.

"No . . ." There was a long pause.

"I didn't pay any attention to that when I bagged up all of his belongings for you that day. There was so much going on that I didn't even notice." Added John.

"Well, no big deal. It's just the only thing missing that's all. Look, if it shows up, let me know. Otherwise, forget it." Concluded Toby.

"Gotcha. I have to go. Old lady McGruder down the road died last night, unexpectedly. I have to do an autopsy today. If I find the shoe, I'll call you. Goodbye." John finished.

As Toby hung up, he heard a car start up outside the door and walked over to the window and watched Dick pull away in the car that he had gotten earlier from Stan's. Just then, the portable two way radio on his desk came alive. It was Dick checking in. He said that he just wanted to see if everything was working and asked Toby to keep the radio with him at all times so that they could stay in touch.

"Ralph and I are going to take turns shadowing Jimmy Cuthbert around the clock. He may lead us to something sooner or later. Whenever those three get together we want to be there close by. They're our only leads right now."

"Will do," Toby said.

"So for now you won't be seeing much of us around. When Jimmy's at home, he'll be under constant surveillance. When he's driving we won't be far behind either. We'll work in shifts. Eight on, eight off. You know."

"Yeah, I know," Toby acknowledged.

"Good hunting."

"Thanks. See ya." With that Dick shut down transmission.

Jake came into the office just then. He seemed excited about something. "

"Jake, what's up?" Toby asked..

"Dunno". They're picketing the store down the street. "Whole gang of people." "Picketing?" Toby repeated. "Yeah. I think you ought to take a look.

Chapter Six

A Call for Help

Toby stepped out onto the porch outside of his office and briefly surveyed a small group of people walking in the direction of the store where Beth worked. He sighed heavily and hitched up his trousers. He knew what this meant at once. Walking briskly down the street toward the store, he acknowledged the greetings of passers-by. There was a ring of sign-carrying picketers completely surrounding the General Store. They were peaceful enough on the outside, he noticed but old man Johnson and Beth were in the midst of a heated exchange on the inside with two men and another woman. Toby pushed inside. The five saw him enter and the conversation stopped.

"Howdy folks," Toby greeted them. "What's the problem?"

"We're here to demand that Mr. Johnson fire this woman," said the lady with the two men, pointing at Beth.

"For what?" Toby asked.

"She's giving the town a bad name."

"Yeah," agreed one of the men. "She's been cavortin' around with one of them there killers and it's wrong. She's even turned on her own family. It just ain't right," he repeated.

Mr. Johnson objected vehemently.

"You've got no right to accuse her of something like that and you definitely have no right to interrupt my business and then try to tell me who I should and shouldn't have working for me."

"Just remember. You're only in business because we shop here. That can change real quick, you know," threatened the other man.

"Wait a minute," Toby cautioned. "If you came in here to buy something, fine. But if not, I'm gonna ask you to take your protest outside with the others. I will not allow intimidation by anyone of these two. If you're not a customer, you're trespassing."

The three angrily acknowledged Toby's warning moving grudgingly toward the door.

"You ain't heard the last of this," one of them shouted in Beth's direction. Then he pointed at Mr.Johnson.

"We'll force you to close the place up. Wait and see."

With that, they left the shop and joined the others outside.

Toby explained to Mr. Johnson and Beth that there was nothing that he could do as long as the assembly outside was peaceful and the law was not being broken. They both conceded that they knew that beforehand. Beth added that she was not surprised. Mr. Johnson confirmed his conviction that Beth would stay on. They talked for several more minutes and Beth told Toby that she would stop by to visit Jeremy when she finished for the day. Toby nodded and left the shop, walking through the picket line outside.

"Just keep it peaceful," he warned them. "If anyone comes into my office complaining that they were harassed trying to go inside, I'll have the picketers arrested and I'll get a restraining order against any further demonstrations. Understood?"

Mumbles of acknowledgment greeted Toby's ears.

"Good," he added walking away toward his office once again.

Back inside, Jake told him that the courthouse had called while he was away. The pre-trial hearing had been set for two weeks from tomorrow.

"They didn't give us much time, did they?" he remarked.

"Doesn't look that way," Toby responded, drawing himself a cup of coffee.

"Keep an eye on the picketing, Jake," he told his deputy. "If you see anything illegal, let me know right away. I'd better call Harold about his court date."

"Right," Jake responded.

Toby called Harold and broke the news. He sounded upset about the quick date of the hearing. He was going to fight for more time but was not very optimistic about winning.

The rest of the day passed rather uneventfully with Jake keeping a watchful eye on the demonstrators and Beth coming in later that afternoon to visit Jeremy. Dick had called Toby on the two-way and reported that he and Ralph had Jimmy Cuthbert under 24-hour surveillance. So far, nothing had resulted from their work.

Down the street, Doc Cuthbert was cleaning up his laboratory after finishing his autopsy. His mood was one of uneasiness. In the back of his mind, the thought of the missing shoe kept eating at him. Such a trivial detail, he thought to himself. Why was Harold Steinmetz bothered about that? What could a missing shoe tell him? Still, it was a piece of the victim's belongings that was unaccounted for. What if the question about its whereabouts surfaced at the trial? He certainly had paid no attention to it when he had brought the body to the morgue. He dismissed the thought with a heavy sigh. He would tell Jimmy about it later tonight and have them look for it tomorrow. If they found it, he would have them get rid of it. It wasn't important anyway. It would look awfully suspicious if they found it and took it back to the original site, especially after Toby and his deputy had failed to find it too. Still he couldn't help but wonder why Harold was even interested in it in the first place. Must be a lawyer's mentality he decided.

The McCutchins and Blakes were up early the next morning. After meeting in the lobby of the hotel, they planned to have breakfast and visit Jeremy.

"We haven't heard from the Sheriff in over a day," John was saying to James Blake.

"He hasn't phoned since the hearing," he added.

"Well, he told us to relax and take it easy for a day or two, remember?" his wife reminded him.

"I agree with John, Harriet," James was saying. "If that was Rodney in town, I'd be there too."

"Men! Always worrying about their sons," quipped Mary Blake.

"Speaking of sons, where's the kids?" James asked.

"Probably still asleep," Mary offered. "I'll call Andrea. James you call your precious son."

"Yes, ma'am," he mocked.

Rodney answered the ring of the telephone, his voice thick with sleep.

"Holy cow, Dad, what time is it?"

"Eight thirty."

"Man, old folks never seem to sleep," he complained.

"We've got a busy day planned," his father told him.

"We're going into town and see Jeremy today along with talking to the Sheriff and our Attorney. We want you and Andrea to get dressed and meet us in the lobby so we can go have breakfast before we leave."

"Okay Dad. Give me 25 minutes." He hung up.

By the time he got downstairs, everyone was waiting for him, including Andrea.

"How'd you beat me?" He asked her.

"Oh, I've been up. I just didn't call you. You always talk about how slow I am, so I decided to let you sleep and be last," she teased.

"Cold blooded," Rod mumbled shaking his head.

They all left together and went to the nearby restaurant where they enjoyed a hearty breakfast before loading up in the van for Midway. There was an air of excitement about the prospect of spending time with Jeremy. They had not seen him in a couple of days letting things cool off since the incident after the arraignment. They talked excitedly as they drove. Mr. McCutchin had already telephoned Toby to let him know they were coming.

Meanwhile, back at the Sheriff's office, Toby was concluding a conversation he was having with Jeremy about the recent developments involving the case.

"I'm only telling you because you're behind bars and can't do or say anything to damage the case. Rod doesn't even know and we want it to stay that way. We don't want any slips of the tongue, no change in attitudes, nothing!" Directed Toby.

"Don't worry about me," Jeremy promised, "I want out of this mess too bad to do anything that might jeopardize our chances."

"Good," Toby added, "your folks will be here pretty quick. Just remember what we talked about." With that, he left the cell block leaving the door opened.

Within five minutes, the Blakes, Rodney, Andrea and the McCutchins all came through the door. Rodney was wide-eyed as he talked intently with Toby about the picket line around Beth's shop. Toby explained to them that it was outgrowth of what they encountered a couple of days ago outside of the courtroom.

"People are upset about Beth's relationship with Jeremy. Unfortunately, he didn't help himself any by fighting with her brother. They've demanded that Mr. Johnson, who owns the store, fire Beth. So far he's refused. He's a stubborn ol' cuss. But I don't know how long he can hold out. His business has already slowed to a crawl." Toby said.

"That's not fair," Harriet McCutchin said.

"She's such a nice girl."

Toby reassured her that Beth was being made the scapegoat.

"The real problem is that these people are resentful of outsiders. They don't trust them. Put that together with the situation that Rod and Jeremy are involved in, makes it a sticky thing. Anybody who knows Bobby McCallister knows that he's always getting into scrapes. But he lives here. Jeremy doesn't. That makes a difference. So, in turn, they pick on Beth." Toby pointed out.

"How's Jeremy doing?" asked Rod.

"Go see for yourself. He's expecting you," Toby told them.

With that, everyone hurried down the hallway to the cellblock. Toby went ahead of them to unlock Jeremy's cell. He left them all in the room closing the door behind him. He smiled faintly at the noise on the inside. He was beginning to feel some optimism about this case after all.

Dick Wingate sat in his car about a half a mile away from Jimmy Cuthbert's house monitoring the tracking screen. Nothing had happened for the past 12 hours. Jimmy's car had not moved. He talked on the radio to Toby in his office as the visit with Jeremy was going on. It was now a waiting game. Dick told Toby that he was sure that the criminals would eventually return to the scene of the crime if their guess was right.

After about an hour or so, Jeremy's visitors exited the cell block and Toby once again secured him in his cell.

"Did you remember what you talked about?" he asked Jeremy. Jeremy nodded.

"They know nothing," he continued. " In fact, we hardly talked about the case at all. We talked mostly about getting back to school and graduating this year. You know, that kind of stuff."

Toby acknowledged his comments with a smile. When he returned, everybody was leaving. They all waved goodbye and made their way to the waiting van. Toby looked through the office window as they drove away.

The van turned the corner and headed toward the outskirts of town. Suddenly from behind one of the buildings, a group of young people emerged with rocks and stones, shouting obscenities and running with the moving van. A huge rock shattered the window on the passenger right front side causing Mrs. McCutchin to gasp and duck down in her seat. Startled, John swerved as another rock hit the front windshield. Inside, the loud thumping sounds told them the van was under attack from both sides of the street. Rod and his father told the women to lay down in their seats while they scrambled up front to join John, who had now in his anger come to a complete stop. This surprised the attackers momentarily and they backed off slightly.

John rolled his window half-way down and yelled angrily that he would shoot the next one who threw anything at his van. Rod was amazed at his actions. There wasn't even a gun in the van. One of the attackers shouted for Rod and Andrea to get out.

"Give us the niggers," another screamed.

Several of the attackers were upset that a white man was locked up and Rodney was running around free. Rodney jumped up and bolted for the door. His father tackled him and wrestled him to the floor.

"Get your ass back here!" he screamed.

"What the hell do you think you can do against that mob? I thought you were smarter than that."

Harriet and Mary lay sobbing in their seats. Andrea sat staring as if in shock.

"Let hero boy out," one of them yelled after seeing Rodney try to get to the door.

"We'll make a lampshade out of that dark hide," he taunted. One of them yelled at John.

"Hey, mister! You ain't got no gun," he said hurling a huge boulder that dented the side of the van. John cursed and began driving as rocks pelted his vehicle. He turned down the next street and headed back toward the Sheriff's office. Toby saw them pull up and ran outside.

"Holy cow," he exclaimed, "what happened?"

John quickly told him about the attack. Toby disappeared into his office and came back sprinting toward his car.

"Follow me," he yelled to John.

Toby jumped in the squad car and peeled rubber as he made a "U" turn in the direction of the attack. John followed closely behind. When they arrived at the scene, the street was deserted. Rocks and bricks cluttered the dusty road.

"Damn it," spat Toby as he climbed out of his car and checked around several buildings. He whistled softly as he eyed the damage to John's van.

"They certainly did a number on your van. Did anybody get hurt?"

Everyone reported that they were fine. A little shook up but alright otherwise. Toby told them to go back to the station so they could file a report. He suggested that they say nothing to Jeremy about what had happened.

"It'll only give him one more thing to worry about."

They all climbed back in the van and followed Toby back to the station. After the incident report was completed, Toby told them to go back to their hotel.

"I'll check with Stan and call you in the morning to tell you where you can go to have your van repaired. I'm sure it's covered by insurance. We'll arrange for you to get a loaner while your's is being fixed."

After a brief exchange, John, Harriet, Rod, Andrea, Mary and James headed for home. This time they left town without further incident. Weary and battered, they slowly made their way to the sanctuary of the colored section.

It was about five thirty in the evening when the alarm on Dick's surveillance monitor came to life. He jumped—startled . . . the blip on his screen was moving. Jimmy was headed somewhere. Dick maneuvered his car in the direction of the blip until it held steady at SE. As he followed the screen, he called Toby. He told him what was going on and instructed him to stand by. The signals began to become stronger. He knew he was closing in rapidly. Then, he spotted Jimmy's car about a quarter of a mile away. He settled down to a comfortable pace, following the vehicle from a distance. Jimmy led him down the road to the open countryside. Dick followed just out of sight. The car ahead made a slight change in direction and stopped. Dick paused. The blip had stopped. He looked around, then pulled off the road into a clump of trees.

He climbed out of his car and under cover of the trees and thickets, he moved to the edge of a clearing. About 30 yards way, Jimmy's car was parked in front of a huge, comfortable looking farm house. On the front porch, he was talking to someone. Dick called Toby on the two-way. He described his position and the house in front of him.

"That sounds like Hank Peter's place. Is the fellow with Jimmy, a big burly kid?" Toby asked.

"Yes."

"That's Hank alright. I suspect they'll pickup Bobby next. Be careful, Dick. Don't let them see you. I think something's up. Good luck." Toby said.

The two moved in the direction of Jimmy's car. Dick made his way back to his own car and once again took up the hunt. They drove a couple of miles before stopping again. Dick pulled off of the road, got out of his car and stole to the bend in the road. He saw Jimmy and Hank at the front door of a quaint white wood frame house. The door opened and another man stood at the screen. They talked for a moment and the door closed. Dick went back to his car and waited. In a moment, they were moving again. As he drove, he recognized the landscape. Then he passed the first set of stakes that he and Ralph had planted the other day when they had begun their search. his pulse raced and his heart thumped in his chest. He knew where they were headed. The car he was following stopped at about the place where he and Ralph had taken the samples of blood-stained grass.

Knowing the terrain, Dick picked up his camera and made his way through the trees that lined the road. He spotted the three men combing the area. He adjusted the telephoto lens to his camera and began to snap pictures. As they worked, one of the men waved the other two in his direction. Dick crept as close as he dared. He adjusted the lens again and zoomed in for a closer shot. The man was waving something he had found. Dick focused on it as best he could taking several shots. They stopped and talked for several minutes. Then they headed up over the knoll and down toward the creek. Dick followed. From behind the tree that hid him, he photographed one of the men throwing the object into the creek. Realizing that his car would be spotted along the roadside when the three headed back, he made a dash for his car while Jimmy, Hank and Bobby walked back to their own.

By the time the three men were heading for home, Dick was long gone. He drove straight to Toby's office. it was getting dark as Toby and Dick huddled together in his office. Beth was in the back visiting with Jeremy while the new Deputy occupied the front office.

"Did you see what it was they found?" Toby asked.

"I'm not sure. I'll have to blow up the photo to get a clear look." Dick replied.

"I'll bet you anything that it's the missing shoe they found," Toby added.

"If it turns out to be the shoe, that can only mean that the Coroner tipped them off. What do you think?" Dick asked Toby.

He nodded his agreement.

"All of this suddenly happened after I told Doc Cuthbert about Harold being concerned about the shoe this morning. There must be a correlation," he decided.

"Well, we'll know in the morning after these pictures are developed. Of course, you know we were taught how to do that in school too," he told Toby wryly. Toby just shook his head.

"Nothing you and Ralph do anymore surprises me. And to think we had doubts about whether you two could handle the job." He smiled and shook Dick's hands.

"Happy development," he said soberly. "Call me in the morning."

"Sure thing. Good night, Toby."

With that he was gone. Toby looked at his watch. It was time for him to get home. Peg would have dinner ready by now. He had a million things to do tomorrow and he was tired. But it was a good tiredness. Things were beginning to happen in rapid fire order, one right after another. It's funny how one hunch can change things. Several days ago, this whole case seemed hopeless. No clues, no explanations, no evidence, no suspects. Nothing. Then a lucky guess on his part and an inadvertent telephone conversation being overheard had changed things overnight. Toby remembered an old saying that his father used to tell him . . ."It's always darkest before the dawn." In this instance, those words were becoming prophetic. Toby never paid too much attention to providence but it sure seemed as if divine intervention was on their side. He glanced skyward and winked.

"Thanks," he whispered.

As he made his way homeward, he analyzed the current state of affairs. Doc had lied about the time of death to cover for somebody. A person or persons unknown had moved the body to where the boys had reported hitting something. Blood samples had been switched. Bobby, Jimmy and Hank were somehow involved. But how? How did Doc fit into the whole picture? How could they prove which site was the original place of the killing? One thing was sure, he decided. They did have enough proof now to establish a basis for a frameup and collusion even though they had no real explanation as to what really took place that fateful night. At least now, they were miles ahead of where they were several days ago.

Early the next morning, Dick paid Toby a visit at his office. He had developed the pictures taken of Jimmy, Hank and Bobby last night. He had blown up the shots of Jimmy holding an object in his hand. It was the missing shoe!

"This is our third real clue," he said jubilantly to Toby.

"First, there's the Corner's incorrect time of death. Then there's identical blood samples at two different locations, and now this. I think we're getting some place."

Toby studied the photos intently. They were clear as a bell.

"That's some camera you've got," he mused.

"This is great. Fantastic. I'll get with Harold right away about these. Oh, yeah, I almost forgot. Either you or Ralph should go with Jeremy and Rod's parents to Chattanooga where they will have their van repaired today. I can't spare Jake and I don't want anyone else to become involved with anything related to this case. Can you swing it?" Asked Toby.

"Sure. No problem. I'll talk it over with Ralph when I get back to the hotel. We've still got to have breakfast. Why Chattanooga?" he asked.

"That's what Stan suggested. He said that Midway was too small to maintain a full-time body and fender shop. Not enough accidents, I suppose. Anyway, there's a shop there that he usually recommends. Periodically, he sends our squad cars up there for work."

Toby told him that he would call when the van was ready to leave. After Ralph had left, Toby settled down behind his desk and studied the photos again. Just then, the phone rang. He picked it up. It was Mr. Johnson from the general store.

"Toby can you spare a minute or two?" he asked.

"Of course. What's up?"

"I need you to talk to Beth. Can you stop by anytime soon?

"Sure. I'm on my way. Is she okay?"

"Physically, she's fine. It's her mental state I'm concerned about. She seems depressed. Talks about quitt'n and things like that." Added Mr. Johnson.

"Be right over." Toby hung up and told Jake where he was going. He left his office and headed to the store with long strides. The picket line still surrounding the shop was peaceful. No one spoke to him this time as he gently made his way through the demonstrators and inside the store. Toby, Beth and Mr. Johnson talked for long minutes. How the town folks felt about her and the relationship she shared with Jeremy did not phase Beth at all. What seemed to trouble her was what was happening at the store.

"Sheriff, I know what's going on. I do the stock inventory twice a week as well as reordering supplies. We have hardly moved anything off of the shelves since those people began picketing the store. At this rate, we'll be in big trouble before long," she said.

Mr. Johnson had to reluctantly agree as Toby looked at him for confirmation.

"I just don't want to be the reason for the problems," Beth continued.

"Mr. Johnson has a family and a life of his own. I don't want my problems to become his."

Toby said that he understood but Mr. Johnson objected.

"You see, this is where we're having problems. I can't get Beth to understand that there is a higher principle involved here. Our town people are as wrong as they can be about how they're treating her and Jeremy. And look what they did to their parents' van the other day. They have already judged Rod and Jeremy and they haven't even gone to trial to defend themselves. I know that a lot of their anger is directed at Rodney because he's black and is not afraid of them. They call it northern arrogance! If I have to make some sacrifices personally to try and help change these racist attitudes in Midway, I'm willing to do it."

Toby agreed that both of them were right in their own way. Beth was thinking about what was best for Mr.Johnson while he was thinking about what was best for the town people.

"Beth," he said, "you're too young to understand what we older people are fighting for here. We went through this 20 years ago. Man has walked on the moon and can design machines by computer. Yet cannot accept other humans because they're different. It's absurd but true nonetheless. Every moral principle must sometimes be defended even at some personal loss by some people. Mr. Johnson, here, is making that statement."

Beth acknowledged Toby's explanation.

"But it's so wrong. They have no right to do this to us. We haven't hurt a soul."

"Neither has Rod and Jeremy," he reminded her.

"That's true," she responded.

"Look. I think both of you need to know something. I can't give you any specifics but we are making tremendous progress with the case. Tell you what. Give us until after the pre-trial next week. If we can't clear this up by then, Beth, you can quit for Mr. Johnson's sake. Can you do that?" Added Toby.

After a brief pause, she nodded.

"Two weeks."

Toby and Mr.Johnson smiled at each other. Beth hugged them both as tears filled her blue eyes.

"Welcome to the wacky world of adulthood," Mr. Johnson told her in a tender voice. They both thanked Toby and he left once again for his office. As he made his way back through the picket line outside, he was glad that no one said anything to test his patience. He was not in the mood to be diplomatic.

Back at the office, Mr. Blake, his wife, Mr. McCutchin, and his wife were waiting for him. The van was parked outside.

"Where's Rod and Andrea?" he asked them.

"We thought it would be best to leave them at the hotel," Mr. Blake said.

"If my son was seen coming in here it might only cause problems that we don't need." He added.

Toby told them that his deputy would escort them out of town.

"One of my investigators will go with you. Let me call them now. In the meantime, get yourselves some coffee and make yourselves comfortable. I'll only be a minute."

He disappeared into the back room. When he came back, he informed them that Ralph was on his way over. He gave them the name and address of the body shop in Chattanooga along with the directions to get there. When Ralph got there a few minutes later, they got ready to leave. He told them to call if they had any problems as they left.

About an hour after the van left, Dick and Harold paid him a visit.

"Toby," Dick told him, "Harold and I were discussing the case over breakfast this morning. I have a theory that I want to work on while Ralph and the boys' parents are gone."

"Okay. Shoot."

"Well, Harold needs some concrete evidence to substantiate the charge of a frameup. Even though we know that the same blood was found at two different places, we can't prove what really happened. Someone could say that Rod and Jeremy moved the body for whatever reason."

Toby thought for a moment. He had not looked at it from that angle before. It was true.

"I see what you mean," he admitted.

"We have to be able to demonstrate what actually happened in order to convince the jury," Harold was saying.

"Unfortunately, the burden of proof rests in our corner. The Coroner's report forces us to answer questions that the defense doesn't have to," he finished. Ralph then spoke to Toby.

"Here's my theory. If Jeremy and Rod didn't hit the victim at the location of their accident, then they hit something else. Whatever that was, I have to find it. It's the only thing that can clear up this mystery. Whatever blood was originally on their car must have been washed off and replaced with the victim's blood either before or after the body was moved."

Toby immediately wondered why he hadn't thought of that before. He had even mentioned to the boys earlier that they had probably hit an animal or something. When everything else began to happen so fast, that seemingly small detail had gotten lost.

"There must be two different specimens of blood involved in this case. I don't know how I could have missed that." Toby replied.

"Well, don't feel bad," Harold told him.

"Ralph just thought of it himself. We were all so caught up in the riddle of how the same blood could be in two different places that we lost focus on that part of the puzzle."

"If I can find whatever it was they hit, we would have all the proof that we need to prove them innocent," Dick said.

"Except, who really did it and why," Harold responded.

"We would have everything except the perpetrators and the motive. But at least we could establish a reasonable doubt."

"I'm going back to the original site and do some work," Dick said as he stood up.

"Wish me luck." With that, he left.

Toby and Harold talked for several more minutes. When he left, Toby sat down and shook his head. It was amazing. With all of the clues that they had uncovered, everything still depended upon one more piece of evidence. When would it all end? Even with all of the unanswered questions they had raised, they still needed more. He began to have more of an appreciation of the tremendous burden that was placed upon the shoulders of a trial lawyer. They had to have an answer for everything. He could only hope that Dick Wingate would be successful.

Dick soon arrived at the spot where Jeremy and Rod's car had its accident. It was a scenic spot, he observed. In the distance, the green hills rolled endlessly. The sky was a patchy blue and the air was fresh and still. The sweet smell of wild flowers tickled his senses. This is what he missed in the city most of all. It sure beat the heck out of concrete, pavement and the smell of exhaust fumes.

He combed the area meticulously where the blood of the dead man was found. He worked clockwise in a radius of about 100 feet looking for more blood. About half of that space was dirt road and he knew that finding blood in it would be next to impossible. Yet he searched methodically for hairs, blood, anything. He found nothing in the dust. Continuing clockwise until he reached three o'clock, he found a faint trail of blood leading into the surrounding thickets. He stopped to recheck himself as excitement began to build in his stomach. The trail began at least 30 feet from the site of the blood where the body was found. It couldn't be the same blood because the Coroner's report had said that the victim died instantly.

As he followed the faint trail into the trees and bushes, he noticed that the further he went, the heavier the trail became. Whatever it was, it had begun to weaken dramatically. He went on another 20 feet or so. He no longer could see the road. He suddenly stopped dead in his tracks. Directly ahead about 40 feet lay the prone body of a dead adult deer. It's carcass had been partially eaten away by vultures or other animals and the odor was rancid. Dick raced to the corpse. Somehow he had to find a way to preserve the remains until Ralph had a chance to examine it. He hurried back to his car after marking the trail of blood and sped toward town.

In less than a half an hour, he and Toby were back at the site, taking photographs of the trail of blood and the dead carcass. Toby very carefully took several blood stained blades of grass from the trail of the animal's blood and put them in a storage container in his kit.

"Let's hope and pray that this is the animal that the boys killed," he said.

"This is why you didn't find a body that night," Dick told him. "The deer that they hit didn't die until it came this far."

"There's not a whole lot of it left," Toby said, wrapping the smelly remains in a huge plastic bag. The masks they wore failed to protect them from much of the stench of the decomposing carcass. When they had finished, they took off their masks and breathed in the fresh air deeply as they sat in the van. After several minutes of gulping air, they donned their masks again and returned to the thickets to carry the carcass back and put it in the rear of the Sheriff's van. They drove quickly back to town, parking and locking the van in the rear of the station. Once inside, the two got a cup of coffee and went in to tell Jeremy the news.

He was elated to say the least.

"I knew it! I knew it!" he said triumphantly.

"Rod and I looked all over the road that night. All we saw was the blood on the car. In all of the excitement, we must not have heard the deer running away into the trees. When we finally stopped to listen, he must have already died." Finished Jeremy.

Dick told him that they had brought what was left of the dead deer back with them to protect the remains.

"It's all up to Ralph again, isn't it?" Jeremy asked.

"Yep. As soon as they call us, we'll let him know what we've found." Toby replied.

Toby then told Jeremy that he knew how hard it was not being able to share the information that he knew with anyone.

"Hey, that's easy," he said.

"I understand. No problem. I just thank God that this thing is being cleared up. You don't know how tough it is being locked up and looking at five to 20 years at my age. Anything is worth the price." Jeremy confessed.

They all laughed together. Just then, Jake poked his head through the door and informed them that Beth was here to visit with Jeremy.

"She hasn't missed a day since you've been here, has she?" the Sheriff teased him.

"She helps me keep my sanity," Jeremy confessed.

Toby reminded him again not to mention anything to her about what was going on, especially since her brother was a suspect.

"She'll be a little down in the dumps today. I talked to her earlier. She'll probably tell you about it. You'll have to cheer her up without breathing a word." Jeremy added.

"I will, and thanks a lot fellas, for everything." Jeremy said gratefully.

Toby unlocked Jeremy's cell door and he and Dick went back out into the office passing Beth on her way in. Dick watched Beth as she walked past.

"Jeremy is sure lucky. She's quite a dish."

The dust from inside the body shop was thick enough to slice with a knife. The shop was full of vehicles in all stages of repair.

Some were receiving just minor touchup work, while others were practically dismantled. About 10 body and fender mechanics moved about the shop, all wearing masks. The noise of sanders, drills and air guns was deafening. The Blakes, McCuchins and Ralph were crammed into a small, cluttered waiting room with a clerk who was busy running an adding machine and going through piles of work orders. Ralph struck up a casual conversation as the woman worked. He thought that she was kind of cute in a mature sort of way. He noticed that she was married by the ring on her finger but he never passed up the opportunity to talk with an attractive member of the opposite sex.

Most people took him to be the bookworm type, probably because of his glasses and extensive vocabulary. But in reality, he was far from being what the other kids called a nerd. In fact, he was pretty popular with the girls back on campus, having been told on more than one occasion that his aggressiveness contradicted his mild manner.

"Doesn't anyone help you with all this?"Ralph asked.

"Not really. If you want something done right, it's better to do it yourself." Just then the phone rang. It was someone calling for a tow truck. She put them on hold and called out a name over the loudspeaker in the body shop. In a few moments, a big fellow with a thick brown beard opened the door. Not being able to talk over the noise, he stepped inside. The lady at the desk gave him a piece of paper and told him to pick up the car. After he left, she told whoever was on the line that a tow truck was on the way. When she hung up, one of the mechanics came in and handed her a finished work order and told her that he was going to start another job.

Just then, a small man knocked on her door. He was dressed in a suit that must have cost a fortune, Ralph thought to himself. He spoke to the woman at the desk about needing someone to do an estimate on his car outside. Picking up a clipboard and pencil, she said that she was the person that he wanted to see. They left the tiny office. The Blakes and McCutchins were busy reading magazines, so Ralph stepped out into the shop to look around. He saw the woman outside the shop through the door window examining the man's car. Then he noticed the sign over the tiny office door.

Katrina's Body and Fender Works

He marveled at how methodically she went about her examination. She had to be Katrina, the boss. When she finished her estimate and took the man's keys and came back inside, he asked her.

"Sure am," she replied.

Ralph couldn't believe it. He just never expected to find a woman running a business like this even though he had seen the sign when they drove up earlier.

"My husband runs the towing service. I run the shop," she smiled.

"Don't look so shocked. Anyway, what's going on in Midway these days? This is the second job from down there in a week or so." She headed for the office door but Ralph stopped her.

"I'm sorry, but I need to ask you a question before you go back to work inside."

"Okay. What is it?"

"You said that a week or so ago somebody else from Midway had some work done on their car. Do you remember who it was offhand?"

"No, but if it's important, I can find out in a couple of minutes."

"I'd really appreciate it."

"Why do you want to know?" she asked.

"Just curious to see if it's somebody I know. It'll give us something in common to talk about, that's all."

Back inside the tiny waiting room and office, Katrina reached over and got a handful of old invoices and started going through them. Ralph reached over and took a business card out of the small card holder on her desk and put it in his pocket while she worked. Suddenly the search was over.

"Ah, here it is," she said handing him the invoice. As he glanced at it, a mechanic stuck his head in the door and told Katrina that she was needed out in the shop. She excused herself and left immediately. Ralph took advantage of the opportunity to jot down the date, total, name of the account and account number. When he had finished, he put it back on top of the others.

"Anyone you know?" she asked upon returning.

"Uh-uh. Don't know a Jimmy Cuthbert," he lied.

"Well, from what I remember, it wasn't much. Just a dented front bumper and a busted headlamp."

She told him that they worked on Sheriff Relliford's squad cars periodically. She thought he was nice.

"Yeah, he's well-respected in Midway all right," Ralph replied.

"By the way, you're an attractive woman. Your husband is a lucky man."

She laughed and waved off his remark with a slight of her hand. "Thanks. But I've got a son about your age," she said with a smile and a wink.

You're kidding me," Ralph exclaimed in genuine surprise.

"Nope. I'll be 44 in two months," she winced as if it was difficult to confess.

"I just find that hard to believe," Ralph added, shaking his head in disbelief.

"Believe it," she said. Then directing her attention to the boys parents, she told them that the van should be ready in a couple of hours. Ralph excused himself and went outside to use the telephone to call Toby. He told Toby about the work that was done on Jimmy Cuthbert's car and that he had all of the information written down. Toby was excited about the news. Then he dropped his own bombshell.

"We've got some work waiting for you when you return." Toby added.

"What kind of work?" Ralph asked.

"Dick found a deer back at the site of Jeremy and Rod's accident. We've got the carcass here at the station for you to examine. Hopefully it wasn't shot but you'll have to determine that when you get back. Can you tell exactly how long ago it died when you examine it?" He asks.

"Piece of cake," Ralph said, his voice filled with excitement.

"How close?" Toby asked.

"Within a matter of a few hours or so." Ralph replied.

"Good. how long will it be before you get back?"

"They'll be finished here in a couple of hours. We ought to be back around ten." Answered Ralph.

"Okay. Call me at home if you finish your examination before morning. I'll leave the key to the van with my Deputy before I leave. You and Dick can take it over to your office. Don't let anyone know what you're doing. Okay?"

"Right. See you later." Ralph hung up and went back to the waiting room.

Toby put the phone back on the hook and lit up his pipe. Harold would be over in a minute or two. He had called him shortly before Ralph's call. Toby then called Dick and told him about Ralph's call.

"Don't let Jimmy out of your sight," he told him.

"I'm on him like white on rice," Dick replied.

Just as Toby hung up, Harold strolled into his office.

"Hi," he greeted Harold.

"Sit down, pal. Have I got news for you."

He related to Harold the latest developments. As he spoke, the Attorney's eyes became bigger and bigger.

"Wow!" was all that he muttered.

The Sheriff told him when Ralph would be back in town and how accurate the examination could be.

"That could be the clincher. If it can be proven that the deer died from massive internal injuries at the time of the boys' accident and the fact that Jimmy's car was fixed the next day, I can begin to build a pretty solid case. However, there are still several unanswered questions that we need answers to. For one, who switched the blood samples? Two, could Jimmy provide an alibi as to his whereabouts that night. And three, how does the Coroner fit into all this?" Harold finished. Even with the unanswered questions looming overhead, he was very optimistic nonetheless.

"I think we have enough evidence already to raise a reasonable doubt but whether its enough to win over a biased jury is another question all together. We still don't know who did what and why." Harold concluded.

"We've only got until next week to answer your questions," Toby told him.

"I think that in the meantime, I'll instruct Dick to change his course of investigation. He's shadowing Jimmy Cuthbert around the clock but I'm not convinced that that's the direction he ought to be taking. Jimmy has already implicated himself, Hank and Bobby by disposing of the victim's missing shoe. What more can he provide us with? The area's clean now." Toby said.

Harold suggested that maybe he could begin to try and find out where the three suspects were that night and what they were doing. Toby agreed with him. He called Dick on the two-way and told him what he and Harold had decided.

"We have the circumstantial evidence," he relayed,"now what we need is to place Jimmy at the scene of the crime. Oh, Ralph will be in about ten. He'll need your help." Toby directed.

"Gotcha," Dick replied. "I'll start on it right away."

"Those three hang out a lot at The Silver Dollar. You might want to start there" Toby suggested.

After they had finished talking, Harold told Toby that he was going to have dinner and then begin to put a preliminary case together. Toby decided that it was about time for him to knock off as well.

"As soon as Ralph finishes his work, I'll be in touch," he told Harold as the Attorney was leaving.

"Fine. See ya later."

Toby was on his way home ten minutes later.

Dick Wingate stepped inside the door of The Silver Dollar. The strong smell of beer saturated the air but the place was clean and neat. It was sparsely populated with people sitting at tables throughout the room. There was little congestion as they sat sprawled out over the entire place. Dick looked at his watch. It was still pretty early for the night crowd. He had a couple of hours before Ralph was due in. The music was loud but nice. He momentarily watched two couples dancing then walked over to the bar and sat down. In a moment the bartender came over.

"Let me see some I.D. son," he demanded.

Dick reached for his wallet and extracted his driver's license. The bartender looked at it closely, then handed it back.

"What'll it be?" he said.

"Draft beer, please," Dick replied.

The bartender left and drew him a glass of beer from the dispenser.

"From New York I see."

"Yes. I'm a student at Wayneville State University there."

"Down here on vacation too?"

"No sir. The other two guys involved in that accident a couple of weeks ago are classmates of mine."

"Oh, I see. You come down for the hearing next week?"

"Well not exactly . . . Yes and no," Dick began.

"I came down to give them some moral support but also to help them if I can. They're friends of mine."

"How so?" The bartender wanted to know.

"I'm a pre-law major at school and I'm working with their attorney as a legal aide."

"Uh-huh. Gettin' a little experience to boot as well. That's pretty smart. Those two fellas of yours don't seem to be bad sorts but they're sure in a heap of trouble as you know." The bartender said.

"I know. That's why I need as much help as I can get. Can you help me?" Dick asked.

"I'll do what I can."

"The people who are here right now, can you remember if any of them were in here the night of the accident?"

The bartender scanned the room intently with a furrowed brow.

"Well, it's been a while but I think Jill and Walt over there were here," he said pointing at one of the couples on the dance floor, "and Fern and Mike as well," he added directing Dick's attention to another couple seated at a nearby table.

"The rest of them I'm not so sure but you're free to talk to anybody you want to," he added.

Dick smiled his approval.

"I was hoping that you'd give me that opportunity. Now seems to be as good a time as any since it's not too crowded and noisy. Thanks a lot."

"Don't mention it, kid," came the reply. "Good luck."

Dick got up and headed in the direction of the couple seated nearby. He introduced himself and asked if he could talk with them for a few minutes.

"Sure," Mike said pointing to an empty seat at the table. Dick sat down after thanking them and began the conversation by asking them what they remembered that Tuesday night, two weeks ago.

"Just the usual thing," Mike began, "It's always crowded in here late but I remember that for a Tuesday, it was unusually crowded."

"Did you notice anything unusual that night out of the ordinary?"

"Nope. Nothing that I can recall."

Dick paused. He wanted to ask them about Jimmy, Hank and Bobby but did not want to arouse suspicion.

"Anybody especially rowdy or drunk that night?" he ventured.

"Nothing unusual. You remember anything, honey?" he asked his wife who sat silently.

"No just the same old crowd. Nothing exciting ever happens around here."

Dick asked them how long after that was it that they first heard about the accident.

"A couple of days later," Mike replied.

"Nothing else that either of you can remember? Anything?"

Mike's wife suddenly sat up.

"Only thing I can remember was Ned, the bartender. He had a little rumble with some of the guys who always come in here. Nothing much though."

"Oh? What was that about?" he queried.

"Nothin' really," Mike said. "Just Jimmy, Bobby and Hank blowin' off steam as usual."

"Okay," Dick said as he stood up. "Thank you very much."

He shook their hands and headed back to the bar and his beer. The bartender seemed like a nice guy and the most logical person to talk to about Jimmy and his friends. He didn't want to create anymore attention than he already had toward the three. He sat down again and finished his beer. Soon the bartender came back and he asked for a refill.

"Have any luck?" he asked Dick, refilling his glass.

"Nope. nothing of importance," he told the bartender, "except that I understand that you had a little run-in with a few guys here at the bar that night."

"Oh, yeah. Doc's boy and a couple of his friends. They always stir up something. More of a nuisance, those three, than anything else."

"What kind of problem were they causing you?" Dick dared to ask.

The bartender never hesitated to answer as he continued to dry the glasses he was holding.

"Just drank too much and started a loud argument. Jimmy, the Doc's boy was really tanked. I had to shut off his drinks. He didn't care too much about that either. Let me have it with both barrels."

"You made him mad, then?"

"Yeah," the bartender chuckled with a twinkle in his eyes. "It worked though. He stormed out of here maddern' hell. Why he could barely walk a straight line."

Dick finished his beer, stood up and shook the bartender's hand.

"Thanks. You've been a big help."

"Ain't done nothin'," was the reply. "I hope your friends come out okay. Come back soon. We can always use the business."

"You bet. Thanks again."

As he was getting ready to leave, he suddenly remembered the most important piece of information that he needed.

"Oh, about what time was it that those three left The Silver Dollar?"

"Around two thirty or so," he answered. "Why do you ask?"

"Just curious. Well, I'll see you later."

Outside, Dick breathed in deeply, gulping down the fresh country air. He had gotten the information that he had hoped for. Exactly 24 hours after Rod and Jeremy had reported their accident to the Sheriff, Jimmy, Bobby and Hank had left The Silver Dollar drunk. The exact time difference between Ralph and the Coroner's two times of death.

While this was not conclusive evidence in itself, it did add one more piece to the puzzle. The three men involved would have no alibi that could be used to exempt them from being bona fide suspects in the case. In fact, it can now be pointed out that they had to be prime suspects when coupled with Beth's story and the repair to Jimmy's car. The very next day after the homicide, Dick's photograph of the three tossing the missing shoe of the victim into the creek was even further evidence of their involvement. If necessary, the bartender could be called in as a witness by the prosecution.

If the findings of Ralph's examination of the deer carcass found at the site proves favorable, Dick was confident that Harold would be ready to take his case to trial. When Dick arrived back at the office, he found Harold still at his desk.

"Ralph just called from a gas station outside of town," Harold told Dick as he came in. "He'll be here in half an hour. How'd your interrogation at The Silver Dollar go?" he asked whimsically.

"Better than expected. Jimmy, Bobby and Hank were all drunk that night the bartender told me. In fact, he had to ask them to leave. Harold, they had to have been on the street, driving at the time of the original accident. It was around two thirty in the morning, the time that Ralph said Mr. Detmer was killed."

Harold audibly breathed a sigh of relief. He settled back in his chair, his mind racing. This took care of any alibi that the suspects might come up with as far as their whereabouts at the time of the homicide. This was exteremely important. The chain of events in the past two weeks concerning this case was staggering. His notebook was filling up rapidly. All missing pieces were falling into place at an alarming rate. His pulse quickened as he spoke.

"I've got about five days left, Dick, to get a case ready for pre-trial. Only one thing stands in our way."

"Ralph's examination."

"Right."

The two decided that now was the time to have a late dinner. Once Ralph arrived and began his work, nobody would be able to eat anything.

"He'll probably be in here working by the time we get back," Harold said as they were leaving.

"Let's keep our fingers crossed," Dick replied as they headed toward Sarah's.

They phoned Toby from Sarah's and broke the news. Toby was beside himself. He instructed them to call him the minute Ralph was through with the work. He didn't care what time it was. After their conversation had ended, the two weary warriors sat down to a huge meal. They laughed and talked casually as they ate.

The now newly-repaired van rolled into Midway about half an hour later under the cover of infant darkness.

"Nine thirty, exactly," Ralph noted, looking at the clock on the dashboard. "We made good time."

He told the boys' parents to take the van back to the hotel because he had some work to finish.

"We'll call you first thing in the morning. I'll let Jeremy know that we made it back all right," he told them.

After saying their goodbyes, the van slid into the blackness. Ralph headed toward the van parked in back of the Sheriff's office after he got the keys from the Deputy. It was a warm night and as he opened the door to the van, the stench on the inside screamed out at him.

"Good heaven," he exclaimed choking. The odor was devastating. He went around to the other door, opened it and rolled down the window. He left both doors open for about five minutes before he dared climb inside. He drove as quickly as possible the short distance to the office. He was busy at work when Harold and Dick returned from Sarah's.

"Good grief, Ralph, where's the air freshener," Dick complained holding his nose.

"Kinda makes you hungry, doesn't it?" Ralph kidded with a wide grin.

"That's sick," retorted Dick.

Harold laughed robustly as the two went at it.

"Where's the information from Chattanooga on Jimmy's car?" Dick asked Ralph as he worked.

"In the notebook on the desk," he replied making another incision. Harold and Dick studied the notes intently. It was Jimmy's car all right. Ralph had taken down all the pertinent information that they needed. When they had finished, Harold put the notes in his briefcase. Ralph worked meticulously into the night, paying attention to the slightest of details. He analyzed and reanalyzed. Harold and Dick waited patiently without disturbing his work. He jotted down every finding and charted his every move. He knew very well the gravity of his findings and was determined to leave nothing to chance.

Harold called Toby while Ralph busied himself with the smelly carcass and within the hour, Toby ambled into the office joining the three men. Dick made a pot of coffee and joined Toby and Harold at a table as they plotted their next move.

"We'll need to get Rod and the parents together in order to prepare for the pre-trial. I'll bring Jeremy up to date tomorrow on everything," Toby was saying.

"Yes, that's where we need to go from here," Harold agreed. "If the results of Ralph's work prove favorable, we'll have done all that's necessary in our preparation for the pre-trial. We just now need to recheck our findings together and make sure nothing is overlooked."

Toby informed them that the witnesses at the hunting lodge had all left forwarding addresses in case they were to be called later. Dick also gave Harold the information of the persons at The Silver Dollar he had talked to. They all agreed that with the corroborating testimonies of the other witnesses, it probably would be unnecessary to have Beth testify against her own brother.

"That will make Jeremy a happy young man," Toby responded soberly.

Harold then led the group through a detailed evaluation of all the physical evidence and data that had been gathered during the investigation including Dick's photographs, the blood samples from each accident site of the victim as well as the dead animal's found at the original site. Ralph's notes from the body shop in Chattanooga were discussed as well. They once again reviewed the discrepancies of the two autopsy reports relative to the time of death of the deceased as well as that of the dead animal. Toby's preliminary investigative reports were also gone over in detail.

"Even though we can't place Jimmy, Bobby and Hank at the site of the crime, we can establish sound probability," Harold told them. "That remains the most tenuous part of our defense, along with proving that the Coroner actually switched the blood samples. And even then, we have enough evidence to establish probable cause and opportunity. Gentlemen, I would say that we're as ready for trial as we'll ever be. If we lose this one, it'll be a surprise to me. I want to take this time to thank each one of you for your excellent work and dedication to this case. Two weeks ago, I wouldn't have bet a dime on our winning. Now, I'll be shocked if we don't. We have a pretty strong case for the boys' defense. But a word of caution! We are all outsiders here with the exception of Toby. It will be difficult at best, to discredit Doc Cuthbert among his own people here. Remember, we must convince the Judge and jury of our clients' innocence I've seen some strange verdicts handed down before. Need I remind you of the Rodney King trial in Los Angeles?"

Harold's speech brought a sober and stark silence to the table. Everyone looked at each other. Harold continued after a brief silence.

"If Ralph's findings are conclusive about the time and the nature of death of the dead deer, we most likely can prove reasonable doubt about Rod and Jeremy when weighed together with the rest of the evidence. However, we may not be able to prove the guilt of the real criminals as well."

"Why is that?" Dick asked.

"Well, we can only prove that Doc Cuthbert had a reasonable opportunity and motive to switch the blood samples but nobody actually saw him do it. Likewise, Jimmy, Hank and Bobby, because of their whereabouts within the proximity and the time of the homicide, makes them strong suspects—again, there are not actual witnesses. The photographs Dick took of them throwing the dead man's shoe into the creek, is really our strongest evidence linking them to the crime. And even then, they could claim that they stumbled upon it accidentally and simply threw it away."

"Yeah, I'm beginning to get the picture," Toby agreed. "It will be easier to prove innocence by the preponderance of evidence than guilt."

"Exactly," Harold acknowledged.

Dick whistled. "What does it take then to convict somebody?" he wanted to know.

Harold chuckled. "The most effective way without a confession is eye witnesses. Without either,it becomes paramount that the trial lawyer in his or her opening and closing arguments, convince the Judge and jury of guilt. But here's the clincher—even that must be beyond a reasonable doubt and unanimous."

"So what you're telling us is that all it takes is for one juror not to be convinced of guilt or innocence and you could lose a case," Dick added.

"Well, yes and no," Harold added. "A hung jury can result in a new trial but the case would continue. Then it's neither won nor lost."

Dick shook his head slowly from side to side in disbelief. "Man, I sure don't envy you at all," he mumbled.

"It's tough all right," Toby agreed. "I can't imagine a guilty verdict against Doc and the boys here in Midway."

"That won't happen anyway," Harold corrected.

"This trial is not about the guilt or innocence of the Doc and the boys but rather the guilt or innocence of Rodney and Jeremy.

If they are found innocent, then another trial would have to be ordered and charges made against the others."

The three were so wrapped up in their discussion, they failed to observe that Ralph had joined them, standing quietly off to the side. When he cleared his throat, they all jumped simultaneously.

"Well," Dick asked springing to his feet. Ralph grinned mischievously at him but said nothing.

"Come on man. Stop clowning," Dick demanded shoving him playfully.

"He doesn't have to say anything," Toby smiled knowingly. "We were right. Jeremy and Rod killed a deer, not Mr. Detmer."

Ralph nodded with a smile. "Right on," he said simply.

Jubilation erupted spontaneously within the small office. Toby danced with Harold. Ralph and Dick exchanged high fives and embraced. They all hopped it up for several minutes. When the celebration finally subsided, Ralph spoke.

"Without a doubt, Rod and Jeremy almost missed him. They hit him a glancing blow on his right hindquarters breaking his right leg and crushing some ribs. After running and dragging himself as far as he could, he bled to death from hemorrhaging and massive internal injuries. It must have been a slow and agonizing death. I feel sorry for the poor fella."

Ralph told Toby that he would get x-rays in the morning to give to Harold for the trial. He indicated that even if the animal had been shot, it couldn't have died from the wound because no bullet was found lodged in the bone.

"A lot of the carcass had been eaten away and any gun shot would have ben superficial. He was killed by the impact of a vehicle without question."

Chapter Seven

Quest of Truth

The small courtroom was crammed with spectators and reporters. An almost carnival atmosphere existed as it had been years since anything of this nature had happened in this small southern town involving outsiders. It was almost exclusively the single topic of conversation in Midway for the days leading up to this point. Many people had already chosen up sides on the issue of the probability of an indictment being handed down. Judge McGill felt it necessary to retain absolute control over the upcoming proceedings because of the excitement and publicity connected to the hearing. He spoke in a deliberate and measured way.

"First of all this is a pre-trial, not a jury trial. No indictment has been handed down at this point! That is the purpose of this proceeding. We are here only to ascertain whether or not the prosecution has sufficient evidence to warrant charges against the two defendants. I will tolerate no disturbances or interruptions from any onlookers at any time. I will hear the evidence presented and will render my judgment at the trial's conclusion."

The Judge's remarks brought an instant hush over the courtroom. It was as if everyone present held their breath at the same time. You could literally hear a pin drop. After a brief pause and being satisfied that he had accomplished the end results that he desired, Judge McGill continued.

"Are both the counsels for the prosecution and defense present in the courtroom?"

John Sterns and Harold Steinmetz stood. The Judge nodded and they both sat down.

"Are both defendants present in the courtroom?"

Jeremy and Rod both stood, casting long glances at each other. When they were acknowledged, they too became seated.

"Let's proceed then by hearing the Prosecutor's opening argument."

John Stearns rose deliberately from his seat and strode confidently to the front of the courtroom. He was a tall, handsome and well-groomed man of 45 with sideburns that were grey at the temple. His dark blue suit was immaculate, highlighting the steel blueness of friendly, but penetrating eyes that scanned the courtroom. He was the epitome of professionalism, the kind that you wanted in your corner rather than as an adversary. He had a reputation of being an astute and deadly trial lawyer, one who went directly for the jugular in his presentation. His courtroom tactics were sometimes shrewd but never unethical. He was what is known as a "hard hitter."

The spectators watched his every move as he approached the bench to begin. His voice matched his appearance.

"Your honor, ladies and gentlemen of Midway, the Prosecution will produce conclusive evidence to warrant criminal charges of Vehicular Homicide against the two defendants seated here before you. The evidence that will be submitted is real evidence and not circumstantial. On Tuesday morning at approximately 2:30 a.m., the day of August 16th, the two defendants did in an automobile driven by one, Jeremy McCutchin, strike and kill one, Arnold Detmer, who was staying nearby at the Elkhill Lodge."

"Objection," Harold shouted, jumping to his feet. "The Prosecution is drawing a conclusion."

"Sustained," acknowledged Judge McGill. "Strike the last statement from the records. Be careful, John. You know the rules," he warned the Prosecutor.

John Stearns apologized to the court and then continued as he walked back to his table to pick up a folder.

"Your honor, I would like to submit to the court the autopsy report of the County Coroner, Dr. John Cuthbert." He walked back to the Judge and handed him the file. Judge McGill accepted it with a nod and told him to continue.

John Stearns then called his first witness, Doc Cuthbert, to the stand. John strode nervously to the witness stand and was duly sworn in.

"Please state your name and occupation to the court."

"John Cuthbert, County Coroner."

"Doc Cuthbert, would you please tell the court the circumstances surrounding your autopsy report and its findings."

His eyes came to rest momentarily on the Prosecutor, then for a fleeting second, on Rod and Jeremy. He quickly looked away and spoke to the Judge.

"Your honor, late Monday night, or rather at about two or three Tuesday morning of the 16th , Deputy Jake Aldridge called me at home to report an accident. He told me that the Sheriff and Deputy Bivens failed to find anything. I called the Sheriff's house but he hadn't come in yet. Since there was no body, we didn't see a need to rush at the time. I examined the defendants' car sometime the next day. That would have been on Tuesday." John Cuthbert added.

"Why did it take you so long to examine the situation surrounding the accident?" Probed John Stearns.

"I was backed up with higher priority work at the time. I told the Sheriff this and he wasn't too concerned because it only involved analyzing some blood on the defendants' car. He guessed that they probably hit an animal or something. We handled it pretty routinely." Replied Doc. Cuthbert.

"How long was it after the accident that you gave Sheriff Relliford your report?" John continued his questioning.

"About a day later, I believe."

"And what were your findings?"

"The car in question was impounded at Stan's Garage. When I analyzed the blood on it, I found it to be human blood."

"What happened then?" Continued John Stearns.

"I took my report to the Sheriff and we discussed it at great length."

"What was Sheriff Relliford's reaction?"

"One of disbelief," John began. "He said that he and Deputy Bivens had checked the scene of the accident and had found no body. He admitted, however, that the search was conducted in the middle of the night and was not very extensive because they were certain that it was just an animal that was hit."

"How could he have been so certain of that?" John pressed.

"Well, probably because no Missing Person Report was filed. News travels fast in this town. If someone was missing, the Sheriff would have been notified." Replied John.

"So, it was assumed that if someone was injured or killed that it must have been someone from Midway?"

"I guess so," John said. "That didn't seem to be so unusual to me at the time."

"But that assumption proved false, didn't it, Doctor?" John pressed.

"Yes."

"What happened next?"

"Well, after Toby . . . er-r-r . . . Sheriff Relliford and I talked, he told me that they would do another investigation of the site the very next morning during broad daylight because, by this time, it was getting pretty late in the evening." Responded Doc.

John halted his questioning for a moment and walked over to his assistant and conferred for a brief time. Nodding his head, he walked back to John.

"Please continue," he instructed him.

"The next morning, I got a call from Sheriff Relliford. He and Willie Joe had found a body off the roadside behind a thicket. He asked me to perform the autopsy and to see if it was the same blood that was on the defendants' auto."

"And?"

"They were the same. Absolutely." Doc replied.

Gasps were audible from the spectators in the courtroom. There began a low rumble of murmurings and whispers. The Judge rapped his gavel twice and silence once again ruled.

"By the time all of this had taken place, how long would you say that the victim had been dead?"

"About two days."

This time the noise in the courtroom grew louder and some protests could be heard. Judge McGill banged his gavel again and spoke in a stern voice this time.

"I will clear this courtroom. This is a hearing, not a circus. We will have it quiet. Counsel, continue." The judge demanded.

A faint smile could be traced around the corners of John Sterns' mouth. Just barely. He had to seize this moment. He had to stall to allow further time for the Coroner's words to set themselves in the minds of the people. He conferred once again with his assistant.

"Your honor, I have no further questions of this witness. I would now like to call Sheriff Toby Relliford to the stand."

Harold Steinmetz knew what John Sterns' was doing and deliberately decided to be out of order so that he could minimize the impact of Doc Cuthbert's testimony. He stood up and asked if he could cross-examine the Coroner.

"Mr. Steinmetz, you know the difference between this and a "trial by jury." The Prosecution is presenting its evidence and will be afforded all the time it needs to do so. This is as fact-finding proceeding. You will get your chance . . . Doctor Cuthbert, you may step down."

After John Cuthbert was once again in his seat, Attorney Stearns called Toby forward to be sworn in. He took his seat on the Witness Stand, remembering his training at the academy to breathe deeply during questioning, collect his thoughts, speak slowly and control his emotions. He knew to answer only the questions asked him. Volunteer no information, he reminded himself.

"State your name and occupation, please," John told him.

"Toby Relliford, Sheriff of Midway."

"Sheriff Relliford, please tell the court in your own words, the events and circumstances surrounding this case."

"Rod and Jeremy there, come into my office about ten on Monday night of the 15th reporting that they had struck something in the road about two miles outside of town. They didn't find anything but there was blood on the front of the car and the fender and a headlight were damaged. Since there was no body at the scene, I advised them to stay in town for a few days. I had their car impounded so that it could be examined and told them we would investigate their story."

"And when did you investigate?"

"That same night. Willie Joe and myself went out to the scene. It was pitch black and we really couldn't see very well. We looked up and down the road with flashlights but found nothing."

"How extensive was your search?"

"Not very extensive. Like I said, it was awfully dark. All we saw were skid marks in the road and some blood. We guessed that the boys had probably hit a deer or something."

He ached to tell Stearns that that was exactly what had happened but Harold advised him to say nothing yet. They still had no proof that the car actually hit the animal. John Stearns would eat him alive on the stand and accuse him of trying to protect Rod and Jeremy. His advice was soon to be proven accurate. John continued his questioning.

"Why were you so convinced that the two of them had not hit and killed a human being?"

"Because of the severity of the impact, a person would have been killed at once."

"Oh?" John queried. "Exactly how fast were they going?"

"They weren't sure," Toby said. "Jeremy estimated about 40 or 45."

"Sheriff, as you know, the speed limit in Midway is only 35. By your own admission, the defendants were speeding, weren't they?"

Toby was caught totally off-guard. The fact was never discussed or even considered before. He paused, not knowing exactly how to answer without further incriminating Rod and Jeremy. Harold Steinmetz raised another objection. He was overruled this time.

"Did you cite them for speeding, Sheriff?" John demanded.

"No."

"Why not. Isn't that your job?"

Toby bristled. "I don't need you to tell me my job, Counselor. The boys were outside of the city on a deserted country road at night. Practically everyone in this courtroom travels at that speed outside of town."

"How about you, Sheriff?" John asked with a smile.

"I don't have to answer that."

Snickers could be heard throughout the courtroom. Toby knew he was being baited. With Doc Cuthbert's previous testimony and the line of questioning that he was now receiving, he had a good idea of what John Sterns was up to. He had always thought of him as somewhat of a friend. Not close, but friendly. They had mutual respect for one another but now Toby realized that relationships don't mean much in a court of law. A prosecutor is a prosecutor and his sole purpose is to prosecute. John was simply doing his job and Toby had to concede that his reputation was well deserved. John went on.

"So Sheriff, in actuality, you not only failed to cite the defendants for speeding but your investigation that night was done rather haphazardly because you were convinced that the defendants story was true. Isn't that right?"

"Not exactly," Toby answered. "I felt that by the fact that they came in and reported the ccident when they really didn't have to stop at all, said a lot about their character and integrity."

"Then, you believed their story?"

"I trusted their judgment, yes."

"If they had been escaped felons, would your investigation that night have proceeded any differently?"

"I object," Harold blurted. "This line of questioning is irrelevant and is an attempt to discredit the witness."

John immediately turned to Judge McGill.

"Your Honor, the Prosecution is gravely concerned about the passing of two whole days before the victim's body was found. I'm convinced that the relationship between the Sheriff and the defendants affected his investigation."

"Objection overruled. You may continue."

"Thank you, your Honor. Now Sheriff, would you have conducted a more thorough search with less reliable suspects?"

"Probably, yes."

"When the Coroner presented you with the facts of his report that the victim's blood matched that of the blood on the defendants' car, what did you do then?"

"I had Rod and Jeremy placed under arrest."

"Sheriff, I notice that you often refer to the defendants by name. Why is that?"

Harold squirmed in his seat. Toby had made his first big mistake. If John was successful in showing fraternization between him and the defendants, it could have a lasting effect upon the defense by suggesting possible collusion, thus soliciting further sympathy for the Prosecution. Damn it. He didn't miss a trick.

"I call them by name because I got to know them during the time before the arrest was made. They were simply hanging around waiting for word from me about the accident. They're nice kids. Yeah, I call a lot of people by name, even you, John."

Laughter quickly filled the room and disappeared with the Judge's hammering the gavel. Score one for Toby, Harold smiled. Still he was concerned. John was painting Toby as an obstacle to the Prosecution, a move that if successful, would place more burden of proof upon him and his clients.

"In fact, your relationship with the defendants caused a major stir in the town, didn't it?"

"Objection, your honor. I object strongly," Harold cried standing behind his desk. "I demand to know the logic behind this line of questioning! The mood of the town is in no way relative to the purposes of this hearing!"

"Yes, I quite agree," Judge McGill said turning to look directly at John Stearns. "What is your point counselor?" he asked John. John knew that this was a crucial point in his case. He didn't know what the defense had planned but he knew Harold Steinmetz's reputation as a plush, successful and astute big city trial lawyer. He also knew that he would have agreed to a plea bargain earlier if he didn't feel that he had a reasonably strong defense. He, John Sterns, needed every morsel of support and sympathy that he could muster, just in case.

"If it pleases the court, I want to show 'just cause' why Sheriff Toby Relliford should be removed from having anything else to do with this case in any manner. No further investigative work or contact with the defendants since this is merely a pre-trial hearing. Toby Relliford is a good Sheriff with a spotless record but in this case, we have reason to fear the possibility of obstruction to justice, even if done inadvertently because of his protective nature of the defendants."

Bedlam broke out in the courtroom. Flashbulbs burst to life. Reporters scribbled furiously on notepads. People looked at each other stunned. Judge McGill banged his gavel loudly and demanded order. It took him a full minute to settle the courtroom. Harold sat quietly in his chair while all of this was going on until he caught Toby's eye. He nodded and winked reassuringly at him. Then waved a hand slightly to tell him that everything was okay. He was not surprised at John's tactics knowing all along that Toby's relationship with the boys would be a problem. Hell, that's why he had suggested two weeks ago that he back off the case and bring in Ralph and Dick. John Stearns was doing exactly what he himself would have done in the same situation! The problem was that he was succeeding all too well. Without a doubt the people were quickly swinging to his side.

Jeremy and Rod sat disbelievingly. They were in shock. Their mothers wiped their eyes with handkerchiefs. Beth was stunned and completely numb. Bobby McCallister smiled. Jimmy pinched his father's leg. Hank stared blankly ahead. Toby couldn't believe what John was doing to him. After order was restored, Judge McGill called both attorneys before his bench and whispered sternly to them. He spoke directly to John.

"Young man, if you fail to prove "just cause" for Sheriff Relliford's dismissal from this case, I swear, I'll call a mistrial. This is unprecedented in Midway. I hope you know what you're doing. Mr.

Steinmetz, do you have any objections to this line of questioning?" he asked Harold.

"None, your honor."

"Very well, then. Proceed."

Harold and John exchanged brief glances. Each seemed to be reading the other's mind. John knew instantly that he was right about Harold. This was going to be a dog fight for sure, clear to the bitter end. Composed, both lawyers left the bench and assumed their previous positions. John knew that everyone in the courtroom eagerly awaited his next words, even the Judge sat on the end of his seat. All was going well, extremely well, in fact. Yet he knew that he couldn't afford a mistake. Toby Relliford had a lot of friends here and he could not risk alienating himself with those persons. He did not like what he was doing because he considered Toby a friend and respected him deeply. But his job was to gain a conviction for the county with the evidence submitted and all that he had was the Coroner's autopsy report. He had no witnesses to the accident or anything else. He also knew that Harold was aware of this too.

If the autopsy report was all conclusive, Harold would have given in to him before the pre-trial but he didn't, and this bothered John. He was convinced that Harold must be holding an ace up his sleeve. This is why he was so intent on gaining every ounce of advantage while he had the opportunity. When Harold refused to object as they both stood before the Judge, he knew that the only person in the courtroom not shocked by his method was Harold. He was good. Damn good. John had to admit. John now turned to Toby who sat patiently on the witness stand.

"Sheriff Relliford, what is transpiring here is in no way a reflection on your competence or integrity as a law officer. I have nothing but the highest regard for you and your work here. But because of some unusual circumstances that have occurred since this case began, I must in all fairness do what I feel I have to do."

Turning to Judge McGill, John told him that he had no further questions of the Sheriff.

"You may step down, Sheriff," the Judge said to Toby, "and thank you for your patience."

Toby nodded, stepped down from the witness stand and went back to his seat.

"The prosecution now calls former Deputy Willie Joe Bivens to the witness stand."

As Willie Joe made his way forward, again there was murmuring in the courtroom. After the former Deputy was sworn in, John began his questioning again. "Please state your name and occupation to this court please."

"Willie Joe Bivens, hardware store stock merchant."

"Willie Joe, would you please relay to the court, the circumstances involving your dismissal as Deputy Sheriff."

Willie Joe fidgeted nervously and cast a pleading look in Toby's direction. Toby simply nodded to Willie.

"Well," he began, "after Doc Cuthbert and the Sheriff had talked about the blood on the car of the defendants over there, I called the Prosecutor's office to tell him."

"How did you know about it? Were you with the Sheriff and the Doc at the time?"

Willie Joe flushed.

"No. They were in the back room with the door shut. I heard some of the conversation but not much. After the meeting was over, the Sheriff told me that he would have to arrest the two men."

"Why?"

"Because the dead man's blood matched the blood on their car."

What did you do next?"

"When he left the office to make the arrest, I called Mr. Sterns and told him what had happened."

He paused for a moment, wiping perspiration from his brow with the back of his hand.

"I shouldn't have done that. I know that now," he continued.

"Why not, Willie Joe?"

"Because it was not the right time yet. There was no arrest or charges filed at that time. I should have waited and let the Sheriff do it. That's his job."

"I see," John said. "Is that why you were fired?"

Again Willie Joe looked at Toby. Again he simply nodded back.

"I guess so."

"For making just one mistake?"

"It was more than that, sir. You see, because I didn't like the colored boy, I was too anxious to have them convicted. I thought at the time that I would do everything I could to get him and his friend behind bars. I hated it when the Sherriff Let them go."

"What did the Sheriff say to you when he found out that you had called the Prosecutor's office?"

"He warned me not to get out of line again. But that night, still angry, I went to The Silver Dollar and had too much to drink. I accidentally told some people at the bar some details about the case. Sheriff Relliford suspended me the next day."

"What was his explanation?"

"He said that he could not risk me damaging the case any further. He didn't want to take any chances . . . of the boys being accused of something that no one was sure they did."

"Did you feel that he fired you to protect the boys, or because you acted unwisely?"

"At the time, I thought it was to protect the two. But now I know that it was probably both."

"Why did you feel that he was trying to protect the two?"

"Well . . . he liked them, it seemed. He drove them places, they talked all the time. I resented that. I thought that it was wrong for him to be so nice."

"I have no further questions. Thanks Willie Joe."

Willie Joe left the stand, looking at Toby apologetically. Toby winked at him and smiled.

"I now call Mr. Nate Jefferson to the stand."

When the huge black man stood up, flashbulbs popped. His wife gave him a reassuring pat as he walked forward toward the stand. Several people whispered to each other. Some giggled at private jokes. All watched him. After being sworn in, he took his turn with John Stearns.

"Please state your name and occupation to the court, please."

"Nate Jefferson, Restaurant Owner in the black section," he stated with pride. Mrs. Jefferson beamed.

"Mr. Jefferson, do you know the defendant, Rodney Blake?"

"Yes."

"Would you tell the court how you came to know him."

"Sheriff Relliford brought him to my house a couple of weeks ago and asked me and Gloria to kinda look out for him that day. He stayed with us, ate and just hung out until the Sheriff came back for him that evening."

"Is the Sheriff in a habit of bringing people like that to your house to take care of?"

"No."

Mr. Blake went on to explain the circumstances surrounding the incident.

"Would you say that the Sheriff had more than a casual interest in Rodney?"

"I can't say for sure, I'm not the Sheriff," he answered.

"But he did have the Sheriff's private escort to and from your home, didn't he?"

"Yes."

"Did you think that the Sheriff's actions were official business, or more of a personal nature?"

"I didn't pay it no mind."

"Even though he brought him to your house to just 'hang out'?"

"That's right. What's okay for the Sheriff is okay with me."

"That's all Mr. Jefferson. Thank you."

John next called Will Travers, the owner of the hotel in the colored section to the stand. He questioned him at length about why the Sheriff personally brought Rod and the two young men's parents to his hotel to stay.

"What was wrong with the hotel here in town?" he asked.

Mr. Travers explained that because Rod's parents and girlfriend were black, that the Sheriff felt they were better off at his hotel.

"Well, what about Jeremy's parents who are white, staying in a black hotel? Weren't you concerned about that?"

"Not really. The Coloreds respect Sheriff Relliford and I certainly had no problems with it."

"How many times has the Sheriff brought people to your hotel like that?"

"That was the first time."

Mr. Travers was dismissed. John then turned his attention to Judge McGill who sat looking on interestingly.

"Your honor, I think that it is clear that Sheriff Toby Relliford took it upon himself to make decisions relative to the defendants and their families that were purely personal in nature. His role as a private escort and personal ombudsman are totally out-of-line. By his actions, he implied that Midway was not only unsafe for Black visitors but white ones as well. It helped set the tone for the racial unrest now surrounding this case. Not only that, but the same night that the accident was reported, he had dinner with the two suspects and personally put them up at the hotel. All of these things together prove that there is an intimacy here between the Sheriff and the two defendants and their families that go beyond his duties as an impartial law officer, including having special meals catered to these two while they were incarcerated."

Bobby McCallister sprang to his feet at that instant and shouted angrily.

"Yeah, that's right, Judge! He even brought that one by my house to pick a fight with me," he screamed, pointing in Jeremy's direction. Jeremy jumped up and angrily called Bobby a liar. Beth futilely tried to shout above the noise about the encounter she had had at the restaurant. Bedlam broke loose. Judge McGill stood up instantly hammering his gavel and screaming at the bailiff to restore order. Newsmen jostled each other for room. Flashbulbs popped from every angle. It took the bailiff and three uniformed guards several minutes to calm the room. Judge McGill shouted redfaced that the court was in recess until two that afternoon.

He then told everyone present that if there was the slightest indication of disruption when the court reconvened, that it would then be closed to the public for the duration of the hearing.

"I hope that I have made myself perfectly clear," he said harshly. "Now clear my courtroom! We are recessed until two this afternoon. Counselors, I want to see you both in my chambers immediately." With that he disappeared behind closed doors. The furor in the courtroom continued in scaled-down tones for several minutes as people slowly made their way outside the courthouse. It spilled onto the courtyard and into the streets. The crowd seemed divided over the strategy of Prosecutor John Sterns. One side felt anger and indignation over the treatment and allegations brought against Toby Relliford. One man was overheard saying, "The Sheriff has always been a people's person. He treats everybody with respect and hospitality. Those two boys are no different. They came here as visitors. What was the Sheriff supposed to to do? They were not charged with anything at the time."

Another man in the crowd disagreed

"John Stearns was absolutely correct in what he did! It is his job to protect the integrity of the case. The Sheriff's actions were more friendly than professional. He'll try to protect those two anyway he can."

And so it went. It was beginning to become obvious that the Prosecutor was successful in a least casting suspicion on Toby concerning his ability to remain objective in this case. The conversations went on and on as the sun stationed itself directly overhead. Meanwhile back in the Judge's chamber, Howard McGill was having his say.

"John, although you are legally within your rights to press for the Sheriff's removal from this case as a possible investigator after this pre-trial is over, I don't approve, in the least bit, the way you went about doing it. You could have come to me privately with your concerns. Toby Relliford is a good sheriff and I don't like his office becoming suspect. This could have very negative repercussions."

John nodded. Inwardly he knew the Judge was right but he had a foundation that he wanted to lay. He glanced at Harold next to him and wondered if he had allowed himself to be intimidated. Finally, he spoke.

"I won't argue that point, your honor," he conceded. "I didn't think about that."

The Judge further cautioned both attorneys that sensationalism needed to be avoided whenever possible.

"We have a potentially explosive situation here. The people are already upset that the colored boy has been running loose, scot free while the white one is behind bars. The incident with him and Bobby McCallister was most unfortunate."

He turned to Harold who, so far, had said nothing as he scolded the Prosecuting Attorney.

"Mr. Steinmetz, what are your intentions when we reconvene? I have yet to hear from you."

Harold told Judge McGill that he would wait until after John was through presenting his case.

"I would, however, like to cross-examine the Coroner before we conclude today. We have cause to dispute the autopsy report and its findings. Also at some point, I have several witnesses to call as well."

"Very well," Judge McGill responded. "I'll see you two at two sharp." Harold and John left together going back into the new empty courtroom to pick up their briefcases.

"How about some lunch?" Harold asked John.

"Sounds good," John replied. He looked at this adversary and smiled. "You've got something, don't you? Any other lawyer would have been screaming at the top of his lungs about what I did in here earlier."

"Well, it was shrewd but very smart. Your whole case rests upon the Corner's report and circumstantial evidence concerning the defendants' blood-stained auto since there were no eyewitnesses who actually saw the accident. On the surface, it appears open and shut. In fact, two weeks ago, I didn't give our side a chance but since then, we've found out that Doc Cuthbert lied about facts in the autopsy report."

John raised an eyebrow and peered surprisingly at Harold.

"Of course, you're kidding."

"Not at all. It's now my job to prove it," Harold cautioned.

The two left the courtroom walking and talking like old friends as they made their way toward Sarah's.

During the court-ordered recess, Toby Relliford sat behind his desk sipping a cup of coffee while talking with Jake.

"It's a good thing that Harold warned you last week that your involvement with Jeremy and Rodney might come up," Jake was saying.

Toby nodded. After Jeremy's fight with Bobby, he knew that there would be trouble. Even though he was surprised and caught off-guard by John in court, the two of them had known and respected each other long enough that he knew it was not a personal vendetta against him. Still, John didn't have to hit so hard. He could have pulled his punches . . . a little.

"I guess John was just doing his job. I shouldn't have forgotten his reputation as a tough guy in court. His style has won us a lot of convictions here over the years," Toby acknowledged.

He knew that he would be barred by Judge McGill from further involvement in the case but he had already distanced himself from it anyway. Ralph, Dick and Harold had gathered together all of the evidence possible to present their defense. He felt confident that the boys would be set free and that he would be vindicated in the end.

"What are you smiling about, Sheriff?" Jake asked noticing Toby's musing.

"Oh, nothing really. Just thinking," he said wryly. "Have I still got time for a sandwich?"

"About a half hour," Jake replied.

"Okay, see you later," he said as he picked up his keys and headed outside.

There was not enough room for air when the hearing resumed. A sardine would have complained. As Judge McGill scanned the courtroom, he was thankful to hear the dull humming of the air conditioner. He rapped his gavel twice and a hush fell over the room.

"Let me begin by informing the court that during the recess, I have decided to grant the motion of the prosecution and dismiss Sheriff Toby Relliford from further involvement with any part of this case. Let it also be stated that this decision in no way is a reflection upon his competence and integrity as the Sheriff in this town. Secondly, no matter what transpires on the floor of this courtroom, I will not tolerate anything resembling the chaos of this morning! This is the only time that I will issue this warning. If you, the public, wish to be a part of this pre-trial as spectators, then the rules of this court will be adhered to without exception. Now, let us proceed. Mr. Prosecutor?" he concluded looking directly at John Sterns. John rose and took center stage once again.

He had done some thinking about his lunch-time conversation with Harold Steinmetz since he had returned to the courtroom. He didn't know exactly what to prepare for but if the defense had reason to believe that the autopsy report was inaccurate, it just might involve the car in question.

"the prosecution would now like to call Mr. Stanley Merritt to the stand."

Stan made his way to the witness stand and was sworn in. He took his seat.

"Please state your name and occupation to the court."

"Stanley Merritt, owner of Stan's Auto Repair and Storage."

"Mr. Merritt, the vehicle connected in the death of Mr. Detmer has been impounded at your place since the accident, is that correct?" John asked.

"Yes, sir."

"Is this unusual?"

"No sir. I do this quite often for the Sheriff when vehicles are involved in legal matters."

"Why is that?"

"Well, with the high chain link fence around the yard, which is locked each night, it's the most secure place in town to store vehicles for a short period. We also keep the cars that we work on there as well." Stanley answered.

"Has there ever been any thefts or vandalism involved with any of your vehicles?"

"No sir, never. I've operated that shop for over 15 years and have never had any trouble whatsoever."

John smiled and nodded.

"No more questions. Thank you Mr. Merritt."

Stan left the witness stand with a puzzled look on his face. John then turned to Judge McGill.

"The prosecution would now like to call Mr. Jeremy McCutchin to the stand."

As Jeremy rose to take the stand, he glanced quickly at Harold Steinmetz, Rod and Sheriff Relliford. His Mom and Dad held hands as he came forward. Beth had her hands together under her chin as if praying. Mr. and Mrs. Blake along with Andrea stared blankly ahead. Jeremy was sworn in and seated before the Prosecutor. He was asked to state his name and did so.

"You're a student at Waynesville State in upper New York , are you not?"

"Yes sir. I'm a senior."

"Tell the court the circumstances that brought you to Midway and the present situation in which you now find yourself. Take your time, there's no hurry."

"Well Rodney, there," he said nodding in Rod's direction, "and me were on our way back to school from Florida after our last time together outside of school before we graduate and go our separate ways. We were initially planning to make it to Chattanooga, Tennessee to spend the night but were getting low on gas and were tired anyway. We decided to stop at the nearest town instead which happened to be Midway."

"Who was driving at the time?"

"I was."

"And how long had you been driving?"

"We were driving in shifts. I guess I had been at the wheel for about five or six hours at the time."

"That's quite awhile," John noted. "Weren't you fatigued?"

"Yes. I said that we were tired."

"Were you drinking?"

"No, Rod and I never drink and drive. That's foolish."

"I quite agree. What happened as you approached Midway?"

"Well, Rod and I were talking when a blur of something suddenly flashed in our path from nowhere."

"Did you see what it was?"

"No. Not really. It all happened so fast and I wasn't really too alert . . . I mean . . . I wasn't expecting anything to happen way out there in the middle of the night."

"How fast were you going at the time?"

"I . . . I don't know for sure. I didn't check the speedometer."

"50?"

"Not that fast, I know. Maybe 40 or so."

"How often do you check your speed while driving?"

"Pretty regularly most of the time but like I said, we were talking and it was late."

"What happened next?"

"We hit whatever it was. I am positive that it was not a person, though."

"I thought you said that you didn't know what it was you hit."

"Well . . . I mean, if it was a person, Rod and I would have found him in the road."

"Young man, if an auto strikes a pedestrian at 50 or 40 miles an hour, don't you think that it could throw him well off the road?"

"I wasn't going that fast."

"Oh, no? You stated earlier that you didn't know exactly how fast you were going. Let's move on. What did you do next?"

"Well, Rod and I got out and checked the road for whatever it was we hit. We didn't see or hear anything. When we saw the damage to the car and the blood on the fender, we decided to go to the Sheriff and report it just in case. We thought it was probably just an animal or something."

"Why didn't you check over where the body was found?"

"We were panicked and not really thinking at the time. I still cannot believe that I was going that fast to knock someone that far," Jeremy said shaking his head.

"But you did," John stormed, "the Sheriff found the body himself. The dead man's blood was the same as the blood on your car. How do you explain that?"

"I can't," Jeremy confessed.

"It's apparent that you were not the only ones who didn't find a body. The Sheriff and his Deputy didn't find one either that night. They evidently believed you when you told them that you were only going about 40."

Harold Steinmetz objected to the conclusive statement by the Prosecutor about the Sheriff. His objection was sustained.

"Let me rephrase my last remark," John continued. "It appears obvious that the Sheriff's search of the area was no more extensive than your's was by the fact that they checked virtually the same area. Wouldn't you agree?"

"I don't know."

"When you first reported the accident to the Sheriff, did he say anything at all about deer?"

"Only that it was not uncommon for deer to be hit around here at night."

"Uh-huh . . . no further questions."

Jeremy was released from the witness stand and Rodney Blake was called up and sworn in next. Noise from the spectators rose to a low rumble.

"Mr. Blake, can you add anything else to what your friend has told the court?"

"Not really. It was just like he said. It all happened so fast. But I would be willing to stake my life that we didn't hit a human."

John turned his back on Rodney and paused for a moment.

"You might be doing just that, young man," he suggested.

Harold sprang to his feet and objected on grounds of badgering the witness with threats. Again, his objection was sustained. John continued.

"Now think before answering the next question. It is very important. Did you notice at the time of impact how fast the car was going?"

Rodney paused and took a deep breath "No sir. I did not. But I know it wasn't as fast as you claim."

"No you don't KNOW! You think, Mr. Blake. You think!"

Blood rushed to Rodney's face and he started to rise to his feet,but having second thoughts, he resettled himself. Jeremy's fight with Bobby had already caused enough damage.

"Yessir. I think," Rod mumbled holding down his anger.

John nodded. "I have nothing else. Thank you."

As Rodney made his way back to his seat, John began his summary to Judge T. Howard McGill.

"Your honor, by a clear preponderance of the evidence submitted and the subsequent testimonies following, it is clear that the charge of Vehicular Homicide in the death of Mr. Arnold Detmer should be handed down against the defendants. The Coroner's Report directly links the defendants' car with the death of Mr. Detmer. The body was found at the scene of the crime by the Sheriff himself. The two defendants themselves admit to striking an object at that time and at that location. Furthermore, their vehicle has been impounded under lock and key by the Sheriff's department. Although there were no witnesses to the crime, all available evidence places them at the scene along with the body. No one disputes this. The position of the deceased when found, clearly indicates that an excessive rate of speed is evident, thus proving negligence. again, this fact was not refuted. Therefore, the prosecution insists that an indictment be handed down and that the defendants be bound over to a Grand Jury accordingly. Thank you you honor."

John Stearns strode confidently back to his table as murmurs and polite applause greeted his ears. He acknowledged the crowd with a slight nod of his head as he sat down. Judge McGill then turned to Harold Steinmetz and asked him if he was ready to present the defense. Harold rose to his feet but didn't move.

"Your honor, due to the hour and the excitement of the day, the defense requests a recess until tomorrow morning at which time we wish to recall Dr. John Cuthbert to the stand." Harold wanted to begin his cross-examination of the Corner when the onlookers were well rested and their minds fresh and uncluttered. Such a delay would only serve to whet their appetites and increase anticipation. Judge McGill granted his request and called for a recess until nine in the morning. Court was then adjourned. The room emptied quickly and soon only the two lawyers remained, gathering up their files and packing their briefcases. Harold offered his congratulations to the Prosecutor as John prepared to leave.

"Thanks," the Prosecutor acknowledged. "I just regret that I had to be so hard on Toby. He's a good Sheriff, a good man."

"Well, don't apologize," Harold told him with a wry grin. "When I finish with your man tomorrow, what you did to Toby will pale in comparison. His hands are dirty, John, and I'm going to prove it."

"I don't have to tell you that his reputation in this county is impeccable. The people will be on his side. I don't envy you, that's for sure," John commented.

"I'm being paid well," Harold responded with a smile. "Take it easy. See you bright and early in the morning."

The two men shook hands and exchanged pats on the back as they walked out of the courtroom and into the evening air.

Darkness had settled over the colored section of town and there was little activity. The hearing of Rod and Jeremy hung over the village like a shroud. The residents were kept well informed by the Jeffersons who met with crowds of people in their shop that evening. They were the only blacks to attend the hearings at the advice of the Sheriff who told the Jeffersons that any confrontation between blacks and whites would only work against the two boys.

All through the evening many of the town folks stopped by the hotel to wish Rod, Andrea and the boys' parents well. Some prayed for them and offered their support. It was an act of goodwill that deeply touched John and Harriet McCutchin.

Although by all intents and purposes they should have been considered outsiders, they were never treated as such. In fact, they felt pretty much at home. When they wandered around in their spare time, there was never any fear for their safety. Passers-by tipped their hats or spoke politely. Many stopped to just chat. The past Sunday, they had accompanied the Jeffersons to the Baptist church. They had a fantastic time. They were asked to stand and introduce themselves, and were greeted with warm applause. During worship, they were treated to good old-fashioned Gospel music and strong fervent black preaching. It was the first time that John had seen a preacher actually sweat.

"He sure works hard," Harriet had said quietly.

As they sat in their room that evening reflecting over the events of the past few weeks, John told his wife that he planned to donate a gift to the Jeffersons' church as a contribution towards adding a new roof to the sanctuary.

"Regardless of how the trial comes out, this is going to be my way of expressing our appreciation to these people," he said.

"I think that would be nice," Harriet agreed. She thought about their own church at home with its cavernous and plushly carpeted facilities and huge endowment funds and wondered how warmly Rod, Andrea and the Blakes would have been greeted there. She glanced pensively at her husband who sat at her side and sensed that his thoughts were much like her own. She sighed audibly.

"How do you think things will go in the morning?" she asked changing the subject.

"I wish I knew," John replied hesitantly. "Harold is pretty confident,though, and that makes me feel a little better. Toby sure took his lumps today, didn't he?"

"Oh, that man! What's his name, John Stearns? He made me so angry. I still can't believe what he did," she frothed.

"He did a job all right," John agreed. "Harold will really have to go some to overturn what he did. He literally had the people eating out of his hand. Did you see their faces? Even the Judge looked convinced."

They sat silently for several moments before deciding to shower and retire for the day.

"Well, tomorrow's our day," John said as he made his way to the towel rack.

Rod and Andrea listened quietly to the crickets that chirped in the night as they sat huddled together under a big oak tree. The moon bathed their faces in silvery light as they gazed into each others' eyes.

"Scared?" Andrea asked.

"A little," Rod replied as they embraced.

Midway was lost in a blanket of ink that night, save for the lights of three buildings: Harold Steinmetz's tiny office, the Sheriff's office and The Silver Dollar. It was as if the night had stolen everything and spared only these three places. Because of the early trial time the next morning, everyone had turned in for the night except, of course, the regular party animals at The Silver Dollar. No one wanted to miss a thing in the morning. A cough would have been heard for blocks.

Harold, Ralph and Dick had just about finished checking and rechecking all the material for their presentation the next morning. Harold was giving some last minute instructions to the two students.

"Remember, both of you are my assistants, working under my jurisdiction. Which reminds me . . . I'm going to have to figure out how much to pay you two. If you're like I was when I was in school, you could use some extra cash."

Both boys displayed full toothed grins.

"Ralph," Harold continued, "I'll have to call Doc Williams, the other Coroner, to the stand as an expert witness to validate your work. Once that's done, your findings of the deer carcass will not be disputed. Dick, your work will stand on its own merit. The photos were excellent and I have all of your notes. Any questions before we go?"

Ralph and Dick shook their heads.

"Well, I'll see you gentlemen in the morning. Let's lock up and go home."

Beth lay in her bed unable to sleep. Her visit with Jeremy earlier at the jail had left her disturbed. He had really clung to her. She was convinced that being behind bars while all of this was going on was starting to affect him. Except for her and Sheriff Relliford, he had no one to really talk to. He didn't want to worry his parents, especially his Mom. So, he always played the role of being supremely confident in their presence. but what had happened today in court really scared him. When he was later escorted back to his cell by the Bailiff and locked up, for the first time he had begun to feel like a real prisoner. being locked up by the Sheriff was entirely different than being locked up by the court's bailiff.

She could see fear in his eyes for the first time and his conversation about their predicament was tinged with doubt and uncertainty. Still, he managed to remain fairly composed, she guessed, for her sake. But she could feel and sense his anxiety. For long moments they had simply clung desperately to each other without uttering a single word. She had begun to wonder what she would do if anything ever happened to him. They were now inseparable. Sheriff Relliford was very liberal with her visitations but now that the trial was underway, he had to limit her visitation times. Tonight, she had not wanted to leave when he came for her. Outside the cell block in his office, she broke down. He let her cry,comforting her as best he could. he had encouraged her to get it out of her system and had later dried her swollen eyes.

"I'm glad you did that out here instead of in there," he had said. "You're a strong woman and that's what Jeremy needs right now. Just hang in there. He's going to be all right. Trust me."

His words of reassurance had really helped. After they had drunk some coffee and talked for several minutes, she felt a great sense of relief. Later when she arrived at home, her parents and Bobby had barely spoken to her. That was fine as far as she was concerned because she wanted to be left alone. All she could do now was wait and hope. As the hours stole away, she fell into a troubled but much needed sleep.

The next morning, Harold began his opening argument for the defense before Judge McGill and a packed courtroom. It was difficult to imagine but the room seemed more crowded now than it did yesterday. Even with the air conditioner going full tilt, it was already uncomfortably warm.

"Your honor, if it pleases the court, I would like to first state that my clients are innocent of the charges against them. We will prove beyond a reasonable doubt that they are the victims of a frame up. exactly who killed Mr. Detmer is still a mystery but one thing is certain, it was not Jeremy McCutchin or Rodney Blake."

The courtroom instantly came alive. John Cuthbert, his son Jimmy, Bobby McCallister and Hank Peters who were all sitting together exchanged nervous glances. Beth noticed their discomfort and nervousness. She sat with Sheriff Relliford and the boys' parents. Jeremy and Rod smiled faintly at one another as they sat together behind Harold's table. Ralph and Dick sat near the back of the courtroom casting intent gazes in Harold's direction.

"The defense calls Doctor John Cuthbert to the stand."

As John rose from his seat, the murmuring in the courtroom stopped. He strode nervously to the witness stand where he was subsequently sworn in. following Harold's instructions, he identified himself as the County Coroner.

"Mr. Corner, according to your autopsy report which I now hold in my hand, you listed the time of death of the deceased at approximately 2:30 a.m., the morning of August 20th, is that correct?"

"Yes."

"Are you sure about the time of death, Doctor?"

"Of course I'm sure. I've only been doing this sort of thing for over 20 years."

"Would you say that an autopsy of this sort is pretty much routine considering?"

"Yes, I would say so."

"What would be the chance of making an error in such an examination for a Coroner, in your opinion?" "Pretty slim," John answered somewhat puzzled. "It's a relatively routine procedure."

"And you're sure about the accuracy of this report?"

"Of course I'm sure. I've stated that before," John Cuthbert answered, irritation creeping into his voice.

Harold then changed his course of questioning.

"Dr. Cuthbert, your examination of the accident site where the victim was found is recorded as being one and a half miles outside of town off of the main road leading to Midway. Is that correct?"

"Yes."

"Is that where the victim died?"

"Absolutely."

"How can you be so sure?"

Exasperation etched the face of John Cuthbert. He looked first at Judge McGill, John Stearns and then back to Harold.

"The man died at the site because he suffered massive internal and external injuries. It's all in the report," he said icely.

"So he couldn't have been struck there and died later somewhere else?" Harold pressed.

"Objection," shouted John Stearns. "The witness has already answered the question twice already. This borders on badgering."

"Objection sustained," Judge McGill responded. "Mr. steinmetz, where is your line of questioning leading?"

"Your honor," Harold began, "I want to give Doc Cuthbert every opportunity to be sure of the facts recorded in his report about the time and place of death.:"

"He's already done that Counselor. One question will be enough," Judge McGill concluded.

"Yes,your honor," Harold complied.

"Doctor," he continued," you also examined the blood found on the defendants' car did you not?"

"Yes."

"And what were your findings, for the court's sake?"

"The blood on the defendants" car was identical to the blood of the deceased that is also in the report."

Did anyone else examine the car other than yourself?"

"No."

"How do you know that?" Harold asked.

"Stan, the owner of the garage told me the car was not bothered. the Sheriff had it impounded under lock and key."

"I have no more questions at this time, your honor."

The Judge dismissed the Coroner who shot a disgusted look in Harold's direction. Harold acted as if he didn't notice and called his next witness.

"The defense now calls Mr. Ralph Simon to the stand."

All the heads in the courtroom looked around at once to see who Ralph Simon was as he slowly made his way toward the center aisle. He had been seated almost in the center of the row in which he sat. He was dressed in a baggy but neat brown suit and sported a yellow shirt casually open at the collar. His youthful appearance was refreshing. His hair was immaculately combed and his dark-rimmed glasses gave him a Collegiate look. Harold smiled to himself as he came confidently to the front of the room. After responding to courtroom procedure, he sat down and nodded to Harold.

"Mr. Simon, would you please state your name and occupation to the court."

"My name is Ralph Simon and I'm a graduate student at Waynesville state University in upper state New York. I am currently working as a legal assistant to Attorney Harold Steinmetz."

"Will you explain to the court the nature of your work for me and the reason you are here."

"I was asked by Attorney Steinmetz's office in New York to come to Midway and assist Mr. Steinmetz as a forensic examiner.

"Exactly what does that entail?"

"I gather samples of blood, tissue cultures, hair fibers, and things like that for laboratory investigative analysis. Much the same kind of things that a forensic pathologist does in a crime lab."

"And what are your qualifications for this line of work?"

"I am in my final year of Medical School at Waynesville State College of Medicine. I begin my internship at the New York City Police Department's crime lab in January of the coming year."

"Exactly why were you called here?"

"I was called here to examine blood samples found in connection with the death of Mr. Detmer."

The room came alive with noise as Judge McGill rapped his gavel for quiet. The response was immediate. John Stearns immediately stood up and registered his objection.

"Your honor, this is madness. How can a med student check the work of a qualified County Corner?"

"Yeah, that's right!" someone in the crowd shouted.

Judge McGill warned the onlookers that outbursts would not be tolerated and then turned to Harold.

"Counselor?" he asked him.

"Your honor, Mr. Simon was notified because my investigator found blood involving a hit and run at a different site than the one where Mr. Detmer died. We didn't know at the time if the two accidents were related, so we took measures to find out. Now, Mr. Simon, please tell the court of your findings."

"The blood that I examined was found in the clearing at the bend of the road leading out of town only about a quarter of a mile down the road," he said pointing. "The area is still marked and under the watch of the Sheriff's department."

Harold then asked Ralph to disclose the details. By this time, it was so quiet in the room that one wondered if anybody at all was even breathing.

"When my examination was complete, the blood I checked was then compared to the blood analysis done by the Coroner, Doctor Cuthbert, on the now-deceased Mr. Detmer. They were found to be exactly the same in every detail."

Again the room rocked with bedlam. Cries of "no . . . no . . . no . . ." and "fraud" were echoing like a giant wave. People turned to each other all talking at once. Flash bulbs from cameras had a blinding effect. It was long moments before Judge McGill moved into action. Even he was momentarily caught off-guard. This time he would let the crowd blow off steam. He waited about twenty seconds before restoring order with just two knocks of his gavel. Some people who had stood up, sat down immediately.

"My patience is running thin," he cautioned the spectators. "Mr. Steinmetz, please continue."

Harold nodded to the Judge while noticing that Jimmy Cuthbert was making his way toward the restroom with his hand over his mouth. His father, strangely enough, sat staring straight ahead, expressionless. Bobby and Hank covered their faces with their hands but only Harold noticed. He knew right then and there that somehow they were involved. He had suspected it all along during the investigation, but now, here in the courtroom, he surely knew! He continued his questioning.

"Mr. Simon, you said that the blood samples which were found at the two different locations were exactly the same in every aspect, are you sure?"

"Yessir. They were completely identical except for one thing."

"And that was?"

"The blood samples that I studied, those I found just outside of town, showed a time of death about 26 hours later than the time shown on the Corner's report. But, other than that, they matched perfectly."

"But how can that be?"

"I don't know. All I know is that the same blood was found in two different places with two different times of death established."

"Are all blood specimens different all the time?" Harold asked.

"Yes, always," answered Ralph. "Blood types may be identical but the DNA composition of blood is like genetic fingerprints. No two are alike. That's what is strange. The DNA on both samples were identical. There is no question."

Judge McGill squelched the murmuring before they started. John Stearns was on his feet, petitioning the bench.

"Your honor, how much stock can we put in the testimony of a medical student who is not qualified yet to be an expert witness? I move that this testimony be stricken from the records at once."

Harold then took his turn addressing the bench.

"Your honor, in anticipation of such an objection by my distinguished colleague, I have taken the necessary action to have the work of Mr. Simon corroborated by an expert medical witness. If it please the court, I would now like to introduce this gentleman at this time."

Noise and undercurrents once again started to resurface. As Judge McGill called for order in the courtroom, he motioned for both attorneys to approach the bench. John and Harold responded. When they stood within whispering range, the concerned Judge told them in a hushed but urgent tone that he was inclined to call a short recess.

"Because of the sensitive nature of such a witness and the ramifications that his testimony may have on all the parties involved in this hearing, I want the opportunity to have his credentials verified before his testimony is heard. Any objections?" he asked looking at John and then Harold. Both men shook their heads.

"Very well," Judge McGill told them. Then looking out over the courtroom, he informed the court that a recess of one hour would be called. He instructed the clerk and the two attorneys to join him in his chambers, and then dismissed the court.

As the room began to empty, newspaper reporters unsuccessfully attempted to gain entrance to the Judge's chamber, being restrained by the bailiff. They created quite a bit of commotion for a brief period. Several decided to try and talk to Doc Cuthbert during the recess instead. However, the Coroner, his son and the two other boys were now heading out of town toward his home. He had figured correctly that this situation might occur. He had called his office to let his staff know to keep his whereabouts confidential until court was resumed. Jimmy had become sick to his stomach during the proceedings earlier and Hank and Bobby were in a fretful state. He had to get them away and help them to regain their composure.

"Look," he was saying as they sped down the dirt road, "nobody even connects any of you with what is going on, but if you don't stop acting like something's wrong somebody will start to get suspicious. And another thing, while the hearing is under way, we need to split up in the courtroom. You all sit in the back. I'm staying near the front so I can be close to everything that's happening."

"But Dad," Jimmy began urgently, "they found the spot where I hit the guy. They know!"

"They don't know anything," he snapped. "All they know is what they've found. They have no answers. No suspects. Just let me handle this. They'll contest my report but that's all they can do. I can get around the inconsistencies easy enough. We don't have to prove anything, they do."

"Yeah, that's right," Bobby agreed hopefully.

Hank sat quietly not saying anything as the car rolled out of sight of Midway.

Beth sat talking with Rod and their parents in Sarah's restaurant as they fiddled with lunch. The tiny restaurant was packed with people but no one paid them any attention. The talk of the hour was centered on the surprise witness of the defense and the obvious discrepancies in the Coroner's report. The place was abuzz with noisy conversation. Having failed to find the Coroner at his office, a couple of reporters now approached their table and wanted to know if they knew anything about the surprise witness or the defense's argument.

"We know absolutely nothing," John told them. They grudgingly accepted his reply and did not press the issue any further.

Judge T. Howard McGill, Harold Steinmetz and John Stearns sat together in the Judge's chamber discussing the upcoming proceedings.

"I know Doctor Stanley Williams well," he was telling them" I have no reservations about accepting his testimony as an expert witness at this hearing. In fact . . ." he paused looking at John, "if his testimony substantiates the findings of Attorney Steinmetz's assistant, you've got real problems, John."

"It will certainly change the focus of the hearing, that's for sure," John acknowledged. "If we find out that the Corner's report is not accurate in all details, where does that leave us?" he finished looking at Judge McGill.

"That's up to the defense," the Judge responded rising from his chair and glancing in the direction of Harold. "Right now, I'm going to have some soup and sandwiches sent in. I've got a feeling this is going to be a long afternoon." He went over to a desk phone and rang his secretary as John and Harold looked at each other.

Mr. and Mrs. Blake, the McCutchins, Andrea, Rod and Beth were all getting a bite to eat during the recess at Sally's. As they sat at a make-shift family table constructed by pulling two tables together, they were talking excitedly about the trial.

"I had no idea that so much was going on," James Blake was saying." Evidently we were being kept in the dark about everything," he complained, a little irritated. Rodney sensed his dad's exasperation.

"But Dad, Jeremy and me are as much in the dark as the rest of you. Think how much worse Jeremy has been feeling. He's been locked up!"

Beth, however, was sympathetic to Mr. Blake. "Rod, I agree with your dad. Somebody could have told us something! I visit Jeremy practically all of the time and talk with Sheriff Relliford every day. Even he said nothing to me about the investigation. Nothing. That hurts."

Andrea nodded her head in agreement with Beth. John McCutchin who sat silently observing the others felt that it was time for him to say something. He knew Harold Steinmetz well and knew also the way that he sometimes operated. Shrewdness and cunning were part of his reason for hiring Harold to take this case.

"I'm sure Harold has good reasons for the way that he is handling this case. It's not as if he has kept us in the dark completely. Remember how he and the Sheriff talked to all of us before he suggested that Toby back off of the case. That seemed to be a turning point with him. He must have felt vulnerable. I trust his judgments without question. I wouldn't have hired him if I didn't."

"Well, the trial is going better than I thought it would be up to this point," Harriet confessed pensively.

"Yes, I wholeheartedly agree," Mary chimed in. "The Corner's report is in question and that is what's doing our boys in. I think that there is cause for some hope."

John looked at his watch. "Trial resumes in 15 minutes. If we want a seat, we'd better start getting back."

"Yeah, you're right," James agreed, standing up. "We'd better get moving."

Doc Cuthbert and Jimmy were speeding back to the trial at that very moment.

"If you can't sit through this without doing things to call attention to yourself, then you probably need to stay home," he scolded his son about his unexpected trip to the bathroom.

"I'm okay," Jimmy told him.

"All we have to do is just keep our cool. this is not the first time a Corner's report has been questioned during a trial. I'm just surprised that all of this was going on and I had no idea. Toby never gave me a clue. For the life of me, I can't figure out what led them to even search for the other spot. My report was thorough in every detail. Something must have happened, unless, it was discovered purely by accident."

With his words hanging in the silence of the speeding car, they made their way toward the outskirts of Midway.

At five minutes past the hour, the pre-trial continued with the Judge lecturing the onlookers about proper conduct during the proceedings.

"This is a pre-trial, I remind you. I alone will make the determination based upon the facts presented, whether or not a jury trial will be necessary. I can conduct these hearings with you or without you. The choice is yours. If I have to clear the courtroom again for whatever reason, it will become a closed hearing from that point on. I've been lenient to a fault up to this point because a town like ours is not used to such sensational events as this. but I will not stand for any more disruptions in my court. I hope I'm understood." He then nodded to Harold to begin his case.

"Thank you, your honor," Harold said striding toward the witness stand. "The defense would now call Doctor Stanley Williams to the stand."

As Dr. Williams made his way through the courtroom, a sinking feeling went to the bottom of John Cuthbert's stomach. So this was their surprise! Stanley was a colleague of spotless reputation from a big city that he knew well. His credentials were unquestionable. John knew immediately that he would have to begin to cover his tracks. Nothing could be taken for granted from here on out. He glanced at John Stearns who stared at him intently but without expression. John did his best to appear indifferent.

After Dr. Williams was duly sworn and seated, Harold asked the witness to state his name and occupation.

"Stanley Williams, Coroner for the City of Chattanooga, Tennessee, your next-door neighbor."

This brought some chuckles from the floor. Stanley Williams bore a remarkable resemblance to Mark Twain, the poet and writer. His thick heavy white mustache was badly in need of trimming but his thin, wiry frame exuded a strength that belied its slenderness. His brown suit was a size too large but was neatly pressed. He gave the appearance of a slightly eccentric but studious professor of mathematics. You knew he was a pipe-smoker by just looking at him.

"Doctor Williams, would you please tell the court why you were called to Midway," Harold asked him.

"Well," he began slowly, "Ol' Toby, I mean your Sheriff Toby Relliford, was one up on me, meaning I owed him a favor for helping me crack a case six years ago in Chattanooga."

Toby smiled.

"He called me some days ago to return the favor. Said that a legal Assistant here in Midway was working on some blood samples that he wanted me to examine myself."

"Is that Legal assistant present here today in this courtroom?" Harold asked. Stanley Williams stood up and carefully scanned the room until he saw Ralph near the back of the room and then sat down.

"Yesiree, that's him back there," he said pointing towards Ralph who stood up with a wide-toothed grin, waving.

"Thank you, Doctor," Harold acknowledged. "Now if you will, tell the court exactly what you did and where."

"Of course as you know, I did my examination at your office where that young man had his laboratory. Quite a nice setup for such a small room. Well, anyway, I examined the samples found in his lab as well as taking my own samples from the defendant's' car. My findings matched those of Mr. Simon's exactly."

"Are you aware that Mr. Simon's conclusion and your own are at odds with the Coroner's report here in Midway?"

"I am now," Stanley answered.

"Did you at any time know that the Corner, John Cuthbert, had already conducted an examination of the same specimens?"

"No, I did not. What the Sheriff did was to get a second opinion."

"Do you in any way feel compromised or taken advantage of by Sheriff Toby Relliford?"

"Quite the contrary. Toby came to my aid once and I simply returned the favor." Then looking at Toby, Stanley said aloud with a wink, "Now we're even."

Laughter broke out spontaneously in the courtroom. Even Judge McGill smiled faintly. When the noise died down, Harold continued his questioning.

"Now, Dr. Williams, you conducted two independent tests. One on the blood samples used by my assistant and one on samples taken from my clients' car. What were your findings of both?"

"Well, like I said. My analysis of Mr. Simon's work found no differences. But my analysis of the blood taken from the car in question produced one discrepancy."

"And what was that?"

"The time of death from those samples were the same as that of the samples I analyzed in your office."

"Then the blood on my clients' car and the blood found a the second accident site were one and the same. Correct?"

"That's correct. Absolutely!"

Harold then walked over to his table and retrieved a document file returning slowly to the witness. He held them before Stanley.

"Have you seen the Coroner's report on this case?"

"No."

"I have here a copy of Doc Cuthbert's analysis of the blood taken at the original site as well as those taken from the defendants' car. Will you examine them?"

"Sure," Stanley said taking the document offered to him. After several minutes of study, he handed them back.

"What's your conclusion?" he asked Stanley.

"They're the same."

"Now your examination of the same samples which I have here were found to be identical with the Coroner's findings here," Harold continued, "but with one exception, and that was the time of death. Is that correct?"

"Yes."

"In fact, Doctor Williams, did not your findings agree with Ralph Simon's and disagreed with Doctor Cuthbert's?"

"Yes."

"As an expert witness, then, the Coroner's report is in error about the time of death."

"I would say so. Yes."

"No further questions, your honor. The witness may be excused. Thank you Doctor," Harold said as Stanley Williams stepped down and made his way back to his seat amid muffled conversations and the flashing of bulbs from photographer's cameras. Harold then turned to Judge McGill.

"Your honor, I would like to submit these documents as Exhibit B for the court," he said handing the Judge the folder.

"Very well. You may call your next witness."

"The defense will now recall Doctor John Cuthbert to the stand."

John Stearns rose immediately to object.

"this is a hearing, not a trial. My client has already testified. Cross-examination is not in order."

Harold was quick to respond.

"You honor, this is not a cross-examination. The Defense would only like additional information from Doctor Cuthbert about the possibility of an error on his part or something that may shed some light on this problem."

"I'll permit the recall. Proceed," said the Judge.

"the Defense would now like to recall Doctor John Cuthbert."

After retaking the stand with an uneasy feeling of uncertainty, John prepared himself for the coming questions searching mentally for a way to alter his testimony without compromising his integrity or perjuring himself. In other words, he was looking for a good lie. Harold's question interrupted his thoughts.

"Doctor Cuthbert, is there anything in your autopsy report that you would like to change in light of the conflicting testimonies just given?"

"No."

"Nothing?"

"Nothing."

"Well, then, please tell the court how you account for the fact that a thoroughly trained Med student and a qualified medical examiner both disagree with your established time of death, while agreeing with every other aspect of your report's analysis."

"Objection!" shouted John Stearns. "Council is trying to bait the witness. How can he answer without mere speculation?"

"Objection overruled. Please answer the question, Dr. Cuthbert?"

"I can't. I made my decision based on my investigation."

Harold continued to press the issue.

"A difference, Doctor, of over 24 hours cannot be merely happenstance with a person of your qualifications. There must be an answer somewhere. Just help us to understand."

"The only possible thing that could have been an error on my part was in confusing the day I reported. You see, Sheriff Relliford called me on Monday, in the middle of the night and I wrote it down that night. I didn't do an autopsy, however, until early Wednesday because I was booked up with work the following day. It's possible that I wrote down Tuesday instead of Monday. That's all that I can think of."

As soon as he spoke, he instantly felt relief and surprise. His explanation was spontaneous and done on the spur of the moment, yet he knew that a better explanation could not have been found if he had thought about it beforehand. Anybody can make an innocent mistake.

"So, you admit that it is possible that your time of death recorded in your report could be in error."

"It's possible. Yes. It's the only thing that could have happened that will, as you say, shed some light on the discrepancies involved."

"I need to tell you, Doctor, that the actual time of death is most crucial here, as two lives are at stake. There can be no margin for error! Do you understand the severity of your mistake?"

"Objection! Objection," screamed John Stearns. "Council is leading the witness. Doctor Cuthbert didn't say he made a mistake. He only said that it was possible."

"Objection sustained. Mr. Steinmetz, please stick to the facts," Judge McGill cautioned him.

"I'm sorry, your honor. Let me rephrase my statement . . . Doctor Cuthbert, since you have admitted under oath that it is possible that your time of death could have been wrong, do you understand how that admission could effect the outcome of this case?"

"Objection," John countered again. "the witness is the County Corner not a trial lawyer."

"Sustained," the judge agreed.

Harold decided that it was time to go in another direction. He had established his point to his satisfaction. Any more such small victories for the Prosecution could prove damaging.

"Doctor, in your report, you said that the deceased was killed instantly at impact, did you not?"

"Yes."

"If that is the case, how then do you explain that the same blood of the victim was found in two places almost two miles apart?"

"Of course, I have no answer to that question. How could I?"

"I don't know, Doctor. You tell me. You did the report."

"Objection. Council is badgering," John Stearns begged.

This time Harold responded to his colleague. "Your Honor, I'm growing weary of my colleague's behavior. If I can't ask simple questions to try and understand how a man can be killed instantly in two different places, please tell me what I can do?"

"Objection overruled. Please continue."

"Doctor?" Harold asked.

"Of course he couldn't have been killed twice."

"Then, Doctor, can I assume from the facts thus far, that it is possible for Mr. Detmer to have been killed in one of two different locations?"

"That's reasonable, yes."

"If so, can I also assume that my clients could have been framed for this killing?"

John Stearns leaped to his feet at the same time that commotion was beginning to brew among the spectators. Judge McGill immediately restored order and called the attorneys before the bench. In hushed tones, he warned Harold that he was close to crossing over the line.

"You have gotten the technical information from the Coroner that you asked for and you can't ask him to speculate beyond that point. If you don't have any more medical information to obtain, I'm going to ask you to excuse the witness," he said firmly.

Harold conceded that he had gotten what he needed. He agreed to dismiss John Cuthbert. As the Coroner was dismissed, Harold knew that it was now time for Toby's testimony about his investigative search and his theory that led to the hunt for the original killing site. He had used Doc Cuthbert to introduce the feasibility of a possible frameup, but he almost went too far. When both attorneys had taken their stations, Harold called his next witness.

"The Defense now calls Sheriff Toby Relliford to the stand." Toby's reappearance on the witness stand, this time for the Defense caused a rush of excitement among the onlookers. Harold went back to his table and picked up another folder of papers and returned to the stand where Toby now sat. He handed the document to the Sheriff.

"Sheriff Relliford, would you please identify these documents to the court?"

Toby looked through the folders briefly. He returned them to Harold stating that they were the reports of his investigation of the accident in question.

"Your honor, I would like to submit these documents to the court marked as Exhibit C," he said handing the folder to Judge McGill. Harold then asked Toby to relate to the court the details of his investigation. The courtroom was held captive as he spoke.

"When did you first become suspicious that something was not right during your investigation?" Harold inquired.

"Well, when I didn't find a body at the scene that night and nothing was reported by anyone for over 36 hours following the accident, and then having a body mysteriously turn up at the site later, just didn't feel quite right to me."

Toby then went on to explain that once a body was found, he ran a check on the victim's belongings. Finding out that the man was a guest at the nearby lodge raised the question in his mind as to why he would have been walking so far from the lodge in the middle of the night.

"It just didn't make sense to me at all," he added.

He went on to tell about his visit to the lodge in search of some answers.

"I found out there from several witnesses who have sworn signed affidavits that the deceased was still at the lodge on the night of the defendants' accident. He was not discovered as missing until the next day."

This brought a low rumble of noise from the spectators in attendance. Then there was a stony hush. Harold asked Toby to continue.

"Now I was really becoming suspicious because the men at the lodge also told me that when Mr. Detmer, the deceased, was found missing, his car was also missing. Now, I had a corpse at the accident site over a day later and no sign of his car." Toby then explained that he next launched a search to find the dead man's vehicle.

"I was convinced that if I could just find it, it would offer some clues as to the man's whereabouts at the time he was killed."

"Sounds logical. Go on," Harold stated.

Toby then recounted how he and his deputies had combed the back roads leading into town on the assumption that maybe the man had been hunting and accidently ran into the path of the defendants' car.

"We finally found his car just outside of town next to the abandoned warehouse, at least a mile or more from where he was killed. Not only was he near Midway the night that he was killed, he was there a day or more after the defendants had first reported their accident. It was at this point that I was convinced of the boys' innocence."

"What happened after that to confirm your suspicions?" Harold asked him.

Toby then related how the search of the deceased's car revealed that the man had actually been walking towards town while intoxicated to get help to fix his flat tire.

"It's the only thing that made sense. Being that close to town with a flat,he certainly would not have been walking almost three miles back to the lodge and gotten killed on the way. It was at this point that I became convinced that Rod and Jeremy had become the victims of a frameup."

Harold then turned to the Judge.

"Your honor, it was at this point of the Sheriff's investigation that he proposed to me his hunch about an alternative site of the actual hit-and-run." Then turning back to Toby, he asked him to go on.

"My hunch was that the man was killed somewhere between his car and Midway. it was at this point, that Mr. Steinmetz informed me that he would get investigators to carry on the investigation from there. So, I withdrew at his request."

"Is there anything else that you might want to add Sheriff?" Harold asked.

"Just one thing," Toby noted. "Jeremy, while he was free on bail before his fight with Bobby McCallister had told me that he thought the blood on his car had been tampered with. When I checked it out myself, I found that he was correct. Someone had definitely messed with his car."

"Objection, your honor," demanded John Stearns, "No evidence has been presented that shows tampering of said vehicle. Such conclusions are speculative and inconclusive."

Judge McGill briefly scanned through the documents before him. Failing to find a reference of tampering, he told Harold that he was in agreement with the prosecution.

"Yes sir, your honor, I know. But because of the Sheriff discovering this, it leads us to another part of our investigation which I'm sure the court will be anxious to know about. However, because of the lateness of the hour, I respectfully request that we recess until tomorrow.

Judge McGill asked John Stearns if he had any objections. When there was none, he ordered a recess until the next morning.

That night around eight, Harold gathered his troops together in his office to map out the rest of his plans. Present in the tiny room was Harold, Ralph and Dick. Harold was concerned about wrapping up his case with nothing on Doc Cuthbert, Jimmy, Hank or Bobby but circumstantial evidence.

"We haven't caught them actually doing anything," he said. "No one saw the accident. We can't prove that Doc switched the blood samples on the boys' car but we can attempt to show inclination, opportunity and motive if somehow we can get his son, Jimmy, to implicate himself as a suspect."

"But how can we do that?" Ralph asked.

"I don't know," Harold admitted. "I called everyone together so that we could try and work out a plan of action to get our suspects to tip their hand. There must be something that we can come up with. The ball's in our court."

"Yeah, but what ball?" Dick muttered questionably to no one in particular.

"I'm going to call the rest of my witnesses tomorrow and try to wrap this thing up. We will present a strong enough case to establish a reasonable doubt about the guilt of Rod and Jeremy but that's no guarantee that the charges will be dismissed. We need something else just to be sure. Anything."

"Well, let's get busy," Ralph added.

Meanwhile, John Cuthbert sat in the living room of his home racking his brain feverishly trying to guess what this new line of evidence was that the defense would introduce tomorrow. He was convinced that whatever it was, it would be substantial. He had a new-found respect for this defense lawyer from New York, and ol' Toby had really fooled him. Toby had to suspect his involvement in this whole thing by now, he decided. This may help to explain why the Sheriff kept everything a secret from him.

In his haste to cover up his son's crime, the questions that plagued Toby never occurred to him. He never thought about why the man was out walking that night. At the time, it didn't appear to be important. He never thought about a car and that was the very thing which eventually led John to come up with the theory about the other accident site. John had to admit to himself that was ingenious on the Sheriff's behalf. Had it not been for that one, simple thing, there would have been no reason to doubt or second guess his report. John felt like kicking himself for his carelessness as he looked back over the whole thing. He had been an honest man all of his life and just did not possess a criminal mind. He now knew that his assumption that his report would never be challenged was in error. What he didn't know was that the only reason that his son was connected to what had happened was because of a telephone conversation overheard by, one, Beth McCallister. Yet, if she was not romantically linked to one of the young men involved in the affair, chances are that they might not have paid too much attention to that phone call.

About this same time, Toby was busy scurrying around the office making preparations to leave for the night. As he worked, his mood was upbeat. Jeremy had eaten real well that evening for the first time in days. He had just finished talking with him and they had both shared moments of subdued elation over the events at the trail earlier. There were signs of hope beginning to emerge which led to a marked change in Jeremy's outlook. At least, there was light at the end of the tunnel.

Toby wondered if he had omitted anything important during his testimony today. After a few moments of reflection, he decided that he had done okay. It was satisfying to know that his theory about what had actually happened that night had played an important role in the investigation. He sighed.

"Jake, I'm history," he called out to his Deputy. "See you in the morning."

"Okay, Sheriff," he yelled back from the rear office just as the phone rang.

Bobby McCallister, Hank Peters and Jimmy Cuthbert sat in Jimmy's car drinking beer and talking in the front yard of Hank's house. It was dark and they were alone. Hank was talking nervously.

"We're in trouble. They know more about that night than I ever dreamed they knew."

"Yeah, but not about us!" Bobby said emphatically.

Jimmy reassured them that they were in the clear. "Dad said that nothing that has happened has implicated any of us. They are building a circumstantial case. He also told me that anybody could make a mistake on a report and that was the only thing that the defense has actually proven. He told us not to worry."

Hank didn't buy it.

"if they found out about the real place that the guy was killed, they'll dig up something else."

"Like what?" Jimmy challenged him. "There's nothing at that place that can be traced to us. Nothing."

Hank and Bobby looked at each other. Jimmy was right. No one had seen anything. Jimmy's car had been fixed and they were not suspected anyway.

"Let's drink up and get some sleep," Bobby suggested. "We've got to get up early in the morning."

Harold's final thought that night as he prepared to turn in was centered on the importance of this presentation in a few hours. What he had accomplished so far was probably adequate to establish a lingering doubt as to the guilt of his clients but it was not a determinant. That is what troubled him. Everything hinged on producing other suspects to strengthen his case.

Every morning edition of the local news was devoured the next day. People stood in the street reading the events of the pretrial. On sidewalks, and in front of the stores, it was the conversation piece over the breakfast table and in the restaurants. A steady stream of people had already begun to make their way toward the courthouse over a half an hour before the doors opened.

Sarah, herself, had decided to attend the hearing this morning. As she gave her staff last—minute instructions about lunch, her ears never tuned out the conversations going on around her. Long ago, she had learned the art of listening while talking. Many of her customers were taking the defense counsel's arguments seriously for the first time since the hearing began. Could Doc Cuthbert be covering up something or had he simply made a mistake like he said? If the two boys didn't do it, who did? When Sarah finally arrived at the courthouse, she was lucky to get in.

Toby Relliford was the first witness to testify that morning. He was recalled to the stand to talk about one important part in the case that was overlooked initially—the missing shoe!

"Sheriff Relliford," Harold began, "in looking over the report of your investigation, I noticed something that troubles me. You stated that when the belongings of the deceased were brought to your office for investigation by the Coroner, one of his shoes was missing. Is that correct?"

"Yes."

"Why didn't you say anything about that yesterday in your testimony?"

"I just overlooked it, I guess. It didn't seem to be important at the time."

"It seems very odd to me that every single item of clothing from the deceased was accounted for except one of his shoes. Didn't that strike you as odd?"

"Yes, somewhat," Toby answered. "I asked Doc Cuthbert about it because he brought me all of the man's clothes but that."

"So, the Coroner was the one who rounded up everything. Isn't that your job?"

"Well, it could be," Toby began, "but since my investigators had photographed the scene, I just left everything else to Doc Cuthbert. He pretty much cleaned up the site after his examination. We had already finished our work."

"What did the Coroner say when you asked him about the missing shoe?"

"Not much really. He didn't seem too concerned, so neither was I," Toby lied.

"Isn't it true that often during the course of an investigation, the very thing that is overlooked, no matter how small or insignificant, can be the very thing that cracks a case?"

"Yes."

"Case in point. The victim's car. Isn't that what triggered your mind to look for an alternative explanation of what else could have happened in this case?"

"That's right," Toby answered.

"Couldn't the same apply to this shoe?"

"Yes, it could, but I don't see how," Toby answered.

"I hate to disagree with you Sheriff since I'm not an investigator but everything is important here," Harold scolded.

"Yessir," replied Toby.

"No further questions. You may step down. Thank you," Harold told him.

As Toby made his way back to his seat, Harold called his next witness. As Philip Martin, one of the three men who were at the lodge with Mr. Detmer, made his way to the stand, Harold noticed that John Cuthbert was busy whispering something to his son, Jimmy, who was sitting next to him. From the back of the room, this did not escape the eyes of Dick either as he looked on expectantly.

Unlike the first time that Toby first met Philip at the lodge dressed in hunting togs with a grizzled appearance and gruff demeanor, he was clean-shaven, dressed in a neat business suit and his thick brown mustache was neatly trimmed. He appeared to be a man in good physical condition. Harold questioned him at length about information Toby had written in his report and the sworn affidavit that he and two of his friends had signed in Toby's office. Everything that Toby had stated earlier about the dead man's time of disappearance was substantiated by Philip's testimony. As he testified, Jimmy Cuthbert turned around in his seat and motioned to Hank and Bobby McCallister. A few minutes later, he got up and left and was soon followed by the other two. No one paid any attention to their leaving except Dick. And, of course, Harold, who watched them out of the corner of his eye. It was not necessary for the other two men from the lodge to give their stories but Harold called them to the stand anyway in order to buy some time as well as to firmly establish the fact that the deceased could not have been missing at the time his clients had reported their accident. After interrogating the three men, Harold then turned his attention to Judge McGill.

"Your honor, I think that it has been clearly established by testimony and sworn affidavits that Mr. Detmer could not have been at the site of the accident where he was allegedly killed by my clients. To further substantiate this claim, the next witness that I intend to call will give us proof of what my clients actually killed that night when their car struck something in the road. I would now like to recall to the stand, my medical assistant, Ralph Simon."

The courtroom once again came alive with conversation and activity. Judge McGill looked on intently as Harold once again handed him a series of documents for exhibit. After Ralph had retaken the stand, Harold began.

"Your honor, earlier, this man's investigation of the blood samples taken from a place different than the one of the initial site and validated by an outside medical examiner to be one and the same at both locations, did his own research of the original location and has uncovered conclusive evidence that my clients, indeed, did not kill Mr. Detmer."

This led to a temporary disruption in the courtroom that the Judge quickly halted. He instructed the bailiff and both attorneys that there would be a 15-minute recess while he examined the new report in his chambers. He then left the courtroom immediately. The courtroom transformed into one ball of noise and activity which was held somewhat in check by the bailiff and security guards. Harold, meanwhile, conferred with his two clients at the table where they were seated.

"I know that all of this is a complete surprise to both of you but we had to keep our investigation a complete secret so that there wouldn't be any leaks."

"What did Ralph find back there?" Jeremy asked wide-eyed. Rodney sat looking disbelievingly.

"You boys killed a deer. You didn't find him because he didn't die immediately. He ran off a little way into the thickets. Since it was so dark out there, nobody found him until days later. Because of Sheriff Relliford's theory that the man had to have been killed somewhere else, we knew that there must be something else back there that you two had hit."

"Wow," was all Rod could utter.

"Where does this leave us now?" Jeremy asked.

"I don't know," confessed Harold, "but in a lot better shape than you were before. At least now, there's room for reasonable doubt. Ralph's testimony will establish that I hope." Rod and Jeremy looked hopefully at each other.

"But if we didn't kill him, who did?" Rod asked Harold.

"We don't know, but we have some suspects. Hopefully we can implicate somebody before the day's out. We're working on that right now.

Doc Cuthbert was beginning to look pale as he sat watching and listening to everything going on around him. The place was like a bee hive. For the first time since he had covered up his son's accident, he began to worry. His stomach was in turmoil and he took a couple of antacids to calm the storm churning inside. He was still confident that although things seemed to be falling apart, he and his son were not suspected of anything foul. Even if the two outsiders were found innocent, no one knew who was guilty of this, he was certain. Still uneasiness stole over him. There was no telling what this New York attorney would spring next. Then a cold chill hit him! He suddenly realized that if the next witness could convincingly show the Judge that the deer was what the two boys had really killed, the next logical step would be to show tampering of the suspect's car. That thought caused him to shudder visibly.

For a moment he panicked. No one would ever suspect him, he thought. He had left no clues whatsoever when he had switched the blood that night. Anybody could have done that. All he had to do was stick to his story. He breathed a sigh of relief just as Judge McGill reentered the courtroom. As soon as he was seated, Harold resumed matters by recalling Ralph.

After identifying himself again, briefly, Ralph recounted the events of his findings. He began by stating that the Sheriff had officially opened up the location to himself and Dick to do a further investigation of the area at the request of the defense counsel. As he put it, "Everything was done legally." He went on to explain that the search was the logical thing to do since the man couldn't have died in two different places.

"We knew that the blood on the car had to come from something. So Dick and myself went over the area with a fine-tooth comb. When we found the dead animal, Dick marked the area and took a series of photographs depicting the carcass and the exact geographical location. Those photos are a part of my report, your honor," he said looking at Judge McGill nervously.

The Judge simply nodded, smiling.

"I've examined the evidence, young man," he said reassuringly, "your testimony is credible. Continue."

Well, we, then, notified the Sheriff who subsequently came out and gave us permission to bring the carcass back to the lab for analysis."

John Stearns interrupted at that point.

"Your honor, I object. That privilege should have been the domain of the Coroner who is the official examiner involved here. I question their protocol." John knew that this was a wild shot in the dark.

"Your honor, I beg to differ," countered Harold. "The Coroner's jurisdiction lay only in the examination of the deceased at the site. Mr. Simon's examination of the animal was totally separate and distinct from the Coroner's autopsy report."

"Objection overruled." Ralph continued.

"Upon examining the remains, conclusive evidence showed that the deer had died from massive internal wounds and bleeding which were the direct result of being struck by a large moving object."

"Could the animal have been shot and killed?" Harold asked.

"We found no trace of a bullet. However, a lot of the carcass had been eaten by predators."

"Could those predators have eaten the bullet along with the missing parts?" Harold asked.

"It's possible. But a bullet could not have crushed several ribs and broken the hind quarters. The animal had dragged himself hundreds of feet before he collapsed and died."

"How do you know this?"

"We followed the trail of blood from the location of where he was struck. We photographed that as well," he added looking at the Judge who nodded once again.

"Where was the deer struck?" Harold queried.

"About 20 feet from where the deceased man was struck. We found the animal's blood that far from his."

"So, there were two pools of blood at the scene instead of just one."

"That's correct."

John Cuthbert cursed silently to himself. He had worked in total darkness that night and had never thought in his haste to look for other blood trails. That was a big mistake. If only he had had more time before daybreak that night! Still, he reflected, even after he had submitted his report to the Sheriff, the thought had not occurred to him then. His thoughts were broken by Harold and a voice telling Ralph to continue.

"After a thorough analysis of the carcass, the blood of the animal showed that it died approximately the same time that the Sheriff's accident report had indicated.

"Approximately?"

"Well, yes. There was a difference of an hour or so. That was probably due to the fact that the animal was not instantly killed."

"So then, your two reports would show that the times of death of both the deceased and the animal were different?"

"Absolutely. At least by the same amount of time shown between Mr. Detmer's death and the accident report. Approximately 26 hours or so."

"Now let me go back a little," Harold requested. "You have shown a day or so difference in the time of death of the deceased in the Coroner's Report and that of your report, and now your finding further suggests that the deer was killed at or about the same time that the defendants first reported their accident?"

"Yes."

"So then, we can conclude that the deer died at or near the time that the defendants reported their accident and Mr. Detmer did not?"

"That's my findings. Yes."

It took Judge McGill several moments to restore order in the courtroom. He then told Harold to continue.

"If that's true, Mr. Simon, how can you explain Mr. Detmer's body being found at the scene a day later, the time that you found he actually died and which has already been verified by Doctor Stanley Williams?"

"I can't. I know only that he couldn't have been there at the time that the defendants hit that animal."

"How do you know? Tell us again, please," Harold demanded.

"Simply because he died a day earlier."

"Where, Mr. Simon. Where?" Harold repeated.

"I don't know. But not there."

"Why do you say that so assuredly?" Harold pressed.

"Because I also found his blood at another location as well," Ralph answered boldly. Harold then turned his attention to Judge McGill with Ralph still on the stand.

"Your honor, with the testimony that we have just heard, I'm convinced that something stinks here. Mr. Detmer died at least a day later than my client's report of an accident. A deer was found later, dead at the scene that died about the same time of their report to the Sheriff. The dead man's blood was unexplainably found also a mile or so closer to town. He couldn't have died twice.

"What are you suggesting, counselor?" the Judge asked him.

"My clients struck and killed a deer that night. Not finding his body, they reported the incident to the Sheriff who rightly impounded their auto. While the auto was being held, somebody hit and killed Mr. Detmer the next day. Knowing that an accident had already been reported, they took his body to where the defendants had killed the deer and placed him there. Because of where the Sheriff found the deceased man's car and the fact that his blood was also found not far from it, all evidence points to the fact that he was killed there and later transported to the other location."

John Stearns objected profusely.

"That's pure conjecture counsel and you know it," he shouted above the noise. Harold challenged him.

"Then Mr. Prosecutor, you explain how a dead man's body can be in two different places and also die two different times?" he blurted out savagely. John failed to respond. Judge McGill then asked Harold to explain why the defendants' car had human blood on it and not that of the deer's.

"Because someone changed them, your honor. Whoever killed Mr. Detmer put his blood on their car after washing off the animal's blood. My clients were framed pure and simple."

"That's yet to be proven," the Judge corrected him. "Nevertheless, it does raise some interesting questions. Assuming that you are correct, who could have known about the accident? The Sheriff's report stated that it was held confidential until after the autopsy which was not completed until late the following day. The body would have had to be moved prior to that because immediately following the Coroner's report, the Sheriff and his deputy went back and discovered the corpse."

"That's a mystery all right," Harold admitted, "but I think maybe the Sheriff can help us here." He dismissed Ralph from the stand who had sat passively through all this and recalled Toby to the stand. Toby then told the court why he had to suspend Deputy Willie Joe.

"So before the accident was officially released, it had already been let out of the bag so to speak?" he asked Toby.

"That's right."

"Was this prior to the autopsy?"

"Yes."

Then I guess that explains how the guilty party or parties could have found out. Thank you Sheriff," Harold said dismissing Toby from the stand.

As Toby stepped down, John Cuthbert had another chilling revelation. Toby, Harold Steinmetz and his staff had known all along that Mr. Detmer was not killed at the time and place in question. That could only mean one thing—the missing shoe was used as bait. He had been baited! Now that all of this had come out, they had to have suspected his involvement somehow all along. He nearly fainted when he remembered that at this very moment, his son and the other two were down at the creek to get the missing shoe and dispose of it. He had been certain that the defense would try and find it by possibly even dragging the creek in order to prove that the man was killed there. He had thought that the shoe was their only hope! He had not known at the time about the deer being found. Now the first time, stark fear washed over him like water cascading over a broken dam.

He was so wrapped up in his thoughts, that when he paid attention to what was going on at the hearing, he had missed much of Stanley's testimony about how it would have been possible for someone to tamper with the vehicles on his property.

"Even though our vehicles are locked up in the yard, there's no guard dogs or alarm system if someone either climbs over or cuts their way through the fence. Since it wasn't cut, somebody could have climbed over," he was concluding.

Just as Harold was finishing his questions with Stanley, he noticed that the Sheriff's Deputy had come in and was beckoning to him. The trap had been sprung! He dismissed his witness and asked for a moment to confer with his staff. He returned shortly to the bench.

"Your honor, we have just been informed of a new and startling development in this case that will give the defense information concerning possible suspects in the death of Mr. Detmer." All hell broke loose.

Chapter Eight

Continuations

Jimmy, Bobby and Hank were free on bail within an hour of the recessed hearing. They had been charged with tampering with court evidence. The pretrial was scheduled to resume at ten the next morning. They had been caught red-handed by two of the Sheriff's deputies fishing the missing shoe from the creek. The deputies had been instructed by Toby to stake out the area, undercover, and to apprehend anyone taking anything out of the water.

Toby had no idea that Harold, Ralph and Dick had plotted the scheme the night before. As he sat at his desk sipping a hot cup of coffee, he smiled to himself. He had to take his hat off to Harold and his boys. He had sat through the entire proceedings that afternoon and had no idea what was being done. Looking back now, he marveled at how Harold had baited the trap. He didn't understand at the time why the attorney had made such an issue over the missing shoe while he was on the stand. But what strategy! Right after introducing Ralph's findings at the real scene of the crime which came as a total shock to everyone, Harold then brought up the issue of the missing shoe as being the clue that could unravel the mystery as to what had actually happened. He shook his head in wonder. He was glad that he was on the right side of the law and didn't have to have this man hunting him. He was an amazing man, Toby had to admit.

John Stearns had accompanied John Cuthbert to the office earlier to make arrangements for the release of the Coroner's son and the two others. He had looked subdued and drawn. Unlike the sure and confident prosecutor, he had always known. He looked almost beaten. Almost. He knew John. He would always come out swinging but he was now on the ropes.

Sarah failed to get into the courtroom this next morning. Like everyone else, she had gotten there at least an hour early but even then she was too late. Reluctantly, she slowly made her way back to the restaurant as the spectators standing in line were let in one by one in the order that they had lined up. With less than half of the people waiting in line allowed in, the door to the courthouse was closed.

Inside the crowded courtroom, Harold was preparing to resume his presentation for the defense. because no formal charges involving the case were filed against Jimmy, Bobby and Hank, other than tampering with court evidence, a misdemeanor, the Judge was going to allow Harold to question the three. John Stearns had failed to block the defense from questioning them about the tampering, much to the chagrin of John Cuthbert. Now as they both looked on, Jimmy was on the witness stand, looking scared and alone.

"Mr. Cuthbert," Harold began, "are you related in any way to the County Coroner, Dr.John Cuthbert?"

"Yes, He's my father," Jimmy answered haltingly.

"Oh, I see," Harold said pausing purposely.

"Would you please convey to the court, why you were apprehended by the Sheriff's deputies yesterday, along with Hank Peters and Bobby McCallister?"

There was as long pause by Jimmy which only accentuated the hush that had fallen over the room. His eyes darted nervously about the room and he ran his fingers nervously through his hair. When he finally spoke, his voice was barely audible and Harold asked him to speak louder. He laughed to himself quietly in a nervous attempt to appear casual as he spoke up.

"Me, Hank and Bobby were just horsing around yesterday down by the creek. We didn't have nothing else to do. We certainly didn't know at the time that the area was under the protection of the Sheriff's department. We were just wading around and having fun.

"Didn't it occur to you that the creek was only a stone's throw from where the blood of the victim was found?"

"No."

"Weren't you, Bobby and Hank at the hearing yesterday when all of this was revealed?"

"Well, yes, but we didn't associate that with the creek. We didn't see any connection."

"I noticed that the three of you left together yesterday during the trial. Why did you do that?"

John Stearns objected immediately holding that the question was irrelevant. His objection was sustained. Harold apologized to the Judge stating that he had thought it was a little unusual for the three to get up and leave together and then later be caught tampering with court evidence.

"Why were you taken into custody, then?" he continued.

"Because of a stupid old shoe that we found down there," he answered defiantly. "Can you believe that?" he added looking mockingly at Harold.

"No, I don't find that stupid at all," he countered, "especially when the three of you left the courtroom yesterday only minutes after hearing about the missing shoe of the deceased."

"Objection!" John cried. "Counsel is leading the witness. Mr. Cuthbert is not on trial here. What is the defense insinuating here?" Harold interrupted.

"Your honor, I wish to beg the indulgence of the court at this point. Before I'm finished here this morning, I hope to furnish you with proof that the three men who were caught fishing Mr. Detmer's shoe from the creek had more than just a fleeting curiosity."

"Okay Mr. Steinmetz, I'll be patient for a reasonable period of time. But, please keep in mind that these three are not currently suspects in this case. Proceed."

Harold breathed a sigh of relief.

"Thank you your honor . . . Now, Mr. Cuthbert, you have stated and I quote, 'The three of you were just horsing around down at the creek', is that right?"

"that's right."

"Nothing else?"

"No."

"Where were you on the night of August 19th around one in the morning?"

Jimmy looked up at the ceiling for a moment and rubbed his chin thoughtfully.

"The 19th . . . hmm . . ."

"Yes, the day before your father performed the autopsy of the deceased," Harold clarified for him.

"I'm not sure, but I think that I was with Hank and Bobby," he answered.

"And what were the three of you doing around one or two that morning?"

"We are at The Silver Dollar having a few beers."

"A few beers . . . I see. In reality, you three had more than just a few beers, didn't you? In fact, weren't you all drunk?"

"Objection," complained John Stearns.

"Denied," Judge McGill answered.

Jimmy fidgeted back and forth in his seat. Harold repeated his question.

"No we weren't drunk," Jimmy challenged. "We were just a little high, that's all."

"Remember, Mr. Cuthbert, you're under oath to tell the truth. I have a witness that I can call to verify the fact that you were so intoxicated that your drinks were cut off and the three of you were asked to leave. Do I have to put him on the stand or will you stop before you perjure yourself?" Harold threatened.

"That's not necessary," Jimmy conceded. "We were asked to leave because the bartender felt that we were a little out of control. We were arguing about something that I can't remember what it was."

"Why didn't you just calm down when he asked you to?"

"I got mad about something, that's all," Jimmy repeated.

"Didn't you in fact tell him that he knew where he could put his bar and that you didn't need him and his kind?"

"I could have. I don't remember."

That doesn't sound like a sober statement to me,"Harold added, "especially when he was looking out for your better interest."

"He was bugging me," Jimmy said acidly.

"What did the three of you do after you were thrown out of The Silver Dollar?"

"We weren't thrown out. We were asked to leave."

"Okay . . . after you left, what did you do then?"

"We just drove home. I dropped them off."

"What time was that?"

"About one thirty or two, I guess."

"And you went straight home?"

"That's right."

"Mr. Cuthbert, if you drove the others straight home right after leaving The Silver Dollar around two that morning, how do you explain the fact that Bobby McCallister did not get home until around three thirty, an hour and a half later?"

Jimmy was caught off guard. He was not prepared for this question. He panicked momentarily.

"Mr. Cuthbert? I'm waiting," Harold pressed.

"I don't know," Jimmy stammered. "Who told you that?"

"He woke up his sister, Beth, at around that time. He was drunk and woke her up as he stumbled to his room which is down the hall past his sister's."

"Maybe he didn't go right in after I dropped him off."

"Now, why would anyone sit in front of his house for an hour and a half at two in the morning, Mr. Cuthbert? Come on, now. The court's not that naive."

"Objection. How can the witness answer for someone else?" John Stearns asked.

"Sustained," agreed the Judge.

Harold had no more questions for Jimmy. He then later proceeded to call Bobby and Hank to the stand. They both told the same story as Jimmy, that they had gone straight home after they had left the night club.

"Maybe my sister was wrong about the time," Bobby had suggested.

Harold then called the parents of both Hank and Bobby to testify as to the time that their sons came in that morning. Neither could be sure, because their boys had their own door keys and they were asleep at the time. Harold wanted to establish the fact to the court that the hour and a half was crucial to account for. He pleaded this point to Judge McGill.

"Your honor, the hour and a half in question is critical in this case because it is the actual time that Mr. Detmer was killed. The evidence submitted has shown that. The Coroner has even admitted that he could have recorded the wrong day but not the time on his report. Both his established time of death and that of my assistant correspond. Therefore, the times between two and four that morning hold the key to this case. Now, the three young men who just testified were up and around about those hours. The only proof that is available about the actual time that they got home is from a witness who doesn't want to take the stand against her own brother, which I can understand. But before I'm finished, I'll prove to you and this court that the three of them are lying about their whereabouts that morning after they left the bar. May I approach the bench, your honor?"

Judge McGill consented. After a brief whispered exchange, the Judge announced that following the next witness by the defense, that the court would be in recess until the next morning. Dick Wingate was the next to be called. After he was duly sworn in, Harold questioned him.

"Mr. Wingate, would you please tell this court why you are here and what are your qualifications as my investigative assistant."

"I am a classmate of the defendants in question and I was summoned here by Mr. Steinmetz's New York office, along with Ralph there," he said pointing to his classmate.

"I will graduate after the upcoming semester with a degree in Criminal Investigation. I have already been hired by the FBI pending graduation."

Dick then proceeded to tell how Jimmy, Hank and Bobby became suspects in this case, based upon his studies of the Sheriff's investigative report.

"Actually, Bobby's sister was the first to suspect that somehow they were involved in this case, or at least knew something about it. Based upon that lead, I put them under around-the-clock surveillance. I watched the three of them rendezvous several times at each other's homes following the homicide."

"How long did this surveillance go on?" Harold asked.

"A day or so," he answered.

"Did this lead to anything that could be used as evidence in this case?" "Yes, sir. It sure did!" He said emphatically.

There was a distinct break in the silence of the courtroom. Judge McGill quickly brought it under control as Dick continued.

"After Sheriff Relliford came up with the theory about where the man was actually killed, and with Ralph's work at the alternate site, I changed my course of investigation."

"How so?" Harold quizzed.

"Well, in most cases, the criminal will always return to the scene of the crime if he thinks that there is a good enough reason and if he can do it and not get caught. I waited for them to show up."

"Where was this place you're talking about?"

"The creek where they were apprehended."

Again the room became full of noise. Judge McGill immediately intervened.

"What made you so sure that they would go back there?" Harold led him to explain.

"Initially, the Sheriff informed the Coroner that he was puzzled as to why everything of the victim was accounted for except the one shoe. When I radioed to check in with the Sheriff, he told me that he had talked with the Corner earlier about the shoe because I had asked him to earlier."

"What happened next?" Harold asked.

"Well, a couple of hours later, Jimmy picked up the other two. I followed at a distance until I knew where they were headed. I beat them to the creek site and hid my car in the woods off the road. Hiding in the bushes, I took several photographs with a telephoto lens of them searching the area, finding an object, and throwing it in the creek."

"What was it they found?" Harold quizzed.

"I couldn't make it out from where I was at the time, but when I developed the pictures and blew them up, it was the shoe of Mr. Detmer."

The bailiff had to restrain Jimmy Cuthbert who had jumped up out of his seat screaming "Lie . . . lie." It appeared as though he was attempting to climb the railing separating the onlookers from the trail floor. His outburst this time was an isolated event as the rest of the crowd looked on in stunned silence. When order was restored, Harold handed the Judge a large manila envelope containing the photographs and some notes written by Dick. After looking at the information handed him, he nodded for Harold to continue. Harold turned back to Dick.

"What happened after that?"

"Well, I knew then that there was as connection in this case between the Coroner, his son and the other two. It was more than pure coincidence that the shoe was disposed of immediately after the Coroner was told about it."

"So what did you do then?"

"I called Mr Steinmetz, Ralph and Deputy Jake Sharpod together with myself and planned a way to get the three to implicate themselves in the crime. Our plan was to bring up the subject of the shoe again in court, hoping that they would once again return to the scene. Yesterday, they did and were caught."

John Stearns objected immediately, claiming that the throwing of the shoe into the creek and its retrieval was inconclusive for implicating the three with the actual crime. The Judge, however, countered his objection by stating that the actions of the three were highly unusual and would not have occurred in the manner that they did without sufficient motivation.

"I will give the defense every opportunity to bring this mystery to a conclusion. If there are no further questions of this witness, I will call the court to recess until tomorrow morning." He looked at Harold.

"No further questions, your honor."

"We are recessed then until tomorrow," he answered, leaving the bench immediately and disappearing through the back door.

John Cuthbert lay awake that night unable to sleep. The sound of a distant train rumbling over the tracks at a high rate of speed, periodically sounding its horn of warning was the only noise that broke the night's silence. He had tried in vain to force himself to fall asleep, but the harder he tried, the more awake he became. Finally he simply gave up the struggle. His world was coming apart piece-by-piece. All of the sweat, sacrifices and years of hard work now appeared to be for naught. He knew that the noose was closing rapidly around his neck. His stomach churned and gurgled audibly. He was afraid that the sounds would awaken his wife, so he carefully stole out of bed and went downstairs to fix a pot of coffee.

As the coffee perked, the only light he turned on was the dim one over the stove. He sat at the dinette table in darkness alone with himself. A tear crept into the corner of one eye. He was not feeling sorry for himself, he was beyond that, but he was regretting what he had done. During the trial, he had become painfully aware of the life and death struggle of those two innocent boys being waged by their attorney. He had been able to live with himself these past several weeks only by not allowing himself to think about what his actions had done to them. His concern was not even for himself, but for his boy. He had been so busy double-checking behind himself that he gave everything else little thought. His work occupied the rest of his time, so he was able to survive.

Watching the faces of the two boys' parents during the hearing was enough to break through his own callousness and indifference. He realized then for the first time that they loved their children as much, if not more, than he loved his own. What right did he have putting them through such torture and agony? He realized more now than ever before, that no matter how intelligent, competent, or well-trained one might be, in a crisis our emotions push common logic aside. By and large, we are emotional creatures. When you look at the ills of mankind, such as crimes, prejudices, dislikes and the sort, most of them are based on emotional responses. The sad part of it all is that too often, we don't even understand our own emotions. We just act,spurred on by some unknown source.

What he had done was purely irrational. He knew that now. At the same time, he also knew that he had gone too far to turn back now. He was not afraid for himself. He had lived most of his life and had enjoyed many of the fruits of success sand security. His family was well-provided for and he found comfort in that fact, yet if one cannot be at peace with himself, what is it all really worth in the end? If only he hadn't panicked that night and simply took the blame for Jimmy by turning himself in, things would be different. He would gladly have traded places with his son. If only he had thought of that then! Unfortunately, he hadn't and now he was living to regret it.

As he was buried deep in his thoughts, he was jarred back to reality by the sound of rushed movements in the next room. He sprang to his feet and rushed into the dark living room. Before he could find the light switch, a shadow rushed by him to the front door.

"Jimmy? What the hell's going on?" he barked, finding the switch and instantly flooding the room with light. His son was trying to unhook the safety latch when John grabbed him.

"Let me go, Dad. I thought you were in bed," Jimmy demanded.

"The hell I will. Keep your voice down before you wake up your mother . . . now where do you think you're going at this time of the night?"

"I'm leaving . . . gettin' outta here. They know, Dad . . . they know!" he exclaimed. "I don't want to be locked up. I didn't mean to do it . . . I didn't!"

He struggled to free himself from his father's grip. John was startled by his son's strength and had to use all of his might to restrain him. Just then, his wife came down the stairs gathering her housecoat around her.

"John . . . what's wrong? . . . Jimmy?"

"It's nothing, Martha. Just Jimmy and his drinking again," he lied. "Go on back to bed, I'll talk to him outside," he said, shoving his son out of the door and onto the dark porch. Jimmy began to cry at this point as his father forced him to sit down in the porch swing.

"I'm scared, Dad," he sobbed.

"Where were you going?"

"I don't know. I was going to call you later."

"Running is an out and out admission of guilt. That's the best way in the world to hang yourself."

As he spoke, he instantly heard the echo of his words. Again, he had reacted just as before—protecting his son at all cost. He winced as he continued, nonetheless.

"Look. They still have nothing to pin on you. So they caught you, Bobby and Hank tampering with the dead man's shoe. That's bad, but it still doesn't answer their question. The burden of proof is with them, not us. All we have to do is stick with our stories. They want you to panic and do something foolish. We made one mistake with the shoe already, let's not make another."

He got up and walked to the edge of the porch, his mind racing. He reminded his son that nobody had actually seen what had happened.

"They'll only know if we tell them. Look, the evidence by the defense is pretty strong in favor of the two boys. They'll probably succeed in having the charges dismissed against them. At least they'll go free, so there's no need to give yourself up now. The man died accidentally. It's not like you murdered him or something. Giving yourself away now won't bring him back . . . will it?"

"I guess not," Jimmy muttered, drying his eyes.

"Let's just see where things go. I just wish I knew who their witness will be tomorrow . . ." he finished, his voice trailing off into the night. He was glad that he had talked to Hank and Bobby earlier because they were coming apart too. Since they were not the ones driving that night, their anxiety was not as acute as Jimmy's but they needed to be reassured as well. He had told both of them not to change their stories for any reason. If he was recalled to the stand again, he knew what he had to do.

The courtroom was abuzz that morning as Harold called his surprise witness.

"The defense now calls Mrs. Katrina Miller to the stand."

John Cuthbert and his son's mouths dropped open at the same time. How did they find her?! My god! John gasped. This was a total shock. As the shapely body shop owner made her way to the stand, Harold noticed the look of surprise on their faces and faintly smiled with satisfaction. When she was duly sworn, crossing her shapely legs, he began his quest.

"Mrs. Miller, are you the owner of Katrina's Body and Fender Shop in Chattanooga?"

"Yes, I am."

"On the 20th day of August, did your garage service the vehicle of one Jimmy Cuthbert?"

"Yes."

"Please tell the court exactly what was done."

She proceeded to hand Harold a work order who, in turn, handed it to Judge McGill.

"Well, it was very minor damage compared to what we usually handle. But when his father called me, he said that it was urgent that it be fixed as soon as possible. I have done work for him before, as well as for the Sheriff here in Midway."

"Exactly what was the damage?"

"The left front fender was dented pretty good and the headlight was busted."

"Is that all?"

"Yes. Otherwise, the care was in good shape. Now the van from Midway that came in later was a different story. That was more in our line of work."

"Thank you, Mrs. Miller, that is all." As she made her way back to her seat, every man's eye in the room followed her every move,, including Ralph's. She sure looked a lot different in as dress than in those baggy overalls, he noted.

"Your honor," Harold said turning his attention to the Judge. "The next day after the established time of death of the deceased, Doctor John Cuthbert made an appointment in Chattanooga to have his son's car fixed to repair a damaged front fender. Keep in mind, this was the same vehicle that was driven that very same night that the deceased man was struck and killed. It is also highly probable that the same vehicle was on the road much later than the time that its three occupants claimed they were at home. Now what is even more mystifying, is that all of this took place before Doc Cuthbert even performed the autopsy on Mr. Detmer. It just doesn't make sense to me that a man in his position would be more excited about getting a dented fender fixed than examining blood on a vehicle that was involved in an accident!"

Needless to say, the response in the room to Harold's words was predictable indeed. Shouting over the noise, Harold called for John Cuthbert to retake the stand. When the Coroner's name was heard around the room, it became instantly quiet. The Judge didn't even have to wield his gavel.

"Thank you, counselor," he told Harold grimly.

John was visibly shaken but did a good job of gathering himself as he stood. When John was seated, Harold attacked him vigorously.

"Doctor, a few hours before you telephoned Chattanooga about your son's car, you were in the Sheriff's office weren't you? At about five thirty in the morning to be exact?"

"Yes."

"Wasn't it still dark at that time?"

"yes."

"What were you doing at the Sheriff's office when everybody else was asleep?"

John Stearns objected to the question as being irrelevant. His motion was denied.

"I was behind in my work and wanted to get an early start that day because I knew the Sheriff was getting impatient about my examining the car."

"What did that have to do with the Sheriff's office?"

"I wanted to get some information about the reported accident so that I could have some idea as to what had happened."

"Was that absolutely necessary in order to examine the impounded vehicle," Harold demanded.

"No. Not absolutely."

"Then why did you do it at such an ungodly hour?"

"I just told you. I got an early start. I knew that I had to wait until daylight to examine the car, so I just made good use of the time until then."

"What kind of information were you looking for, Doctor?"

"Speed at impact, that sort of thing in order for me to make a proper assessment."

"What about the time of the accident. The exact location. Weren't they important as well?"

"Yes."

"But, you didn't mention those. Why?"

"It's obvious that those things were important too. They're a given."

"No, Doctor," shouted Harold a vein rising on his forehead. "They were the very reasons why you visited the Sheriff's office that morning! Just hours before your visit, your son, Jimmy, and his two pals were out driving dead drunk and ran over Mr. Detmer. They didn't dare call the Sheriff, so they called you. You then went out to the site and put the dead man into the trunk of your car and drove to the Sheriff's office to find out the exact location and time of the accident. Sheriff Relliford had already told you about it, so you were the only one who knew."

John interrupted Harold angrily.

"I wasn't the only one who knew about the accident. Deputy Willie joe told the whole town," he shot back.

"No sir! No Sir!" countered Harold, "That didn't happen until that night, not that morning. At that time, no one knew about the killing except you. No, you needed that information to stash the body where the defendant's had reported their accident. Deputy Jake and the Sheriff didn't suspect anything when you came by that morning because at that time there was no body."

"That's absurd," John barked.

"Is it? What did you do next?" Harold challenged more than he asked. "After you got the information from the Sheriff's file that you needed, the next thing you had to do was dump the body at the site. Once that was done, you had to beat it back to Stan's and change the blood on the defendant's car with that of the victim's. You had to work fast, didn't you, because daylight was approaching. You made just two mistakes, Doctor! In your haste that night, you missed one of the victim's shoes and we used that missing shoe to trap all of you. The second mistake you made was in sending your son to Katrina's Body Shop in Chattanooga the very next morning with a rush order to fix the car as soon as possible. A dented fender is not an emergency unless you're trying to hide something."

Doc Cuthbert sat back in his chair and stared expressionless at Harold.

"All of that makes a neat little story, but it doesn't prove a thing. Nothing you've said contains as shred of truth," John replied.

"Oh, about the blood on the vehicle that was switched. The very next day after you completed your examination of the vehicle, both the Sheriff and Jeremy McCutchin noticed that the blood on the car had been altered in some fashion. But they didn't know by whom. You say that all of this is absurd, huh! answer another question for me. Since the evidence presented here in this court has proven that Mr. Detmer probably did not die at the site of the defendant's accident, nor even on the same day, but rather they had struck and killed a deer instead, how then is it possible for you to have examined human blood on that vehicle?"

"You've got all the answers, suppose you tell me," John answered beleagueredly.

"I'll do just that, Doctor. Whoever examined the impounded car, had to have had the body containing the victim's blood. He had to be an expert in this field because every trace of the original blood was removed and replaced with new blood. Since no one had cut through the fence at Stan's, the human blood had to have been carried in by the perpetrator in storage vials that only a professional would have access to. Wouldn't you agree?" he asked John.

"I don't know how who did what." he murmured.

"Who else could have done it, Doctor? Let's look at the facts. If someone other than your son had killed Mr. Detmer besides the Sheriff, he, his deputies or you, how could they have known enough to frame my clients that morning?"

"I don't know."

"Only you and they knew about the reported accident Doctor. The incident was so new that you hadn't even checked the car yet. It couldn't have been anyone else but you, the Sheriff, or one of his deputies. Now isn't it ironic that the very same day you send your son out of town to have his car fixed, is the same day that you examined the car in question. Coincidence, Doctor?"

John said nothing. He dared not.

"Do you actually expect the court to believe that all of these occurrences involving two different places where the same blood was found, an apparent mistake in your autopsy report, the switching of blood on the defendant's car, your son's damaged auto and his tampering not once, but twice with the victim's only missing piece of clothing is all merely coincidental?"

Again John said nothing.

"I assume by your silence, then, that you agree with me?"

"No., I don't," John said evenly, "I just don't have anything else to say."

"Very well," Harold told him, "you may step down."

Having dismissed John Cuthbert from the stand, Harold informed the Judge that he was now prepared to give his closing argument. Judge McGill consented to his request. Ralph, Dick, Rodney, Jeremy, their parents, Andrea, Beth, Toby, and everyone including Sarah, crossed their fingers and held their breath as he began.

"Your honor, with all due respect to the distinguished prosecutor, John Stearns, the case against my clients has not been established. Everything they presented rested solely upon the accuracy and credibility of the Coroner's report which we have proven by the preponderance of evidence to be in error as well as being suspect. The Coroner's report is simply not correct as written nor are the circumstances of events drawn from it by the prosecution. The time of death is in error and the blood that the Coroner examined according to his testimony, was not the blood originally on my clients' car. Those are simply the facts of this case. Not only that, the victim died over a mile from where my clients had their accident. We have proven also that it was a deer that was indeed killed by them; not a human person."

Harold paused to catch his breath and to let his words soak in. He walked slowly to his table and then back toward the bench as he continued.

"There are still several unanswered questions about this whole setup that bothers me. Since there were no witnesses as to what happened, we have presented the only viable alternative. Although we proposition likewise is inconclusive, it does however, establish enough evidence to reasonably show motivation, opportunity and inclination to indict Doctor John Cuthbert, his son Jimmy and his two friends as prime suspect in the killing of Mr. Detmer and the subsequent cover up of their crime. Someone killed the deceased a day later than originally recorded just outside of town. Jimmy Cuthbert, Bobby McCallister and Hank Peters are prime suspects having been on the road and drunk at the time. The fact that Jimmy's front fender was repaired the very next day further implicates him.

The body of Mr. Detmer was moved from just outside of town to the place where my clients killed a deer. The person who moved the body was also the one who switched the blood on the vehicle in question. That person was the same one who visited the Sheriff's office that same morning only hours after the deceased was killed, one, Doctor John Cuthbert, as no one else even knew at the time what had happened other than he and the Sheriff's office. Nobody else was in a better position to do all this than the medical examiner handling the case. His motive? To protect his son.

Adding further guilt to the parties involved is the whole scenario involving the dead man's missing shoe and the incriminating actions of all four of them, involving tampering, not once but twice. It was more than sheer coincidence. Therefore, with all things considered, I humbly request that the charges against my clients be dismissed and that the four individuals named, be bound over to a grand jury for further investigation into the death of Mr. Detmer."

When Harold had finished, the silence was deafening. Judge T. Howard McGill sat thoughtfully silent for several moments. Even the press agents present did nothing to break the mood of the moment. Finally, the Judge spoke.

"I want to thank both the prosecutor and the defense for excellent presentations and to you who have observed this proceeding. On the whole, considering the nature of this case, you conducted yourselves well. I have heard both sides and will now call a recess until four this afternoon at which time I will render my decision. I want to see both attorneys in my chambers immediately following this hearing."

With a rap of his gavel, court was dismissed. Harold and John followed the Judge through the back door to his chamber. In his office, as serious-faced Judge McGill greeted them.

"Sit down, gentlemen," he said beckoning to a couple of seats at the conference table. When all three were seated, he started his own post-trial hearing in total seclusion. He began by looking in John's direction.

"We have a potential crisis of monumental proportions as far as Midway is concerned, John. How do you feel about what has been presented by Harold, here, concerning your client?"

"While the allegations against Doc Cuthbert and his son are not conclusive, they are nevertheless noteworthy, if not impressive. I think that there is enough circumstantial evidence to warrant a further grand jury investigation, though."

Both the Judge and Harold nodded their agreement.

"That's what I want to avoid if it's at all possible, for the sake of this small town. At the same time, I want justice to prevail above all else. Any suggestions?"

Both attorneys looked at each other. Harold spoke first.

"My first and foremost concern is that justice be served my clients. That's why I'm here. I'm convinced that whatever killed Mr. Detmer did so accidentally and that the Coroner knowing this, acted out of parental concern. Nevertheless, he is guilty as an accomplice after the fact as well as attempting to thwart justice. However, I'm open to any suggestions from John who after all, is the prosecutor for the county."

John thanked Harold for opening the door to him.

"Judge, if I agree to having the charges against Harold's clients dropped, and can get the Doc, his son and the other two to agree to a plea bargain, would that be satisfactory to you?"

"what kind of plea bargain do you have in mind?" Judge McGill asked.

"A guilty plea to accidental vehicular homicide for the three boys with a thousand dollar fine for each. This would also include as a six month suspension of driving privileges for Jimmy Cuthbert as well as probation for each of them coupled with 12 months of community service."

Judge McGill looked at Harold who nodded his approval.

"What about John Cuthbert?" he asked John.

"John abused the duties of his office so he must be asked to resign immediately as County Coroner. If he refuse, we prosecute. For his role in the coverup, we can request a suspended six-month jail sentence in lieu of a ten thousand dollar fine."

Harold nodded at John and the two of them then looked at Judge McGill. As he stood up, so did Harold and John.

"Gentlemen, it's settled then. John, I'll give you one week only to convince your clients to plea bargaining. Good work." Then looking at his watch, he recommended that the two attorneys use part of the remaining two hours getting something to eat.

"I'll see you both at four sharp," he finished. They all shook hands, smiling and then Harold and John left the room together.

"Well, I guess now that the war is over, there's no reason why two civilized lawyers can't share a meal together," John said putting his arm affectionately around Harold. The two men laughed as they made their way back across the now empty courtroom to the front door.

At exactly four p.m., Judge McGill emerged from his chambers and took his seat on the bench. A mosquito didn't have room enough to fly.

"Ladies and gentlemen, I have reached a decision on this case. After carefully weighing the evidence at my disposal, it is my verdict that the charges brought against Mr. Jeremy McCutchin and Rodney Blake be dismissed. Thank you. Court's adjourned."

Rod and Jeremy sat in stunned silence as pandemonium broke out all around them. All of the women: Harriet, Mary, beth and Andrea broke into tears. The men, John and James hugged each other and danced in the aisle. Ralph and Dick exchanged high fives. Harold and john shook hands as reporters converged upon them with flashbulbs popping all over the place. After several moments had gone by, Jeremy and Rod had gathered themselves enough to embrace each other as their tears flowed freely. Finally, they were together again—and free! The Jeffersons had already bolted for the door to take the news back to the black side of town.

"Sheriff Relliford told me so much about this place that I decided I waned to spend my last day with you up here," Jeremy told Beth as his car made its way over the scenic countryside toward Elkhill Lodge.

Beth suddenly realized that just like the Sheriff, she too had never been up to the lodge. Going there now with Jeremy would certainly make it extra special. She watched him as he drove their bodies snuggled up as close as they could be without interfering with Jeremy's control of the vehicle. This was the first time in over three weeks that they were alone together . . . and it was to be their last. it just didn't seem fair, but she knew that he had to leave tomorrow. He was already a week behind in his classes, and it was only the influence of Harold Steinmetz's New York office that he and Rod were granted permission to start school late.

Jeremy noticed a hint of sadness in her face as he drove.

"having second thoughts?" he teased.

"You mean going up here with you? . . . You can't be serious," she said, a look of surprise showing in her wide blue eyes.

He chuckled softly. "You don't have that radiant look that I was hoping to see," he said mockingly.

"I know, and I'm sorry," she said remorsefully, squeezing his large hand tightly. "you just can't see on the inside. I've never been happier in my life."

"Well, your heart needs to get the message to your face," he joked. They laughed.

"You were thinking about my leaving tomorrow, weren't you?" he stated more than he asked.

"Sort of . . . yes," she responded hesitantly.

Jeremy couldn't help but remember what she had told him earlier about her ill-fated romance in high school sand her determination to make the next time a special time with a special person. Could she be feeling that experience was happening all over again?

"You don't fell pressed into this, do you, Beth?"

"Don't even think that, honey," she said brushing her lips caressingly against his cheek, "never! Nothing is forced with you. You're different than any man I've ever known. You'll always be special to me, even if we never see each . . ."

Jeremy interrupted her. He was right after all!

"For pete's sake, Beth. How could you even think about us not being together again after today?"

She avoided his probing look and the hurt in his eyes. It was as if he saw right into her deepest thoughts. She gazed at the floor as tears began to well up in her eyes. She didn't trust her voice not to crack, so she said nothing. She felt Jeremy stop the car in the middle of the road, not bothering to even pull over to the side.

"Geez, Beth. I don't believe you," Jeremy said exasperated, as he tilted her chin revealing the tears that now stole down her face. She turned her face away, looking at the road ahead.

"Well, it does happen, Jer . . ." she choked fighting back the tears. "You're a man and men are different about those things sometime. I believe that you really care . . ."

"Care? Care?" he repeated. "Is that what you call it? After all that has happened, the help that you have been to me, all of the visits and times that you were all that I thought about and you call it caring? Beth, you're kidding me, right? Tell me you're kidding, Beth!"

Beth stared at the floor. "I just don't want you to feel obligated, that's all," she sobbed.

Jeremy put the car in park, took his foot off the brake and gathered Beth in his arms.

"Beth, honey, don't do this to me. Please don't do this. I couldn't stand it if I thought for a second that you could possibly even think that I would try to take advantage of you." He crushed her sobbing body against him, covering her hair, face and wet eyes with tender kisses. They sat together for long moments like this, saying nothing. They both began to realize that their relationship had lacked moments just like this. Moments alone, devoid of troubles, confusion and time restraints, but most of all privacy. The next 24 hours were theirs and they needed it more than anything else. Jeremy understood Beth's apprehension and lingering feelings of doubt. After all, tomorrow he would be on his way to New York with Rod. He spoke softly to her.

"Honey, it was not my intention to suggest that we come up here for the purpose of lovemaking. I just want those last hours to be ours, that's all. If we make love before I leave or not, that's not important. You are important to me, period."

"But, if we do make love now, what else do I have to offer? " Beth asked him in a whisper, wiping her eyes.

" A lifetime," Jeremy said simply. "When I finish with school this spring, I'm coming back to Midway. If you still want me then, I'm taking you back with me. I can't imagine the rest of my life without you a part of it. That's just the way it is . . . What I'm trying to say is that I know my feelings. I love you with all my heart. I might not yet understand all of the why's and wherefores, but I do know my feelings and that's enough for me. All I need to know is how you feel in your heart about me," he finished looking deep into the depths of her eyes.

Beth laid her head on his shoulder and squeezed his hand tightly.

"You know how much I love you, Jeremy. I have never been so sure of anything in my life. If I didn't allow my own family to come between us, nothing else will. Whatever happens between us tonight and the next few months is meant to happen. If we truly love each other, nothing will change. I believe that."

"That's my girl," Jeremy smiled. "Let's go."

As they drove on toward the lodge, Beth's fears began to slowly fade away. She had never trusted a man so completely.

"My mom and dad apologized to me this afternoon. They both felt bad about misjudging you. They were only concerned about me. You will never know how much that meant to me."

"What about Bobby. Did he say anything?" Jeremy asked her.

"I haven't seen him since the hearing. Jeremy, I'm worried sick about him. What's going to happen to him?" she asked her voice tinged with fright and a sense of panic.

"I don't know, sweetheart. Maybe before I leave, we'll get a chance to talk with Attorney Steinmetz together. I heard him mention something about a possible Alford plea for the Doc and the boys. That's where a guilty plea can be accepted without actually confessing the acts themselves."

"That would be nice," she murmured snuggling up to him once again. They drove the rest of the way in silence, sharing the closeness of each other, their hearts racing in joyful anticipation of the hours ahead.

When Toby pulled his cruiser up in front of the Jefferson's store, several of the residents rushed up to greet him as he climbed out of his car. They were all preparing a celebration in the back and he had been invited. People were everywhere. Some of them bugged him and others shook his had vigorously. They knew that without his help and protection, things might have been very different. The Jeffersons had kept them informed on a daily basis. His work during the investigation had almost achieved legendary proportions. They hailed him as a modern-day Sherlock Holmes. It was all very flattering and he had to work hard to keep from becoming flushed with embarrassment.

Eventually, he wound his way to the back of the store where two huge barbecue pits were going full-tilt. People were bringing in food from every direction, placing succulent dishes on tables set up in the yard. A group of young men were busy putting up a sound system. Another group scurried about stringing up streamers to nearby trees. They were preparing for a party, big time. Everyone was talking excitedly. Toby couldn't help but smile to himself. It was as if these people searched for excuses to throw parties and dance the night away. He could not imagine this kind of festivity taking place in Midway under similar circumstances—especially for outsiders. Very seldom did blacks have cause to rejoice over legal proceedings in the deep south. This was a victory of sorts for all of them. The fact that he was here to celebrate the occasion with them, gave him a sense of euphoria.

His thoughts were interrupted when Rod and Andrew popped up next to him.

"Bulldog Drummond, super sleuth!" Rod teased him, extending his hand with a smile. Andrea hugged him warmly,kissing his cheek. Toby playfully warned Rod that he had a weakness for pretty women, especially ones who kissed him. They all laughed.

Jeremy's mom was so busy with Mrs. Jefferson and the other women that she had failed to notice all of the attention that Toby had drawn. Likewise, Jeremy's father and Mr. Jefferson were completely absorbed in tending to the grills. It was one of those special moments when people were just people. Toby made his way over to the men and joined them.

"I need to make myself useful," he said to them, causing both to look up at the same time.

"Sheriff Relliford," Mr. McCutchin spoke warmly, shaking his hand. "I haven't had the opportunity to thank you for what you did for Rod and my boy. It was your work that really broke the case for Harold. I'll always be grateful to you for that. Let me make you an offer.

My wife and I would like to offer you and your wife a full-paid vacation to New York whenever you choose to come. I'll charge all expenses to my corporate account. This is our way of saying thank-you."

He went to his back pocket for his billfold and took out a business card to give to Toby. Toby took it with a smile.

"Why thank you. Peg and I have never been to New York. You can bet your bottom dollar that we'll come."

"Hold it, Sheriff!" said a voice form behind. They all looked around at Mr. Blake.

"I don't own a corporate business, but we have some sustenance. My wife and I too will forever be indebted to you and what you mean to our family and to Rod. When you do come to New York, use this for some of your expenses as well."

He placed a check in Toby's hand for three thousand dollars. Toby gasped. His first reaction was to give it back.

"Don't even think about it," Mr. Blake said, knowing what he was about to say. "This is our way of saying thanks."

Toby stuffed the check happily in his pocket.

"No problem," he responded with a laugh.

Toby then talked to the Jeffersons about the possibility of having ten minutes to talk to everyone in attendance prior to Reverend Trembull's blessing of the food when it was time to eat. It was put immediately on the agenda. Just then, a young black man's voice came over the P.A. system announcing that everything was set for music and dancing. The sound of his voice attracted dozens more people who were milling around nearby. Rev. Trembull's appearance signaled that it was now getting close for things to begin. Mr. Jefferson then took the microphone and called for everyone's attention. All activity ceased and everyone's eyes were cast in his direction.

"Before we eat and begin our celebration, Sheriff Toby Relliford has asked for a few minutes to speak to you after which Reverend Trembull will bless the food and we can eat and party."

A cheer and rhythmic chants greeted his ears. Toby stepped up to the microphone. Everyone became quiet and attentive.

"Let me begin by saying that it has been a pleasure being your sheriff over the years. It was your votes at the last election that helped me win another four years in office."

His remarks were interrupted with applause and cheering. He waved his hand in acknowledgment and continued.

"I just want to say thanks and also to express my admiration of the way that all of you handled yourselves over the past several weeks during the pre-trial. I regret that I had to ask you all not to come to town while the hearings took place, but we just couldn't afford to have anything go wrong. On the behalf of the white people in Midway who feel that all of you had every right as citizens to be there, I offer you our apologies."

He was greeted with a thunderous applause. By this time, there was over 100 town folks assembled.

"As you know, I will not always be Sheriff here, but I do intend to run again in the next election."

Before he could finish, he was interrupted again by applause.

The response to Toby's plea was deafening. No white person had ever spoken to them so candidly and openly. Even during the election years, Toby had simply let his reputation of being a fair person speak for itself. He was deeply touched by the way these people now responded to him. Toby spent the rest of the afternoon in the colored section eating and having a merry old time. Several of the young women insisted that he dance with them as the day wore on. A few beers helped him overcome his hesitancy. He was a white middle-aged white anglo-saxon male and not a very good dancer, especially when compared to the dancing going on around him. He was always taught dance steps as a youngster but as he soon came to realize, no one did steps anymore. They simply gyrated to the music and did whatever they felt like doing. If Peg saw him now, she would faint, he thought to himself, smiling. He left late that afternoon heading back to town, feeling better than he had felt in years.

For the first time in a while, he felt like he had really accomplished something worthwhile. He was sure that Midway would not be unaffected by the events of the past month. It would be a better place as a result in many ways. And he had played a key role! He was damn proud of his detective work. He hadn't had to use those skills in ages and he was glad that he hadn't lost them. As his car bumped down the unpaved road, he reminisced about the investigation and smiled slightly to himself.

After all, it was his hunch that launched the investigation on the right course! He couldn't wait to get home and share all of the details with Peg. She had always believed that he was never happy being a sheriff in a small town after the experience of being a cop in a large metropolitan area such as Atlanta. And she was partly right, of course. Many times he had griped and complained about literally wasting away in obscurity. No police work. No shootings. No risk of life and limb. No drug busts. No high-speed chases. Well . . . it'll be different now. His foot unconsciously pushed the accelerator pedal harder.

Harold, Ralph and Dick had spent that afternoon rounding up their equipment and cleaning out the tiny office that had almost become like home over the past month. As he worked, Harold was filled with mixed emotions. This case had done more to invigorate him than any case that he had handled out of his New York office in years. For one, he worked right in the midst of real people, instead of an insulated environment of expensive furnishings and high priced lawyers. Here, he was totally on his own, practically naked. His staff had been made up of college students! He could not have imagined before he agreed to take this case, of depending upon the work of a small town southern sheriff to provide the groundwork for his case.

As he reflected backwards, he wondered if it had not been for his friendship with John McCutchin if he would have ever taken a case like this. When he had accepted it, he thought he would be able to use his own professional staff. He hadn't anticipated the use of undercover agents, and was not prepared for the obstacles that a small southern town presented. In many ways, he was thrown to the mercy of his own creativity, just like he was over 30 years ago when he had started his career. He now realized that success had made him a little too comfortable and as a result his creative juices had all but dried up. If a case did not meet certain criteria, he simply wouldn't take it. He had allowed himself to become such a specialist that his career had become predictable and thus boring to a great extent. Until now, he was beginning to feel restless and unfulfilled.

His home life had begun to suffer as a result. He became too critical of his wife and children, claiming that they lacked initiative and motivation. His wife was a graduate social worker who had never worked because she never had to. His children, now grown, were all college graduates but had struggled with their grades most of the time. He had become cynical, accusing them of lacking the courage to accept challenges. It was only now that he realized that much of the frustration levied against his family was really his own discontent with himself and his work. He had allowed himself to become stale with success.

From now on things would be different. This case had awakened him from his sleepwalk and rekindled in him the desire to risk being an underdog. He had mistakenly allowed himself to believe that being an underdog was an indication of inferiority. But here in Midway, he had been a decided underdog and this had now made the victory all the more satisfying. He felt like a kid again at heart and he liked the feeling. A month ago, he was scared . . . really scared . . . because not only were the cards stacked against him, he was also out of his element. He was used to the big corporate world not a small country environment with a simple, common mentality. Somehow, John had never lost faith in him. When he called, he had told him that he wanted the very best lawyer around to free his son. As he had put it, "You're the best man for the job, Harold. If anyone can do it, you can."

He smiled to himself as he remembered John's words while packing his suitcase. Just then Harold and Dick came back into the room, talking excitedly about getting back to school. He listened to them for a while, remembering his own college days.

"Dick, Ralph, let me talk with both of you for a second," he told them. They stopped their activities and walked over to where he was and sat down on the couch nearby. He started talking to them about how important it is to have fun in whatever it is that they would be doing in their future careers.

"When it stops being fun, it's time to get out. Change directions You two have helped me discover this."

They looked at each other with puzzled expressions.

"How could WE help you?" Ralph quizzed wide-eyed. "We couldn't believe who they told us we'd be working for when they asked us to come down here. No attorney in New York is any more well-known than you, Mr. Steinmetz."

"And that's precisely my point," Harold responded. "Success can be intoxicating to the point that it becomes all consuming. I didn't become a lawyer just to become successful. Oh, that was a part of it but I really just wanted to help people have a better life and receive justice at the hand of the law. that's why I became a defense attorney rather than a prosecutor. But when being successful becomes more important than what you got into the business for in the first place, then it can become a hindrance to happiness. You two have helped make me feel better than I've felt in years. This case was the first one in ages that made me feel vulnerable enough to have to hustle. It was actually fun!"

"But you've always been a winner, Mr. Steinmetz. What's so different about now?" Dick asked in genuine puzzlement.

"Dick, my boy, life is not about winning, but about enjoyment. Yes, I've been a winner in court most of the time but there has been little fun and excitement to it, because winning had become too important. I gave the difficult cases to my junior partners in order to maintain my reputation as a winner. But this case has changed all that. From now on, I'm going to start handling some of those myself. I've rediscovered that the true joy of competition is not in the winning, but in the competing. We worked against some pretty big odds down here and won in spite of them. Without the work that both of you did, we wouldn't have had a prayer in this one."

With that, Harold reached into the inside pocket of his blue suit he wore, and took out a couple of white envelopes.

"These are for your outstanding services rendered." He handed each one an envelope.

"Can we open them now?" Ralph asked excitedly.

"Doesn't everyone look at their paychecks?" Harold teased them.

Both boys opened their envelopes and withdrew. the checks inside. Dick's mouth dropped open and Ralph's eyes bugged out of his glasses. Harold smiled.

"I hope it pays for your books this semester."

Each boy had received a check for $2500. Dick had never held this much money before at one time and Ralph had only exchanged this amount of money from his hand to the medical school. But this was his. Harold left the two like that and moved over to the phone on the desk at the other end of the room. before he picked up the phone, he had one more thing to tell them.

"Dick, I know that the FBI is waiting for you to graduate and I want to wish you a successful career with them. Ralph, if you have any trouble finding a police department that satisfies you, call my law firm. We can always find a spot for someone with your skills. now, if you'll excuse me, I have to see if my office is still in business."

As he dialed the phone, Dick and Ralph exchanged high fives, grinning from ear to ear. Harold got his office and both of them overheard him ask for someone in the library.

"Jim? Harold. How's everything going?"

Pause.

"What's our caseload?"

Pause.

Harold made several sounds of acknowledgment as the man on the other end went through a brief litany of cases.

"Which one appears more problematic?" he probed.

"Pause.

"Save that one for me. I'll get on it as soon as I arrive."

Pause. Harold laughed.

"No, the weather's fine down here. I haven't come down with anything."

Dick and Ralph laughed as they listened to the telephone conversation. Harold gave them a knowing wink as he laughed once again.

"Bill, just do as you're told, okay?"

Pause.

"Fine. See you later."

Harold explained to them that what they had just observed was an example of the rut that he had allowed himself to fall into professionally.

"My assistant just couldn't believe that I actually wanted to take a case that would demand hard work on my part. Up 'til now, I was content with just being involved, not in competing. That's what you two have helped me change. That's what I meant by 'having fun'. Thanks fellas."

The two of them looked at the checks they held in their hands. "No. Thank YOU!" They chimed together. All three shared one final laugh together.

Harold finished gathering up his belongings and left the boys in the room wide-eyed and grinning. Dick's eyes once again riveted on the two grand he held tightly in his hand. His first real paycheck! Man, this was wild. He felt ten feet tall. When Harold's office had first called his home and told him what had happened to Rod and Jeremy and what they wanted him to do, he was petrified. Totally. The news about his two friends, at first, had shocked him. But what followed had literally scared his socks off.

"Attorney Steinmetz has requested that you go down and handle all of the investigation work for him."

"THE Harold Steinmetz?."

"Yes."

"For real? . . ." He let his voice trail off.

"Yes for real. He said Rod and Jeremy had recommended you to him. He wants you to fly down as soon as possible. We've already attained permission from your school to go. We'll see that you have all the equipment necessary to do your work. Well . . . what do you say?"

"Cool . . ." he muttered.

"I take that to mean yes?"

"OH, YES. THAT'S RIGHT . . . YES!"

Thank you, Mr. Wingate, we'll be in touch."

He was snapped back to reality by Ralph's waving hand in front of his face and his mocking gesture as he bent down peering into his eyes.

"Hello? . . . anybody home in there?"

"Stop clowning," Dick responded with a smile.

"I was just thinking about how I got into all of this and now I'm a paid professional. Hell, I'm tough now."

"Yeah, I know. Isn't it cool? I don't know if you were as scared as I was when Harold's office contacted my folks and told me to call their office. I was out in the field doing some lab work and I couldn't even get to a phone when they handed me the message. I couldn't keep my mind on my work from wondering what would a big time lawyer want with me?"

"I know the feeling."

"When I finally called and they told me everything, it blew me away. First about Rod and Jeremy and then to do forensic work for Steinmetz. I thought I was dreaming."

"Well, it ain't no dream, just look at our hand,"" Dick finished eyeballing their checks.

"Ralph, you were fantastic, man."

"So were you, buddy. You know what really makes me feel great? . . . to have my work verified as being exactly correct in every detail by a qualified big city Coroner who didn't know me from Adam, tells me I'm really ready to get it on!!"

They embraced and did a little jig as they showed their excitement; two budding careers now coming to full blossom. Boys—now men.

Toby sat in his office, smoking his pipe and sipping on a cup of coffee. He was going through a list of court appearances that his deputies had to attend in traffic court but his mid kept wandering over the events of the past month. Jeremy and Rod would be going home for sure this time, first thing in the morning. John Stearns was now representing the prosecutor's office in the continuing investigation into the death of Mr. Detmer. The two had talked at length earlier about the case. John had told him that he had accumulated enough evidence concerning Doc Cuthbert and the three others that he was almost certain that they would accept the plea bargain offer.

"I don't think that they could stand a grand jury investigation," he had told him. This had satisfied Toby as far as having justice prevailing in this instance. He felt sorry for John Cuthbert, however. Over the years, they had established a good professional working relationship. John was a good medical examiner but he had allowed himself to become trapped by his own emotions. Now, for all intents and purposes, his career as a coroner was over. After serving his sentence, he would probably move from Midway and go into private practice elsewhere. John had agreed as part of the plea bargain, that he would not pursue the revocation of his medical license. His resignation of office and the subsequent humiliation that he would suffer was punishment enough.

Harold remembered how remorseful Doc Cuthbert had been during their earlier conversations. He had always been a nice, professional and courteous man. He loved his kid more than anything else. Probably too much. He had admitted as much. Even though he never verbally admitted his guilt, John had observed him talking to the priest at church on several occasions and knew that he had confessed to Father Machielson. About what, he didn't know but it was not hard to guess. He knew that he would eventually have to leave Midway.

"If you resign your office, I won't push for revocation of your license to practice medicine," Stearns had told him. "I believe that what you did was more an error in judgment than anything else."

Doc Cuthbert merely nodded his head but had said nothing. The Alford plea would allow him to assume this posture. As for Jimmy, once his debt to society had been paid, he would retake the medical exam. Bobby and Hank had both sworn off drinking and carousing. Bobby had decided that once this was over, he would take that second-chance offer to play football again at an upstate junior college. It wasn't a big-time college scholarship offer, but he was good enough that a junior college would take a chance with him to put them on the football map. With his father's failing health, Hank had to retreat to the family farm to look after things.

There was only one loose end to tie up now. Bobby McCallister's parents had already come in and dropped the assault charges against Jeremy, apologizing to him for the inconvenience that they had caused. Now as Toby sat at his desk, the one loose end was now coming through the door.

"Hello, Willie Joe. Come on in and have a seat," Toby said to his former deputy as he stepped into his office. "We have a lot to talk about."

"Thanks, Sheriff."

Toby invited Willie Joe to share a cup of coffee with him. The two sat down in his office with the door shut.

"Willie Joe, what brings you around?"

"Just stopped by, Sheriff Relliford, to tell you that you did one heck of a job with this here whole thing."

"Well, thanks Willie Joe. Nice of you to say that. How's that job coming?"

"It ain't much but it's better'n than nuthin'. Not like my deputy job that I had. I also came by to tell you that I now know what a stupid thing that was for me to do."

How so, Willie Joe?" Toby asked, leaning back while lighting his pipe and looking intently in his direction.

"Well Sheriff, to begin with, I talk too much when I'm drinking. I realize now that information from this office should be safeguarded at all costs. People are too unpredictable. I hadn't the foggiest notion that they would make such a fuss."

"Do you know why they did now?"

"Yes sir. They were like me, I guess. They didn't really like the nigger . . . er, colored boy being involved in the whole thing. Why shucks, if both them fellers had been white, it wouldn't have been such a big deal and I was the one who made it a big deal."

Toby leaned forward a little, took a deep drag on his pipe but said nothing.

"Why, heck," Willie Joe continued, "all of my life it was nigger this, nigger that, around my house. I just kinda accepted them as no-count, I guess. I never went in the colored section. Never . . . but I've learned through all this, they're people too, just like us."

"What did you think of Rodney's folks, Willie Joe?"

"They were nice people. They sure as fire, love that boy of theirs. I was always told they didn't have feelings about that, like we do, you know, fathering and mothering, those sorts of things. I apologized to both of them after the trial for my part in puttin' their son's neck in jeopardy. And I meant it too, Sheriff, really."

"How about Rodney?"

"Him too. Why, we even shook hands" He admitted.

Toby paused for a moment, pampered his pipe and leaned back again. He really liked this kid, always had.

"Willie Joe, it's hard not to be affected by what we're taught all of our life. It takes a hold even without us sometimes knowing it. I was taught many of those same things. But, I had an advantage over you. I was forced to serve with the coloreds in the Army. Eat with them. Sleep with them. Work with them. Hell, I found out they were no different then I was. They weren't lazy, it's just that nothing was really expected of them. They didn't get promoted like the rest of us, so they were always being told what to do. Some of them even stopped trying after a while."

"I can't say that I blame 'em none," Willie Joe responded.

Toby nodded.

"Thing is, when are things between our races going to change?" Toby asked. "I don't have the answer."

"Me neither. But Sheriff, you're not to blame. Why you treat colored folks just like white folks."

"Well, I have to Willie Joe. It's my job. We, us, we're the ones who are trusted to see that justice is done to everybody, regardless of race or religion."

Willie Joe shook his head in agreement vigorously.

"I really learned that at the trial, Sheriff. I wished a hundred times that I could have taken back what I said that night."

"Well, that's behind us now, Willie Joe. You made a serious mistake as an officer of the law. No question about that. But you've learned a lesson from your mistake and that is all that counts, really. Everyone makes mistakes and all that we can do is to try not to make the same mistake twice."

Willie Joe stood up and held out his hand.

"Well, I'm a fixin' to go, Sheriff. I sure feel a lot better after our talk."

Toby shook his hand warmly.

"There's a town meeting coming up next Tuesday, maybe I'll be able to convince the boys to consider giving you a second chance at getting your old job back."

Willie Joe's eyes grew surprisingly large and he grinned ear-to-ear.

"Do . . . do you really think so , Sheriff?"

"Well, I don't know for sure. Don't count on it. But this is a small town and the people are pretty forgiving, especially to its own."

Two men on the inside, one black and one white, talked excitedly as they drove.

"Man, this sure feels good, doesn't it?" Rod was saying.

"You mean being free again?" Jeremy replied.

"No, I mean heading for home AND being free."

"That's for sure," Jeremy acknowledged checking his speed. Rod noticed his partner's action and kidded him about learning his lesson. Jeremy grunted.

"You know the thing about driving is that you can never afford to underestimate the suddenness of the unexpected happening. I don't worry about me because I know my driving ability. But it's the other guy, or the unusual that I'll be on the lookout for from now on."

"Yeah, I know what you mean. Man, things happen so fast that you can't afford to become careless or not be alert," Rod agreed. "You know, I'm gonna miss 'ol Toby," he added as an afterthought.

"Me too. He's some kinda sheriff alright. You know, if he had not believed us when we walked into his office that morning and went about his work on the assumption that we were guilty outsiders, we'd still be down there."

"You know what? The amazing thing was that while all of the time you were in jail and I was on the other side of the tracks, I didn't give a nickel for our chances. I was really beginning to get depressed and Andrea was scared stiff."

"Well, look at me! I was right under the nose of everything and was completely in the dark. I mean, the Sheriff didn't let on to me about anything."

They talked as they drove on about how shocked they were about the way the case had unfolded in court.

"Boy! Mr. Steinmetz was brilliant with the way that he trapped those three with the missing shoe bit," Jeremy said admiringly.

"Yeah, that was solid," Rod replied. "But what about Ralph and Dick? You know, the best thing that we did in this whole affair was to suggest to Mr. Steinmetz to contact them. even so, I would have never imagined that they would be that good. It was a shot in the dark when we mentioned them. Thank you good 'ol Waynesville State!" Rod exclaimed casting his eyes upward.

Jeremy laughed at his friend's gesture of thanksgiving.

"What was neat was bringing in that Coroner from Chattanooga to verify Ralph's work. When he was on the stand testifying, I just knew that the prosecutor would shoot his work down. I was really nervous then. At that time, I thought that his report was all that we had going for us."

"Well, it was actually," Rod analyzed. "Ralph's testimony had challenged that of a professional medical examiner. If it hadn't been for the outside examiner's testimony, they would have thrown out Ralph's report."

"That's true. I never began to relax at all until after the other coroner had testified. The prosecutor, until then, had me even believing if we were guilty or not."

"Boy, he was tough, wasn't he?" Rod murmured. "He really raked Toby over the coals. Wow! I thought we had had it at that point. He had convinced everybody that he was either protecting us or trying to shield us."

Jeremy went on to acknowledge that he hadn't helped matters any by getting into the fight with Bobby McCallister.

'Yeah, you almost blew it," Rod agreed. "But, hey! If I were in your shoes, I'd have done the same thing. He sure pasted Beth a good one . . . umph," he finished remembering the shiner that she had worn.

"Uh huh. And if the Sheriff hadn't pulled me off of him, I'd still be whipping him." Rod guffawed.

"Speaking of Beth. What happened last night at the lodge, buddy?" he teased Jeremy, nudging him with an elbow. Jeremy's face flushed. "Uh oh. This is gonna be good, I know it!" Rod said with saucer eyes. "Come on, man. Let's have it. Don't leave nothin' out."

Jeremy was really dying to tell someone about what had happened the night before and the following morning. His whole life had begun to change but the things that had happened were so private and personal. He hesitated about sharing them with anyone. He didn't have time to talk with his parents because by the time he and Beth got back to town, Mr. Steinmetz and the Sheriff had left for the colored section with Ralph and Dick to pick up the boy's parents to take them to Chattanooga for the flight home. He said his goodbyes when he had left to pick up Beth and had told them that he would see them when he got home. They had all left town together, leaving Rod behind for him to pick up later. When he had picked up Rod, they ate breakfast and then took their car to a mechanic at Stan's to be checked out for the trip home. They had been so busy getting ready, that there was little time for much else. Until now.

"You don't just talk about things like that, Rod," he answered wryly.

"Yeah, right," he quipped. "Not to just anybody, I agree. But this is me!! Are you gonna tell your dad?"

"Sure."

"Why?"

"Because he's my Dad, that's why."

"Who's your best friend?"

"You."

"And you can't share the most exciting event in your life with your best friend? That's hypocritical, Jer," Rod challenged. He had to smile. He and Rod had always shared their innermost secrets ever since they became friends. Plus, he didn't know how long that he could hold everything inside without bursting.

"Okay. Let's make a deal."

"Shoot."

"I'll tell you about yesterday, if you tell me about you and Andrea. I know you two. You celebrated last night too, didn't you?"

"Yep. I can't lie," Rod confessed.

Jeremy told Rod about Beth's reluctance at first. Once they got to the lodge, they spent the rest of the day hiking and taking archery target practice. Beth was amazingly accurate. She and Bobby had been taught the art of archery by their father when they were very small. He was an avid hunter and when he had heard Ralph's testimony at the trial about the deer that they had found, he told Beth that the animal had not been killed by a hunter. That night they had made love for the first time and now Jeremy confessed that he was hopelessly in love." when are you and Andrea tying the knot?" Jeremy asked Rod as they sped over the highway.